BATTLEFIELD 3
THE RUSSIAN

BATTLEFIELD 3
THE RUSSIAN

Andy McNab
and Peter Grimsdale

Swordfish

For Lawrence

Copyright © Electronic Arts Inc. 2011

This edition first published in Great Britain in 2011 by
Swordfish
an imprint of the Orion Publishing Group Ltd
Orion House, 5 Upper St Martin's Lane,
London WC2H 9EA
An Hachette Livre UK Company

1 3 5 7 9 10 8 6 4 2

A CIP catalogue record for this book
is available from the British Library.

ISBN: 9780857820679 Hardback
ISBN: 9780857820686 Export Trade Paperback

Typeset by Input Data Services Ltd, Bridgwater, Somerset

Printed and bound by CPI Group UK Ltd, Croydon, CR0 4YY

The Orion Publishing Group's policy is to use papers
that are natural, renewable and recyclable and made
from wood grown in sustainable forests. The logging and
manufacturing processes are expected to conform to the
environmental regulations of the country of origin.

Every effort has been made to fulfil requirements with regard
to reproducing copyright material. The author and publisher
will be glad to rectify any omissions at the earliest opportunity.

www.orionbooks.co.uk

Author's Note

I have been invited to work alongside many different gaming companies in the past, but up until now, I have always turned down their offers. But the opportunity to work with DICE and help develop Battlefield 3 was an opportunity I didn't want to miss. Not only did it mean I'd get to work with gamers whose track-record of ground breaking games is world renowned, but it was also clear right from the start, that BF3 had something special, something that other games didn't. The only word I can think of that explains it, is 'substance'. BF3 wasn't going to be a simple shoot 'em up – it was going to be packed with emotion, grit and the sheer physicality to take any gaming experience to another level.

I was first asked by the development team to help weave together the different storyline strands which make up the levels of the game. I worked alongside them providing ideas on how the action might play out, and just as importantly, giving possible reasons as to why the action might go in a particular way. I gave advice on how soldiers talk, act and think. For example, soldiers within the game needed to have the exact words and inflections to accurately reflect how soldiers in the real world speak. Words like 'maybe', 'we will try to' or 'we will attempt', don't exist in a soldier's world. We use words like 'you will', 'I will', 'we will'. All dialogue is absolute because soldiers in the real world must be positive in everything they do. After all, real lives are at stake, so there is no room for failure.

The second part of my role was to work alongside the team's graphic designers to make sure what you see and hear as you play the game feels 'right'. We would sit for hours talking about how men and machines move tactically and how they look, even down to making sure that the soles of soldiers' boots were dirty and worn. A desert camp that is attacked by US tanks within the game is an exact replica of a camp on the Iraq/Iran border that I flew over four years ago. Authentic detail is so important because our brains are very good at telling us when something isn't just right.

The third part of my job was to work with the actors and stuntmen in the motion capture studios, to ensure the game's characters moved like men who had been handling weapons and fighting with them for all of their lives. I also explained their lines to them, so that they could do their job and display the appropriate emotions like fear, anger and determination as they carried out the task ahead.

BF3 is the most sophisticated game ever because it gives the player a far deeper, more physical presence within the world in which he/she is playing. An ex-US Tank Commander who has seen the game said the whole experience was better than any simulator he had ever been in, and that it gave him flashbacks to the Iraq war. In a positive way.

But the game is just one window into the BF3 experience – this book is another. It seemed a natural progression to write a novel to complement the game as there was still so much more of the story to tell. That story is Dmitri 'Dima' Mayakovsky's, a Russian ex-Spetsnaz Special Forces soldier. He finds himself in a world that no longer has the certainty of the old Communist dictatorship he once served.

Dima will certainly never win a humanitarian award for the role he plays in BF3, but he's a character its impossible not to feel drawn to. The novel gives you the opportunity to see things from his point of view, and maybe understand the decisions and actions he takes when he finds himself in this most impossible of situations.

I hope you enjoy the book and game. I think they work really well together.

Andy McNab

Prologue

Beirut, August 1991

They'd been stood on alert since 0600. Moscow didn't call until three, the hottest part of the day, in the hottest month, in what must have been the last non-air-conditioned hotel in Beirut. But that was the GRU's style: they never failed to disappoint. Dima swung his legs off the bed, felt his head swim. Picked up the receiver. Two thousand kilometres away, Paliov's voice, full of anticipation.

'*You set?*'

'*For the last nine hours.*'

'*A red Peugeot, Jordanian plates.*'

'*Where?*'

There was a pause. Dima pictured him, his desk in Moscow littered with memos and telexes, all stamped 'Urgent – most secret'.

'*Four blocks from Khalaji's hotel, the Majestic Palace, a parking lot on a bomb site.*'

'*That narrows it down. Half the city's a bomb site.*'

'*The whole Iranian nuclear delegation's at the hotel, so it'll be swarming with their own security. But they're not permitted out of the grounds. Our information is Khalaji's all set. You won't have any problem.*'

'*You always say that and we always do.*'

Paliov sighed.

'*I assure you, everything's in place. Khalaji thinks the Americans are coming for him, so there'll be no resistance. Just get in and drive. Tell him there's a plane waiting just across the border and show him the documentation as we agreed. Once you're on the move, if he realises who you are, what can he do? Just have the autojet ready.*'

The chemical cosh: always the GRU's answer to any problem.

'*And if there is a problem?*'

'Kill him. Better Iran's nuclear prodigy dead than the Americans really do get their hands on him.'

Paliov rang off.

Dima dropped the phone back on to its cradle and looked across at Solomon.

'It's a *go*.'

Solomon sat cross-legged on his bed, the disassembled pieces of his US-sourced Colt 45 laid out in front of him. He didn't react, just glared – his default expression. Still so young – twenty – but projecting an intelligence that would have been intimidating in someone twice his age. Once Dima had been his mentor but Solomon didn't need mentors now. Beside him Dima felt old and inferior, not a good feeling before a hit. For a few seconds neither spoke as they listened to the overhead fan stirring the soupy city air. Near the window a fly was noisily trying in vain to separate itself from a slow gluey death on the wax ribbon. Outside in the traffic, horns blared, the collective frustration of Beirut's drivers at the permanent gridlock. Then, without warning, Solomon's face split into a mirthless grin.

'You know the part I'm looking forward to? When Khalaji realises he's not headed to the land of the free. I want to see that look.'

Not for the first time Dima wondered about his protégé. Particularly disturbing was the pleasure Solomon took in others' misfortune. And on this, his first GRU field assignment, how come he manages to stay so cool, Dima wondered. He got up, went to the bathroom, sneaked a sip of vodka from the flask in his washbag. Just a small one to see him through the next few hours. He returned to the room, picked up his 45. Holstered it. Solomon frowned.

'You cleaned it?'

'Yes, it's fine.'

Solomon raised the barrel of his own gun and examined it for the umpteenth time. 'With all the dust here. Plus these 45s are notorious.'

Know-all, thought Dima. It was the ammunition they should be worrying about. Bootleg bullets with a weak charge. Why should they use this American crap anyway? Paliov's obsession with disguise. Never mind the weapons, just get the intel right.

He glanced at the ejected mag and the rounds. Solomon had scored a cross on the nose of each bullet. He was using JHP rounds for maximum damage. Dima's hope was that no shots would be fired today.

'Let's do it.'

They took a cab, an Opel with several different coloured panels. The interior stank of sweat and the driver's lunch. Solomon sat, arms folded, sullen as a teenager forced to take out the trash.

'If we were CIA we'd have our own car and our own driver,' he said, in his perfect American English. 'And our own radio net.'

'Maybe you chose the wrong side.'

He said nothing, as if he was thinking the same.

'Look on the bright side.' Dima tapped his chest. 'At least we get to keep these polo shirts with the logo. And the chinos.' He slapped Solomon's thigh.

'Yeah, courtesy of the souk, run up by a kid cross-legged at a sewing machine who should be at school. They look about as American as falafel.'

'Khalaji won't notice. He's a physicist.'

'He's been in America once. You haven't.'

Dima gave him a reproachful look. Solomon's attitude had nearly got him flung out of his fast-tracked Spetsnaz training. From day one he'd been marked down as trouble. Always awkward, always challenging his tutors, always a better idea of his own. They complained to Dima, to Paliov, and then to Dima some more. Dima could only blame himself. Solomon was his find, plucked by him from the blasted slopes above Kandahar in the dying days of Russia's futile occupation. He had been part of the great diaspora of youth who flocked to Afghanistan to help defeat the Evil Empire. Dima, operating undercover, spotted the boy's potential and turned him. His calm, his discipline, his amazing facility with languages, and his ruthlessness were precious assets. The GRU needed him, *Russia* needed him, Dima insisted. Okay, they said. When his two years are up, he's on your watch. This was Solomon's first assignment and Dima was having doubts.

3

They left the cab a few blocks from the hotel, took a walk past it, found the bomb site parking lot. Just the short distance through the sticky smog had already drenched him in sweat. There was no sign of the Peugeot, but he spotted a small bar opposite. As if pulled by a magnetic force, Dima headed straight for it, slammed a five dollar bill on the counter and ordered a double.

'What are you having?'

Solomon lurked by the doorway.

'Just water.'

'You have any vices at all?'

Solomon gave him a blank glare that seemed to say, '*Does it look like it?*', and again Dima felt uneasy.

On a shelf above the bar was a small black and white TV. An image of Gorbachev, released from house arrest, but neutered, humiliated. The great hope – now hopeless as the Soviet Union crumbled around him, the revolution he had started careering out of control. Where would it end? All Dima could envisage was chaos. Hardly the great socialist dream he had promised Solomon he was signing up for.

'Maybe Khalaji will help put us back on top.' Dima tapped the bulge under his jacket. 'Think about it: portable nuclear capability.'

Dima's irony was lost on Solomon. For the first time that day, the boy's eyes lit up. The idea had caught his imagination as it had fired up Paliov and the rest of their masters back in Moscow. Dima slapped down another five dollar bill and ordered the same again.

He'd warned Paliov there'd be a problem, and now, as the Peugeot came into view, he saw what it was. Coming slowly up the street, it almost ground to a halt as a wheel hit one of the many potholes. The car was more than fully laden.

'Fuck. He's got his whole family in there.'

There was a fresh scrape all down the side, exposing bright metal, and the offside end of the front bumper was bent forward as if it had got entangled with another vehicle. The car swerved erratically before bottoming as it mounted the curb.

'Wait,' Dima hissed at Solomon, who was starting to cross the street. 'We need to check if he's being followed.'

That second vodka didn't feel so great now.

From the other side of the road they could see Khalaji at the wheel, his wife beside him, heads twisting round, looking, panicking.

That's Plan A out of the window, thought Dima. What the hell was Plan B?

Nothing else came up the street behind them. Dima and Solomon walked towards the car. As soon as Khalaji saw them he leapt out. A wiry man, his shirt collar way too big for his scrawny neck.

'Hi, hi. Over here!'

This guy has no idea! Dima motioned to him to cool it, get back in the Peugeot. As they got nearer they could see the back seat was full of children.

Dima felt the contents of his stomach rearrange themselves.

'We'll have to kill them,' said Solomon. 'Sedate him first. Then get them out of the car. He'll never know what happened.'

Another fucking fiasco. Blame Paliov as he might, in the end Dima knew it was his own fault for agreeing to the mission. It just wasn't in his nature to say no – especially these days with all the old guarantees of employment being torn up.

Khalaji was back in the car, window down, eyes bulging with expectation. One of the children in the back was wailing.

'Mr Khalaji, I'm Dave,' said Dima.

'Dave ...' repeated Khalaji, frowning, as if he was trying out the name. 'The message said Dean.'

Shit, thought Dima. What had they agreed? Dave, Dean, Dima, not a lot of difference. He felt his head clouding. Maybe the vodka hadn't been such a good idea. Or maybe he should have had a third.

The wife leaned across her husband, frowned at Dima from under her veil, snapped at Khalaji in Farsi. '*I can smell liquor on his breath.*'

Suddenly Solomon was at Dima's side, edging him away from the car window, wearing a broad grin like he had never seen on his face before.

'Hey folks, how y'all doin' today? My name's Dean and we'll be taking you from here on to your destination. Ma'am, if you'd step out of the car please, and your little ones.'

If there was any more to Solomon's sales patter Dima wasn't going to hear it, nor were the Khalajis, because what happened next rendered their feeble cover story redundant. A pair of new but dusty Chevy Suburbans swung into view and slewed to a halt in the middle of the street. Eight doors swung open and eight Caucasian men in T-shirts, shorts and shades stepped out, all armed. Four covered, four approached. Two of those covering took aim at Dima. Khalaji's wife screamed so loud Dima's ears sang.

Solomon was no longer at his side. At the first sign of trouble he had made himself invisible among the parked vehicles.

'Hands in the air, cowboy,' one of the shaded ones shouted, repeating the order in Arabic for good measure. Dima fumbled for his 45, aimed, squeezed, missed, aimed again – and it jammed. A fraction of a second later and the gun was gone from his hand – which was now spurting blood. The Yank had shot it clean out of his grip. Dima dropped to the ground as the Americans got to the other side of the car, opening the doors, reaching in and scooping up the Khalaji family into the bosom of democracy. Dima cursed Paliov for his stupid, ill-planned, under-resourced missions, he cursed the 45, the one or two too many vodkas and pretty much everything else about his shitty life so far.

A flicker of movement between a parked Datsun and a Mercedes – Solomon, behind the cars, choosing a position. And from under the Peugeot he saw one of the Americans inching towards him round the car, taking no chances. With his good right hand, Dima wrestled the Beretta from the left pocket of his chinos and fired at one of the American's feet – just as he lifted it.

He heard doors slamming, the Americans retreating.

'Family secured. Good to go. Go now!'

Better dead than the Americans get their hands on him. Dima hadn't shared that with Solomon. Didn't need to. Solomon would know. The bullets, that family ... The American whose foot Dima had just missed swung into view, big jaw, Zapata moustache, mirror shades.

'You Commie cunt.' The American lifted his M9, took aim. The air between them exploded.

The American sank to his knees, his forehead cratered by the bullet that had entered the back of his head and chewed its way out front. His mouth had turned into a perfect O as if preparing to sing. He hovered there a second, then he slumped on top of Dima, pinning him down, the contents of his smashed head emptying out over his face.

There were more shots from Solomon's position. More screams and shrieks –

'*fuckoutahererightnow*!' Doors slamming and furious wheelspin – and then silence.

Solomon lifted the corpse off Dima, wiping his face with the fake polo shirt.

Dima breathed out.

'You got Khalaji? You stopped them taking him, didn't you?'

Solomon shook his head slowly.

'How come?'

He prodded the American corpse with his toe.

'It was either shoot Khalaji or him.'

Dima let a couple of seconds pass while the meaning of what Solomon was saying sank in.

'You saved my life.'

No comment from Solomon, just a glare of contempt. Eventually he nodded.

'Yes. I fucked up.'

1

Dima opened his eyes, a second of blankness before he remembered where he was and why. The call could come at any time, they'd said. It was just after three. Bulganov's voice was thick with fatigue. He told him when and where. He started to give directions, but Dima shut him up.

'*I know where it is.*'

'*Just don't fuck up, okay?*'

'*I don't fuck up. That's why you hired me.*' Dima hung up.

Four-thirty, a stupid time to choose to swap a girl for a suitcase of money, but he wasn't making the decisions. 'Remember: you're just the courier,' Bulganov had said, trying to swallow his pain.

Dima called Kroll, told him twenty minutes. He took a cold shower, forcing himself to stay under until the last traces of sleep were gone. He dried, dressed, gunned a Red Bull. Breakfast could wait. He gave the case one last check. The money looked good: US dollars, five million, shrink-wrapped. The price of oligarchs' daughters was going up. Bulganov had wanted to use counterfeit, but Dima had insisted – no tricks or else no deal. Barely a dent in the man's fortune – not that it stopped him trying to beat them down. The rich could be very mean, he'd learned – especially the old ones, the former Soviets. But the Chechens had set their price. And when a fingernail arrived in the post, Bulganov caved.

Dima put on his quilted coat. No body armour: he couldn't see the point. It weighed you down and if they were going to kill you they'd aim for the head. No firearm either, and no blades. Trust was everything in these exchanges.

He handed in the key cards at reception. The pretty brunette on the desk didn't smile, glanced at the bag.

'Going far?'

'Hope not.'

'Come back soon,' she said, without conviction.

The street, still dark, was empty except for clumps of old snow. Moscow under new snow he liked: it rounded off the sharp edges, covered up the grime and the litter, and sometimes the drunks. But it was April, and the frozen remnants clung to the pavements in long, winding fortifications, like the ones they'd been made to dig at military school. The tall, grey buildings disappeared into low cloud. Maybe winter wasn't over just yet.

A battered BMW swung into view, weak lights bouncing off the glaze of ice. The tyres slid a little as it shuddered to a halt in front of him. It looked like it had been rebuilt from several unwilling donors, a Frankenstein's monster of a car.

Kroll grinned up at him. 'Thought it would remind you of your lost youth.'

'Which part?'

Dima didn't need any reminders: any idle moment and the old times crowded in – which was why he did his best never to be idle. Kroll got out, popped the trunk lid and hefted in the bag, while Dima took his place at the wheel. The interior smelled of sauerkraut and smoke – Troikas. You wouldn't catch Kroll with a Marlboro. He preferred those extra carcinogens that came in Russian tobacco. Dima glanced at the ripped back seat: a bed roll, some fast food boxes and an AK: all the essentials of life.

Kroll slid in, saw the expression on Dima's face.

'You living in this crate?'

Kroll shrugged. 'She threw me out.'

'Again? I thought you'd got the message by now.'

'My ancestors lived in yurts: see, we're going up in the world.'

Dima said it was Kroll's nomadic Mongol blood that got in the way of his domestic life, but they both knew that it was something else, a legacy of having lived too much, seen too much, killed too much. Spetsnaz had trained them to be ready for anything – except normality.

He nodded at the back seat. 'Katya has standards, you know.

One look in here and she might decide to stick with her captors.'

He shoved the shift into drive and they took off, fishtailing in the slush.

Katya Bulganova had been snatched in broad daylight from her metallic lemon Maserati, a vehicle that might as well have had *'My Daddy's rich! Come and get me!'* embossed on the hood. The bodyguard got one in the temple before he even saw what was happening. One onlooker said it had been a teenage girl brandishing an AK. Another described two men in black. So much for witnesses. Dima had little sympathy for Katya or her father. But Bulganov didn't want sympathy and he didn't just want his daughter back. He wanted his daughter back and revenge: 'A message to the under-world: no one fucks with me. And who better to deliver it than Dima Mayakovsky?'

Bulganov had been at Spetsnaz too, one of the generation that bided its time then cut loose in the free-for-all Yeltsin years, to grab its share. Dima despised them, but not as much as those who came after, the grey, lifeless micromanagers. Kushchen, his last boss, told him, 'You played the wrong game Dima: you should have shown some restraint.'

Dima didn't do restraint. On his first posting, in Paris as a student spy in '81, he discovered that his own station chief was preparing to defect to Britain. Dima took the initiative and the man was found floating in the Seine. The police settled for suicide. But initiative wasn't always appreciated. Enough people higher up thought he had done too well, too soon, which was how he ended up in Iran training Revolutionary Guards. In Tabriz, near the Azeri border, two recruits on his watch raped the daughter of a Kazakh migrant worker. They were only seventeen years old, but the victim was four years younger. Dima got the whole troop out of their bunks to witness proceedings, then made them stand close enough to see the look on the boys' faces. Two shots each in the temple. The troop excelled in discipline after that. Then in Afghanistan, during the dying months of the occupation, he witnessed a Russian regular soldier open up on a car full of French nurses. No reason – out of his head on local junk.

Dima put a bullet in the corporal's neck while he was still firing, tracer rounds arcing into the sky as he fell.

Perhaps if he had shown more restraint he would at least still be at Spetsnaz, in a civilised posting where he could use his languages, a reward for the years of dedication and ruthlessness, not to mention the chance to reclaim a bit of humanity. But Solomon's defection in '94 had done for Dima's reputation. Someone had to take the rap. Could he have seen it coming? At the time, no. With hindsight, maybe. The only consolation – he'd packed in the drinking and that had been the toughest mission.

The streets at this hour were almost empty, just as they used to be all day long in his childhood. Under the throngs of imported SUVs, Moscow's vast avenues lost their grandeur. There was a queue to get on to the Krymsky Bridge, where a beat-up Lada had been rammed by a Buick. Doors open, two men shouting, one wielding a crowbar. No police in sight. Two drunks staggered along the pavement, joined at the head like Siamese twins, plumes of vapour rising from them into the frozen air. When they reached the BMW they paused and stared. They were men from the past, probably no more than fifty years old, but with faces so ravaged by drink and bad diet they looked much older. Soviet faces. Dima felt an unwelcome sense of kinship, not that they would have known. One spoke, inaudible through the glass, but Dima lip-read: 'Immigrants'.

Kroll tapped him on the shoulder – the lights had changed.

'Where are we going, anyway?'

He told him. Kroll snorted.

'Nice. Residents sold the window glass so the authorities put up plywood instead.'

'Capitalism. Everyone's an entrepreneur.'

Kroll was off. 'Fact: There are more billionaires in Moscow than any other city in the world. Twenty years ago there weren't even any *millionaires*.'

'Yeah, but probably not round here.'

They passed rows of identical blocks of flats, monuments to the workers' paradise, now filled with the drugged and the dying.

'Tombstones in a giants' graveyard,' said Kroll.

11

'Easy on the poetry: it's a bit early for me.'

They parked between an inverted Volga, stranded on its roof like an upturned beetle, and a Merc, the passenger compartment burned out. The BMW blended right in.

They got out. Kroll lifted the trunk lid and reached in. Dima moved him aside.

'Careful with your back.'

He lifted the bag out of the trunk and set it on its wheels.

'Big bag.'

'Big money.'

Dima handed Kroll his phone. Kroll tapped his shoulder where his Baghira was holstered.

'Sure you want to go in naked?'

'They're likely to scan me. Besides, it will impress them.'

'Oh, you want to look like a tough guy. Why didn't you say?'

They exchanged a look, the look that always said it could be their last. 'Twenty minutes,' said Dima. 'Any longer – come and get me.'

The lift was dead, its doors half-closed on a crushed shopping trolley. Dima collapsed the grab handle of the case and lifted it. The stairs stank of piss. Despite the hour, the building was alive with the thump of rap and domestic disputes. If it came to an exchange of fire, no one would hear or even care. A boy of no more than ten came past, with the low nasal bridge and pinched cheeks that Dima recognised as foetal alcohol syndrome. The grip of a pistol stuck out of his hoodie pocket, a dragon tattoo on his gloveless white hand. The kid paused, glanced at the bag, then Dima, considering. Behold the flower of post-Soviet youth, Dima thought. He wondered if he had been right not to bring a gun. The boy, expressionless, moved on.

The metal apartment door made a dull clang as he thumped it. Nothing. He thumped again. Eventually it opened half a metre to reveal the muzzles of two pistols, the local equivalent of a welcome mat. He stood back so they could see the case. Both of the faces behind were shrouded in ski masks. The men stepped back to let him enter. The apartment was dark; candles on a table gave out a ghostly glow. The smell of fried food and sweat hung in the hot dry air.

One man pressed a pistol into Dima's forehead while the second, shorter one patted him down, squeezing his genitals as he went. Dima had to force himself not to kick out. He sent a stern command to his foot, ordering it to stay on the floor while he collected all the data he could. The shorter one was probably late twenties, left-handed, stiff movement in his left leg, which bent awkwardly, probably from a wound to the left lower abdomen or hip. Useful. The other, straight and tall, almost two metres, looked younger and fitter, but being a terrorist had lived on a poor diet and had neglected to exercise. The sight of their faces would have helped, but the job had taught him to assess character from movement and body language. A mask was a sign of weakness – another useful pointer. A slight tremble from the gun trained on him: inexperience.

'Enough.'

The voice that rang out from further in the gloom, followed by a low cancerous chuckle, was instantly recognisable. The room became clearer: empty except for the low table strewn with candles, a take-away pizza box, three empty Baltica cans, a pair of aged APS Stechkin machine pistols and a couple of spare mags. Behind the table squatted a huge red plastic sofa that looked like it had come from a cheap brothel.

'You've aged, Dima.'

The sofa creaked as Vatsanyev hauled himself to his feet with the aid of a stick. He was barely recognisable. His hair was grey and ragged and the left half of his face had sustained severe burns, the ear almost gone under shiny, livid scar tissue that twisted round to one end of his mouth. He let the stick drop and opened his arms – the knobbly fingers splayed. Dima stepped forward, let himself be embraced. Vatsanyev kissed him on both cheeks then stepped back.

'Let me get a look at you.' He grinned, half his top teeth missing.

'At least try to act like a terrorist. You sound like my great aunt.'

'I can see some grey on you.'

'At least I have all my teeth and both my ears.'

Vatsanyev gave another chuckle and shook his head, his black eyes almost disappearing into the folds of flesh. Dima had seen men in all of the stages between life and death. Vatsanyev looked closer to the latter. He let out a long sigh and for a moment they were comrades again, Soviets united, brothers in arms for the Great Cause.

'History's not been kind to us, Dima. A toast to the old days?' He gave a theatrical wave at the half-empty bottle on the table.

'I've given up.'

'Traitor.'

Dima looked to his right and saw two corpses, both women, half covered with a rug – overdone, doll-like make-up on the one who still had a face.

'Who are they?'

'The previous tenants. Behind on their rent.'

They were back in the present. Vatsanyev stepped back to reveal the huddled bundle on the sofa.

'Allow me to introduce our guest.'

Katya was barely recognisable from the glamour shots Dima had been shown. Her stained hoodie almost obscured her face, which was a blotched mess, eyelids swollen from tears and exhaustion. The ragged bandage on her left forefinger was grey, topped with a dull brownish-red stain. Her blank eyes met Dima's and he felt an unfamiliar stab of pity.

'Can she stand? I'm not carrying her down those flights.'

Vatsanyev glanced at her. 'She walks and talks, and is now maybe a little wiser as to how the other half lives.'

Katya's eyes focused on Dima, then her gaze moved slowly to the doorway to her left, and then back to him. He made a mental note to thank her later – if there was a later. He gestured at the case. He wanted them to start counting soon.

'You're getting greedy in your old age, Vatsanyev. Or is this your pension?'

Vatsanyev gazed at the money and nodded thoughtfully. 'You and me Dima, we don't do retirement. Why else are you here in this godforsaken shithole at this ungodly hour?'

They looked at each other and for a second, the years that separated them vanished. Vatsanyev reached forward, clasped him by the shoulder.

'Dima, Dima! You need to move with the times. The world is changing. Forget the past, forget the present even. What's coming will change everything. Trust me.'

He let out a barking cough, exposing gums where teeth had once been. 'We're in what the Americans call the End Times – but not in the way they think. God won't be there, that's for sure. Three letters: P – L – R. Time to polish up your Farsi, my friend.'

They had served together in Iran during the war with Iraq, comrades and rivals. Dima had to arrange Vatsanyev's release from the Iraqis, but not before they had stamped on his back and pulled out all of his fingernails. They had even stayed in touch after the break-up of the Soviet Empire, but Vatsanyev had gone underground after Grozny fell to the Russians. Now they faced each other in a dead hooker's flat, mercenary and terrorist – two professions that were on the up.

Dima swung round suddenly. The two ski masks jumped. He bent down and unzipped the case, and with the flourish of a black marketeer presenting his booty flipped back the lid to reveal the neatly packed dollars. Bulganov wanted it all back but that might have to be Kroll's task. The ski masks stared in wonder. Good, more signs of innocence. Vatsanyev didn't even bother to look.

'Aren't you going to count it?'

He looked perturbed. 'You think I don't trust my old comrade?'

'It's Bulganov's money, not mine. If I were you I'd check every one – front and back.'

Vatsanyev smiled at the joke then nodded at his boys, who knelt down and eagerly started to pull at the tightly packed bundles. The atmosphere in the room relaxed a little. Dima noticed that a dark stain had spread from under the rug that had been thrown over the dead hookers.

The shorter Chechen holstered his pistol but the other left his on the floor by his left knee. Less than two metres away. Dima wished he knew who or what was in the next room, but it was now or never.

'I need a piss. Where's the toilet?'

Dima leapt forward, appearing to trip over the table which tipped it on its side. He slammed down hard on top of the younger thug who folded in on himself like a book. As he landed, Dima lunged for the pistol on the floor with both hands, found the trigger with one, racked the top slide with the other and without raising it fired first at the taller one, hitting him in the thigh. The man sprang backwards, offering Dima a better target. The bridge of his nose exploded with petals of bloody flesh. Still with the gun under him, Dima aimed another shot into the groin of the man beneath him and felt the explosion as he went slack. Without pausing, Dima rolled himself over the open case of money and across to the corner diagonally opposite the open door. Looking back, he saw the sofa was empty. Vatsanyev was bent over the upturned table trying to reach one of the guns with his stick. Dima lost a whole second as a remnant of embedded kinship stopped him taking a shot. He recovered enough to put a bullet into Vatsanyev's shoulder.

Katya was nowhere to be seen. She had to have gone into the other room. Had she taken shelter there or been pulled in by whoever was in there? He didn't have to wait long. She appeared in the doorway, head pulled back, her face contorted in a fresh convulsion of fear. Just behind her, another face half-hidden, even younger. No question who this was: the same black eyes as her father's, only wrapped in an exquisite porcelain doll's face. Dima did a quick calculation: Vatsanyev's daughter Nisha, his only child by his last wife would be – sixteen. Nisha had had the choice, could have gone to America with her mother and could soon have been heading for Harvard. Instead she was here, sucked into her father's desperate struggle. He glanced at Vatsanyev on his side, eyes open, watching his daughter on the other side of the money he would never get to spend.

Dima's eyes locked on to Nisha's. She kept her body behind Katya, gripping her captive's hair tightly with one hand while the other held a breadknife against her throat. Half a second passed. Dima had been here before. There had been younger targets than Nisha. An eight-year-old boy in northern Afghanistan wielding an AK like it was joined to him, and a girl, a trained sniper sent to assassinate

16

her own informant father. On a rooftop where he had cornered her, the building beneath them burning, he made a last attempt to persuade her to switch sides. But she made it clear that the idea disgusted her and insisted on going down fighting.

Another half second. There were no choices here, no second thoughts, no opportunities for negotiation. Her father had been like a brother once; Dima had even held Nisha as a baby. The best she could hope for was that his aim wasn't what it was, that his bullet would hit Katya and then they'd all be fugitives.

Dima raised his arm. It seemed to take a huge effort, as if some subterranean force field was exerting itself. Nisha was slightly to Katya's left, face half-shadowed by her captive. Dima fired wide, predicting that Nisha would dart behind her human shield, then he fired again to Katya's right, catching Nisha on the rebound. Katya crumpled forward as Nisha dropped her and fell back into the darkness. He sent a further burst into the other room, then stepping across the debris and bodies he lifted Katya into his arms.

In the sudden silence he could hear the rapid breathing of one of the Chechens. Dima turned, about to put a bullet in him, when he heard something shuffling outside. He looked up just as the apartment front door exploded. Three AK muzzles and, not far behind, three figures: faces pointlessly blackened, their helmets and body armour fresh and untarnished by action. An internal security SWAT team – famous for their ineptitude. Trying to take in the scene that confronted them, they froze. For a moment, nobody spoke.

'He's down there,' Dima said, gesturing at Vatsanyev but keeping his eyes on the men. He could hear Vatsanyev struggling to lift himself, and his wheezing whisper, 'Dima, Dima, don't let them take me.'

One of the SWATs stepped forward, lowering his weapon. 'Dima Mayakovsky, you're to come with us.'

'On whose authority?'

'Director Paliov.'

'Am I under arrest?'

'No, you have an appointment.'

'Can we make it later? I'm a bit busy.'

17

Kroll appeared in the doorway, behind them.

'Sorry I wasn't able to warn you. Shall I take the goods?'

At the word 'goods', one of the SWATs fixed his gaze on the money. As the SWAT nudged his pal, who'd clocked Katya as part of the package, Dima swung his own weapon up into his face. The second one, weighing up whether to ditch his nice steady job for a case full of dollars, left Dima plenty of time to ram the gun into his balls.

Dima looked round at Vatsanyev and gave him a single nod. Looking back at the men, he said, 'Just a moment'. Then he looked once more at his old comrade, and put a bullet in his head.

2

Paliov folded and unfolded a corner of the report as he read. With two fingers of his other hand he smoothed a patch on his forehead, as if trying to eliminate part of the network of creases that was ranged across it. The pendulous folds of skin under his eyes reminded Dima of the nosebags the carthorses wore in winter on the farm where his mother once worked. The big empty desk should have been an indication of Paliov's status, but Dima thought it had the opposite effect. It made the Chief of Operational Security look small and shrivelled.

The incident at the apartment was less than two hours old, but the hastily concocted document looked like it ran to over twenty pages. Paliov appeared to be studying every word, frowning as he read. Dima offered him a summary.

'To save your valuable time, Director, it's simple: Went in, got the girl, kept the money, shot them all. The End.'

'Vatsanyev could have been a useful source.'

'How?'

Paliov looked up from the report and glared.

Dima hadn't expected this. Typical: you sort out a mess for these people and they suddenly decide they need someone who's already been stored in the big, chilled filing cabinet with a tag on his toe. Anyhow, they'd never have got anything out of this one. Did these people never learn?

He laughed. 'If we'd lopped off his other ear? Snipped off his damaged fingers one by one? You could have pruned every limb, and his bollocks, and served him up his own cock on a blini; he wouldn't have given you a thing. He's a Chechen for God's sake.'

'And then there's the matter of my men. How do you explain that?'

'Explain what?'

This was getting tiresome. Dima hadn't expected a medal and the massed ranks of the St Petersburg Symphony, but couldn't Paliov at least pretend to sound grateful?

'I'm informed that they were beaten up in an unprovoked attack.'

Dima restrained himself with difficulty. 'Use your imagination. After those jokers brought me here, they'd have banged the girl and vanished with the money. You should congratulate me on purging your service of corrupt elements.'

Hadn't this occurred to him? He seemed to shrink further behind the desk. Dima glanced around the office. He hadn't previously been inside the GRU's new 'Aquarium', opened by Putin himself in 2006 and thoughtfully placed within sight of the old one. No one was sure how it had got its nickname – you certainly couldn't see in, that was for sure. One theory was that it was the reputed birthplace of waterboarding. Either way, and despite this latest attempt to finesse the past, the old name had stuck.

The presence of foreign furniture and new technology was striking: an Italian chair, Apple computers, on the wall a slightly bleached print of Nattier's portrait of Peter the Great. And by the window, a plant that was actually alive. An agent repatriated after long years away might be forgiven for wondering which country he was in. But the frosted glass of the internal windows and the lingering hint of pickled cabbage in the recycled air was a giveaway.

Dima nodded at the fat file under Paliov's nose. 'If that really is a report on the incident, I congratulate your staff on their creative writing. The whole thing didn't last as long as it's taking you to read about it.'

Paliov didn't respond, looked down again, continued to read. Dima wished he had managed to stop for some breakfast after all. Six dead, two in casualty, and it wasn't even nine-thirty. An armoured GAZ SUV – at least that was Russian – and an official Audi, blue light flickering on the dash, had been waiting outside when they came out of the apartment block. Two more goons jumped out of the Audi with a view to helping Kroll with the case. Kroll tried to dissuade them with a couple of punches but they didn't get the message, so Dima had to slam them against the car a few times, and in the case of the one who grabbed Katya, shut his arm in the trunk.

Dima had taken the SUV and delivered both Katya and the money to her grateful father. At least that was one satisfied customer. He had urged Kroll to help himself to the Audi. It was top of the range – heated seats and integral Bose music system, even a cute little circle of beige leather on the end of the cigarette lighter – but Kroll said it was too loud for him and besides, he said, disabling the tracker was a pain.

It was still dark, so Dima had turned on the sirens and the blue lights and had enjoyed a quick spin down the wrong side of the road – a metaphor for his whole life, now he came to think of it. He had thought of skipping the appointment with Paliov altogether, but a twinge of curiosity had prevailed. It had been so long since his former masters had come asking for him, it was a wonder they even remembered him. At the famed 'tank-proof' barrier, a guard waved the GAZ through without even checking who was at the wheel. A shocking lapse in security. He parked it in a space reserved for the Deputy Secretary of Paperclips or some such. Only when he presented himself at the desk and saw the pained expression on the pretty receptionist's face did he hesitate. The parking space? He was just preparing a snappy excuse when she nodded slowly towards a floor to ceiling mirror. His face was still peppered with a fine spray of blood from one of the exploding goons, the first lot.

'Sorry,' he said. 'Busy morning.'

She reached into her bag and produced a packet of baby wipes. He smiled. 'Bet they come in handy.'

'Every day.' There was a mischievous look in her large dark eyes. 'On my twins.'

For a fleeting moment he wondered whether she meant the pair of delicious breasts straining against the cotton of her shirt. Now he had another incentive to miss the appointment: a quick fuck over the desk would have more than made up for the missed breakfast.

He dabbed his face and held the wipe up in tribute as he walked towards the lifts.

Paliov finished reading, took off his spectacles and rubbed his eyelids with his thumb and forefinger, as if he was trying to make what he'd just read go away. Then he turned to Dima and shook his head.

'How much did Bulganov pay you?'

'It was a favour. For old times' sake.'

'Ah, old times.' There was a mournful faraway look in Paliov's eyes as if he was recalling his first fuck, which may well have preceded the Siege of Leningrad if not the Revolution itself.

'The good old days. We must get together some time and reminisce over a few bottles.'

Another man entered without knocking: slim, wiry, taut frame, early forties, tailored English suit. Paliov made a move to rise but the suit waved him down. 'Carry on – don't mind me.'

Dima recognised Timofayev, Secretary of Defence and Security, Paliov's political master. He lunged forward and took Dima's hand, a Tag Heuer watch sliding into view as his cuff moved back. Timofayev was one of the new breed of apparatchiks on whom Western accessories looked almost normal.

'So good of you to come. I hope we haven't taken you away from other assignments.'

'Only breakfast.'

Paliov winced but Timofayev laughed heartily, like a good politican, which caused Paliov's face to move unnaturally as he tried to form a smile in response.

'In fact, Secretary, Dima Mayakovsky is not currently on our—.'

'Ah, a *freelance*,' Timofayev cut in, pronouncing the English word without a trace of an accent. 'Are you familiar with that term?'

Dima replied in English.

'Yes, Secretary.'

'A man without allegiances, without loyalty. Would you say that describes you, Mayakovsky?'

'The former only,' said Dima, rather too pointedly for Paliov's comfort. He receded further into his seat.

Timofayev looked Dima up and down.

'So, Paliov: tell me all about your *freelance*. Impress me with his credentials.'

Timofayev settled himself on the edge of the huge desk and folded his arms. Paliov took in a deep, wheezy breath.

'Born in Moscow, father a career soldier, mother the daughter of a French Communist Trades Unionist driven into exile by De Gaulle. Graduated first class from Suvarov military school, youngest of his year's Spetsnaz intake, which did not seem to hinder him from coming top in most subjects and disciplines. First posting Paris, where he perfected his English through contact with the American expatriate student community and infiltrated the French interior ministry with the help of a charming young—.'

Dima gave Paliov a look. He coughed. 'Subsequently transferred to Iran as instructor to the Revolutionary Guard.'

Timofayev roared with laughter, exposing expensive dental work. 'Promotion or punishment?'

Dima let his face go blank. 'Both: my station chief turned out to be working for the British. I executed him. You could say the posting was a reward for showing initiative.'

Timofayev hadn't finished laughing, but there was a cold gleam in his eye. 'Ah, don't you miss the old days?'

Paliov pressed on. 'After an undercover assignment in the Balkans he advanced to Afghanistan where he was responsible for developing a close rapport with Mujahideen warlords.'

Timofayev was still giggling, like a battery operated toy that wouldn't switch off. 'All the choicest jobs. You must have made a real nuisance of yourself, Mayakovsky.'

A shudder from Paliov, followed by an exchange of looks between the two apparatchiks – then a silence which Dima didn't like the sound of. A silence while they remembered Solomon, the one who got away.

Dima wasn't going to rise to it. 'I accepted all assignments in the spirit in which they were given.'

'Like a true hero, I'm sure. And then? What excuse did they find to pension you off? Don't tell me. Too much initiative? Too "creative"? Or did they suddenly uncover some "unpatriotic tendencies?"'

Timofayev turned and glared at his Head of State Security, as if Dima's departure from Spetsnaz had been Paliov's doing. Paliov's round shoulders slumped further under the burden of his superior's disapproval. 'In fact, Secretary, Comrade Mayakovsky was awarded both the Order of Nevsky and the Order of Saint Andrew—.'

Timofayev cut in: '—"for exceptional services leading to the prosperity and glory of Russia", though probably not the prosperity of Comrade Mayakovsky, eh Dima?'

'I did all right.'

'But still a tall poppy nonetheless. My predecessors had a fatal tendency to be suspicious of excellence. Mediocrity was their watchword.' Timofayev swept his hand through the air. 'Like Thrasybulus, who advised Periander to "Take off the tallest stalks, indicating thereby that it was necessary to do away with the most eminent citizens."'

He turned to Paliov, who looked blank.

'Aristotle,' said Dima.

But Timofayev was warming to his theme. 'You were too good, my dear Mayakovsky, and you paid for it. It's a credit to your patriotism that you didn't go West in search of better terms and conditions.'

He put his face close to Dima's. His breath was mint fresh with a hint of garlic. Dima's desire for breakfast evaporated.

'How would you like a real reward?' He squeezed Dima's shoulder, eyes blazing. 'You'll find our terms are much improved these days – entirely competitive with the best private security outfits. Your chance to get that Lexus, or the nice little hunting lodge you promised yourself. Somewhere comfortable and private to take the ladies: Jacuzzi, satellite porn, roaring log fire . . .'

Both of them looked at Dima who showed no reaction. Eventually Paliov gave a short cough.

'It may well be, Secretary, that Mayakovsky is not motivated by, er, remunerative compensation.'

Timofayev nodded. 'Fine sentiments, rare in our brave new

Russia.' He got up and paced over to Peter the Great, his handmade shoes squeaking very slightly. 'For a chance to serve, then.' He seemed to be addressing the portrait. He wheeled round and fixed his gaze on Dima. 'Your chance not only to serve your country – but to *save* it.'

The words failed to have the desired effect. The suits could never believe it, but persuasion seldom worked with him. If anything it had the opposite effect. He had heard it all before; too many opportunities for glory and reward sold to him in the past had turned to shit. His stomach rumbled as if by way of response.

Timofayev strode over to the window and jutted his chin at the view. 'Did you know that on the Khodinka field there, Rossinsky became the first Russian to fly an aeroplane?'

'In 1910.'

'And Tsar Nicholas the Second had his coronation there.'

'In 1886.'

He wheeled round. 'You see Dima, you can't help yourself. You are a Russian through and through.'

'Twelve hundred were killed in the stampede. They say their patriotic fervour got the better of them.'

Timofayev pretended he hadn't heard. He strode back over to Dima and put a hand on each arm of the chair. 'Come back to us for one last mission. We need a genuine patriot – one with your skills and experience, and commitment.' He glanced at Paliov. 'We could even – overlook the matter of the operatives this morning.'

New furniture, new computer, same old threats. Your country needs you to get your bollocks shot off, if you wouldn't mind. Your choice naturally, though if you say no we have ways of making you change your mind. What the hell was he doing listening to this crap, when he could have been at Katarina's Kitchen, eating pancakes with Georgian cherry jam? Or better still, screwing the receptionist, whose fiery red hair framed a perfect white skin in a delicious vision of purity, with the promise of some very sluttish behaviour to come? Why not both? He'd done his bit, and deserved to enjoy himself for a couple of days – for good. Yet in some obscure part of his brain a small pulse of curiosity was beating.

Dima got to his feet and glanced at his watch, which still had a small smear of blood on the face, turning the '12' into a shape very slightly like a heart. He gestured at the frosted glass and the ghostly shapes of minions moving about in the outer office.

'You have a whole army out there. Young fit men and women jockeying for a chance at the big time, desperate to climb the career ladder. Whatever it is, the answer's no. You retired me. I'm staying that way. Besides, I'm hungry. Good day, gentlemen.'

He marched out.

For a few seconds neither of them moved. Then Paliov gave his master an 'I told you so' look and reached for the phone. Timofayev put his hand down on top of the old man's. 'Let him go. Forget about your casualties. But find something to make him agree.'

'He's immune.'

'Nobody's immune. There must be something. Find it. Today.'

3

It was a 104°F inside the Stryker and the smell wasn't getting any better. The shift had just stretched into its thirty-second hour, which would do nothing to improve the personal hygiene of the inmates in full kit: Kevlar helmets, bullet-resistant glasses, heat-resistant gloves, body armour, knee pads, elbow pads, 240 rounds of ammunition for their M4s in pouches attached to the body armour. It was like being in an armour-plated coffin, but not so spacious. Up until a few weeks ago they'd been leaving the body kits at the base. But things had changed.

Marine Sergeant Henry 'Black' Blackburn reached up and lifted one of the hatches, then another. It didn't produce much of a breeze, however, as they were keeping to a steady 25 miles an hour. In the early days they used to go full pelt, until it became clear that they stood a better chance of avoiding trouble if they saw it before they drove into it. He put his head out and squinted at the sun-bleached landscape around them. It had been years since outright war had devastated this part of Iraq but the damage remained. None of the trillions of dollars spent on reconstruction had made it to Al-Sulaymaniyah, or if it had the myriad layers of middlemen and subcontractors had got there first. The sheer number of them made your head spin. They all creamed off their cut, producing paperwork for men who were never hired, buildings that were never built. True, a few roads had been resurfaced, sewers relaid, but after a few months they all sank back into the same state of decrepitude as before. Any unrest and the first casualty after the local population was the infrastructure. They passed the remains of a freshly shelled gas depot, whole sections of concrete hanging by the rusting steel reinforcement rods. Two small children in nothing but T-shirts were throwing small rocks at nothing in particular from the top of a mound of rubble. Half a dozen goats looked on, grazing in the carcass of the depot.

Campo was mid-story. '... And I'm, like, on station ready for deployment, and she says, "Honey do you have any protection?" so I say, "Baby I left my M16 at home, but if you wanna see it I'll go get it ..."'

No one responded. They'd all heard it at least twice before.

Montes reverted to his favourite refrain.

'I mean, who even wants to be here? TV say soldiers want to be here. Where they get that from? Make folks feel better? Maybe if you wanting to get your star, make some rank. All we want is get the fuck outta here, right Black?'

Black shrugged, not because he didn't have an answer: he just didn't want to have this conversation right now. He was thinking about the email home he would write tonight. *Dear Mom and Dad. Today was 115°F. That's the hottest we've had.* He spent another ten minutes trying to come up with the next line. Three positives. That was his rule. His mother could find a silver lining in a tornado. *The school they built just by the base has opened.* He'd leave out the fact that no kids had turned up, that the deputy head had become the head because the original head had been shot in front of his family. He couldn't think of two more positives right now. He abandoned that and considered writing to Charlene. *Just to let you know I'm still sane* ... Perhaps she'd take it the wrong way, think he was in doubt. She'd always known he'd enlist from the get-go, all through Senior High, but when it came to it, she said it had to be her or the army – not both. There wasn't going to be any waiting for him. *You may come back* – she'd struggled for a word – *different.* She thought his father would sway him. She knew what he thought about the whole army thing. She just didn't get it. But Blackburn still loved her, still hoped she'd come around.

He had been counting the days to September 1st, when they were due to go home, crossing off the days on a grid he had drawn in the back of his log. Since last week he'd stopped. Home didn't seem to be getting any closer.

28

Black's radio squawked: Lieutenant Cole.

'*Misfit 1–3 this is Misfit actual. Listen up. We lost contact with Jackson's squad in grid eight zero, ten klicks west. You're the only element I got to send. Last known position Spinza Meat Market. Bad freaking part of town. Go find 'em, got that?*'

'*1–3. Copy that.*'

Jackson was out of contact. That could only mean something bad.

Black looked at the crew. They'd all heard the order on their headsets. No one spoke for a few seconds, as if they were conserving every last grain of energy.

'So, anyone else don't get what we're doing here?' Montes was off on his high school debating society riff again. Blackburn wished he would shut up and just do his job. He was tired, and this was making him feel tireder.

'Quit being a fucking hippie, Montes.' Chaffin ripped the wrapper off a stick of gum and folded it into his mouth.

Montes loosened his grip on his weapon.

'All I'm saying is we're here to keep a lid on things, not start a fucking war with Iran.'

'The PLR's not Iran.'

'Man, we been over this a hunnert times.'

Chaffin put his hands over his face.

Black continued. 'They're *in* Iran though, because that's where they're coming from. And Iran is just' – he cocked his head leftwards – 'right over there.'

'You got that now, Montes, you fucking tree hugger? We want your opinion, we'll give it to you. All right?'

Blackburn hoped this wasn't going to evolve into something full-blown and personal between Chaffin and Montes. Debating the relative merits of twin cheerleaders or a one-on-one with the new British princess was a pleasantly pointless diversion. Questioning their entire purpose in this hellhole could develop into a discipline problem.

They'd served in the same platoon for eighteen months. They were family. But the terms of engagement had changed. They'd gone in thinking they'd be the last American deployment in the area, and Chaffin wasn't the only one whose patience was running out. The whole place was sinking back into chaos. Montes was becoming the target for his frustration, and Blackburn didn't blame him. Privately, he knew Montes had a point. He wondered what a man like him was even doing there, when he should have been handing out flyers about the decline of capitalism on a leafy campus somewhere. But Blackburn didn't have time to be anyone's camp counsellor. Jackson's Stryker had gone silent and they had no choice but to go look for it. It's what you did. What you didn't do was sit in a 104°F sardine can discussing it like a bunch of liberals on PBS.

He raised his voice a notch.

'Look at me. Montes? This is our job.'

'Yeah, baby, I hear that.'

Black raised a hand.

'And to finish the job, we gotta deal with the PLR. And to do that, sooner or later we gotta go cross the border.'

Chaffin opened his mouth to speak, but Blackburn silenced him with a look.

They dismounted from the Stryker and fanned out. The Spinza Meat Market was an old cloistered building with a gallery on the upper level. A week ago it had been swarming with activity. Today it was deserted: not a good sign. Campo tapped Blackburn on the shoulder. 'Check this out.'

A freshly painted mural of Al Bashir, the PLR leader. A good likeness, Blackburn thought: someone had taken their time.

'They sainting him here. He their man, now.' Montes was next to them. The artist had given the Iranian former Air Force General a fierce glare of certainty. 'Dude looks like he means business.'

'Jerkoff. It's just a painting. He's gotta be as old as your granny. They just left out the wheelchair.'

'Ever ask yourself how this part of the world got so fucked up all the time?'

'Hey I just work here, Montes. Other people work that shit out.'

Montes persisted. 'How long before we rolling ourselves into Iran?'

Blackburn waved them forward. 'That's way above my pay grade. Let's go find this patrol.'

The old man was squatting in a doorway. Montes was crouched down, talking, his weapon pushed behind his shoulder, out of the way. He held up ten fingers, made fists, then another ten, and then another ten, then mimed using a machine gun. To give him his due, he was trying to be useful.

'He's saying there were thirty, all armed. Came through half an hour ago.' He turned back to the old man. 'Thank you, Sir.'

'Thanks, I'll take it from here.'

Black leaned down, continued in Arabic.

'*Were they PLR?*'

The old man shrugged.

'*Local boys?*'

He shook his head, although it could have been more of a tremor, and pointed at the westward gate of the market.

'Well, let's go the way the man says.'

The gate led into a narrow street of three-storey buildings. Blackburn heard a couple of shutters close and a baby crying. A Toyota pick-up lay sideways across the street, the front fender torn away as if it had been swiped by a much heavier vehicle and in a hurry.

Black signalled to the others to hug the walls. 'Big cross street here, exposed.'

They all heard the rumble at the same time. Tracked vehicle. Blackburn flattened himself against the corner wall and peered round. He saw the vehicle nose out of a gateway, a block up the cross street, and turn left, moving away at patrol speed.

Black got on the radio.

'*APC, no markings, headed north, taking its time like it owns the place.*'

'*That's some serious metal.*'

'*Flag him down, ask what side he's on.*'

'*Shut up Montes. Take a right up that street, where he just came from.*'

They crossed the road in twos.

'Keep it moving!'

'So quiet it's like they got the whole place on lockdown.'

'Or the Pied Piper's just been through.'

'I no like this shit.'

'Okay, that's a Combat Indicator. Take it slowly guys.'

The side street the APC came from was narrow, a chasm of tall buildings with overhanging upper storeys, throwing it into dark shadow. At the other end it opened into a small plaza. A group of women were huddled down behind wicker baskets in a deep doorway near the plaza entrance. They were waving them forward, pointing upwards.

'Okay, let's not do what the lady says just yet. Get visual on the rooftops.'

They froze, scanning the rooftops and every shuttered window. Blackburn saw the silhouetted figure first, just as the masonry beside him shattered. 'Sniper! Cover, cover!'

Black wheeled round just in time to see Chaffin's shoulder explode. 'Man down. Smoke cover. Now!'

Campo tossed a white phosphorus grenade to block the sniper while Blackburn and Montes grabbed Chaffin and pulled him into a doorway, but he didn't want to go, wrestling them with his dissipating strength. 'Get me back up. I can still shoot. Let me at him, the fucker.'

'Easy soldier.'

Matkovic was screaming down the radio.

'Fucking smoke. I had visuals on three more!'

The wound was bloody but not deep. Blackburn let Chaffin get to his feet. He swayed, then grinned. 'I'm fucked up but I'm up. Let me at 'em.'

Through the smoke, ahead, Matkovic loosed off a mag at the rooftop where Chaffin's sniper had been. Paused, waited.

As the smoke cleared, Blackburn saw the sniper fold up on himself and drop like a bad guy in a Western. The body thumped into the street ten feet from Matkovic, who stood in a doorway. But Matkovic didn't react. He was static, staring ahead into the plaza. Something about his stance, weapon down, told Blackburn that Matkovic had seen something he was going to have trouble forgetting. Without altering his gaze he beckoned to Black.

'Think we've found what we came for.'

Two dead marines were sprawled at the gates to the plaza. One, helmet gone, face half off, looked like he'd been closest to an RPG. The other, a wide red crater in his chest, had a pensive look in his eyes, which were fixed on the blazing sky. Blackburn leaned down, took the tags off one, then the other, and pushed them into his top pocket. 'Fuck this day.'

'Black, look up!'

Matkovic was first into the plaza. Bodies and body parts had been thrown in all directions. The Stryker was on its side, its ramp down and its tyres on fire, with all eight wheels twisted at different angles. Close by was the chassis of what might have been a small truck or bus, the bodywork vaporised by the IED it had been carrying. A low, rhythmic groaning was coming from inside the Stryker.

Matkovic was already on the radio ordering CAS-EVAC, trying to keep his rage under control as the voice on the other end pressed him for more detail, eventually exploding. *'Just get the fuck here yesterday, okay?'*

He turned to Blackburn. 'Going to check inside the Stryker.'

'Stop.' The word was out of his mouth before Blackburn knew why he'd said it. There were several other damaged vehicles in the plaza, two minibuses, glass all gone, peppered with shrapnel dents. Blackburn motioned them back, tracked right until he could see another vehicle, a Nissan pick-up, on the other side of the Stryker. Like the others it was a mess, its windows and lights gone, every panel dented. But something was wrong.

It was the tyres. Still inflated. They should have been shredded. Matkovic looked at Black, then the pick-up. Some civilians were starting to appear at their windows, looking down on the plaza. Matkovic waved his hands in the air like he was doing the breast-stroke, screaming in Arabic: *'Back inside!'*

Black tracked further right, scanning what he could of the area round the pick-up, looking for detonator wires. Whoever planted this was waiting until as many US as possible were crowded around the Stryker tending the dying and wounded. A woman, only her large brown eyes visible under a dusty grey burka, was watching him from behind a fruit stand: a young woman – his age, maybe younger. He watched her gaze move slowly, deliberately, away from him and up to a first storey window on the south side of the square, then back down to him again. Then she slipped into the shadow of her doorway and was gone. He scanned the pavement again. It was strewn with bits of brick and metal and flesh. Amongst the mess he saw the wire snaking across to the building that had been pointed out by the woman's eyes.

All the crew were stopped, waiting. They knew what he was doing. That was the upside of having been together in this shithole for so long – they could practically read each others' minds. He'd miss that when it was over, when he was home. Where else would he ever have that closeness, that rapport? With a woman maybe? A family? Or would he be too fucked up by then. Maybe he'd become too good at this, and blow his chance of having a life. *One thing at a time*, he said to himself: *focus*.

He took his time, backed out of the square, fixing the building in his mind before he checked out an approach to it from its rear. Out of view, he slid swiftly through a passage that would lead to the back of the houses. He had cleared so many properties like these he could guess the layout, even though he had never been in this square before. Side entrances in the alleys were common. The stairs usually went sideways, the first floor front rooms, usually the largest, stretched across the building. There was music coming from this one, from inside the ground floor. He stepped in through a curtained doorway: a kitchen, two clean tea glasses on the draining board and a radio, playing that high pitched music. He reached in and, very slowly, turned up the volume. He thought of taking off his boots, decided against it. There were two bodies on the stairs, a woman and a girl. Both shot through the head, proof he was on the right track. He didn't pause, but the split second's vision was still sickening. He tiptoed up the stairs, listening to the blood hammering through his veins, adrenalin blocking every impulse but what he needed to get the job done.

At the top of the stairs he paused, about to step into the room. He saw the car battery, the wires, the jaws of the jump leads, one attached, one waiting. But nothing else. He just had enough time to see that it was empty before a blow to the back of his neck flattened him, his head inches from the battery. On his way down he managed to twist to one side and reach for his KBAR knife, his M4 too unwieldy in the narrow space. The figure was in shadow, a blur of fabric. As it lunged for the battery, Blackburn put the knife deep into a thigh – hitting the femoral artery. The scream was piercingly high. Too high for a man. A boy?

As he struggled to a kneeling position his assailant slammed down on to the floor beside him. Not a man or a boy, but a girl, a lake of blood gushing out from under her shalwar kameez, writhing like a beached marlin, seemingly unaware of the blood draining out of her. In between gasps she let out a torrent of Arabic. Blackburn could only make out *scum pig* and *hell*. But the message was clear. She went on struggling, sliding in her own blood. If he was going to save her he had about twenty seconds.

'*Let me help you. Or you will die.*'

How many times had he said that, and how many times had his help been rejected? They had come to help. But it didn't always look that way. As he reached down to her, she lashed out.

'*PLR?*'

'*The PLR will destroy you all. You are finished. Finished.*'

She tried to repeat the word again but nothing came and Blackburn watched helplesss as the life emptied from her.

4

It was after two a.m. when Dima got back to his hotel room. Getting out of the Aquarium had been more difficult than getting in: one tradition that had been kept on. When he left Paliov, he'd found a trio of Internal Affairs heavies in the outer office. Hoping they were merely for decoration he started to move past them, but they blocked his way. He decided to deploy the sweet talk before punching anyone. A bit of foreplay, he thought to himself as he sized up the leader of the three, a face he recognised from way back.

'And what can I do for you gentlemen?'

Two of them looked out of practice, their muscles gone soft from years of hitting those too weak to fight back. The one he had to worry about was Fremarov, a Mongolian who had served with him in Afghanistan. The once proud soldier was now in the slow lane, eking out his time up to retirement doing the shit jobs reserved for older operatives who hadn't been smart enough – or unpleasant enough – to progress up the greasy pole. Just the sight of him made Dima thankful that he'd got out when he had.

'Fremarov, old friend. How's life treating you?'

The pair of bookends looked bemused, thrown by this unexpected greeting from someone they'd been sent to detain.

Eventually Fremarov spoke. 'This is awkward.'

'What did they tell you? That I've broken ranks, failed to follow orders, spun out of control?'

'Something like that.'

'A simple misunderstanding: bit of a crossed wire that's all. Right hand doesn't know what the left hand is doing. You know what they're like.'

'Yeah.' Despite his instructions, Fremarov gave a shrug. With

36

fifteen years to go till he could collect his pension, why not use up another five minutes? The bookends looked less convinced.

'Your comrade here is a bloody good bloke,' said Dima. 'Saved my life on more than one occasion.'

Fremarov smiled. They both knew it was crap, but it sounded good. 'It was the other way round, you bastard, as well you know.'

'Was it? I can never remember. Well, it was a laugh anyhow.'

'Do you two know each other?' said Bookend One. Fremarov rolled his eyes.

'The trouble with our superiors,' Dima continued, watching Bookend Two and shifting his weight on to his other foot in readiness, 'is they have such short memories. They forget who's done them a favour.'

'True,' said Fremarov, just as Bookend Two chose that moment to make his move. As he swung a clumsy right at Dima's jaw, Dima bent and flipped him over his back like a sack of potatoes and shoved him hard against the wall. He collapsed on to the thin carpet, panting. Not wanting to be outdone on the initiative front, Bookend One tried to knock Dima off balance by hooking one foot round his left leg while simultaneously slicing him hard across the solar plexus. Dima swung round to see Fremarov's huge hand squeezing the man's neck. He carried on squeezing while Dima stepped neatly out of the way.

'I'll say you fought us off and gave us the slip,' said Fremarov.

'Yes, three against one – I like that,' said Dima. 'Nice to run into you. Give my best to your beautiful daughter.'

'She's married now.'

'Shame.'

When he reached the hotel, the pretty brunette at reception had finished her shift, to be replaced by a severe-looking type, possibly with potential if you liked the feel of stilettos on your back, which he didn't. He walked to the Polezhaevskaya metro and took the purple line back into the centre. It had been a funny old day – handling $5 million one minute, taking the metro to breakfast the next. Not to mention all the killing in between.

He let himself into the room. The curtains were open, the neon sign of the club opposite – The Comfort Zone – striping the walls with red and green in hectic succession. He left the light off, threw his coat on the bed. Sometimes he wondered what it would be like to be one of those people on the metro, getting up, going to work, arguing with the wife, leading a normal life. Nothing about his life had been normal and it was too late to change that now. He was who he was, for better or worse. The question was whether he could live with himself.

5

Dima spent the rest of the day with Kroll. Breakfast had merged into lunch, which meant Kroll was too out of it to drive, so Dima took him home. While his old friend napped, Dima flipped between news channels. Vatsanyev had been right. The PLR were clawing their way up the news agenda. Al Jazeera had footage of a big rally in Tehran, the PLR leader saluting the crowd as if he'd already taken over.

He turned and addressed the mirror.

'For fuck's sake put that toy away: I'm too tired to do a runner.'

Paliov got up stiffly, emerging out of a shadow by the window; the XP9 semi-automatic looked absurd in his gnarled hand.

He pocketed the pistol, went over to the TV and turned up the volume: more Iran, and CNN footage of Al Bashir in his air force days before he went rogue, saluting a flypast.

Dima rolled his eyes. 'Is that really necessary?'

'You never know who's listening.'

'Thought that was your job.'

Paliov's lipless slit of a mouth widened into what could have been described, at a push, as a grim smile.

'These days . . . It's complicated.' He shrugged, then gazed round the room from under his heavy-lidded eyes. 'Rather modest surroundings for someone of your reputation.'

'I like to keep things simple.'

'This is a bit extreme.'

'I like extreme. You know that. That's why you fired me, remember.'

'Oh Dima, that was a long time ago. Water under the bridge, eh?'

'I think the bridge got swept away in the flood.'

Dima flopped on to the bed and kicked off his boots. 'So what is it that your shiny new politician wants you to get me to do?'

'You know I wouldn't be here if it wasn't serious.'

Dima lay down anyway and stared at the ceiling. 'Tell you what, you begin my bedtime story and I'll see how quickly it puts me to sleep.'

'We have a situation.'

'*You* do: *I* don't.'

Paliov wafted a hand at the TV, still playing pictures from Iran.

'I noticed.' Dima sighed and slid his hands under his head. 'You only have yourselves to blame. You've been supplying Iran ever since they fell out with America. T-72 tanks, MiG 29s, SA-15 Gauntlet surface-to-air missile systems, TOR-M1 air defence missile systems, S-300 anti-aircraft missiles, VA-111 Shkval torpedoes. Arms transfer agreements to the value of $300 million between 1998 and 2001, $1.7 billion between 2002 and 2005. You couldn't help yourselves.'

'Arms exports have kept this country solvent; we're outselling the Americans two to one. We are the majority supplier to the developing world. It's a great source of national pride.'

'Now you sound just like Timofayev. If you go on like that I may have to shoot you.'

'Okay, okay.' Paliov rubbed a gnarled hand over his face. 'It doesn't get easier, you know. The Cold War was a lot simpler.'

'You're tired Paliov. Take a tip from me. Get yourself sacked.'

'That may be sooner than you think, if I get this one wrong. What do you know about Amir Kaffarov?'

'Ethnic Tajik, mediocre air force lieutenant who helped himself to a fleet of Antonovs during the Glorious Liberation, when everyone was looking the other way. Filled them with stolen kit and flew them off to destinations unknown. Now Russia's foremost and dodgiest arms dealer. You want him killed I take it?'

'Rescued actually.'

Dima laughed. 'I've been on the wrong end of Kaffarov's merchandise in three different theatres. Half the boy soldiers in Liberia and Congo are toting his AKs, he's putting weaponry into the Tribal

Areas faster than the Coalition can take it out with their drones. The guy's an A-list merchant of death.'

Dima glared at Paliov, a man of the past trying to keep up, out of his depth. He raised his hands and let them drop on to his knees.

'He's in Iran. We have to get him back. Now.'

'He's in cahoots with Al Bashir?'

'Was: they fell out over a deal. Al Bashir's holding him, demanding a ransom.'

'Leave him. Let Bashir do his worst. He'll be doing the world a service.'

'The Kremlin doesn't see it that way. The Americans find out, that would be bad for us, which together with the international loss of face . . .'

Paliov didn't sound convinced by his own words. For all his rank and status, he seemed pathetic.

'Go away, will you? I'm tired. It's been a long day.'

Paliov looked up. 'Don't get me wrong, I admire your principles. God knows I envy your freedom to pick and choose from the jobs that come your way.'

'You know me as well as I do – probably better, easily well enough to know I'd never consider something like this. You've got hundreds on your books who'd jump at the chance to die pointlessly for the Motherland.'

Paliov slowly got to his feet. 'I don't have a choice here. As you say, I know everything about you.'

Dima felt the indignation boiling up in him. 'If you're about to bring up Solomon – don't. You hung his defection round my neck nearly twenty years ago. I've done my time for that one, believe me.'

Paliov shook his head. 'Not Solomon – though he might turn out to be in the mix.'

'What does that mean?'

'In Iran. There's been a sighting.'

'Just go. Get out of my life and don't come back.' Dima lunged forward and grabbed the old man's lapels.

'Hear me out, Dima. I've got something for you – that could mean a lot more than Solomon.'

He took a slim manila envelope from his inside jacket pocket. 'Something that may help you decide to – reconsider.'

Those old Soviet euphemisms – so hard to give up. He let the envelope drop on to the bed.

Dima kept his eyes on the ceiling. 'Compromising photographs? You really do live in the past. I've not done anything exciting enough for too long. And anyway I'm not interesting enough for anyone to care.'

'Open.'

Dima sighed, lifted himself on to an elbow, flicked on the bedside light, tore open the envelope and shook the contents on to the bed. A pair of photographs fell out. The first was a long-range close-up of a young man, mid twenties, tall, strong frame, black hair, good suit, among a crowd of commuters on a bridge. Dima didn't register who he was at first. He examined the background, then recognised the Pont Neuf: Paris. Dima felt his pulse shift a gear. He looked at the other photo: the same man, in a park, sharing a joke with a pretty blonde, pushing a buggy with two children.

Dima sat up. Held the photos under the light. He stared at the young man for some time but it was the child's face – the image of his mother – that left him in no doubt. Now his heartbeat was smashing against his ribs. He looked up. Paliov had managed to contort his mouth into something resembling a smirk.

'Do what we ask and his name and address is yours.'

Suddenly Dima wasn't tired any more.

6

The Ops Room stank of sweat and smoke. If there was a 'No Smoking' sign it wasn't visible through the exhaust from Kroll's Troikas. He and Dima had been there since seven a.m. At first they'd had the place to themselves, then a swarm of archivists and researchers had descended, armed with dossiers, maps and photos, until the big polished table where they were seated disappeared under an avalanche of intelligence. Two technicians arrived to fire up the big screens that lined the walls, each one displaying satellite images of Iran. Then came a platoon of uniformed young men who took their places at the row of consoles that ran down either side of the room. Seeing Kroll puffing away gave them an excuse to light up as well. What else they were doing was a mystery.

Kroll glanced at the massed ranks of the GRU's finest. 'Well, at least if World War Three starts we're ready.'

Dima coughed. 'If we don't all die of lung cancer. Maybe we should decamp to Chernobyl for some fresh air.'

Now it was past ten and the air conditioning had given up the ghost. Portable backup units were wheeled in, which just wafted the smoke around while filling the room with more noise. Also disturbing Dima's concentration was a trio of Ops Room supervisors, supposedly standing by to fulfil his every need. Lavishing manpower on a job like this was out of character, not just for Paliov but for the GRU in general, with its reputation for stinginess and corner cutting.

He pored over the shots of Al Bashir's compound near Bazargan, north of Tabriz, close to the Azerbaijan border, all taken by satellite in the last forty-eight hours. The intelligence team had gone to town with a three-dimensional plan of the compound and all of its buildings, plus a full analysis of how many rooms, whether there were any basements, where the power lines came in, what the door and window frames were made of, if there were any security bars, whether the glass was strengthened or bullet-proof and finally if there were any drains.

A black Mercedes G-Wagen, believed to be Kaffarov's, was clearly visible among a cluster of trucks and pick-ups. Without looking up, Dima addressed the trio.

'Nothing from the ground yet?'

Arkov from Reconnaissance stepped forward.

'Sir, these images were captured by the very latest SSR 809 and bounced back to us just two hours ago. We can live-link and show movement minute by minute.'

'So at least we'll know if they're sending out for pizza.'

Irony hadn't been on Arkov's syllabus. At a loss to know what to say next, he drew a pointer from under his arm and traced lines on the photo. 'The perimeter walls are clearly visible from above, Sir.'

It amused Dima to be addressed as Sir, though he couldn't help but detect a hint of scorn in the inflection. He knew that for the likes of Arkov his presence was a breach of protocol. This inner sanctum of the GRU was the preserve of the permanent staff, out of bounds to outsiders, and Arkov was having trouble concealing his disapproval. Dima found the man's movements irritatingly robotic, as if he was being operated by remote control. He had an urge to knock him off course and pull out his wiring.

Kroll, his twentieth Troika of the day burning close to his yellowed fingers, looked up from his laptop and addressed the robot. 'He needs to know how *high* the walls are.'

Arkov gazed imperiously at him, as if he was a vagrant who had come off the street in search of somewhere warm. Considering he lived mostly in a car, Kroll had made a creditable effort to look normal, reliable even. For once his jacket and trousers looked like he hadn't slept in them and he had even had a shave.

Arkov's nose seemed to rise as he opened his mouth to reply. 'As I said, we are not in a position to determine that at this time.'

Dima was prepared to expend only as much energy as was needed to cut through this crap. Computers and cameras had their place, but his natural habitat was the field, the real world, not this glorified stationery cupboard manned by shop window dummies who wouldn't know their arse from the White House. In parts of Africa there were boys Arkov's age who'd already seen several lifetimes' worth of action, who knew as much as he did about how to make war, yet couldn't even read. To Dima, he personified everything that was wrong with the new Russia. A triumph of arrogance over experience.

Arkov wasn't getting the message. 'Our information based on special analysis is that there is a clear case for helicopter insertion.'

Kroll's face contorted with menace. 'He'll be inserting something else if you don't get the information he needs. NOW.'

Without looking up Dima added, 'Also, I want a full analysis of all movements of vehicles, plus numbers of visible personnel on-site. Look for any uniforms, insignia and arms.'

'That will take—.'

'You've got half an hour, starting now.'

Flushed with indignation, Arkov flounced out.

There were a whole lot of uncertainties about this mission, Dima thought, not least why it was being mounted at all, why he had been singled out, why Paliov had gone to such trouble to make him commit. That's why he had insisted on having Kroll at his side, someone he could trust absolutely, who knew how his mind worked. Maybe Paliov understood, but to most people inside the GRU Dima's regard for his old comrade was a mystery. For a start Kroll didn't look anything like your typical Spetsnaz veteran, but Dima regarded that as an asset. Kroll had the sort of colouring that meant he could pass for a whole variety of nationalities, and his unmilitary, stooping frame gave no hint of his training. To say he was battle-scarred was an understatement. His hearing had been permanently damaged by a car bomb in Kabul; he bore several livid scars after being tortured in Chechnya and he had taken a bullet in the Beslan siege. He had his weaknesses, chiefly a fatal attraction to volatile women. He was a terrible shot and harboured a fixed-wing pilot's innate suspicion of helicopters. *If God had meant them to fly he would have given them proper wings*, was a favourite refrain of his. But he had an almost supernatural ability to anticipate whatever Dima was thinking and they shared an impatience with the military rulebook that had been the undoing of so many missions.

Kroll waited till the last possible moment before extinguishing the cigarette, pressing it down with his thumb into the five-sided Pentagon souvenir ashtray. Someone, Dima noted, had emptied it at least once since they arrived. 'If we go in from above we'll wake the whole place up and lose any element of surprise. I'm thinking we could get on target with vehicles.'

'You would be. Time to face up to your fear of helicopters. Besides it's most unpatriotic: you know they're a Russian invention.'

'Sikorsky fled to America first. That makes him a traitor in my book.'

There was no point trying to reason with Kroll. Besides, Dima knew that in the end he would always do what he was told. He glanced briefly at his old friend, lost in thought, his fingers pressed against his temples, which exaggerated the slant of his eyes. He hadn't told him about the photographs in Paliov's envelope. Even though Kroll was dismayed when Dima told him he had accepted the assignment, and most probably guessed that there was more to it than he knew, he had the grace not to probe. They knew each other's boundaries instinctively.

Dima reviewed what he had learned so far. The property at Bazargan had once been a monastery. Parts of it dated back to the fourteenth century. Arkov, credit where it was due, had come up with an archaeological survey that showed that the present walls were built on the original ones and were four metres deep. What had those Christians been anticipating? Artillery? Tank rounds? A nuclear strike? In which case they were about six hundred years too early. In the 1950s the Shah had had the place renovated as his northern retreat and hunting lodge. It had acquired a pool and a vast garage that housed some of his exotic car collection. The Ayatollahs probably had these symbols of Western decadence crushed. It was unclear how or when the property had come under Al Bashir's control, or what he had intended it for. A regional command centre was a realistic assumption. Arkov had come back with an estimate of between twelve and twenty-five personnel currently on site. Some of this stuff was useful, but most of it merely raised more questions.

How much of precisely what weaponry Kaffarov had already sold to Al Bashir was also unknown. The compound could be an arsenal. For all Dima knew he might have enough gear in there for a full-blown campaign.

He became aware of a presence in front of him. And a faint scent of something pleasant: jasmine, was it? Or possibly gardenia.

He looked up. She was tall and angular, though not without curves. Around the same age as him but in better condition. Despite the formal, understated tailored Italian jacket, he could tell by the way she stood that she had trained in the field. Probably capable of killing every one of those screen-jockeys if she needed to, and giving him a run for his money. Her badge said Omorova.

She put down a fresh bundle of files.

'I hope I have everything you want.'

He smiled.

'I'm sure you do.'

The warmth in her eyes faded. He cancelled the smile.

'Shouldn't you be operational?'

She took the question as a compliment.

'I wish. But my father's not well and my mother can't cope so I'm taking some Moscow time.' She looked down at the photos and sighed. Dima guessed what she was thinking. Maybe if they were going in, in full kit, but undercover? A six-foot blonde, in Iran? It wasn't going to happen.

'Okay, show me Kaffarov. I want everything, down to which hand he jerks himself off with.'

She didn't alter her expression.

'That may be difficult. He has a very attentive harem.'

'"Many hands make light work."'

Kroll looked up from his laptop. 'What?'

'English proverb. Go back to work.'

Omorova spread out the files and took a deep breath. 'I'll skip to the highlights. He's fifty-four, a sixty a day smoker and despite tennis twice a week is not fit. Don't expect him to do anything physical like scale a wall or run very far. He's nervy, pushy and impatient. He won't be taking kindly to being held but values his life and is not physically fearless. He uses a lot of cocaine so you can expect him to be wired – or strung out if he's separated from his stash. Could be helpful to give him a top-up if you've got time before you lift him. He's also a control freak who hates to be driven. He used to pilot himself everywhere before he did a hard landing in Ghana and ripped the undercarriage off his Falcon.'

'Is he likely to have loved ones with him?'

She raised an eyebrow. 'Interesting choice of words. He's got a second wife in rehab and at least two mistresses, one here in Moscow, another who was in Tehran.'

'Could be with him?'

'Maybe. She's Austrian. Kristen. I don't have her cup size.'

'I'll use my imagination.'

'Put it this way, he's never been over-attentive to any of them. The first wife was kidnapped . . .'

'And?'

'He didn't pay.'

'What was the demand?'

'A million dollars.'

'Cheap. What happened to her?'

'Never seen again.'

'Okay, I'm getting the picture now. Where is he based?'

'Apart from his Moscow house on the Arbat and a dacha in Peredelkino, he's based himself in Iran for the last ten years. And as a Tajik, he gets by in Farsi and has taken full advantage of Iran's non-aligned status, smoothing access to some of his more – unconventional clients.'

'By which you mean terrorists. Tell me about his background.'

'Russian passport. Only son of a Tajik assembly worker and seamstress mother. Father worked in the Togliatti Lada plant until an injury put him on crutches. They devoted their lives to his advancement. He's had no contact with them for twenty years but funds all their care.'

'Anything about his time in the air force?'

'Undistinguished. Mostly a tender pilot, passed over for combat training. Always a troublemaker. He was investigated for dealing ammunition to Mujahideen in Kandahar. Unproven, but it was generally accepted that he was guilty. No long-term friends, no attachments to any causes or other individuals. He's believed to have fathered at least three children, none of whom he recognises as his own. He lives for his business. He negotiates harder and longer than anyone else, and when a client can't meet his prices he takes a stake in whatever land or mineral reserves might be going. In fact his property and oil earnings exceed his arms trading, according to our estimates. He's so off the grid it's hard to say, but he's probably Russia's richest man.'

'What does he do for security?'

'It's all handled by a pair of twins. North Koreans known as Yin and Yang.'

'Not really?'

'Really.' Her perfect mouth tweaked itself into the hint of a smile: the Mona Lisa in Armani. 'He used to use a gang of Azeri mafia boys, but he caught them with their hands in the till so they had to be "retired".' She held up her hands and made a pair of quotation marks with her fingers. 'Legend has it he did it himself, with a hacksaw – as a warning to their replacements. The twins have their own posse of Koreans who do the driving and so on.'

'Were they with him?'

She shrugged. 'It's not clear. He certainly counted Al Bashir as a valued customer, so it could be he'd let his guard down, though it would be out of character.'

'What's our contact with Al Bashir?'

'Officially, none.'

'Meaning?'

'One officer in our Tehran embassy has kept a line open with them but it's all gone dead the last fifteen days. Plus we've pulled most of our diplomatic staff out of there because of the crisis. The country's unravelling.'

'So it's about arms the PLR wants access to?'

Omorova blinked. 'Presumably.'

Dima peered at her. 'You blinked.'

She did a kind of I'm-not-smiling smile, sphinx-like. 'I do sometimes.'

'But not until then, when I asked you a question.'

Kroll sighed. 'Oh come on. Leave the lady alone.'

'Keep out of this Kroll. She's a big girl, she doesn't need your protection.'

Dima raised his fingers from the table. She maintained her smile. They had both been too long in the job to pretend. Dima took a moment to consider. He could make a fuss, demand from Paliov that he be given the full facts. He probably wouldn't give them. Perhaps Paliov didn't know them. Omorova and he were doing well so far. It would be a shame to ruin a good rapport. He calculated that she could probably be more help in the long run if he didn't pressure her.

He leaned forward, glanced round. The Ops Room team had retreated. He fixed his gaze on the woman. 'Comrade.' He liked the old nomenclature when it came to people he recognised as allies. 'Are you saying that's all you have or that's all you're allowed to have?'

'I'd say the latter.'

'So if you were my commanding officer, what would your advice be?'

She looked at him like a woman who didn't always get the respect she deserved, but was getting it now.

She blinked – differently this time, a little more slowly. 'Watch your back, at all times.'

She stood up and gestured at the files she'd brought. 'You want these?'

He shook his head. 'Can I reach you if I need more? Information, that is.'

She smirked. 'You'll have to get clearance.'

'From your mother?'

She laughed and swept out of the room.

He watched her go. Supressed a thought or three and turned to Kroll.

'We're going to need all the toys. This job doesn't smell right.'

Kroll sighed. 'You love to do everything the hard way, don't you?'

'Meaning?'

'This is easy. It's undefended. There are no sentries. There's only one way in and out. If they've got manpower there they're not showing up on the images. Those trucks may have kit on board but they won't have time to make ready if we don't give them warning. We go in and slot everyone who isn't Kaffarov, swing him on to your back and pull him out. Job done.'

'Sometimes, Kroll, I honestly wish I was you. You make everything sound so simple. Maybe that's why your life is so complicated.'

'You're going at this as if he was Bin Laden.'

'Because there are a lot of unknown unknowns. Me and Donald Rumsfeld, we no like unknown unknowns.'

'Like what?'

'Like, why is Mother Russia expending any energy on repatriating this shit-fuck? Why has Al Bashir gone to all the trouble of deliberately getting on our tits when we're supplying his kit?'

Kroll went back to his laptop and started typing again.

Dima nodded at the machine. 'Is that your go-plan?'

'Letter to my wife. Won't take a minute. I think this time I might be in with a chance.'

Dima let his head drop into his hands. Kroll paused, fixed Dima with a frown. 'You haven't said why you accepted the assignment. Did they blackmail you?'

'Worse.'

'What then?'

The photographs flashed in front of him for the hundredth time. 'They gave me hope.'

7

Not much got to Black: that's what his buddies believed. Patient when tempers were frayed, calm when others were jittery, measured when they were up to their armpits in the shit. It was a source of private pride that he got credit and respect for being what Cole called a 'steady, solid soldier', which was good because Cole didn't do compliments.

At Fort Carter, lined up on the freezing Michigan tarmac before they boarded the plane, the Colonel had told them, *This is no game. You will see terrible things, some you will struggle to understand. It will change you* ... In the week before, at a stress briefing, the Chaplain had said, *You need to be prepared to die, to see your friends die.* He counted himself prepared. His mother, who always told him how strong he was, as if willing it to be, told him to make it go his way. *You are always you, no matter who or what they try to make you be.*

He showed early promise, commended in his first week in Iraq for pulling a half-burned Sergeant from a Humvee sinking into a drainage ditch. The FOB Commander, Major Duncan, had told him, 'I see a great future for you in the Marines.' But that wasn't the plan. Once he'd done it, proved to himself he could, he was all done with it. Stay alive, stay sane, get home.

All his life he'd heard his father's screams at night, found him covered in sweat in the cold Wyoming dawn, the same story in the morning. 'Just my goddamn kidney stones, son.' The stones that he never went to hospital to have removed. As a kid he'd accepted the excuse. In his teens he'd begun to question his mother, who just replied with silence and, when pressed, tears. So he did some research. Read up about his father's platoon, about Khe Sanh in

February '68. Michael Blackburn never spoke a word to his family about Vietnam. Henry was determined to understand his father, who hadn't waited for the draft, who loved John Wayne movies, who had grown up listening to Grandfather Blackburn's euphoric tales of the liberation of Europe, of cheering crowds and grateful French girls throwing their underwear at them. But three weeks into his tour, his father, then just eighteen, was cornered along with his entire platoon in the jungle. He and the three others who survived spent the rest of their teens in a Viet Cong bamboo cage not much bigger than a coffin, sometimes immersed up to their necks in a snake-infested tributary of the Mekong. The week he came home, he married Laura, his high school sweetheart, his prom queen, who had promised to wait for him. But the man she married wasn't the boy she'd danced with. He quit college midway through the first semester and by Christmas had been fired from the 7-Eleven he was training to manage. She would never admit it but from then on Laura, the grade school teacher, was the breadwinner.

For Henry, enlisting wasn't about fighting for his country. It was more personal than that, to slay a ghost that haunted his family's life. A validation of his father's decision to go to war, that fighting was a worthwhile and noble choice. And privately – to prove to himself that he could go into battle and come back in one piece, solid and, more to the point, sane.

Today he was having trouble sticking to his plan. He had done the right thing. As soon as the girl was contained he'd gone for the battery. Found the grips. Paused, looked, checked the initiator, picked a wire to disconnect and cut the circuit. Shouted down to the men below: 'Clear!'

But on his way back to the stairs, he'd felt his legs turning to water. He'd stopped, looked down at the girl, reached down, and as he closed her eyes for the last time he saw his hand was shaking. In that moment he heard one of his father's unforgettable screams and realised that it wasn't in his head but in his mouth. He was screaming so loud the walls were starting to shake. And as the walls folded in he crashed down across her body and felt the floor collapse under him. *Could a scream do this?* That was the last thought that had gone through his head.

How much time had passed, he had no idea. It took him a while to remember where he was. The dead girl beside him was a reminder. He replayed the scene: the girl, the detonator, the girl again, closing her eyes, his scream – a grim comfort to realise that it wasn't reality that was caving in, it was the building. An air strike? He thought again and remembered the first tremor, expecting it to be an APC and not seeing one, and the second, prolonged shudder that set him off. Bigger than anything a RPG could deliver.

As his eyes adjusted he could see a triangle of light. No, not light so much as a shape of grey in the blackness. His left wrist was trapped under something metal. Foul-smelling water from a ruptured drain had drenched him, weighing down his fatigues. His body armour had probably saved his life but it was also trapping him in the cavity he now occupied. He reached round with his right hand and unstrapped the ceramic plates to give him more mobility. Then he undid his watch, a present from his mother, which made it easier to work the wrist loose. His hand was numb, and so swollen it felt like a baseball glove had been grafted on. He mentally checked the rest of his body, toes, legs, flexing each muscle, gradually becoming aware of a pulsing throb on the back of his head. He snapped his fingers, heard nothing except the rushing of air – the sound of no sound. His eardrums had been blasted. His ears still worked, though most of what they heard was the pulsing thud of the pain. He inched forward, sliding from his armour as if it were a moulted skin, toward the dull light, quietly thrilled that whatever had happened had spared him – for now. He wasn't religious, but thanked an invisible deity for that triangle of light he was twisting and scratching towards like a low-bellied reptile.

The first thing he noticed was the stars. A clear moonless night. Brighter than he had seen in all his time in Iraq, because most of the time the night had been viewed through NVGs (night-vision goggles). He hauled himself out of the aperture, struggled to his feet and immediately fell down again. Okay, take your time. Was there any time? His watch was gone, his armour was gone, his helmet gone, his M4, all the parts of him that said soldier: gone. He lifted himself on to his elbows and looked round. Nothing familiar, as if he'd been teleported to a different landscape. Then he recognised the Stryker, on its side, the booby-trapped truck, still intact. The IED hadn't detonated. But both vehicles were half-covered in rubble, as if a giant dump truck had emptied its load all over them. He could see an arm, a boot. If there were others under the rubble he was deaf to their cries. No sign of his fellow soldiers, or the wounded in the Stryker.

Still on his elbows he craned round. On three sides of the plaza the buildings had collapsed, as if that same giant truck had flattened them under its wheels. Blackburn had seen plenty of bomb damage, villages razed by bombs, mortar and RPG, but this devastation was on a scale that reminded him of footage of German cities after World War Two, or of Hiroshima and Nagasaki. The sight of it drained what little energy he had left. He rested his head in his arms. Had the PLR taken to the air and bombed them?

Then he remembered the tremors, the first as they entered the plaza. This was no air strike. It was an earthquake.

8

Higher Airborne Command School, Ryazan, Russia

From the air it looked so neat, so full of promise, like an architect's model. A cluster of low-rise buildings with bright red roofs surrounded by perfectly mown grass, bisected by grey metalled roads that radiated out to the edge of the grounds. A place in which there was only order and logic, not a single movement that wasn't regimented, practised and predicted. To the east, however, behind a curtain of trees, was where the action took place. Twelve olive green tents stood among a vast expanse of red-brown mud. Looking out of the grey framed windows, Dima felt as though his life was on rewind, spooling back to an abyss.

Thirteen years ago he'd stood down there, grateful to have crawled out alive. And promised himself he would never go back. And until 48 hours ago, when Paliov had shown him the photograph, he'd kept that promise. Isn't life just full of surprises, he thought. You think you're in control of your life, but fate has an unpleasant trick up its sleeve. I thought I was free, he reflected, but was it an illusion all along?

He had never forgotten the taste of that mud, in his mouth, in his nostrils and the sensation of it drying on his naked, battered body. It was a common belief that the red tinge came not from the iron in the local soil but the blood spilled by recruits.

The theory of how the Spetsnaz training worked was explained like this. Take an empty barrel and push it right down under water, then let it go. The deeper it's taken, the faster and further it shoots up out of the water when it surfaces. At Spetsnaz there was no such thing as too deep. Every man was taken to the depths of exhaustion and humiliation. To learn how to take orders, to control and conserve resources when you were past breaking point. To go beyond the limits of human endurance. Only the best were inducted. And many of them didn't make it. Star recruits with glittering records gave up, broken. Some took their own lives. A few turned their weapons on their instructors. Dima was very nearly one of those.

The whole platoon shared one long tent. In the upper bunks were the *stariki*, the old men of nineteen who had already survived a year – in the lower, the *salagi*: those who had yet to pass six months. New recruits were beaten nightly with belts, sticks and spoons. If they protested they were beaten in the morning as well, and made to sleep naked out on the mud. The *salagi* were the slaves of the *stariki*: they cleaned their weapons and their boots. The *stariki* held jousts, riding on the *salagis'* backs. All part of the process of learning to manage your emotions: contain, control, direct.

New arrivals would be welcomed – or confronted – with a small white towel laid at the entrance to the tent. What should they do? Pick it up? Ignore it? Generally, their instinct was to step over it so as not to dirty it. At which point the inmates would take umbrage at this slight and so would begin the innocent's first night of suffering. Dima remembered the hush, the expectant faces watching his polished boots already caked in mud, waiting to see where he would step. It was a lonely moment, the first of many. He stepped forward on to the towel and carefully wiped the uppers of his boots until they shone again. It bought him a bit of leeway, but not much.

As the Mil Mi-24 lost height he could see them, like ants crawling on the surface of the mud, the new recruits being put through their paces. How many would last? How many would end it all with a bullet – for themselves, unable to bear the shame of failure, or if their anger got the better of them, a particularly hostile *stariki*? It was an unspoken agreement between Spetsnaz graduates – and those who'd fallen by the wayside – never to speak about the training. Dima exchanged glances with Kroll, a look that needed no explanation. Each knew exactly what the other was thinking. Soldiers learn to work together, Spetsnaz learn to operate alone. Once he believed it had been a good training for his life – the best possible. But then maybe if he hadn't been one of the élite, he wouldn't have ended up alone – might have had a real life. But there was no time to think about that now.

Today, it wasn't recruits Dima was after: he had come for the instructors, the hardest and the smartest, full of pent-up energy for a return to the field, men to whom he could leave the more basic task of clearing the compound. Paliov had set no limits on how many men or how much kit, but that in itself bothered Dima. Paliov had made his name as a master of efficiency, never one to use a regiment where a platoon would do, who had fought long and hard against campaigns for better, more expensive, equipment. Why was he suddenly splashing out like this? Was this his last stand? Or something else?

He glanced at the other passengers, all eight of them Paliov's underlings: Baryshev – surveillance, Burdukovsky – logistics, Gavrilov and Deniken, Yegalin and Mazlak – human doorstops. Only Burdukovsky, despite his girth, had the look of a field man, beady-eyed, his expression one of permanent quiet amusement, as if in on a joke to which only he knew the punchline. The rest looked like Aquarium lifers, unaccustomed to being let out into the daylight. He thought of Omorova's blink – what exactly was it she'd hinted at in the Ops Room? All day the news had been full of Iran, Americans on alert along the Iraq border, the PLR consolidating control of at least three centres. And to cap it all, more earth tremors in the east. It was all happening in Iran, and they were going in to snatch a single rogue arms dealer with a small airborne army. Something wasn't right.

They disembarked on to the apron outside the main building. Dima and Kroll were ushered straight to a prepared interview room. Three chairs, one table, a jug of water, two glasses. It was all eerily familiar. The only sign Dima could detect that put them in the post-Soviet era was the slice of lemon floating in the jug.

The door swung open to reveal the Camp Commandant, Vaslov. His gleaming hairless scalp was reminiscent of a baby's, but the resemblance ended there. He had no neck to speak of, so that his head appeared to rise out of his collar like one of those wide, pillar-shaped rock formations Dima had seen once in a picture of Arizona. On his face, the features were crowded round a broken nose, as if reluctant to spread out. The famous glass eye stared fixedly into the middle distance, its predecessor taken out by an Afghan sniper's bullet that was reputed to be still lodged in his brain – some said because it didn't dare ask permission to leave. It was this injury, the last of several, which had eventually condemned him to this administrative role. Now and then, the bullet – or something – provoked him to uncontrollable bursts of temper, victims of which included a clerk, whose wrist had been broken when a document was found in the wrong file. He ran a tight ship, you could say. He lived on the camp all year round; he had nowhere else and no one else. Spetsnaz was his life, his family, his reason for being.

Vaslov glared at Dima, who didn't rise. He was just a contractor now. No need for military niceties.

Without meeting his glare Dima spoke.

'I thought someone would have killed you by now.'

What little there was of Vaslov's lips disappeared altogether as he stepped into the room.

'I'd shake you by the hand but I may have some use for it after.'

'I'm glad we see eye to eye, at last.'

Dima couldn't resist the joke. When they had first encountered each other he had just stepped on to the towel. Vaslov was an instructor and from day one he had had it in for him. Dima was smarter than him and they both knew it. Vaslov had made it his mission to break him. He never managed it, but what eventually evolved was a grudging mutual respect.

'Still growing roses?'

Vaslov gave a lipless grin as he nodded and patted his tunic side pocket. He was known to carry a pair of secateurs with him at all times. His favourite humiliation was to order anyone who flunked an exercise to strip in front of his fellow recruits, whereupon he would produce his rose cutters and close them round the offender's cock until he wet himself. He even had a pickle jar on view in his office that contained items closely resembling human penises. No one had ever got close enough to be sure.

He put his hands on the table and leaned forward until his face was almost touching Dima's.

'You seem to have a lot of clout for someone who was *let go*', he said. For once both eyes were looking the same way. 'The powers that be appear to have signed off your request for the pick of my best instructors.' He leaned even closer. 'If any of them don't come back in showroom condition you know what the consequences will be.'

'I've got my titanium underpants on.'

He stood up, dropped a stack of files on the table, turned and marched out. Kroll rolled his eyes, reached for the files and started rifling through them.

Dima felt his phone vibrate. He examined the message and then turned the display towards Kroll. A gallery of pictures of the compound walls appeared.

Kroll's eyes widened. 'Who the fuck sent these?'

'Darwish, lives north of Tabriz. I called him this morning. Got him to drive up and have a look-see.'

'Trust you to have your own spies.'

Kroll took the phone and pored over the images. 'Those walls are massive.'

'Yes, but look closer. Parts of them are patched with brick and breeze block. And see where those cracks are – they're from the tremors. You could knock it down with a mallet.'

Kroll looked up. 'Confirms my feeling – no call for heavy metal. A big entrance, with lots of bangs, bullets flying everywhere – more likelihood of Kaffarov not making it out in one piece. We really don't need all these men.'

They were both spooked by the same thing. Dima was silent for a moment, lost in thought.

Kroll shuffled the files. 'So how many do you want?'

'Three to lead the Go Teams.'

Kroll shrugged. 'Have it your way.'

Dima lifted a finger. 'No, wait: change of plan. Three for an advance team with us.'

Kroll's face brightened. 'By road?'

Dima got up, paced, thinking aloud. 'A heavy Mil drops us first in a neighbouring valley. On board, two cars. We'll recce, confirm what we need, then call in the Go units once we've cut the power. That way we've got more options if there's a change of plan.'

'Change of what plan?'

Dima looked at Kroll. Inside, he wondered what he was getting his old friend into. 'I don't know. I just want to be prepared – in case.'

He nodded at the files. Kroll picked up the phone on the desk. 'Okay, we're ready. Lenkov first.'

The first one marched in. Two metres plus: sandy hair, Nordic features. He didn't even make it to the table.

Dima shook his head. 'We're invading Iran, not Finland.'

Lenkov obediently turned on his heel and left.

Kroll frowned. 'He might be a good fighter though.'

'He looks like a poster boy for the Waffen SS. They need to blend in.'

'Fair enough. Next is Hassan Zirak.'

'Good Kurdish name.'

'A Shi'a from Lachin.'

Zirak entered and stood to attention in front of the table, his eyes fixed on the wall. He was short, no more than 165 centimetres. His prematurely aged face and slightly bowed legs betrayed his peasant origins.

Dima addressed him in Farsi. *'I'll give you four hundred rials to drive me from Tabriz to Teheran.'*

Zirak blinked then answered. *'I shit on my mother first. Four thousand, plus your daughter for the night.'*

Kroll tried to hide his smile, but Dima stared back thunderously, then switched to Tajik.

'A Persian goes on holiday to Africa. Right as he's about to take a swim a gorilla jumps out of a tree and rapes him. He's in a coma for three months; when he comes home reporters are waiting at the airport. One asks if he was hurt. How does he answer?'

Zirak looked down, stroked his chin then looked up.

'He didn't call, didn't write, sent no flowers. Of course I was hurt!'

Dima allowed himself a smile. 'Wait outside.'

The next two flunked the question, either because their languages

61

weren't up to it or they were too distracted by the gorilla. Dima and Kroll examined the remaining files. When they looked up again the next was standing in front of them: Gregorin, another blond candidate. Kroll was about to send him away but Dima spoke first.

'I didn't hear you come in. Go out and come back in.' The soldier obliged, returned to position.

Dima turned to Kroll. 'Did you hear anything?'

'No.'

'Neither did I. How did you develop that skill, Gregorin?'

Gregorin stared at the wall behind them, his face devoid of expression, like an actor waiting to be given a part. 'I studied ballet before I enlisted, Sir.'

'A red rag to the *stariki*. How did you deal with that?'

'After I killed one of them it ceased to be a problem.'

'In a fight?'

He lowered his eyes and met Dima's. They looked cold and dead. 'I made it look like that.'

'Premeditated? Why weren't you court-martialled?'

Gregorin kept his gaze on Dima. 'No one found out.'

'But you're telling me.'

'If I'm to be accepted for this mission Sir, it's probably better we have no secrets.'

Kroll looked up from Gregorin's file. 'Impressive. How did you do it exactly?'

'Following the fight, the man in question was hospitalised. I was concerned that he might make a full recovery, so I obtained access to the facility and administered a lethal dose of diamorphine.'

Dima reached for his file. Nothing run of the mill in there either. As well as tours in Afghanistan and Bosnia, he had worked undercover in Brussels, infiltrated a drug cartel in Dubai, carried out assassinations in the Dominican Republic and had been put in quarantine for a period over allegations, unproven, of collusion with the CIA while operational in Pakistan. Most commanders, Dima knew, would keep this man at a distance. He was perfect.

'Thank you for being so candid. Wait outside.'

Gregorin saluted and left without a sound.

Kroll took a deep breath. 'Better not get on the wrong side of him.'

Dima ignored him. His mind was elsewhere. Eventually he spoke. 'I want Vladimir.'

'You said you'd never work with him again.'

'I said the same about you. Look where that got me. Do you have an actual objection?'

Kroll pushed out his lower lip. 'Not at all. He's in prison though. Drug trafficking.'

'Then let's get him out.'

'Paliov could have a problem with that.'

'He needn't know. Which facility is he in?'

'Butyrka.'

Dima let out a long breath.

'Great. We'll be lucky if he's not dead from TB or AIDS.'

'We'll get Vaslov to order him transferred to a military facility and stop off on the way.'

'He considers Paliov to have been a brake on his career. It'll be an opportunity to get one over on him.'

'You know everyone's weak spot, don't you?'

'Except my own.' Paliov's photos had flashed up again.

Kroll stood up. 'While I get it sorted, don't you think you should put those two through their paces?'

Dima nodded. Kroll picked up the phone. 'Send Zirak and Gregorin back in.'

The two candidates stood side by side, an unlikely pair. That was good, thought Dima.

He peered at each one. 'The mission starts now. Your first task is to deliver Vladimir Kamarivsky to me by first light tomorrow. He's incarcerated in Butyrka. You'll find his details on the database. If there's anything blocked to your report level, Vaslov will open it. I don't care how you do it. Just bring him to me.'

Zirak looked mystified.

'The "Jewish Ayatollah"?'

Vladimir, a Latvian Jew, was a legend at Spetsnaz for infiltrating the Iranian Supreme Leader's staff. He prided himself on his knowledge of the Koran and his grasp of the intricacies of Iranian power was second to none.

Dima nodded. 'Yup, that's the one. Be back here by dawn.'

When they'd gone, Kroll turned to Dima and looked at him warily. 'Is there something you're not telling me? Don't fuck about now.'

'Just a feeling that this is going to be my last mission. I want my favourite people with me.'

9

Black had lost all track of time. His watch was gone, his radio smashed, his headset also gone. To escape the cavity in the rubble he'd had to strip himself of all the things that were designed to keep him alive. The sixty extra pounds of weaponry and bulletproofing the soldiers carried was useful, but also a liability. Even his water bottle had gone. His mouth felt as if someone had emptied a sack of brick dust into it, and the wind was full of particles that shot-blasted his features. The light was failing fast: it had to be around 1900 hours. That meant he'd lost six hours in the rubble. Once he managed to get on his feet he found cover under a pair of pillars that were drunkenly holding each other up. He stood still. He couldn't hear anything so he looked for movement. The devastation was total. It reminded him of his grandfather's pictures of Dresden, an entire living, breathing city reduced to nothing but rubble.

A dog came past, skinny and limping. It looked at him, hesitated as if uncertain as to whether he was friend or foe, thought better of it and padded away. Blackburn thought about his crew. Buried as well, or had they made their escape? The wind noise of his deafness was lessening. He became aware of a low intermittent moan and decided to head towards it. Perhaps there was something he could do. The street was strewn with debris and his balance was still uncertain. As his eyes began to focus he was able to pinpoint the source of the sound. A figure in military fatigues lay sprawled on the street, half hanging into one of the fissures that the quake had unzipped. Once he recognised the battledress as US he quickened his pace.

Black was less than a block away from the stricken soldier when he heard the vehicle. Definitely heavy duty, probably military. Help on the way? Something about the sound slowed him to a halt. The engine note – not the Stryker's familiar Caterpillar diesel but a lower guttural thrum, more like a V8. Definitely not a Stryker or any other friendly vehicle he could think of. He crouched down behind a half-crushed van as the first of three Russian-made BTR-152s – six-wheeled APCs – nosed into view, alongside them a crowd of young men in improvised combat gear.

What followed was something he would never forget. Like all soldiers, he had seen some things in Iraq that he would have pre-ferred not to, but that was part of the job. If you didn't like seeing innocent people get killed and mutilated, don't join the army. Then seeing the light go out of that girl's eyes in that kitchen had upped the ante somehow: he had held her, the first and last man in her life, in a single intimate embrace before death. And now, even that would soon be subsumed by what came next. Sometime later he would grimly acknowledge that it had served his purpose. After that, he would no longer entertain any of that shit about the nobility and rightness of war.

The injured soldier, hearing the convoy, had managed to haul himself up on one elbow and was waving. The BTR shuddered to a halt. One of its armoured doors flew open and a figure clad in a shalwar kameez, face masked by part of his turban, jumped down and spoke to him. Several others armed with AKs tumbled out of the machine and took up positions around him. More young men, similarly dressed, crowded round. The turbanned guy and the Marine appeared to have found a common language – presumably English – but then the turbanned guy signalled to one of the crowd, who came forward with a camcorder and started filming. The turban stepped back and produced a blade, serrated like a breadknife but longer, as if specifically designed for what he was about to do. He grabbed the Marine by the hair and slashed at his neck, blood flying as he sawed with such ferocity that the decapitation was over in twenty seconds. Blackburn felt his lungs fill with breath for a shout, but self-preservation took over. As the man held the Marine's head aloft for his comrades to admire, the flap of his turban slipped and Blackburn took a mental picture of the face – clean-shaven, which was unusual, high cheekbones and small eyes narrowed to slits. He bared his teeth and bit off the nose of the beheaded Marine and spat it out. His crew went wild, firing their AKs in the air and chanting something Blackburn couldn't make out, then he waved them back into the vehicle and it moved off east at walking pace, the crowd chanting behind.

10

However good it looked, Dima didn't like what he was seeing. He watched from his temporary Ops Room as the giant Mi-26 'flying slug' he'd ordered, the world's largest chopper, eased its way down on to the apron. Able to carry eighty troops with ease, it could even swallow an eight-wheeled APC. He wondered briefly whether Zirak and Gregorin would arrive to find Vladimir with his bags packed, all ready and waiting for them at the gates of Butyrka.

Half of him marvelled at the speed with which whatever he wanted was provided. The other half – the doubter, the sceptic, the half he listened to the hardest – knew this was all too good to be true, which was why he had called Paliov.

'We have to talk.'

'We're talking now.'

'Face to face, not over your phone. Or else it's off.'

He'd hung up before the old man could protest.

Dima's plan had come together quickly. The Slug would drop them and their transport ten klicks from the compound, well out of earshot. Burdukovsky had sourced a pair of Peykans, Iran's most popular car, for his advance party. They would conduct a final recce before cutting the compound's power. Then they would rappel in over the walls – and with silenced weapons methodically clear each room until they had Kaffarov. Meanwhile, the Slug would have moved to the location ready to lift them all out. Back before breakfast.

But the team who had choppered in with him made him suspicious. Then he learned he had been 'given' a team of fifty airborne 'for backup', plus a second chopper team from a separate agency.

The GRU's 'executive' Mi-8 parked by the Slug. Its passenger door flipped open and out stepped Paliov. As he watched the old man progress stiffly to the building, he saw the Commandant striding out to greet his unexpected guest. Paliov appeared to be alone. That was telling. People of his rank usually never travelled without aides and security. Vaslov directed him to the building where Dima had set up his post and started to walk alongside him until Paliov waved him away. This was going to be a one-to-one.

Dima was back behind his desk when Paliov came in. As if it was an unconscious reflex he did a quick recce of the room, his eyes darting to each corner.

'I've already swept it; you have nothing to worry about.'

Paliov lowered himself carefully into a chair as if he'd walked from Moscow. 'Have you been getting all the assistance you require?'

'My every whim fulfilled. Imagine that.' He smirked at Paliov. 'Thank you for opening all the channels.'

He accepted the compliment with a nod.

'If this doesn't work out the way you want it, I'm still expecting you to keep your half of the bargain.'

'Ah, the photographs ...' He sighed. 'If this doesn't work out I doubt you will see me again.'

'I thought as much. You're so desperate for this not to go wrong you're throwing everything you've got at it. And there's more to collect than just Kaffarov, isn't there?'

Paliov folded his hands in his lap. 'I've no idea what you mean.'

Dima slammed his hands down on the desk. 'Dont fuck with me.'

'There are ... operational obstacles. Even Timofayev has to tread carefully. One foot wrong, even at his level, and we all go down the crapper.'

The sheen of sweat on the old man's brow told Dima his instincts were correct. 'Okay, then I'm going to tell you. There's another team who go in when my lot come out. Because Kaffarov's left something precious there.'

Paliov looked ashen.

'The Chernobyl cleaner team landed their chopper here an hour ago. They're repatriating warheads.'

Paliov raised his hands and let them fall on his knees. He smiled wanly. How pathetic, Dima thought. To be so high up, at such an age, and to be so scared. Perestroika, the transformation of the evil old USSR into the shiny new Russian Federation. Nothing had really changed. They might as well be back in Stalin's time.

'And Timofayev insisted I wasn't told.'

Paliov had managed to stop the flow of sweat down his forehead.

'Their existence is classified at the highest level. Only three people in the Kremlin know of it. It is therefore most embarrassing for those who do know that this has come to pass.'

'Al Bashir gets his hands on this, he gets the nuclear capability his country's been craving, to put them in the game with Israel and Pakistan. The Americans get wind of this, if they haven't already – they're going to be seriously pissed off with Russia for supplying a rogue state. I mean, seriously.'

Paliov reached into his jacket and pulled out a packet of cigarettes. He helped himself, lit up and drew on it deeply like a man enjoying his last one before the firing squad.

'As I recall, the smallest we ever made weighs in at over 90 kilos and is about the same size as a medium-sized domestic refrigerator.'

Paliov shifted in his seat and gazed at his knees.

'There have been developments. The use of carbon fibre and the miniaturisation of key components has brought the size down to that of a normal suitcase. The blast potential is the equivalent of 18 kilotons of TNT – about the same as the Hiroshima bomb.'

'How do you know it's still there, in the compound?'

'It gives off a signal, which Kaffarov seems not to be aware of. He's lucky. That's how we knew where he was.'

Paliov drew again on his cigarette. Already past his sell-by date, he seemed to have aged another ten years just in this meeting.

Dima felt a small flicker of contempt. 'Your job's on the line, isn't it, pension even threatened. I do so feel for you.'

Paliov let out a smoky, sardonic laugh. 'My life, more like.'

Dima pursed his lips and blew out a long sigh. 'And fuck the rest of us. Right, now listen to me. The photographs: I want a name and an address, and when they were taken. You tell me now, or do the job yourself. I've had enough of being fucked around by you people.'

'Timofayev has that information.'

'And he doesn't even trust you?'

Paliov shrugged. 'No one trusts anyone.'

'Then why should I trust you? What do you take me for?'

He wanted to kill him there and then, squeeze the life out of his contemptible, wobbly, time-serving little body. But then he would never get the photographs.

Paliov leaned forward, elbows on his thighs, his hands pressed together as if in supplication, the cigarette jutting between them. 'Give me back twenty years and I'd be going in with you. If you succeed, I will give you every assistance to help you find ... that which caused you to accept this mission. I know what those photographs mean to you. If it was in my gift you'd have it all now. Oh, and by the way, Timofayev has promised you thanks in person from the President.'

'I hope you told him I don't give a shit about that.'

Paliov stood up and offered Dima his hand. 'But, if this goes wrong, my honest advice is – don't come back.'

11

By the time Blackburn got to the dead Marine there was nothing on him. Helmet, M4, body armour, ammunition: gone. Fatigues, gone: tags, gone. Even his boots, watch and wedding ring. Even his underpants. The crowd had picked him clean. Headless, naked in the shattered landscape, surrounded by rubble, he looked like a fallen statue. Only the dust-specked delta of blood oozing out of him was proof that he had ever been a living man.

A few feet away, like discarded candy wrappers, he saw a couple of crumpled photos. He reached down and picked them up. One was of a girl sitting on the hood of a blue Firebird, the other a labrador leaping in the air to catch a stick.

There was nothing Blackburn could do for him. He smoothed out the photos and put them in a pocket. Then he whispered a prayer, and inwardly promised himself he would put a name to the dead man and somehow avenge his horrible, inglorious death. He knew this image would remain with him forever and that in the future he would never speak about it, because nothing good or positive could ever come from communicating it. Now, for the first time in his life, his father's silence finally made sense.

It was dark now. The temperature was falling. He was weak and desperately thirsty. The deafness had turned into a steady buzzing in his ears like a malfunctioning radio. He turned and started heading east back towards the border from where they had come he didn't know how many hours before. He had been walking for an hour or so, stumbling along what was left of the road, when above the buzz he heard the welcome throb of an Osprey. He doubled his pace and immediately tripped and fell on some rubble. He got back up and continued more slowly. The Osprey disappeared over the horizon, but it had given him some hope, something to focus on. As the sound died away he became aware of other sounds in the darkness: shouts, a vehicle being furiously manoeuvred, gears screaming, then shots and a flash. If there was fighting, he reasoned, there had to be good guys as well as bad.

In the area he was now walking into, the quake damage was less intense. The street was still strewn with rubble but most of the buildings were intact. He heard a voice and aimed for it. It was coming from a vehicle, a crashed Humvee. He could see a figure leaning out of it as if waving him on, but the angle was wrong. The soldier, hanging half out of the cab, was dead, his arms splayed. Blackburn focused on the source of the voice. It was several seconds before he registered that it was American, coming from somewhere on the ground – a radio.

'... *Roger that, we're engaging in the vicinity of two two four eight six grid.*'

'*Misfit 1–3, that's a Roger, rotating in for CAS-EVAC...*'

He grabbed the radio. The outer casing fell away. He tried to open a channel, no go, so he tossed it aside as right on cue the Osprey reappeared, clattering overhead, its twin rotors tilting into position for a landing. Blackburn found energy he didn't know he still had as he half stumbled, half jogged in the direction the chopper had gone. He kept it in sight, a dark cutout against the night sky, until its lights came on, flooding the area beneath. He tried to manage the outpouring of relief he felt. He wasn't there yet, and the lights had provoked a volley of small arms fire followed by a blast and a fireball to the west of where the Osprey was landing. Now it was out of sight behind the buildings.

Suddenly it occurred to him that no one on board knew he was out there heading for it. With fire around it would be on the ground for the minimum time to take on its cargo of wounded. He had to get there before it lifted off again. Not far now: he could feel the wind stirred up by the rotors, the furious crashing sound of the propellers slapping the air. He was running now, with better vision and a powerful turbocharge of adrenalin, leaping over boulders and bodies in his path, not pausing to look at the carnage he was passing –

from the quake or the fighting, it was impossible to tell.

The Osprey put down in what had been a square, its rear ramp lowered, two sentries on guard as medics hauled the casualties aboard. He heard the engine revs climb, the air whipping up a tornado of dust. The sentries backed up the ramp as the suspension of the landing gear slackened and the chopper started to lift. He was shouting at the top of his voice but it was pointless against the roar of the rotors. Something clanked off his shoulder and he felt a sting as if from a huge wasp. The ramp was waist high as he reached it: arms outstretched, he scrabbled for a grip, felt himself slipping back until four hands from heaven reached down and hauled him aboard by his epaulettes. Only then did he allow himself one look back at the receding devastation as it sank into the gloom of the night.

12

They were standing in the vast metal cave that was the Mil's hold, Zirak and Gregorin a few paces away, a look of quiet triumph on their faces, Kroll lounging against a mound of camo net. As trucks came and went on the floodlit apron, a steady stream of men, purposeful, focused, loaded kit on to the deck of the hold. Several glanced at the group in their Iranian standard issue men's clothes – dark suit jacket, loose trousers. One gestured discreetly at the new arrival, then muttered something to his comrade, whose face registered a mixture of awe and disbelief. Vladimir was notorious, a Spetsnaz legend. Dima hoped to God the reality still lived up to the mythology.

The prison van had screeched up to the Mil at ten-thirty. It looked like it had travelled through a war zone. Its windscreen was cracked and one side mirror hung drunkenly from its mounting. Zirak and Gregorin stumbled out of the cab wearing stolen prison guards' fatigues, with their captive looking dazed and moving stiffly. As they led him up the ramp into the hold of the Mil where Dima was standing, Vladimir threw his head back and erupted in laughter.

'Tell me this is a joke.'

'No joke.' Dima grabbed Vladimir and kissed him on both cheeks. He smelled rancid.

'You spring me from one of Russia's baddest prisons. Did everyone else turn you down? I get it, it's a suicide mission and you figured I'd prefer it to another five years in there. Nice sense of humour you have, Dima Mayakovsky.'

Dima studied his old comrade. Prison had not been kind to him. His weight was down, his skin was an ugly pallor from lack of sunlight and there was a livid scar on his cheek from a recent knife fight. He'd arrived in jail with several teeth gone and had since lost several more. Dima gestured at his T-shirt. 'Off.'

Vladimir peeled off the grubby garment. Dima circled him, studying his frame, which to his relief didn't look as bad as his face. He thumped him hard in the abdomen. Vladimir barely flinched.

'You found time to visit the gym then.'

'Nothing else to do.' He dropped on to all fours and started rapid push-ups.

Dima nodded to Kroll.

'Take him away, brief him and get him something decent to eat. The man's not had a proper meal in two years.' Then he nodded at the other two. 'Well, you passed the initiation. Lose the van somewhere.' Gregorin started to speak, but Dima shushed him. 'Tell me later. We've got to get this show on the road.'

Another pair of vehicles drew up to the ramp. Burdukovsky, the logistics man, stepped out of one and beckoned Dima over to it. 'Happy?'

Burdukovsky slapped the hood like a car salesman. 'Peykans. The Lada of Iran. Finest examples available.'

Dima knew them well from his tour. They had been the commonest car on Iran's roads and these two looked authentically weary. One had a bashed door, the other two different coloured front wings and a roof-rack that was entirely rusted. They would blend right in. Burdukovsky gestured at the licence plates. 'Genuinely from Tabriz, more or less.'

'You've surpassed yourself. Do they work?'

'New engines and drivetrain. You should have no trouble. And I've thrown in full tanks of gas. If you can, bring them back in one piece: usable ones are getting harder to come by.'

He waved them on to the ramp then gestured to Dima to join him on the tarmac.

'There's more.'

He walked backwards until he'd got a decent view of the Mil, then beckoned Dima again. Like a kid in a Ferrari showroom, Burdukovsky bristled with excitement. 'You're very privileged. See those?' He pointed at the dishpan-shaped cowling on the rotor.

'Noise suppressor. Top secret. The Americans used it on the Black Hawks when they went to get Bin Laden. They don't know we've got it. It's a big bus but it has all the toys off the combat Me-28s. Low-level and extreme terrain-following capability with a combined radar and thermal imaging system. Duplicated hydraulic and control systems, armoured cockpit's got a separate, ceramic fuselage, bullet-proof windshields and armoured partition between crew members, self-sealing polyurethane foam-filled fuel tanks.'

He strode forward and smoothed his hands over the fuselage as if it were the flanks of a prize racehorse. 'Feel.'

Dima felt.

'Special paint to suppress infrared detection. First time we've used it.'

Dima pointed at the Nuke team's Mil-24. 'And that?'

Burdukovsky shrugged, the first sign of a chink in his armour of enthusiasm.

'Standard issue, so keep them back till you've secured the site.'

Dima walked over to the other aircraft. Shenk, the Nuclear Recovery team leader, was doing final checks on radiation gear with his crew. When he saw Dima he stopped and stood with his arms folded as if barring the way. He had a long tombstone of a face, more suited to an undertaker. If there was a Mrs Shenk he felt sorry for her.

'Something you need?' He jutted his chin out.

Dima suppressed a desire to give it a good whack.

He tried a warm smile.

'Came to wish you good luck.'

'You do your bit right, we won't need luck.'

The rest of the crew stopped what they were doing.

Dima pressed on. 'I need pictures of the device I can show the team. They need to know what they're looking for.'

Shenk shook his head slowly and deliberately.

'Classified.'

'Ha ha, very funny.'

Shenk jutted his chin. 'Very serious. All pictures, diagrams and descriptions are only for those cleared by the Defence Secretary himself. You secure the area and find your target. We do the rest.'

Dima walked over to the kit laid out in the hold of the chopper. Geiger counters, wouldn't want to go in without those. And a slim tablet-style PC: bit odd. He decided to find out if there was any more to it, like a scanner.

He picked it up, turned it over and scrutinised it doubtfully. Shenk grabbed it out of his hand.

'Only for those authorised, I'm afraid. Extremely delicate.'

Dima picked it up again, peering slightly as his grandmother might, confronted with the same object.

'It doesn't look much.'

'Look,' said Shenk, taking it back again. 'This begins by being used as a normal sat nav to give directions, but it's been customised to pick up the signal from the devices. It will then pinpoint the suitcases by giving the longitude and latitudes of their positions to within less than half a square mile, from a distance of up to 400 miles. This information is then converted when this tab is touched, and this point on the appropriate menu here, to a grid reference that can be used on the map. It's more accurate than a scanner and thus ten times more out of bounds to the likes of you.'

Dima changed his expression to look guilty, and memorised the instructions to tell Kroll when the moment came.

'Now if you'll excuse me,' said Shenk, 'I have to prepare for this mission.'

'Yes, of course. Sorry.'

Dima watched for a bit longer as Shenk and his team fiddled with their kit. Russia bred them in their thousands. Men who spent most of their waking hours in a state of ingrained dissatisfaction, who thought they deserved better but never actually went for better, who spent their lives furiously guarding their precious bit of territory. The Russian military was full of them. Shenk's life was about dealing with the mistakes of others, the cock-ups, the negligence, whether it was the fallout from Chernobyl or the countless warheads well past their sell-by date, seeping radiation. Russia needed its share of Shenks. So much of Russia's nuclear arsenal was older than anyone liked to admit, incapable of being used in anger if it came to it. But in the mad world of Mutually Assured Destruction, it was the nations with the nukes who got to sit at the top tables. This was the root of Shenk's self importance, saving the world from its own folly. Clearly he thought he should be running this show, not Dima.

'See you at the LZ. I'll get it all nicely prepared for you.' Dima gave him a cheery salute and walked away. But something still told him it wasn't going to be as simple as that.

13

Azerbaijan Airspace

The Mil Mi-26 lumbered upwards, curving away from the base as its rotors clawed the air, battering Dima's ears with its thunderous throb. The temperature in the hold plummeted. Under their flight suits, Dima's advance crew were already in their Iranian kit. Dropping them had to be executed with maximum speed. The landing zone they had chosen was a scrap of land surrounded by forest, fifteen kilometres from the compound, but a forty-five minute drive on the unmetalled roads threaded along the steep valley sides. It was good cover, but the sooner the Peykans were unloaded and separated from the Mil, the less danger of the cars being in any way connected to the fat black Russian chopper.

Kroll and Vladimir had taken refuge from the cold inside one of the Peykans. Vladimir was fast asleep after his first good meal in two years, his face a better colour, though the scar on his cheek still stood out. Kroll stared straight ahead, stonily. Helicopters were his *bête noir*. He had survived two hard landings and had made a lucky escape from a third when it had ditched in the Caspian.

Either side of the cars was the Go Team, to be deployed when Dima called them in. Until then they would remain on standby at an Azerbaijani airstrip just across the border. They were in full assault kit, everything black, and they carried AKSUs – short versions of the AK47, fitted with thermal imaging sights that were essential for seeing through smoke or CS gas. The AKSUs were also easier to conceal. With the stock folded they measured less than fifty centimetres. Some would also be packing PMMs or 6P35 Grach pistols. Saiga-12 shotguns would be handy for taking down doors and KS-23s armed with CS gas would help along the process of room clearing. Despite the volume of intelligence, they still had no real idea of how much opposition they would meet.

For some of these men, recent graduates, this would be their first hostile deployment. Dima felt a strong sense of responsibility for taking them on this escapade. I must be getting old, he thought. For a long time now he had worked alone, or just with Kroll. He used to have a reputation as a good leader, the sort men would follow to hell and back – and quite often not back at all. But that was when he was a paid-up Spetsnaz. Now he was a freelance, a gun for hire. He'd heard Kroll say, 'You never *leave* Spetsnaz – even if they fire you. Even if they put you in jail.' Surely a few of these young men had to be asking themselves why they were putting their trust in a man who apparently had no allegiances, whose own masters had long been suspicious of him. But then he thought back to his own early days – when he was desperate for an assignment, any assignment. That was the point of Spetsnaz, to expect the unexpected.

Suddenly he realised that many of them would be the same age as the young man in Paliov's photographs. He tried to put them out of his mind and concentrate on the job in hand. If he couldn't focus, he would never get them and it would all have been for nothing. He had to separate himself from all emotions, completely.

He checked through the kit in each of the Peykans' trunks. The same array of armour. In addition, five SVD Dragunovs – not the most accurate sniper gun but with the ten-round magazine and a 4x scope it was fine for the relatively close range work he anticipated. He'd demanded every kind of night vision optics – binoculars for the recce, goggles for close action. He planned on getting a first-hand view inside the compound walls before calling in the Go Team. That meant a rope kit for climbing and – when they were ready – rappelling. Whatever they had, there would be something they had missed. It was the nature of these operations, balancing enough kit with the need to be nimble.

Dima climbed up to the flight deck, the equivalent of two storeys up from the hold. He put on a spare headset and watched over the shoulders of the pilots as they pressed on into the moonless dark. The low cloud and fine rain almost killed what little visibility there was. The instruments kept them out of trouble, nosing the machine over sudden tall trees and power-lines.

'Still reading quake tremors. It's going to be a mess down there,' said Yergin the co-pilot, waving a printout. 'Keep your tin hat on.' He grinned.

'How long do you need to hold position over the compound to drop the Go Team?'

'They get moving, I reckon three minutes max.'

'You pay good attention to our recce report or you won't know what they'll have pointing up at you.'

'Don't worry: the force is with me.' Yergin swished the air with an imaginary light sabre. 'Get ready. LZ in two.'

14

Near Bazargan, Northern Iran

The rotors swatted the air above as they prepared to disembark the Peykans – Dima, Kroll and Vladimir in the lead car, Zirak and Gregorin in the second. The cars were facing to the rear. As soon as the doors opened and the ramp dropped Dima reversed in a neat arc and accelerated away, night goggles on, no headlights, at least until they were clear of the site and on a public road. They didn't wait to watch the Mil pull away but they heard it all right, and hoped that Kaffarov's captors in the next valley didn't.

'Welcome to Iran. We hope you have a pleasant stay,' said Dima. Vladimir was awake now, lounging on the rear seat. Kroll looked more comfortable now he was back on terra firma. 'And a bloody short one,' he added. 'I want to be back for lunch.'

It was three a.m., but they were pumping enough adrenalin to keep them awake for a week. Once he'd got the measure of the Peykan, Dima put on more speed. He almost lost it on a blind bend when a tanker came the other way, with its huge headlights blazing. Its driver couldn't see them until the last moment, and they couldn't see much but the sudden whiteness, followed by an almighty roar. Taking up almost the whole of the winding, uneven road, it brushed past them with inches to spare. Dima was relieved to find the brakes had been uprated with an anti-lock system, which enabled them to slew to a halt at the only place they could stop without tipping over the edge.

'Quite responsive,' said Kroll. 'I wish my wife was as quick.'

'She is, as it happens,' said Vladimir.

'*Yes*,' said Zirak on the radio. '*And unlike the gorilla, she sends flowers after.*'

Dima smiled to himself. Despite all the danger, his mistrust of

Paliov and the sheer insanity of the mission, he was back where he belonged, leading a team of the best to the very limits of their abilities. There was nothing so bonding as knowing you might all be about to die together – that and a good wife joke.

They went through a small village: a cluster of dozing houses with no evidence of occupation save for a single prayer mat on a washing line. It appeared deserted, yet there was no sign of damage from the quake. A sound, somewhere between a bark and a howl, issued across the cool night air.

'Jackal,' said Kroll.

'Or your wife again.'

Leaving the LZ behind them in the distance, the road climbed out of the valley and did a hairpin left into the next one. Kroll examined the hills with a night sight. 'Got it. Fuck me, it looks a lot smaller in the flesh.'

'Yeah, like your dick,' came the reply from the back.

'The walls are still up. Doesn't look like the tremors have had any impact.'

The road forked where a drive curved up to the main gate. They slowed as they passed, taking in what they could in the gloom.

'Tempting to just go and ring the bell – could be a lot simpler.'

'Yeah, and get your head blown off.'

Two hundred metres beyond the drive Dima slowed to a halt, waiting for the second car to catch up. Once its lights were in view he carried on at a crawl until he found the track to the right that he'd seen on his friend Darwish's pictures. The track was deeply rutted and the car bottomed after a hundred metres. The cypress trees made a good screen. Dima opened his door.

'Okay guys: let's get kitted up.'

The air was damp, and pungent with the aroma of the cypresses. A mountain grouse, surprised by the unexpected visitors, shot into the air from near their feet with a furious clatter of wings, but otherwise there were no sounds, no wind. Vladimir took the rope kit and helped himself to a Dragunov. One of the reasons he was on Dima's must-have list was his climbing skill. As a boy of nine he had escaped from a juvenile detention centre down a four-storey wall. A few years later he was making frequent visits to his girlfriend's second floor bedroom, scaling the outside of the block where she lived while her father waited on guard, oblivious, in the hallway. 'Like Dracula,' he said, grinning with his remaining teeth.

They walked in single file towards the point in the wall that Dima had chosen. They couldn't see any cameras but it was possible they were concealed. Where he had identified a bend in the wall on the pictures, he reasoned there should be a blind spot.

The walls were ten metres higher than even Kroll had estimated, but Vladimir wasn't fazed. With the rope attached to his belt and the guys at the bottom feeding it out in case of kinks, he started up the wall at such a pace that it looked like he had suckers on his hands.

'Nice,' said Kroll. 'Like Spiderman with balls.'

Vladimir disappeared from view, obscured by the trees close to the wall. Two minutes later he was down again, having fixed the rope to a rampart by tying loops round it and then using snail links to join the loops.

'It's a bit busy in there. You better look.'

Dima climbed the wall using the rope. What had he been expecting? A deserted open area, a few vehicles, not much happening. He couldn't have been more wrong.

Since the last satellite pictures he had seen, taken only four hours before, the place had been transformed into a hive of activity. Three large trucks were parked facing the gate, each with its tailgate dropped. There must have been fifty men down there, all very young, looking like they had just been turfed out of the trucks and were waiting to be told what to do next. There were another twenty in semi-military uniforms, carrying a mixture of shotguns and rifles. Far from being the secluded hideaway of Al Bashir, this looked more like an improvised HQ. The wall he was secured to had deteriorated. There was no walkway. He was unlikely to be disturbed by a patrol, nor were there any cameras that he could make out. He pulled on the rope – the signal for the others to join him. It was pointless attempting to mount any assault themselves with those numbers below, he thought. But he also realised that the Go Team making a fast rope descent would be a disaster – unless all those below with arms were seriously distracted. There was just about enough room for the nuke team to land their Mil, but only once the personnel had been cleared.

Kroll peered down at the crowd and sighed. 'Why does life have to be so complicated?'

Vladimir was by his side, reaching down to give Zirak a hand. 'It's what makes it interesting.'

This was why Dima had wanted Vladimir along. He thrived on unpredictability; he lived for it. Dima scanned the crowd below, trying to read what was happening. Someone in uniform prodded an older man with his AK. If these were recruits they weren't exactly being welcomed. Coerced, more like. Where was Kaffarov? They would have to contain these men before they could mount a search. And clearing an area for Shenk's chopper was another problem.

There was no sign of the big boxy Mercedes G-Wagen, identified on the satellite pictures as Kaffarov's.

He turned to Kroll. 'Call up the Slug. Put them on standby.'

A plan was forming in his head, which involved laying down enough fire in one area to provoke the crowd – and the shooters – into taking cover in one corner. But a second later he abandoned it. A prisoner, hooded, half-naked and shackled, was being led by four men towards the far wall. He was not going willingly. Could it be Kaffarov? He was short and from his torso he looked to be the right age. Whatever Dima thought of him personally, the mission was to bring him back in one piece.

He turned to Kroll. 'Tell the Slug it's go-go. Expect armed response. Tell them to be prepared to fire on descent.' Then he addressed the others, pointing at the hooded man. 'If that's what I think it is we have to take out the executioners.'

Above the raised platform towards which the captive was being dragged was a thick beam, from which hung several nooses. His legs were flailing wildly. Despite the hood, he was under no illusion as to what was about to happen.

Dima beckoned Vladimir. 'Prepare five rappels – when we go, we go down together.' He looked at Zirak and Gregorin. 'Which of you is the best shot?' They each pointed at the other. 'OK, G comes before V: Gregorin. Move twenty metres to your right and take out the hangmen. Don't hit the prisoner: he could be Kaffarov. Kroll, how close are the Go Team?'

'One minute.'

He heard the distant thrum of the Mil, but there was too much action down below for anyone to notice yet. In position, Gregorin watched the action through his sights, postponing the first shot as long as he could. Then three things happened in quick succession. A few of the gunmen on the ground looked up at the approach of the still invisible Mil, and Gregorin fired his first shot at the execution team. One fell. The rest, struggling to get the writhing man's head through the noose, thought he had slipped or been kicked – until the second shot took the face off another of them. The others dropped the hooded man like a hot coal and ran for cover, as their victim flopped on to the platform and curled into a foetal position. Then from the corner of his eye Dima saw the lights of a truck come on. It shot forward, forcing its way through the men and the guards towards the gates. 'Shoot out the tyres!' yelled Kroll. 'Stop the truck!'

But the men, panicked, were surging around the vehicle. It was impossible to get a clean shot without hitting the occupants or the crowd. Most of them now had their faces craned towards the sky, as the Mil came overhead, obliterating all sound as it hovered. The ropes came down, followed by the first of the Go Team. They loosed off teargas, but it wasn't enough to cover them effectively as a volley of shots met them. Dima cursed as he saw the first two fall to the ground, wounded or dead.

'Fire at will,' he yelled to the others, but they had already started. 'Take out the gunners.' Then he saw it. Less than a hundred metres from the Slug, ghostly in the thick haze of the night sky, the Nuke team's Mil hovering – drifting closer, as if waiting to land. It was way too early. It had no radar jamming. It wasn't equipped for hostile action. *Why were they so close?* Then he saw the side door open. Shenk's team were firing as well. Some of the gunners on the ground noticed the second chopper and started firing back.

Dima screamed at Kroll: 'Pull back! Get Shenk to pull back NOW!'

But Kroll couldn't hear. He was preoccupied with the shooting. As soon as Dima looked back he saw it. A streak of bright light from the south arcing into the sky and then sweeping towards them, the warhead black and invisible against the blinding blaze of its propellant.

'Missile!'

Dima could only watch as it slammed into the cockpit of Shenk's Mil, shearing the front clean off, the flaming bodies of the crew falling from the wreckage. Meanwhile, the frontless craft turned upwards, dropped its tail and began to spin like a giant boomerang towards the Slug. The Slug pilots, facing the other way, would never have known what hit them. Dima and his team flattened themselves against the wall as the rotors of the two aircraft engaged. The smaller craft fell first, on to the wall opposite Dima's team, wobbled, then slid nose down next to the hangman's platform. The stricken Slug took longer, its sophisticated avionics struggling to compensate for the damaged rotors – but it was all too much for them. The nose of the craft reared up, the draught almost blowing Dima off the wall, as it smashed down into the centre of the compound. A giant fireball swept over them.

15

Forward Operating Base Spartacus, Iraqi Kurdistan

The shower was cold and the pressure zero, but as far as Blackburn was concerned it was the best wash he had ever had. He stood there far longer than his allocated time, and if anyone had a problem with that they could go fuck themselves. Several cuts and scars stung viciously as he smoothed the soap over them. He watched the soupy puddle of dust and soot mix with the congealed blood into the familiar war cocktail that swilled around his feet. But he knew that even if he stood under there for a month, what had happened yesterday was never going to wash off. Is this it, he wondered, the moment when a man changes for ever?

When he'd walked off the Osprey back at the FOB everyone stared. Montes, who had just got the news, came jogging up and slowed when he saw him.

'Man, you look like you came back from the dead.'

Only when he caught his reflection in a vehicle mirror did he realise why. His face and hair were completely grey with dust and soot, mixed with sweat into a paste which the sun had then baked dry. His T-shirt was stiff with his own blood and that of the dead girl. Montes threw his arms round him and several wounds protested in unison.

'We'd wrote you out the script, man.'

As he marched Blackburn to the shower trailer, Montes gave him their end, how after Blackburn had followed the wires into the building they'd felt the first tremor and made for open ground, just as the big one hit and all the buildings collapsed around them. He outlined a mushroom with his hands. 'Baboom. Hello Hiroshima. Place looked like out of some demented game your Mom won't want you playin'. Next thing, they pullin' us out.'

He was doing what all soldiers do after an incident – reprocessing it into an action movie, with all the dark stuff left out. That was for the chaplain or the psych. 'Found the sniper who got Chaffin – had a fat boulder right where his dick used to be and a big look of surprise on his face. Gonna give him a big fucking problem with the virgins upstairs.'

Black looked like he was listening, but other scenes were playing in his head. He wanted the beheaded man ID'd. Montes quit talking. 'Your turn.'

Black tapped his head. 'All fuzzed up.' If only.

When he exited the shower, he noticed things were already changing on the base. Frontloaders were filling a fresh set of Hesco bastions with sand and a truck-mounted jib was hefting them into place, doubling the height of the fortifications. A new guard tower was going up. The base, which had been all about peacekeeping and nation-building, was being put on a war footing.

Blackburn and Lieutenant Cole faced each other across a folding table strewn with maps. Not the familiar ones of their patch along the border, all dog-eared and stained with coffee, but fresh ones of another country – Iran. Cole had his laptop open. He was hunched over it, arms folded, peering at the screen, typing rapidly while he listened to Black's report. Blackburn recounted the scene as it played in his head, as it would again and again for years to come, whether he wanted it to or not, the star exhibit in his gallery of unwelcome memories.

Only Cole seemed to be typing far more words than Blackburn was speaking. 'Back up a second. How far away were you at the moment of the execution?'

'Like I said, hundred yards, maybe more.'

'Behind a slab of masonry.'

'Yessir.'

'You didn't move.'

'That's what I said, Sir.'

Cole looked up from the screen.

What the fuck else could I do? Blackburn wanted to say.

'I had no choice, Sir.'

Eventually Cole stopped typing. Read over his words and closed the document.

'We got an ID. Private James Harker from Cody, Wyoming. Nineteen years old.'

A name.

'Want to see how we ID'd him?'

A cold weight deep seemed to grow inside Black. 'Let me look.'

'You up to it?'

'I was there.'

Cole turned the laptop towards him, clicked 'Play'. The camera was a few feet from Harker's face as his expression moved through relief at being discovered, to dismay, then fear, as he realised what was about to happen. Then it crumpled into helpless outrage.

'Turn up the sound.'

'That's as high as it goes.'

Harker was getting a lecture, or more of a rant, of which only a few words and phrases were audible. 'American pigs ... enter uninvited ... suffer the fate ...' On the screen ran a separate statement rather than a translation. *Invaders who dare to conquer in time of national emergency will suffer a righteous fate. Be warned.* He slammed the laptop shut. He had seen all he wanted. What happened next he would never need reminding of. Blackburn handed him the photographs he had found near the body. Cole glanced at them and put them in a file. Then he breathed out.

For a few seconds neither of them spoke. Then Cole broke the silence.

'Nothing you could do, right?'

Black stared, a surge of indignation rising, but then Cole nodded. It wasn't a question there was an answer to. Cole put the laptop aside and shuffled the maps. Moving on. He smoothed his hand across northeast Iran. Blackburn became conscious again of the sound of the base. A convoy of trucks thundered past outside the tent. The air crackled with choppers stacked for landing.

Cole slapped the map. 'We have one big fucking situation across the border.'

'How bad?'

'Bad-bad. Bashir's taking full advantage of the chaos caused by the quake to consolidate his position. Parts of the south and east have been declared PLR territory. And in Tehran, no one's in charge.'

'You're kidding.'

He drummed his fingers on the table. 'No definitive confirmation yet, but there's shit flying around that Al Bashir has a nuclear capability. If it's true, we're in a whole 'nother game now.'

Cole fixed Blackburn with another glare. Blackburn had been there before. He respected his commanding officer. Beyond that, he wasn't sure. There was a coldness in him that meant he was either just that – cold – or he kept his inner self well-defended.

Cole nodded. 'You did good yesterday, neutralising that IED. We got the casualties from Carter's unit out and had your guys cleared. That wouldn't have happened if it had blown.'

'Just doing my job, Sir.'

'Yeah, well, doing it that well means it doesn't let up for you. It's business as usual.'

'I wasn't expecting it to, Sir.'

Black felt stung. The last thing on his mind was some kind of reward. That was Cole all over. Pat on the back with one hand, slap on the face with the other. Cole stood up and grabbed the laptop.

'Stick around. Briefing at 1300.'

They sat in two rows of folding chairs. The makeshift briefing room, fashioned out of a pair of refrigerated containers and inevitably nicknamed 'the cooler', was very far from cool. Cole stood, legs apart, beside a wall map of Tehran, tapping it with a pointer.

'We got intel that Al Bashir is in the north sector of the city. His people have seized the Interior Ministry; that's now effectively their HQ in the capital. Gentlemen, this one is ours. Our information is that the quake has downed their radar and entire sections of the country are without power. We are going in and we're going to cut this thing off at the head and finish it before he gets dug in. But Al

Bashir must, repeat *must*, be taken alive. The mission will go down as follows ...'

Cole tapped the map emphatically with his stick. The tension rose in the room.

'PLR forces concentrated in the north will be kept occupied by ongoing air strikes. Assault element, call sign Misfit 2–1, will be flown in by Osprey to this location. They will have a sniper element consisting of Blackburn and Campo, call sign Misfit 3–1 as over-watch security. Designated LZ is a quarter mile from the Ministry. Once on the ground the assault team will proceed to the target building.'

Cole turned to another more detailed map of the area surrounding the bank. 'Along the way, Black's team will provide overwatch from these positions. Extraction will be by Osprey. Roger?'

The audience responded. 'Roger.'

Campo grinned at Black. 'This is cool shit, man. Like we Navy Seals all of a sudden.'

Cole slapped the map where the Ministry was. 'I consider it our privilege to be handed this mission. So let's make it good.'

16

They all stared at the carnage. Vladimir spoke first, to Gregorin.

'Well at least you downed the hangmen.'

'And it didn't rain.'

No situation had ever been too bad for Vladimir to extract some sliver of humour from, however grim. But it failed to raise so much as a smile. Eventually all eyes settled on Dima. He was rigid with silent rage.

'Do what you can. Let's get down there. I'm going after Shenk's scanner.'

The smoke swirled around them, an acrid mixture of burnt fuel, rubber and flesh. The high walls had trapped the inferno, containing and concentrating the heat like a coffee pot. For several seconds, as the flames found the ammunition that hadn't erupted, there were smaller explosions and blasts of flame.

Dima's first thought, one that came to him all too often, was: *How can it ever be claimed that these men did not die in vain?* Those who died defending Moscow from Hitler, they did not die in vain, nor did those who fell in the battle for Berlin. The Soviet troops in Afghanistan? When he was too old to do this any more, he promised himself he would write a book analysing Russian military disasters great and small. *Better get on with it*, Kroll had said. *It could take you some time to get through them all.*

What had gone wrong here? Everything: starting with Dima having allowed himself to be blackmailed into taking it on and letting Paliov interfere with the design and the execution. Paliov, terrified of failure, had brought about exactly that, by failing to give Dima control of the whole operation. Dima wouldn't have had Shenk anywhere near the site, a man no doubt competent at dealing with nuclear devices of all kinds in all places – except in the heat of battle. And because time was not on their side, they had only minimum surveillance. It contained a lot of data which appeared to tell them everything but told them almost nothing, especially not the key fact, which was that the compound, far from being a barely populated hideout, was in fact a major PLR base.

He glanced at Gregorin and Zirak, both ashen as they went from corpse to corpse, looking in vain for survivors. They knew most of these men, had taught them all they had learned. They would have good reason to be furious with him for letting this happen.

The carcass of Shenk's Mil was surrounded by flames, its tail pointing straight in the air. Through the open door he could see Shenk in his seat, hanging from the straps, head on his chest, as if he'd nodded off in the midst of it all. Just the impact would have been enough to end his life. He could see the scanner in its housing on the bulkhead in front of him. A sheet of fresh flames erupted between them. Dima lunged forward through the flames, clambered into the fuselage and grabbed the scanner. It was jammed. He got closer, got both hands round it.

'Dima, for fuck sake!' Kroll's shrill yell was just audible over the roar of the blaze. He gave it one last yank and it was out, sending him spilling out into the flames. He rolled through them and got clear just as the whole machine erupted, cremating Shenk and what was left of his crew.

Dima heard himself addressing his team. 'Find the guy they were hanging – we need confirmation if he's Kaffarov. If not, I want it confirmed he was being held against his will. I want it confirmed there are – or were – nuclear devices here. We need this information fast: I don't care how you get it. Go.' He passed the scanner to Kroll. 'Get it working.'

Gregorin and Vladimir had isolated a wounded man. He had rolled off into a space between the structure and the wall, where he had been shielded from both the shooting and the inferno. Lying there bleeding, with three armed Russians standing over him, he had every incentive to talk, but a volley of Farsi invective indicated that his pride was going to be an obstacle.

'Colourful.'

'Did your whore of a mother teach you those words?'

Zirak raised a hand, stepped forward and produced a knife. He sliced through the man's coat and trousers and then his underwear. There was no indication that he was going to stop. The man began to writhe, just like the prisoner he had been dragging to the noose only minutes ago. Zirak took the man's testicles in his hands and pressed the blade against them.

'Hungry?'

The man wet himself, pissing all over Zirak's hands. Zirak squeezed his balls, not quite hard enough to make him pass out. 'Okay, so you can have them with gravy.'

The rage and indignation melted from the man's face. It was still contorted but he was whimpering now, whispering something to Zirak.

Dima, moving towards them, felt something against his boot. A hand reaching out. He looked down. Whoever he was, he was unrecognisable, his features melted. With his other hand the wounded man found the barrel of Dima's AK. Wrapping a single remaining finger round the tip, he pulled it towards his head. Dima obliged. One bullet and the man's agony was over.

Zirak wiped his knife on the man's sleeve and sheathed it. He turned to Dima. 'Okay, it's his version so take it with a pinch of salt, but he says that as of tomorrow this was supposed to be the PLR regional base for the northeast. He reckons the PLR is now in control of the whole country and Al Bashir has been sworn in as President and Commander-in-Chief of the Armed Forces. The man they were about to hang was the district commander, who had been mobilising a resistance, and the guys on the trucks were his supporters.'

'What about Kaffarov?'

'Didn't mean anything to him.'

This couldn't be right.

'Ask if he saw the Mercedes SUV.'

Dima caught a glint of recognition on the man's face. He took out his knife, leaned down, placed the tip of the blade just under the man's left eye. He responded in anxious broken Russian. 'I no know the name, I never heard, please on the head of my daughter.' He started nodding frantically. 'I seen Merc Jeep.'

'You should be worrying about more than your daughter's head. Get up.'

Vladimir lifted him.

'Show me your operations centre.'

The man looked confused. Zirak translated and the man pointed at a doorway, behind which rose a flight of steps.

'Keep him with us.'

With Dima in the lead they dragged him across the courtyard, through the charred remains of men and machines. The stairwell was in darkness. They had never got as far as cutting the power to the compound, so the conflagration must have knocked it out. Dima waved Gregorin forward, who jogged silently up the steps. He beckoned Dima, who followed. A steel door, no handle or spyhole. Gregorin removed his helmet, pressed his ear against the door, signalled with his fingers – five, and five again.

Dima beckoned to the others and motioned for Gregorin to fall in behind him. When they were all lined up, Dima blasted the door frame with the Dragunov, then jammed the weapon right into the hinges and fired again. When the frame splintered, he fired upwards into the room and waited. No response. He peered round the aperture. Gregorin was right. At least ten men had taken refuge, most in some sort of uniform, but three in underwear. They must have been asleep when the choppers arrived.

'*On the ground, face down!*' he barked in Farsi. '*Arms, legs stretched where I can see them. There are a hundred men dead out there. Full co-operation or you die too.*'

He touched the hot end of the Dragunov against the temple of one of the men in underwear. The man flinched.

'Kaffarov. Where?'

'Gone.'

'Nuclear device?'

There was no response to this. What a waste. All that effort, all that planning, for this. Dima felt what little residual patience he had ebb away.

'No, no, please!'

He aimed at the man's head, squeezed the trigger and twisted the barrel a fraction left as he fired. The man collapsed sideways, the remains of his ear running down the side of his face.

'Right. Are you listening, you worthless pieces of shit? I will shoot everyone in this room unless and until I have all questions answered. Whoever's in charge raise your hand. *Now!*'

A grey-haired man looked up at him. Dima's eyes locked on to his. He reached down, grabbed the man by the collar and hauled him to his feet.

'The rest of you, get out and do what you can for those poor bastards out there. Go. Now!'

They got to their feet and Kroll herded them out.

Dima turned to the grey-haired man, who smiled weakly.

'Comrade Mayakovsky?'

17

Rajah Amirasani, former Colonel in the Iranian Revolutionary Guard and one-time cadet under Dima's instruction, stood in front of him. The room was small, yet his old protégé seemed dwarfed by the space around him. Leaving Gregorin on guard outside, he closed the door. They were alone. Rajah came towards him to attempt an embrace, but Dima shoved him away. After such a debacle, the once-familiar face brought no comfort. Rage, frustration, suspicion and the worst feeling of all – impotence – simmered inside him. How had he let himself become part of this?

Rajah slumped on to a chair where he sat legs apart, elbows propped on his knees, the tears flowing freely down his cheeks and on to the floor. He had been the finest in his year, a natural leader who skilfully managed to impress his political masters with his devotion to the cause, without losing all sense of humanity. Now he looked battered and defeated.

'Kaffarov left.'

So he had been there. At least that part was right.

'You let him go?'

Rajah looked up, bewildered.

'He was here. You were holding him here, yes?'

Rajah's brow furrowed. 'Holding him? Why would we do that? He was here to meet Al Bashir.'

'He came here voluntarily?'

'Of course.'

Something was seriously wrong with Paliov's intelligence.

'And Al Bashir is still coming here?'

'Was. But there was a change of plan.'

'A missile from somewhere south took out the chopper. Someone knew we were coming, didn't they?'

'As God is my witness, I have no knowledge of that. Kaffarov took off three hours ago in a big hurry. No explanation. We called Al Bashir's people. One of his staff said the meeting location was changed. No one told us.'

'To where?'

He shrugged, then sighed.

'We had all these —.' He gestured towards where the dead men lay. 'We were instructed to put on a show of solidarity from the local population. The regional governor – we had orders ...'

'To execute him in public.'

Rajah sighed and shook his head.

'The things I've seen happen in my country ... Through the seventies we yearned for liberation from the Shah; after the Revolution, when it got even worse, we hoped again for freedom. But this ...'

'What about Kaffarov's armaments, a nuclear device?'

He shrugged. 'Of that I know nothing.'

Dima reached down, grabbed his chin and forced him to look into his eyes. Once he had counted him as a friend. Not now. 'You say you know nothing about the nuclear device Kaffarov had with him? Fuck with me and I swear I will find you and kill you.'

Rajah looked back into his eyes and Dima saw there was no deception. 'Please understand, Al Bashir gives nothing away. Only those closest to him know his plans. Before, he was – I thought he was – the solution. Now ...' He let out a long despairing sigh.

Dima felt his anger subside a little. This changed everything. The mission was fucked. Paliov had it all wrong. All that waste of life ... Rajah raised his hands. 'Foreign influences.'

'What does that mean?'

'Dima, you told us to respect ourselves, to listen to our instincts ... This country is sinking into madness. Al Bashir has let the genie out of the bottle.'

'What does that mean?'

Rajah shook his head. 'He wants revenge – worldwide – for what he says has been done to our country. Even if he doesn't live to see it. That's why he was so fixated on the weapons – the portable ones.'

He gripped Dima's arm. 'Get away from here while you can. A PLR unit is in the air now.'

'How long?'

'Thirty minutes, fifty at most.'

Dima studied his old protégé's face, embraced him briefly and left the room, collecting Gregorin on the way.

'Forget the search: we're leaving.'

18

Black always addressed his letters *'Dear Mom and Dad'*, but he always sent them to his mother. That way he knew they would get read. She was the one who did the admin, opened the bills, sorted stuff out. To begin with he had written separately to each of them, but once, on home leave, firing up the PC, he looked at his father's inbox and saw his mails unopened. Nevertheless he kept his discovery to himself and it was never spoken about – like so much to do with his father.

He opened his laptop and clicked on 'New Message'.

Please do not ignore this mail. Dad, *he wrote:* Today I saw a man die in front of me and I was powerless to help him. I think that for the first time in my life I am finally beginning to understand what you went through. I just wish that—.

Montes burst in. 'It's go. C'mon.'

Black hesitated, about to click on 'Save', then chose 'Send'. Who knows when I'll get to finish it, he thought.

As they assembled in full body armour, two soldiers he didn't recognise approached Black. Montes whispered, 'Buddies of Harker'. The shorter one raised a gloved finger and pointed at Black's name.

'Did all you could, huh?'

'I'm sorry about your buddy. Sorry for your loss.'

'Your loss too, man. Not just ours.'

The taller but slighter one put a hand on the other's arm, who was shorter but stockier, with a huge neck like a bull. He shook it off, bristling.

'C'mon, Dwayne, don't do this.'

Black stopped, legs apart, squaring up. Having failed to save Harker, was he now going to beat up his friends? It was too pathetic. All the same, he wasn't just going to stand there.

'Look, I appreciate—.'

'You don't appreciate nothin', you fuckin' *coward*.'

The other one put his hand out again, and again was thrown off. This was not an insult Blackburn could let stand. On the other hand, what they had been through, and thanks to modern technology what they had seen, was not in the manual either.

'Men like you are a disgrace to the service. You make me sick, you piece of shit.'

Black took a step towards him.

'Listen carefully,' he said. 'There. Was. Nothing. I. Could. Do. This is a war. People get killed. Six of my own men were killed yesterday and that is war. You got that?'

Both men watched him now, trying to gauge what sort of opponent he was going to be. The short angry one's fist moved up a fraction and before it had gone two inches Blackburn had pinned his arm behind his back. 'Now, take your friend and go and pound the punchbag. Okay?'

He saw Cole approaching and released the man's arm. The three of them saluted and Harker's friends moved on. Cole watched them go, then gave Blackburn a look.

'Just shooting the breeze there, Sir.'

'Okay, Sergeant. Let's get this one done, okay?'

19

Bazargan, Northern Iran

It was in their training from day one. Be prepared for nothing to be what it seems, trust no one you don't have to, and never entirely drop your guard with those you *do* trust. Spetsnaz were trained to do many things that ordinary soldiers wouldn't have a clue about. Part of the selection process was to weed out anyone who showed any tendency to take anything for granted. Working undercover, living double lives, going months embedded in hostile organisations without hearing a friendly voice, living on your wits, thinking for yourself, making life or death decisions about who to kill and who you might save. Achieving this required resources that were beyond most humans.

This one had it all. Dima could blame Paliov for the design of the mission, for its poor chain of command, for the intelligence failures – about Kaffarov, about what to expect in the compound. He could blame Shenk for his failure to wait until the compound was secured, for engaging in the firefight, putting his chopper in harm's way. But above all Dima blamed himself for allowing Paliov to draw him into this catastrophic misadventure, and he particularly blamed himself for recruiting the team around him, who came willingly because they believed in him.

All of these thoughts ran through his head as he led them back to the cars. Already they could hear the PLR helicopter circling, looking for somewhere to land other than the compound, strewn as it was with bodies and debris.

They moved as swiftly as they could, bending low, dodging between branches and leaping over dips in the boggy ground. None of them spoke. He glanced at Gregorin and Zirak, their faces masks of shock, and sorrow for their comrades, roasted alive.

'Anyone see where that missile came from?' Vladimir asked, as they walked. "Cos it sure as hell didn't come from the ground.'

Dima paused, looked at them all. Gregorin nodded. 'He's right. Came in from the west, not from below.'

Dima brought them to a halt and grouped them into a huddle. 'What happened back there – I've seen some fuckups but none of them come close to that. A waste of fine men, for which I take responsibility.'

The others looked at the ground.

Kroll raised a finger. 'Does this mean we're headed home?'

Dima looked at their faces. 'Each man is free to make his choice.'

Vladimir spoke next. 'What's your choice?'

Dima didn't need to think. He already knew. 'Continue. Hunt down Kaffarov, find his WMD.'

Vladimir looked at Kroll, then back to Dima. 'Then I'm in.'

The other three nodded in unison.

For the first time that night Dima had a reason to feel optimistic. 'From now on – our plan: no one else's. We do this thing our way.'

Dima stepped away from the group to get Paliov on the satphone secure line. When he had finished giving the report there was a long silence at the other end.

'*You still there?*'

'*Yes, still here,*' came Paliov's weary reply. '*What do you want me to say?*'

'*Kaffarov wasn't abducted. He was there willingly. Tell me right now you didn't lie to me.*'

A long pause. '*The intelligence was thin. We drew the wrong conclusions. I apologise. Nothing with Kaffarov is straightforward, you know that.*'

'*And he knew we were coming for him. He was tipped off. There was a leak.*'

Paliov's indignation brought him back to life. '*An outrageous suggestion. For all you know he may have just changed his plans.*'

'*If you weren't so defensive I might have believed you. Shenk's chopper was downed by an air-to-air missile. Someone was ready for us. You better take a long hard look at who knew what. Someone told us Al Bashir's come under "outside influences". Any bright ideas from the great Russian intelligence machine?*

Another silence on the end of the phone. The sound of Paliov digesting yet more unpalatable information. They both knew what each of them was thinking. Eventually Paliov groaned. *'That doesn't bear thinking about.'*

'Well you better think about it, but keep it to yourself. If it's true, the longer Kaffarov goes on not realising we know, the better. He'll get to hear about what happened at the compound, but it's better he thinks the mission's been aborted.'

'So you're going on?'

'We still have a deal, remember?'

20

It was starting to get light. They changed out of their kit and put on the local clothing again. All of the kit went into the cars' trunks. Each of them kept a handgun and a knife on them and put their compact AKs in the footwells. Vladimir took the wheel of the lead car with Kroll and Dima sitting in the back. Zirak and Gregorin were in the second vehicle – one at the wheel, the other in the rear watching their backs.

Dima was still seething, but he did his best to keep it from the others. He needed them to be in no doubt that he was keeping it together.

'From now on we do this my way. The signal Shenk was getting from the WMD. Is it still transmitting?' Kroll, the scanner in his lap, shrugged. 'Well find out. If Kaffarov hasn't disabled it I want a grid reference immediately and any changes sent to me by text.'

They took the road going northwest towards Gürbulak. The sooner they put some distance between them and the Bazargan compound the better. Dima called the contact who had emailed him the photos of the compound walls. Darwish gave them directions to a tea shop run by a 'most trusted friend' in Meliksah, a small town eighteen kilometres away. Dima located it on the map and radioed the reference to the second car.

'*Tea shop? What about breakfast?*' was Zirak's response.

At the first crossroads they hit a road block, two pick-up trucks with the letters PLR daubed hastily on their sides, parked across the road to make a tight chicane, and two men with PLR insignia pinned on their jackets, each with an AK.

From the back Dima instructed Vladimir. 'Brake late and hard. Look furious.'

Vladimir snorted. 'They look like they got hired ten minutes ago.'

Before the Peykan had come to a stop Dima was out of the car, shouting furiously in Farsi. 'Are you the escort? Turn these trucks round and take us through to Kharvanah. Now!'

The guards looked at each other.

'Don't you know who I am?'

Dima thrust his dog-eared Iranian passport at them. 'You know what's happening.' He gestured furiously at the hills behind them. 'An entire platoon of foreign insurgents in those hills is what. You should be looking for them, not stopping senior PLR officials. Who's your commanding officer?' Dima pulled out his phone. 'I'm calling him right now!'

The guards looked at each other. The taller bowed slightly. 'I apologise for not recognising you, Sir.'

'So you're not the escort. What a shambles. Move those trucks. Let us through. Do it NOW!'

Back in the car, Dima laughed as he watched the guards recede in the mirror.

'How did I do?'

Vladimir, at the wheel, shrugged.

'You could have waved your arms a bit more.'

'Your turn next time.'

'Where the fuck is Kharvanah?'

'Fucked if I know.'

The main street of Meliksah was rutted and dusty with no sign of any damage from the quake, but the whole place looked neglected. There were no people in sight except for a couple of old men sitting on a bench under a cypress tree, who stared as they stepped out of the cars.

All of the shops were boarded up and the windows shuttered. Definitely too quiet. Gregorin volunteered to keep watch on the cars. Kroll carried a radio so they could stay in touch. The tea shop was up a narrow flight of stairs. Inside there was some life, several men at tables drinking tea. As Dima entered all of them stopped talking and stared. Zirak nodded and spoke first. Once they heard his accent and mention of Darwish's name they seemed to lose interest and went back to their conversations.

A rotund man in an apron came huffing up the stairs and greeted them as if they were his long-lost brothers. Then Darwish entered the room.

'Dear Zima,' said Darwish, embracing him and reminding him of his old cover name. 'Come, I have reserved a room.'

They followed him down a passage to a small low-ceilinged room with peeling walls. In it were a couple of benches, an antique spinning wheel and some hens strutting about, pecking at the sawdust strewn on the floor.

The café owner brought in a tray of tea in small glasses and a plate of flatbread, local white cheese, jam, pomegranates and figs. Zirak could hardly hold himself back.

'Please accept my apologies for the condition of this room,' said the café owner.

'No, no, it's perfect. Your hospitality is too generous.'

Darwish waited for him to go, then shut the door behind him and locked it. All trace of bonhomie vanished. He raised his hands in the air as if appealing to Allah.

'This is big, big trouble.'

'You can say that again,' said Dima.

Darwish clutched his brow and shook his head. 'There's already an alert out for you. No descriptions – just a group of foreigners, all armed. But shoot on sight. Big reward for information about you, even bigger one for your bodies. I sincerely advise you to cross the border as soon as possible. The PLR are using the aftermath of the earthquake to tighten their grip on the whole country.'

'You said "foreigners". Why not Russians? They must know our nationality.'

He shook his head vigorously. 'No no. Much more cunning. They are claiming you are American-backed insurgents. It plays much better with the people, and strengthens support for the PLR.'

He shook his head in disgust and looked at them regretfully. 'So far you are playing into Al Bashir's hands. What you have done —.' He pointed in the direction of the compound. 'That only supports his claims about foreign incursion, which he uses to tighten his grip on us. Why did you let that happen?'

He clutched his forehead and closed his eyes.

Dima put an arm round him. 'First of all, thank you for risking your life to see us. We won't forget. But we're not going home yet. What do you know about Amir Kaffarov?'

Darwish's eyes narrowed. 'Before Kaffarov, people like me, progressive, who wanted change, we were sympathetic to Al Bashir who we believed wanted change also. Peaceful change. But now Al Bashir has lost interest in building a coalition of support and it's becoming clear he wants all the power for himself and his clique. Now it's all about demonstrating the power, a show of strength. Some put that down to Kaffarov. Kaffarov comes along with his wares and he's got Al Bashir addicted. Any trouble in our area he will come back and—.' He made a flattening motion with his hand. 'So Zima, we are very much trying to avoid trouble. So you must go.'

Dima held his gaze. 'Not just yet.'

Darwish started to protest, but Dima put a finger to his lips. He explained Kaffarov's deadly luggage and the aborted meeting with Al Bashir. 'Time is not on our side. We need to get to someone right at the heart of the PLR High Command. We need information from that level. Someone we can pressure.'

He turned Darwish's face towards his.

'You are an influential man. You know people. You can help.'

Darwish shook his head. He reached for the glass in front of him and downed the contents in one, as if it was his last drink on earth.

'One more favour, for old time's sake.'

'Zima, you are like a brother to me. You know I would die for you but . . .'

'We're all going to die if we don't find that bomb.'

Darwish's hands rose and fell. 'Loyalty to Al Bashir is driven by fear. All this time he was the popular leader, the great hope for our nation. Now . . .' He shook his head in despair. 'Many of his oldest allies have been purged. The people round him now – foreign—.'

'Yes I know. Foreign influences. What sort?'

'You know Tehran, all the time rumours. Some say a secret son he fathered abroad.'

This wasn't going anywhere. Humour him. Dima smiled. 'Darwish, you are the man who knows everyone, you have many influential relatives ... Maybe one of them?'

The charm wasn't working. Darwish was sweating, shaking. Showing all the signs of a man who had got himself into something he wished he hadn't.

'You ask I take photos. For old time's sake. Fine. It's dangerous but I do it. Next thing you crash helicopters, kill a lot of people. Now you ask me to betray ...'

Dima butted in, still with the charm. 'You are an operator, Darwish, very well connected. You have played the game well all this time. Very few of us know your true loyalties. The fact that you are able to meet us in the open in a time of national emergency tells me that even now you believe you have nothing to fear from the PLR. No one need know your role. This isn't just for me; it's for your country. Think about it.'

Darwish was thinking all right, but not in the way Dima wanted him to. Not yet. He pressed on, colder now.

'We don't have time to do the research, checking people out, surveillance, finding their weaknesses, compromising them. Instead of weeks, months, we have days, or maybe only hours, to find Kaffarov and his bombs. Brother, don't make me push you any harder.'

Darwish pulled away, a last burst of indignation. 'You're blackmailing me. After all I've ...'

Dima fixed him with a cold stare. Their relationship had always been an unequal one. While posing as a Russian Special Forces instructor to the Revolutionary Guard, Dima had acted as Darwish's handler, running him as a high-value source deep inside the government. The intelligence had been invaluable and Darwish had been handsomely rewarded. Darwish's cover was never blown, but he always knew that he would be in Dima's debt.

Dima piled on the pressure. 'Someone close enough to Al Bashir to know about Kaffarov. We know there's a relationship there because they were scheduled to meet in person last night. And if Al Bashir was prepared to travel up here to meet him that means he regards

111

Kaffarov as valuable. Very valuable. Come on Darwish, think about the old days. "Anything is possible," that was your mantra. "Anything you need Zima, you got." Remember?'

Defeated, Darwish let his head drop into his hands. Then after a few seconds he got to his feet. 'Five minutes, please.'

After Darwish left, Vladimir was the first to speak. 'Nice show, Dima. If you don't mind me asking, what's this going to do for us?'

Dima folded his arms. 'You'll see.'

Then it was Kroll's turn. 'Since we're this short of time wouldn't it be quicker to break his legs?'

Dima glanced at Zirak, who was chewing thoughtfully on his bread.

'What's on your mind?'

'This jam isn't nearly as good as my mother's.'

Two minutes later, Darwish was back. In his hand he held a wedding photograph and a business card. He laid the photo on the table and pointed at the groom, a dashing big-built man in his early forties, stern face. Next to him a triumphant, grinning bride.

'Here is Gazul Halen. He is number three to Al Bashir. In charge of Intelligence.'

Dima pulled the photo closer, studying the face. 'How do we get to him?'

With an index finger Darwish reached forward and circled the bride. 'She is my daughter, Amara.'

21

Half an hour later, Dima had all the information he wanted about Amara and her husband. Darwish, between bouts of tears, explained that although he had gone along with the match he didn't support it.

'We fell out. Very bad. He's no good. All he has achieved is with this.' He made a fist which he banged on the table and with his other hand he made a grabbing gesture at Dima's groin. 'All his people, he has their balls in the blender, his finger on the switch. He's very paranoid. Has his own private security detail twenty-four seven. Not PLR. His own. Same for Amara. They never stay more than few days in each place.'

'She's not happy?'

'So now I'm getting these texts from a number I don't recognise. Always I have to be careful of who is contacting me. But it's my Amara, she has Pay As You Go. "Daddy, please can we make up?" Of course we make up! She is my life! "I'm so sorry I made a terrible mistake, I want to come home." She wants to escape but she is too scared. He keeps her almost a prisoner. Now with all the trouble, the quake, she's desperate. She texts me every day, sometimes five, six times, but what can I do?'

Dima leaned back, folded his arms. 'You tell her you are sending help. She tells us where she is. You get your daughter back, and Gazul takes us to Kaffarov and his bomb.'

Relief swept over Darwish's face. 'Simple.'

'Simple,' repeated Dima, knowing full well it was anything but. The words 'Gazul takes us to Kaffarov and his bomb' echoed ominously round his head. But it was something, and something was a damn sight better than what they had. He stood up and embraced his comrade.

'Darwish, old friend: with you on board, how can we lose?'

22

The Tabriz–Tehran Highway was dead straight: a dark line on the map all the way. Dima drove, pedal to the floor, straddling the two southbound lanes. The Peykan was managing to hold a steady 120 kph. Even though the windows were open and blowing in a steady gale, the heat from the afternoon sun, and what was coming back at them from the screaming engine, turned the inside of the car into an oven.

'You watching for cracks?' said Vladimir.

'I'm watching,' replied Dima.

'An earthquake can unzip a road and before you know it you're in a ravine that wasn't there two minutes ago.'

The southbound lane was deserted. Northbound was a different story: a solid convoy of vehicles of all types heading away from the quake zone, cars piled high with bedding, trailers full of fridges, TVs and washing machines, buses with people perched on top. In one car a granny remonstrated with the driver, presumably her son, from the back seat, while her daughter-in-law scowled in front. She's thinking, let's just wait for the road to open up and throw her in, mused Dima. There had been no sign of serious quake damage so far, but a great cloud of brown dust haze along the horizon, growing ever bigger as they neared the capital, gave a hint of what they would face. They kept the radio on, switching from station to station, each news report predicting more tremors.

Vladimir was slumped across the back seat, finishing a packet of biscuits that was supposed to last them the whole six hundred ks to Tehran.

'How do they forecast tremors, then?'

'They measure the vibrations in the ground or something. Leave some for me, you greedy fucker.'

'I need to keep my strength up. In jail I used to tell fortunes. Ten roubles or five cigarettes, or one joint, and I'd predict whether you'd get beaten or stabbed. If they paid up I'd predict they wouldn't. And I was always right.'

'Tell my fortune.'

'There's an earthquake coming and you're gonna get nuked. And if you survive, the PLR's going to chop your balls off. A thousand rials please.'

'Piss off. You've already had all the biscuits.'

Vladimir screwed up the empty packet and threw it out of the window. After five years in Butyrka, thought Dima, a man was probably entitled to them.

'What was it like in there, anyhow?'

'I was doing all right as it goes. I was kind of sorry when Gregorin and Zirak showed up.'

'Oh, come on. How did they spring you? Explosives? Disguised as a laundry woman? A bloody ugly one.'

'They explained to the Superintendent that I was urgently needed on a patriotic mission. He was quite glad to see the back of me – I can't think why.'

'And have you now seen the error of your ways?'

'Yeah, I shouldn't have got caught. That was an error. Steady, you stupid bastard!'

Dima swerved violently to avoid a cow that had wandered into his path. He glanced in the mirror to see Kroll in the other Peykan do the same.

'How do you rate your chances of finding Kaffarov and his – gadgets?'

'I'm not a gambling man, remember.'

'And rescuing Darwish's daughter? Since when are you anyone's knight in shining armour?'

'If Kroll doesn't fix Shenk's tracker, she's our best hope.'

'Married to that psycho twat: what a hassle. Aren't you glad you don't have kids? Like poor old Kroll.'

'Maybe they're what keep him going.'

'Too bad their mothers don't let him near them.'

'It might be good to have a son and heir. Otherwise, what's it all for?'

'For a laugh, you stupid cunt.'

In the mirror, Dima could see Vladimir's incomprehension: build yourself a future? Who needs another thing to worry about? He focused all his concentration on the road ahead, in the effort to screen out what was going on in his head. Paliov's photographs: confirmation, after twenty years of denials.

They passed through the gap in the Alborz mountains, that stand guard over Tehran's northern suburbs. Above the dust cloud over the city he saw two planes circle and dive. Vladimir sat up.

'Are you seeing what I'm seeing?'

23

Asara, North of Tehran

'Great. That's all we need.'

Gregorin lowered the binoculars and passed them over. 'Brand new F-35 Lightnings, straight out of the box. Only one air force has those.'

'I'm glad one of us is keeping up,' said Dima.

They had turned off the highway and headed up Route 56, west into the Alborz mountains. From there they had a panoramic view of the city, which sat on the plain that stretched out below. Dima watched the fighters circling a giant column of smoke that was funnelling up from a refinery on the southern side of the capital.

'First the PLR, then an earthquake. Now the US fucking Air Force. We've got the full set.'

'Look on the bright side. At least they're attacking the south and west. According to Darwish, Amara's at her in-laws in the northeast.'

'Oh well, that's all right then: no problem. We just ignore the world's biggest superpower laying siege to one part of the town as we rock up to her door and ask if we can take tea with her husband.'

Dima shrugged. 'You got a better idea?'

It was nearly six o'clock. The light was fading. Darwish called. He had spoken to his daughter. She was in Niavaran, a northern suburb, alone in the house. All of her husband's relatives and servants had fled. She had no idea where they had gone, and was hysterical with fear. Darwish had promised her that help was on the way.

'*I told her Daddy is sending some brave men to rescue her: the best.*'

'*No pressure then. But where the hell is the husband – what's his name?*'

'*Gazul.*'

'*What kind of man leaves his wife alone in the middle of an earthquake?*'

'And with the Americans bombing the place.'

'I'm open to suggestions.'

'Let's find the fucker and cut his balls off,' said Vladimir, as Dima hung up.

'*Sensible* suggestions. So far all you've done is scoff all the biscuits so be useful, or we'll find a ravine and chuck you in.'

He turned to Kroll, in the back of the second Peykan, presiding over the tangle of wires from Shenk's tracker, spread all over the seat.

'Why don't you get hold of her first and see how the land lies? See if the guy really has buggered off, and if so where,' said Kroll.

Dima dialled the number Darwish had given him.

'Actually those biscuits were a bit dry. Have we got any vodka?'

'He shoots better when he's drunk, isn't that right Vladimir?'

'Shut the fuck up, will you? I'm trying to listen.'

Dima waited for an answer. He had no idea if she'd be any use, and no expectation that she'd get them any nearer to Kaffarov or his suitcase nuke. If her husband's own family had really abandoned her, were they even in touch at all? He waited for her to pick up. She spoke in a hushed whisper, tearful and breathing in fits and starts.

'*If my husband finds out I've even spoken to you he will have me killed.*'

'*He won't get the chance. Just confirm where you are and where he is.*'

'*I don't know! He went early this morning. I asked his mother if she knew, and she wouldn't even answer. They all hate me. She doesn't even —.*'

Women.

'*Right. Just repeat the address for me, please. Good, OK. Now, are you definitely alone?*'

'*Yes, even my maid has gone.*'

'*And where's Gazul?*'

'*I told you, I don't know! He never tells me anything.*'

As the jets flew overhead, Dima struggled to listen.

'*Okay, Amara, thank you. We'll be there in forty minutes.*'

He chucked the phone on to the car seat.

'She's either genuinely in fear of her life or there's something she's not telling us.'

24

Camp Firefly, Outskirts of Tehran

From a distance the hill rising on Tehran's southwest flank would have looked just as it should, nothing out of the ordinary, which was how it needed to look right now. Hidden under camouflage netting was Black's platoon, trying to take five after the long charge east, deep into quake-blasted Iran.

A rest? Fat chance: over the city, gunships were doing battle with the AA guns on the ground, filling the air with crashes, thumps and the shrieks of rockets. The air was still so thick with dust from the quake they could constantly taste it.

Campo stuffed what was left of an energy bar into his mouth.

'The fly boys putting on a nice firework display there. Just like *Independence Day.*'

Matkovic lay on his back, gloved hands cradling his head.

'Whadya Mom tell ya? Don't talk with your mouth full, dude.'

Montes was fiddling with his night-vision goggles, which were malfunctioning. 'Don't think anyone in Tehran's feeling too independent right now.'

'Button it, Montes. Just try and do the job, all right?'

All the way along the main drag westwards from the border they had seen giant posters of Al Bashir pasted on to billboards.

'Should be keeping them off the streets and in their bunkers.'

'Trouble with quakes, brings everybody out the buildings.'

'Cole says the satellite images are showing a big exodus north. Should just be us chickens.'

'Yeah, real cosy: just us and the PLR high command.'

Closer to their position, on the edge of town, PLR loudspeakers were pumping out the voice of Al Bashir, intermittent bursts of Farsi penetrating the barrage over the city.

'... *we will claim back ... with swords we will strike down the invader...*'

Black nudged Matkovic, who also knew a bit of Farsi.

'He's gonna need a lot more than swords when we ride into town.' Matkovic twitched.

'He don't shut the fuck up I'm gonna stick it right up his loud-speaker, man.'

In front of them at the bottom of the hill, on the other side of an overpass, was an apartment building. On the upper floors, the PLR were setting up a machine-gun nest.

Black stiffened, pointing into the darkness down the hill.

'You see that?'

'Fuck these NVGs.' Montes threw his goggles on the ground. 'Preparing to strike Tehran and we're fresh out of batteries.'

'Gun trucks coming in.'

Matkovic stood up and peered at where Blackburn was pointing. 'The fuck did they come from? We're not even in overwatch position.'

A convoy of five Humvees were headed on the western approach into the city. Cole slid under the camo and snatched up the radio. '*Haymaker actual, this is Misfit actual, we do not have target secured. Say again, target not secured. Hold your position, over.*'

Silence from the radio. Cole's temperature was rising.

'*Come the fuck on, Brady.*'

Hearing the name, Blackburn and Montes exchanged looks.

'The Brady Bunch are rolling into town! We're saved.'

Loved and loathed by equal numbers, Lieutenant Brady had a reputation for pushing his men hard, a habit of putting his own interpretation on orders – and if there was any glory going, grabbing it for himself. A tank-shaped thirty-two-year-old who seemed to have been in the army since he could walk, Brady was the opposite in every way of the wiry, cerebral Cole.

When the answer finally came, Brady's voice was distorted with interference and full of impatience. '*Misfit 2, we are not stopping. So you better get your ass in position and cover our advance, out.*'

'This is so fucked up.' Cole shook his head and got back on the radio. *'All call signs Misfit, we are mission launch, repeat we are mission launch. Hold your position, out.'*

The hill came alive as forty plus marines erupted from under the camo net and moved downhill towards the overpass. In Black's group, Montes and Matkovic led the way, Campo coming up behind with the mortar. As soon as the squad reached the cover of the overpass, Cole was on the radio.

'We need illumination rounds in the air like now, needed down range now.'

Before he had finished speaking the first enemy round came in. Blackburn jumped forward into the scrum of men erecting the mortar, grabbing the tube and angling it.

Campo had the carry case. He slid out the white round with black markings. 'Direct lay. One round illumination. Half load. Elevation one zero niner.'

'Round up!'

Matkovic adjusted the charges at the base of the round.

'Round up.'

'Hang it.'

He slid the round into the tube and held it near the rim.

'Hangin'.'

'Fire!'

In one fluid motion Matkovic slammed the round downwards and ducked below the muzzle. A bright flash of light illuminated their position for a split second before the round popped high above them and lit up the entire area.

They found cover behind a low wall, with the overpass and a ditch between them and the apartment block. It was already heavily damaged by the tremors, the whole structure listing to one side, lumps of concrete swaying on twisted metal rods. The few trees still standing were shredded and leafless. They moved forward to the first wall between them and the building. A mortar swept in and one side of the wall disappeared in a cloud of debris. PLR troops swarmed out of the destroyed structure.

Black was first over the remains of the wall. On the other side was a concrete sewer ditch. There was nowhere to go but down into it. He flattened himself against the opposite side, away from the PLR fire.

Montes jumped down behind him.

'Welcome to Tehran. Please leave the facilities in the condition you found them.'

He tapped Blackburn on the shoulder and pointed. Beyond a pile of rubble that had blocked the canal downstream, the carcass of a cow lay on its side, bloated with gas.

'Better not hit that.'

As he said it the carcass took a direct hit, drenching them in foul smelling fluid.

'Shit and shit again.'

'You said it, man.'

A flare drifted past, illuminating a machine-gun nest on the second floor. Blackburn poured fire into it as they ran to the side of the building.

'Frag their ass. I'll cover. Get that grenade out.'

Montes ripped out the pin, doing a split second check to see that he had both ring and pin, and lobbed the grenade. The machine-gun nest dissolved in a cloud of concrete.

The Humvee column had now advanced beneath the overpass and had made a left turn into the city. A wrecked Nissan truck, half obscured by the rubble from a demolished building, blocked the way. Blackburn was fifty metres away. He could see Lieutenant Brady yelling while half a dozen of his men tried to remove the obstacle. Two gunners gave cover from the Humvee's turret-mounted machine-guns.

Montes closed up behind Black.

'Dickhead shouldn't have gone ahead. What's up his ass?'

Brady spotted them.

'You, what the fuck you looking at? Get down here and help move this fucking wreck now.'

They started to run towards the convoy as one of the Humvee gunners keeled over. Brady pointed up at where it came from.

'Suppressive fire. Now!'

Montes, Matkovic and Campo fired into the building. The

blockage was cleared. Brady was back on the radio to Cole.

'*Misfit 2 this is Haymaker actual, I need back up here right now, over.*'

They heard Cole's reply on their headsets.

'*They're yours, over.*'

Brady pointed at Black.

'You, you're riding shotgun with me. Climb aboard soldier. Next stop Ministry of the Interior. Let's go get a piece of Bashir.' Brady heaved himself behind the wheel, Blackburn beside him. '*This is Haymaker actual, we're Oscar Mike to the Ministry, out.*'

'*Haymaker actual this is Misfit actual, Eagle eye reports personnel running in and out of building. HVT must be secured, repeat secure, copy?*'

'Roger, good copy. Out.'

Brady grinned at Black.

'Let's go fetch.'

They rolled past another set of PLR bullhorns, still blasting Al Bashir's message. Brady swerved into them and laughed maniacally as they were flattened under the Humvee's wheels. Then, without warning, a car appeared right in their path where the road narrowed. Brady flattened the brakes.

'*Ambush! Back up! Back up!*' An RPG whistled over them followed by fresh gunfire. '*Everyone fall back!*'

The convoy shuddered to a halt. Brady's turret gunner poured fire into the car and it erupted in flames, but the bullets were still coming from a window above. Precious seconds went by as each vehicle engaged reverse, while fire rained down on them, dust filling the air as tracer rounds ricocheted into the sky. The turret gunner screamed and slumped to one side, his face gone. Brady grabbed Blackburn by the shoulder.

'Get up there! Make it count, Sergeant.'

The dead man collapsed on to the seat behind Brady as Blackburn took his place and the Humvee roared backwards.

Brady was shouting into the radio again. '*Misfit actual this is Haymaker. Encountering heavy enemy fire. Proceeding to target location.*'

'*Haymaker actual. Secure ground level. Alert for HVT. Birdseye 2 is three miles away, over.*'

They cleared the fire area. Brady yelled up at Black.

'Good work, soldier. Let's go cut this snake off at the head.'

The Humvee surged forward down a parallel street to the one they had just vacated. Ahead, smoke billowed from a tall building, a massive crater in its side as if it had been hit by a plane. An Osprey swooped in and hovered above, the rotors' wash blasting smoke around the building. Blackburn saw the rear hatch open and two gunmen take up position.

'Birdseye 2 on station. Package fast roping in, over.'

The men spilled out down the ropes on to the roof of the smoking Ministry. Brady slewed the Humvee to a halt and was out before it stopped. Blackburn looked round for Montes and Matkovic, saw them and pointed at some cover behind a stranded bus, but the guns round the building had fallen silent.

Black waved them towards the entrance.

'We're with you, Sergeant.'

'Okay you guys: watch for friendlies as you clear.'

Most of the personnel had either fled or taken cover. The lobby was awash with broken glass and abandoned files and boxes. An attempt to evacuate had failed as the occupants simply ran for their lives. Loose paper floated in the air, whipped up by the downforce of the Osprey. Above they could hear the shouts of the men who had roped down, clearing rooms and floors as they went.

'We have a runner on the stairs.'

Black rushed forward as a figure exited a stairwell, hesitated and then turned away from them. Brady, distracted, missed the moment.

'Take him, take him.'

Black threw himself at the man and collapsed on top of him, winding him. A binder shot out of his hands and skidded along the floor. Brady, right behind, thrust the muzzle of his M4 into the Iranian's ear.

'Let me at him.' Brady pushed a boot against the man's shoulder, treading on his insignia. 'Colonel: good. Prepare to die, Colonel. Your war just ended.'

Black turned the Colonel's head to face Brady. For a second he thought Brady was going to let him have it point blank and got ready to jump clear. But Brady had a better idea. He scooped up the file and calmly started leafing through it as he crouched down beside the Iranian.

'Where did you think you were headed just now, Sir? Not many places left to go out there.'

The breath hissed between the Colonel's teeth as Blackburn pressed down on his head.

'... Pigs, bastards ...'

Brady kept his tone nonchalant.

'Yeah, yeah, that's us all over. You want to die now or co-operate and take us to your leader?'

'You attack our defenceless people—.'

Brady slammed the file down on the Colonel's head and screamed:

'Time's up, Colonel! Where's Bashir?'

'Okay; okay. Not here.'

'Where then?'

25

They had spotted the US ground forces from their position in the hills, so Dima's team made their descent into Tehran from the northeast, down the Lashakark Road, which led straight to the Police Park. The streets were littered with rubble and tiles. Some had been blocked altogether by fallen buildings. Every Rakhsh APC the Iranian Army owned seemed to be on the streets, each one wearing hastily-applied PLR markings.

'I finally figured out what's different.'

'Apart from devastation and insurrection?'

'No traffic. Used to be the world capital of traffic jams. A man once died at the wheel of his car. No one realised for two hours.'

The city was now almost empty. Those the earthquake had failed to scare away had been prised from their homes by the bombardment. In the main shopping streets, looters had tried taking advantage of the chaos: pavements were littered with TVs, dishwashers and other goods, pulled out in triumph and then abandoned, for lack of means to transport them. The Peykans were such an effective disguise they proved to be a magnet for desperate stragglers hunting for transport. They kept their AKs prominently displayed to discourage car-jackers as they made their way to Amara.

Kroll radioed from the second car.

'*The tracker. It's working! I'm a genius.*'

'*Okay genius. Get us a grid reference.*'

'*I'm working on it right now.*'

As they closed in on Amara's street, the air filled with the sound of AA fire, followed by the shriek and thud of a massive shell.

'Great. Uncle Sam is homing in. Let's get this done.'

Kroll radioed again.

'*Okay, I'm getting a signal in Central Tehran.*'
'*That's nice and specific. How about a street or a building?*'
'*There's a lot of interference: that's the best I can do.*'
'*Then it's all down to Amara and the charming Gazul.*'

The house was surrounded by gardens and a high wall, but the street gates were wide open. Shutters and security grilles protected the windows. Gregorin and Vladimir made a full circuit of the perimeter wall and reported the area quiet. Dima called Amara again.

'*Are you alone?*'

'*Yes, please hurry!*'

'*Come to the door and let us in.*'

'How do you know you can trust her?' hissed Vladimir, as they approached the door.

'I don't.'

At what precise moment Dima realised his mistake, he couldn't remember. He believed he could trust Darwish, but at a time of chaos allegiances can change by the hour. He could have set them up. Amara could have lost her nerve, aroused her husband's suspicion or even tipped him off. If he was honest, he knew it was high risk to the point of madness, but so was trying to find a bomb in a quake-damaged city under siege.

They stopped about five metres from the door. It opened a crack, and then wider. Dima gestured to the others to wait until he could see Amara clearly. She was shaking and tearful, which was to be expected, but otherwise she didn't move. He looked at her, trying to work out what was wrong. She just stood there, clutching the edge of the door for support. Then after a few seconds she beckoned him forward. The light inside the entrance hall was coming from the right and it was the movement of the shadow she was standing in that made his mind up for him.

Without raising it from his hip, he squeezed off a short burst from the AK. He hoped his aim was as good as it used to be, so the shots would panic whoever was behind the door into thinking she'd been hit. The slugs would have to skim the air just above her head, close enough for the shock wave to blast her right back through the hallway.

They fanned out on either side of the door, ready for a response. Gazul Halen was a man who would shoot first and think later, if at all. Darwish was right. The PLR's Chief of Intelligence – there was an inappropriate title for you – leapt into the doorway brandishing an Uzi like an actor in a cheap TV movie. He sprayed the empty driveway just long enough for Dima to get a fix, so he could put a bullet neatly into his forearm, which travelled on and hit the weapon as well.

The Uzi jumped out of Gazul's hand. As he convulsed on the floor Dima launched himself forward, slamming one boot down on his injured hand and kicking the Uzi away with his other.

'Gazul Halen? Nice of you to have us over.'

He thrust the muzzle of his AK hard into the prone man's groin.

'We're in somewhat of a hurry so we won't bother with tea this time. The Russian government wants its nuke back.'

He glanced at where Amara had ended up. She wasn't moving. He nodded to Gregorin to go and check.

Gazul writhed around like a gored bull, rage, dismay and agony sweeping over his features like bad weather. Dima kept his foot on his hand.

'We want Kaffarov as well. You're going to take us right to them.'

Gazul seethed and hissed. Eventually he managed a response.

'Fuck you.'

Vladimir put his boot on his good hand.

'No, you're not going to be doing any fucking. You're going to watch while we each fuck your wife – alive or dead. Or you can take us to Kaffarov. Can you work out the better option?'

Vladimir leaned on the hand a bit harder. Dima had seen this many times over the years: a man, cornered, nowhere to go but surrender, no options and nothing to bargain with, his brain jammed in pride mode, unable to do the sensible thing. Men who held high positions, who were used to controlling others by fear, were the worst: cowards one and all. He glanced at Amara, who was still motionless.

Gradually the seething and the hissing stopped. Gazul's bottom lip started to quiver and the tears of rage turned into tears of self-pity and fear. His face was pathetic as he looked up at Dima and nodded.

'Okay.'

26

Both Peykans had been great team players, but they knew that one of them would have to be sacrificed.

'Really they should be allowed to draw straws,' suggested Kroll.

Dima, binding Gazul's wrecked hand, rolled his eyes.

'They're cars, for fuck's sake.'

'Where I come from, we say a car is a man's best friend.'

'That's because you ate all the dogs. Get on with it, will you?'

'Goodbye old friend.' Kroll patted the hood as Gregorin and Vladimir climbed in. They had volunteered to hunt down a Rakhsh APC.

'A nice clean one: PLR markings, no punctures, and while you're at it get the crew's uniforms. Remember to strip them off *before* you shoot.'

Vladimir batted Dima's instructions away.

'We have actually done this before – Dad.'

Fifteen minutes later a Rakhsh APC screeched into Amara's drive. Out stepped Gregorin and Vladimir in full PLR battledress.

'Taxi for Mayakovsky party.'

'That was quick.'

He patted his new steed.

'Rakhsh means stallion.'

'Well, you live and learn.'

To Dima's relief, Amara was now conscious. Dima's aim was still good enough to have left her with no more than a scorch mark and a small bald patch on her crown. He prepared her a shot of morphine: it would serve the double purpose of dulling the pain and calming her fears. Whether she had tipped her husband off or been found out, they didn't know. It shouldn't have mattered: they had got what they needed, but Dima had an obligation to her father.

He laid her on a couch by the grand staircase. She was still terrified and tearful, clutching the wound on her head.

'I have to leave you here for a while. But don't worry: it's just a surface wound. It will hurt a bit because of the number of blood vessels in the scalp, but it's not serious, okay? If and when we find what we are looking for and get out in one piece, we'll take you home to your father ...'

Her face changed from terror to self-pity, contorted into rage, in an echo of her husband. She smacked Dima hard across the face. 'You shit. Bastard. My father, he's a prick as well. He always had it in for Gazul, never paid the dowry and now he's turned my beautiful man against me with his scheming. I hope he dies. I hope the house falls on him in the earthquake and crushes him to death.'

He touched the side of his face, which was stinging with pain.

'Okay, well, I'm sorry if I've interfered with your marriage, I'm just trying to stop a nuclear war.'

'You men, always excuses. You expect me to believe that? Get out of my house, you scum! Now!'

He stuck in the hypodermic.

27

The Metropolitan Bank pre-dated most of the buildings around it.
And unlike them it appeared to be unscathed by either the quake or
the bombardment. In fact, it had been built with the express inten-
tion of withstanding a nuclear attack. Whether the architects had
designed it to contain a nuclear warhead was another matter. Gazul,
who was proving a lot more co-operative than his wife, told them
that in the event of an attack Al Bashir's emergency plan was that
only he and his closest aides would take refuge there.

From the forecourt of the building next door, the Iranian Federation of Enterprise and Commerce, a PLR T-60 tank was moving
into position. They surveyed the scene from inside the Rakhsh.

'I've always wanted to rob a bank,' mused Vladimir.

'In the middle of a war?'

'Yeah,' said Gregorin, 'it creates a diversion.'

The plan was breathtakingly unsophisticated. Dressed as the
PLR, Dima, Vladimir and Zirak would rush up to the bank with
the injured Gazul, shouting for them to open up. The sight of their
wounded Chief of Intelligence ought to be enough to get them
through the door. Once in, they would don their facemasks, lob in
a few cans of teargas and get working.

It went like a dream – almost. They hurried past the tank crew,
straight up to the door. Gazul obliged them with a plea to be let in.
As soon as his name was heard one of the huge bronze doors swung
open. Dima expected the next part would be messy: whoever was in
their path would have to be neutralised. The place had to be cleared
of personnel for the bomb to be found. But none of them, not even
Gazul, anticipated what was waiting for them behind the bronze
doors.

At least a hundred soldiers and civilians, maybe more, had taken refuge in the lobby. It was a sea of khaki, interspersed with the bright colours of women and children. How could four of them get the better of this lot? All hopes of a stealth operation melted away. Even if they drove most of them out through the doors and shut themselves in, they would still have the tank to contend with. All of this was running through Dima's mind as he surveyed the crowd. But then he fixed on a familiar face. He couldn't put a name to it. Later he would remember that it was Hosseini.

Dima pressed the point of his knife a little further into Gazul's back.

'Warn them there's a bomb in the vault – be very, very convincing.'

Gazul obliged. 'There's a bomb in the vault below! Run! Run now!'

No one moved. Some of the men turned and looked at each other. Dima shouted,

'Do as he says! Open the doors and get everyone out! It could go off any second!'

Zirak and Gregorin held the doors open, urging people forward. Gradually they started to take the hint. A trickle rapidly became a torrent and then there was a furious crush around the doors, which spilled out on to the forecourt. Dima watched, keeping a firm hold of Gazul, the point of his knife close to his kidneys. Hosseini came towards them, saluted Gazul and narrowed his eyes at Dima. Hosseini was a former student of his – one of the zealots who had joined the Revolutionary Guard's own Intelligence Unit: Iran's Gestapo.

Hosseini pulled his gun from its holster and took aim.

'They're not PLR, Sir. These men are Russians.'

28

Downtown Tehran

Brady drove, with Blackburn in the rear, Campo on the other side, and the Colonel in between, giving directions. He perched on the edge of the seat, head bent forward because of the zap strap which bound his wrists behind him.

'Jafari? You sure that's your name?'

'You shitting us, Colonel, you will surely die. Comprendez?'

Jafari, his pride all that was left, nodded slowly. Brady radioed for an ID check and it came back positive. Pumped with the excitement of snaring the HVT, Campo wouldn't shut up.

'Why does Al Bashir hole up in a bank? Does he think he's going to bribe us with his shitty little rials? I mean if I was him I'd be on the next plane to Saudi or Yemen or some other safe haven.'

'Can't see why we don't just drop a two thousand pounder on it. Smokin' Bashir would solve a whole heap of trouble, 'stead of having him winding up on trial somewhere shakin' his dink at us.'

Black turned to the Colonel.

'How big is this bank?'

He looked at them scornfully.

'Very. The biggest in Iran.'

'Great, so we have to search every room and floor ...'

Brady chipped in. 'Yeah right, Colonel, you gonna narrow it down for us?'

No answer. Brady slammed on the brakes and turned to Black. 'Use a knife if you have to. Cut his dick off and make him eat it.'

Jafari shook his head, nodding emphatically at the ground.

'In vault.'

Brady drove on, taking to the sidewalk to avoid a massive rift running across an intersection. It had half swallowed a bus.

'Sure fucked this place up, Al Bashir or no.'

'Back in '03 they had a quake killed forty thousand.'

'Check out the brain on Campo.'

'You shits did some reading instead of playing *Call of Duty* you'd be less dumb too.'

'Anyone noticed there's no enemy fire?'

'Now you mention it.'

Colonel Jafari nodded again as the bank rose up above the surrounding buildings, a marble monolith that appeared to be unmarked by either the bombardment or the earthquake.

'T-90!'

As they rounded a corner they came face to face with the tank.

'The fuck . . .'

Brady was screaming at the convoy over the radio. '*Back up, back up.*'

The Colonel buried his head in his lap.

Black saw the turret rotate towards them. He jumped out of the vehicle and rolled into a heap of putrid garbage. He felt the air shake as the Humvee took a direct hit, flinging it up into the air and down again on its roof. He rolled over the garbage and on to the sidewalk as a suspension arm with a wheel still attached slammed down inches from his face.

His hearing was shot, just a fine buzzing. He felt a hand on his shoulder, rolling him further away from the blast. Campo.

'How did you—?'

'Followed your example, chief.'

Montes was beside him, grinning. Half his sleeve gone and a patch of blood on his shoulder.

'Brady?'

They only had to look and they knew.

'Like it came straight though his windscreen.'

It was hard to imagine. Brady behaved like he was bullet-proof.

'Nothing left of the Colonel either.'

The tank jolted forward in the direction of the reversing convoy. Montes and Campo dropped behind the mound of garbage. As it loosed off another shell they ducked until it rumbled out of view.

Black, on his feet again, ran half-crouched to the opposite side of the road, where a van was parked. The others followed. From there they scanned the building. There were no lights, and there was no sign of movement outside. The tall metal doors were shut, the small windows fortified with thick steel bars. It had been built like a fortress. Blackburn turned to the others. 'Okay. Let's finish this. Let's do this bank.'

29

It must have been a close one. Dima thought he could remember the muzzle flash of Hosseini's pistol. He definitely recalled thinking that using Gazul as a human shield was probably not going to work. And he was right, inasmuch as the bullet entered Gazul's forehead and passed straight though his skull, brain and more skull and out the other side, clipping the top off Dima's left ear as it did so. Why, he wondered, as he lay under the headless body, had Hosseini not simply fired a second shot straight into his target? He could only put it down to Hosseini's horror at having blown the head off the PLR's Chief of Intelligence, his own ultimate boss.

Anyone might be forgiven for thinking that Dima too was very much dead, squashed under Gazul's lifeless corpse, his face covered with the other's brains. It was hitting the marble floor with such force that had knocked him out.

He awoke to bright light blasting his face and Vladimir peering at him, torch in one hand, a piece of bloodied cloth in the other. There was a powerful smell of antiseptic. The world seemed to be lurching and rolling around him.

'Hold still.'

'What's happening?'

'Just cleaning you up.'

Dima tried to look round. A flash from somewhere lit up Zirak close by, watching the procedure.

'Where am I? Where are we going?'

Vladimir turned Dima's head back again.

'I said hold still. The Chief of Intelligence has very sticky brains, congealed I suppose from lack of use.'

His eyes started to focus. He recognised the khaki interior of the

Rakhsh they had hijacked. Suddenly the life surged back into him as he realised where he was.

'We're in the fucking APC. We should be in the bank. What the fuck are you all doing?'

He pushed Vladimir away and sat up. A massive thudding pain spread out across the left side of his head. For a few seconds he blacked out, then he collapsed back to where he had been lying. He felt the dressing on the side of his head.

'You're going to have a very interestingly shaped left ear,' smirked Vladimir, closing up the first aid kit. 'Something that may make a good conversation starter with the ladies.'

The Rakhsh slewed to a stop. Gregorin was at the wheel, Kroll beside him. The whole vehicle rocked madly as the wash from a huge blast hit it. Then they were reversing, gears whining madly.

'How long have I been out?'

'Twenty, thirty minutes. You missed a good firefight. Some of Hosseini's henchmen came back into the bank when they heard his shot, so we had to deal with them. Then a whole lot more surged up from the floor below. All got a bit much.'

'You retreated. You're pathetic.'

Dima tried to lift himself again. Vladimir held him down.

'Hey. You're alive. We got you out of there. Break the habit of a lifetime and show some gratitude.'

Two massive explosions rocked the vehicle. Kroll leaned forward.

'Oh yeah, we forgot to mention: Uncle Sam's in town. That's the tank having a go at them.'

Dima pushed Vladimir's hand away and raised himself, more slowly this time. 'We had a clear fix on the nuke: we were right in the PLR's lair.'

Kroll craned round. 'It moved.'

'What moved?'

'The nuke.' Kroll patted the device in his lap. 'Told you it worked. Looks like we'll be heading back into the mountains.'

The APC rocked as Gregorin spun the wheel to avoid an obstacle. Flashes of blue and red came through the windscreen.

'Uh-oh. US Humvees ahead. They've just blasted a PLR technical.' He stamped on the brakes and slammed into reverse, sawing at the wheel. 'Fuck, they're moving our way.'

He never completed the manoeuvre. A second later a white flash lit up the inside of the Rakhsh and the front end reared skywards, as if a giant hand had scooped it up and then dropped it on its roof. For a few moments there was silence.

'Out, out. Now!'

'Where the fuck's the door on this?'

'US approaching on foot. Forty metres. Go go go.'

Flames from the smashed front end spread through the windscreen.

'Why the fuck do they make these things so hard to get out of?'

'So you'll stay at your post and fight like a good soldier of the revolution.'

'Well they can fuck their revolution.'

Zirak got the side door open. They spilled out on to an expanding pool of fuel from the wrecked APC. As they rolled across it a bullet from the Americans ricocheted off the pavement and it became a lake of fire.

They were saved by a yawning gap in the street, opened up by the earthquake. A whoosh of flame and heat and the APC became an inferno. They watched their transport disintegrate in front of them. A couple of Marines dismounted from the Humvee and circled the burning Rakhsh.

'We fucked that up good.'

'Yeah, right. Fried Iranian anyone?'

'Fuckin' A, man.'

They ambled off as if they owned the place, got back in the Humvee and drove away.

Dima, tired, hungry, sore, scorched and stinking of gas, found himself in a place beyond rage, beyond swearing. He glanced at his watch, now with a big crack across the face but still functioning. Twenty-four hours had passed since he had taken off with a hundred plus men, two helicopters and two cars. And here he was twenty-four hours later, in a hole in the ground, all but four of his men gone, both choppers lost, no car and no nuke to show for it. As bad days went, this took some beating.

30

The doors were too big to breach. Besides, there weren't enough of them to go in with a bang, guns blazing. Stealth was the only option.

'Every chain has its weak link,' said Blackburn.

'Every dog has its day.'

'Black didn't make Sergeant by being no dog.'

They found the weak link. Someone had added a fire escape to the rear of the building. The lower half of it had been shot away but a vent tube ran up close beside it. Blackburn went first, reached for the lowest rung and caught it just as he let go of the vent. The ladder stopped at a window that was frosted. Blackburn prised it open: a toilet. He put one foot on the top of the cistern and the other on the seat. He peered over the stalls, there were at least five. None seemed occupied. He jumped down and checked each stall: all open. He leaned out of the window and beckoned the other two.

Matkovic was next, Blackburn guiding his feet, then Montes. Campo's foot caught the handle of the cistern. They froze as it flushed, the sound bursting the silence like a shell. None of them moved. There were footsteps outside. Blackburn pointed at his gun and shook his head: no shooting. Quick to right his mistake, Campo ran to the door and stood behind it, knife in hand. An officer – judging by his uniform – stood facing them, his eyes widening. He felt for his holster, about to shoot when Campo reached round, covered his face with one hand and sank his knife into his chest. There was a muffled protest and the body slumped to the floor.

Black was through the door and into the corridor.

'Let's find this vault.'

The lift doors were jammed half open. The car had stalled, leaving a two-foot gap.

'Must be stairs nearby.'

They opened the stairwell door, heard voices coming up from the floor below.

Black pulled them into a huddle.

'We go the quick way. If we rappel down, those guys on the floor below won't know we came past them.'

There was a short silence while they digested this. They didn't look keen.

'Do I look like I'm joking?'

Black went first, slipping into the aperture between the floor of the car and the bottom step of the doorway. They were three floors up but there was no way of knowing how many basement levels there were. As he rappelled down he counted five floors in all. It was pitch dark at the bottom. The lowest doors were jammed shut. He listened hard for any sound from the other side. Nothing. He signalled the others down with his torch. All four of them worked their fingers into the gap between the two doors and eased them open wide enough to slip through.

The doors opened into an antechamber and beyond that was the vault.

Black trained his torch on the huge foot-thick polished metal door. It was wide open.

'Looks like our lucky day.'

They stepped in. It was the size of at least two containers. Safety deposit boxes lined one wall. Several were missing, some were on the floor. A few were wide open.

Black moved further in.

Campo started peering into the drawers.

'I always wanted to rob a bank, y'know, real professional, inside man, tunnel from under.'

Black raised his hand. 'Shut up, Campo.'

He trained his torch over the opposite wall.

'Hey, look: maps,' said Montes. 'This is Al Bashir's command bunker, ain't it? These guys always end up in bunkers, just like Hitler.'

Campo peered at one.

'Uh-oh, planning his world domination, more like.' He moved

closer. 'Hmm. Let me see, what's it to be? Looks like he's narrowed it down to . . . Paris.'

'Or New York. Tough call. Me, I'd go for the one where they speak English.'

'He doesn't speak English, jerkwad.'

Black stepped forward. Circled on the Paris map in a thick black marker was Place de la Bourse, the Stock Exchange. And on the other, Times Square. He raised a hand for silence then waved them back so he could conduct a more methodical search. There were signs of recent occupation: a plate, on it the remains of some nan bread, a tomato and the leaves of a vegetable he didn't recognise. The air was stale with tobacco smoke and an ashtray had fallen off a small folding table. Butts spread out across the floor.

'They left in a hurry all right.'

Campo pointed at a case in the far corner.

'Check that out.'

It was an aluminium container. 'What's that stuff on the side, them numbers? Farsi?'

'That's Russian.'

'Well no surprise there, these dudes got lots of Russian shit.'

'Yeah, but check that symbol. Nothing Russian about that.'

They all stared at the label: a yellow triangle with three cake slice shapes in black arranged round a central dot.

'Shit . . .'

'Jeez, it could be primed.'

Black moved towards it. 'If it is, there's nothing we can do.'

'We should call it in.'

'I'm gonna lift the lid.'

As the others drew back, Blackburn stepped forward and reached down. There were two catches on the lid, both unclipped. He raised it and looked in. Within a thick lining, there were three compartments. Two were empty.

One wasn't.

A single green light flashed frantically. Each of them turned away from the device, instinctively. The power had come back on. A dull yellow light glowed from a cavity in the ceiling.

'Jesus, fuck.'

'Back up lamp. Power must have come back. Maybe the lift's working.'

Montes laughed nervously. 'Anyone else thought that was the big one?'

'I'm calling this in.' Black adjusted his mike. '*Misfit actual this is Misfit 1–3 sitrep, over.*'

'*Misfit actual. Send,*' came the response.

'*Actual 1–3 Haymaker actual is inoperative. We have located vault. HVT negative, repeat negative. Have located what appears to be portable WMD, repeat WMD. Stable. One device in container, evidence of two, repeat two, gone.*'

'Hey, up there!' They all looked at the corner where Campo was pointing. A split-screen monitor showed four views. One appeared to be the lobby.

Two figures, carrying what looked like American M4s, were on their way out, one pulling a wheeled case.

'Fuck! That's our HVT! That's Bashir!'

There was nothing from the radio. Blackburn repeated his message.

'*We have visual of HVT. Al Bashir vacating building. Now!*'

Eventually there was a reply. '*... breaking up. Mobilising assets now.*'

'They can't hear me properly: we're too far down.'

The light went out and they were plunged back into darkness.

31

They'd barely been there six hours, but to the fleeing Iranians it must have looked like the US Army owned the place. Civilian families, a weary, straggling column of them, escaping the quake and the PLR, were now being waved away by the ring of soldiers guarding the encampment.

Cole and Blackburn watched, their faces set in resignation. Also under the camo net, at a distance from the main base, was Gunnery Sergeant Mike 'Gunny' Wilson, the EOD, who was probing the device with a Geiger counter. He had already run it over Black, Campo and Matkovic, plus the tank crew that had extracted them from the bank, and pronounced them safe. Now he was meticulously examining Black's find, in a kind of professional slow motion, as if he had all the time in the world. None of them wanted to think about the fact that Al Bashir was on the run, almost certainly with two of these things. They sat, patience and nerves stretched, waiting for Gunny to make his pronouncement.

Taking their time was all part of the EOD mystique: these were the men who had cheated death time after time, calmly disabling devices with added booby traps designed to catch them out. They were among the most respected men in the field, and among the most frequent casualties. 'Least when it's our time to go, we go. When you're that close and it blows, we're gone baby gone,' Blackburn had once heard one say. But Blackburn wasn't paying full attention to Gunny's investigation. He couldn't stop thinking about what he had seen on the monitor, the man with Al Bashir. Clean shaven, high cheekbones. Just like Harker's executioner.

He wanted to tell Cole but he knew he would be suspicious and start questioning him: 'Still got that on your mind, huh? Eating into

you is it? You watching from a safe distance as that sword …?'
Blackburn got up and paced about, replaying over and over what he
had seen on the vault security monitor.

The images in his mind were as clear as if he had the tapes. Four
views. Two were blank. One showed the main customer floor with
the bronze doors of the entrance. The other showed a second smaller
exit, which was the one that Al Bashir and one other man had
passed through. The second one was carrying two cases. Campo
had spotted it first.

'Holy fuck – you see what I'm seeing?'

They all stopped and stared at the screen. Blackburn glanced back
at the one remaining nuclear device.

'Bashir's sidekick's got the other two …'

Campo shrugged.

'Let's not jump to conclusions.'

Matkovic snorted.

'No: let's not get too worried that America's Most Wanted just
left the building with two WMDs.'

Black raised a gloved hand.

'Just shut up and watch, okay. There's fuck all else we can do.'

His voice trailed off as he stared at the monitor. The two men
exited the building. The camera angle showed a small area of the
street. Al Bashir hesitated. The second man looked round, tall, clean
shaven, high cheekbones, local dress. To Blackburn it looked as if
he was staring straight at him, right through the security camera,
taunting him.

Campo shrugged. 'They waiting for a cab or what?'

Matkovic turned to Black. 'Who's the other guy?'

Campo turned away from the screen. 'Don't know, don't care.
Fuck all we can do about it. We need to secure that nuke.'

After what seemed a month, Gunny set down the Geiger counter
and pulled off his gloves. He chuckled and shook his head.

'It's a nuke Jim, but not as we know it. Fucked if I've ever seen
anything like it.'

Cole, arms folded, sceptical, shrugged.

'Thought they only belonged to James Bond bad guys.'

'Well it's Ruskie, no question about that.' He pointed to the Cyrillic script and glanced in Black's direction. 'Any Russian speakers on your crew?'

Black shook his head.

Gunny peeled off his bomb gear.

'Back in the Nineties, *Sixty Minutes* ran a segment with former Russian National Security Advisor General Aleksander Lebed, claiming that they'd lost track of over a hundred suitcase nukes with a yield of one kiloton – that's equivalent to a thousand tons of TNT. Claimed they'd been distributed to members of the GRU. You know what that is?'

'The equivalent of our Foreign Military Intelligence Directorate.'

'Bonus point, Lieutenant. In fact it was widely concluded that Lebed was shitting us to gain cred in Washington, which he was hoping to make his new home.' Gunny nodded at the device, relishing the opportunity to share his knowledge with an appreciative audience.

'Okay, now figure this: weapons grade plutonium has a market value of over four thousand dollars a gram. So for the Russians to have parted with one of these, well, someone's had to pay them a hell of a lot of roubles – unless they're supplying the PLR for other reasons. I mean, I don't want to worry you guys but it's starting to look an awful lot like Russia vs. US of A all over again. Like the Cold War just came back and got way hot.'

Gunny put the device on a pallet and four of his team took it away.

'Hey, no going over the bumps, okay?'

Cole remained still, staring at the ground. Eventually he looked up at Black.

'You ready for another YouTube moment?'

32

They waited in the crack in the road until the Humvee had gone away, and then waited a bit longer to be really sure the coast was clear.

Dima led, the others followed several metres apart. There were no cars to hijack or steal. Everything on wheels, right down to the last supermarket trolley, had been pressed into service for the mass evacuation of the city. There was a brief moment of excitement when they spotted a Peykan, but it soon faded when they discovered it was missing its engine. Several stray dogs had come up to them, hoping for food.

'Believe me, I know just how you feel,' said Vladimir, scratching the head of the nearest canine. 'Watch out for Kroll as you pass.'

'I once ate a fox,' said Zirak.

'I've had cat,' said Gregorin. 'I still spit up fur balls.'

'In the '50s, when my father was a prisoner in the Gulag,' began Vladimir, 'he and some of the others made a pact that if any of them froze to death, the rest would eat him.'

'I hope there's a funny ending to this story,' said Kroll.

'There isn't,' said Vladimir.

They walked on in silence.

Too tired and hungry to stay focused, Dima let his mind wander further than he had yet allowed himself in these past twenty-four hours. Inevitably the photographs swam back into focus in his head, where he had stored every detail. The young man's eyes, the shape of his smile, the fine crease in his chin and the slight arch to his eyebrows, all confirmed for him beyond doubt who his mother was.

Camille had been the right person at the wrong time, though looking back over his life now, when would have been the right time? Dima had been sent to Paris to befriend the impossibly smart Harvard students, the future powerbrokers of America. She was one of the few French girls who hung around with them.

There was a dinner, one of the secretly Soviet-funded 'Detente' occasions that brought together American students interested in discovering more about the Evil Empire and bright young things from the USSR – those who had achieved the rare privilege of a scholarship to study in France. Of course, like Dima, all the young Russians were recent recruits of the GRU or the KGB or one of the other ministries that could justify the expense of sending its best and brightest to the West. And Farrington James was a standard-issue preppie, with one of those patrician Boston names that looked like it had been written down the wrong way round. Who calls a kid Farrington, for fuck's sake?

Dima had briefly auditioned him with the standard leading questions about China and Africa, until it became clear that James made Ronald Reagan look like a liberal. He was about to strike him off his target list when James introduced his fiancée, Camille. First Dima noticed her hands, fine porcelain-delicate, then her eyes, green-grey, with finely-drawn eyebrows and a smile which, when she beamed it at Dima, made him think that she had created it just for him.

Camille Betancourt was the only daughter of the Marquis de Betancourt, part of the flotsam that bobbed on the surface of French society for no good reason other than seven or nine generations earlier one of them had been given a plot of stolen land – and a title that had probably been snatched as well. What little Betancourt money was left over from the father's monstrous gambling addiction went on keeping his daughter out of trouble and all polished up, in the hope she would snare a rich American like James.

And it had all been going so well. The Marquis toasted Farrington with the last of the family's wine cellar. Dazzled by the father's aristocratic charm as much as by the daughter's beauty, Farrington proposed, but Camille, harbouring doubts about her boyfriend's true sexual preferences as well as his politics, was taking her time to give him an answer. And then Dima arrived in her life.

Holy fuck, he thought, I'm really letting myself go tonight. Trudging through the ruins of Tehran, he realised that he hadn't allowed his memories such free rein since giving up drinking ten years before. But for the first time in ten – no, twenty-five – years, he had a good reason to remember.

James had swanned into the banquet mainly for an opportunity to lecture the Russians on how Marxism was really Satanism for the twentieth century. Lost in the hyperbole of his own self-righteous pomposity, he was blind to what was happening as Dima's laser gaze locked on to the exquisite young French woman at his side, sipping Soviet-bought vintage Dom Pérignon.

Six weeks: that's all they had. Neither Farrington nor the Marquis were going to stand for Camille's affair with a young Soviet, but Camille had already told her father that she didn't care a damn about Farrington or France. As far as she was concerned, she now belonged to Dima, and was ready and willing to elope to Moscow with him. And if he needed any convincing, she was carrying his child.

He never saw her again. All trace of her vanished overnight as if she had never existed. The tiny apartment she had rented was let to another student. Her tutors at the Sorbonne were told that she had dropped out of her course and moved abroad. Frantic, he appealed to his masters in Moscow for leave to go in search of her. But his superiors in Paris had already alerted the Kremlin, and the next thing he knew he was being dispatched on an urgent mission to French West Africa.

A year later a friend in Paris sent him a cutting from *France Soir*: the only daughter of the Marquis de Betancourt had been found drowned in the lake of the family's château in the Loire, whether it was by accident his friend couldn't say. And what had become of the child? 'Channel it,' Paliov had told him. 'Direct that rage into your work. Don't waste it: turn it to your advantage.'

Now, here he was, on the wisdom of that advice. He had compressed all of his feelings into a tight ball of fissile energy that sat deep inside him. Whether it had served him well he didn't know. Perhaps it was what had made him awkward, aloof. 'You're so difficult, Dima: you're your own worst enemy. So much potential, so little to show for it.' How many times had he heard that? He looked over his shoulder at the men following behind. Vladimir, Kroll, had they fared any better? Each of us in our own way is a casualty, he reflected. The GRU's walking wounded.

Kroll caught up with him and clapped him on the shoulder.

'Hey.' He peered into Dima's eyes. 'Uh-oh, I know that look.'

'Kroll, your life is shit. What makes you so fucking cheerful all the time?'

Kroll shrugged. They paused to let the others catch up. Vladimir caught the change of mood and grinned his vampire grin.

'It beats another night in Butyrka.'

Zirak nodded at the street ahead. 'I hope Amara's got the dinner on.'

33

Black sat at the folding table, the field laptop open in front of him and Campo and Montes behind, the light from the screen giving their faces a ghostly glow. The video, shot at night, was almost indecipherable, but there was enough to be in no doubt as to what was happening. Cole stood over them as they watched.

Campo hissed through clenched teeth.

'We got any idea who this cocksucker is?'

The man, tall, with the end of his turban wrapped round his face, stood over the hooded figure, whispering. Then with a magician's flourish he whipped off the hood to reveal the face of the terrified tanker, Miller, before he drove a blade into his neck.

Cole reached forward and slammed down the lid, looked at Black, waiting.

'Same guy?'

Black nodded. 'It's like he's taunting us. Does he think making us this mad's gonna help his revolution?'

'What do intel say? They got a fix on him?'

Cole shrugged.

'Nothing. Okay guys, listen up. We got confirmation Al Bashir's run to the northwest of the city where the PLR forces are concentrated. They'll be kept occupied by ongoing airstrikes.'

Cole broke open a map and spread it over the table.

'Al Bashir and any sub-commanders must be captured alive. Assault element, call sign Misfit 2–1, will be flown in by Osprey. Black, your team will provide overwatch from these positions.'

Cole pointed to two locations on a satellite shot of a large shopping mall.

'Extraction will be by Osprey. Okay gentlemen, get to work.'

Montes looked at Black.

'Do you get the feeling we just missed another night's sleep?'

Campo chipped in. 'No way baby, you've just had eight hours and a nice lie in. Don't you remember that nice nightcap the lady with the big tits brought you in your suite? And how she served it, with whipped cream and—.'

Black wasn't listening. He opened the laptop. Played the video again.

34

'Hey! "Is it a bird? Is it a plane?" Whooh!'

Campo, grinning, watched through a tiny window as the Osprey's rotors tilted from take-off into flight position. He nudged Black, yelling above the roar.

'Man, don't you love it? The first flying machine to combine the vertical take-off capability of a chopper with the cruise speed of a turboprop plane. Is that a beautiful idea or what?'

Black wanted Campo to stop nudging him and shut up but he didn't say so. He knew he meant well. Campo always meant well. If he hadn't damaged an eye in training he'd have been up there in the cockpit. Flying was what he'd signed up for, but his injury had finished that dream. He had accepted it as he did all setbacks, by seeking out the next positive. Blackburn wondered what positives he would have found if he had seen Harker's beheading.

'And you know what's way cool? The enemy can hear us coming but they don't know where the fuck we gonna land. 'Cos this thing can drop on any roof, any playground it wants. They gonna be shitting their girlfriends' panties in that shopping mall when we come out to play!'

Campo gave him another nudge.

'And you know who wanted to kill it off? The Lord of War himself, Dick Cheney, back when he was Secretary of Defense. But know what? He got overruled by Congress. Our elected representatives said, "Go build that bird".'

The relative merits of the Osprey were a subject of heated debate among the Marines. Being able to fly right in and deploy on top of the enemy was a big plus: why fight your way into hostile territory by land when you could just drop regular Marines right on top of their HQ like they were Navy Seals going to get Bin Laden? All good, except for that tense moment they all hated, as the craft hovered teasingly over its landing site while its rotors switched to land position.

'Not so much a sitting duck as a hovering duck,' Campo said.

What was on Blackburn's mind now wasn't the Osprey, but Cole's last words before he boarded. 'You bring us back Al Bashir, the Harker thing is forgotten. Got that?' Cole wasn't letting up.

Black looked out of the porthole as they swooped towards the LZ. Above, a black night dotted with stars, an almost full moon rising over the mountains to the north. It was a long time since he had looked at anything so beautiful. He stared, as if trying to absorb as much of the serenity as he could before the Osprey took them back down into the firestorm.

35

Niavaran, Northeast Tehran

Amara cradled the glass in her hands and stared at the last remaining mouthful of rum.

'Pig scum.'

Dima wasn't sure exactly sure who she was referring to. He decided not to seek clarification.

She had taken the news of Gazul's death with a stoic resignation that he hadn't anticipated. He might have sat beside her and ventured to put a comforting arm round her shoulder, if she hadn't been such a miserable bitch. Plus on the way back into the house he had caught sight of his reflection. Vladimir's attempt at wiping off the remains of her husband's brains had left a lot to be desired, so after the battering he'd received earlier he opted to deliver the news from a safe distance.

'Just to let you know – I let the boys use the facilities to get themselves cleaned up.'

Miraculously the showers in the house still worked, and the electricity was on a generator. Vladimir was in a bath, singing a rousing old Soviet pioneer song, splashing as he raised his fist and slammed it back into the water. *'Forward, people of the Motherland! Fight girls! Fight boys! Slay the fascist beast . . .'* Ah, the good old days.

From the kitchen he could smell a stew being prepared by Zirak, of what it was probably best not to ask. Kroll, who would have to be reminded to wash, was trying to fix the scanner, which had suffered its second near-death experience during the evacuation from the burning APC. Gregorin, freshly groomed, had helped himself to Gazul's wardrobe and was engaged in cleaning their weapons, getting smears of grease on his dead host's best shirt.

The house looked just as the home of the Intelligence Chief's mother should. No one had come looting or even bothered the current occupant, because they were too busy fleeing.

'Pig scum. I hope they are hijacked by Taliban and spit roasted, both ends.' She pointed her two forefingers at each other and made a sharp jabbing motion.

'All the other wives, first hint of trouble —.' She sliced the air with her hand. 'They take the first plane out to Dubai. They'll be round the pool at the Jumeirah Beach now, knocking back the daiquiris at 150 dirhams a time, eyeing up the waiters and thanking Allah their husbands banked offshore.' Her hand flew in a wide circle, indicating the house. 'Mother, cousins, sisters: all gone. When we married they took me into their family.' She jabbed her thumb in the air. 'Fuck them all!'

Dima flinched slightly to avoid the fuming spray from her mouth. He was longing to get under the shower himself and wash the whole lot off, not to mention the last of her husband. He had told her a vaguely plausible story about how her poor hero had been bravely negotiating on her behalf before being tragically cut down in his prime. He wasn't sure she believed him, but now that they'd pretty much run out of options there was potential in playing nice for a bit. That was another thing he'd learned over the years. Spetsnaz trained you to trust nobody, but life had taught him something even more useful: don't stop your dislike of someone from letting them come in handy. As his mother's favourite proverb had it: '*Don't spit in the well: you may have to drink from it.*'

'You think I should have followed my father's advice, don't you? Because he only wanted the best for his little Amara. But you know what would have happened if I'd listened to him? I'd be stuck in that shithole up north, watching Egyptian soap operas all day, pregnant with my eighth child and eating tray after tray of pastries till even he wouldn't look at me anymore. At least this lot left me in peace.'

Dima hoped there was some hot water left, and shampoo, preferably smelling of apples. The receptionist at the Aquarium had smelled faintly of apples.

'I could have one of my men take you back to your father's house. The quake's not hit so bad up there.'

She turned towards him, glaring. 'Why do all you men think we're so helpless, huh?'

Kroll was right about Dima being no one's idea of a knight in shining armour, especially not to this harpy. Anyone less like a damsel in distress would be hard to imagine.

Kroll came in now, clutching the scanner and smiling oddly.

'Want to hear something funny?'

'Why not? We could do with a laugh.'

'Look.' He held it out and tapped the screen. 'There isn't one nuclear device: there's three.'

36

Dima peered at the map spread out on the desk in Gazul's study.

'So, your reading puts one nuke sitting on the edge of Tehran where the Americans are, and the other two halfway up a mountain.'

Kroll had nodded off over the scanner. He awoke suddenly, his elbow landing in the ashtray.

'All I'm telling you is what the scanner's saying. I never said anything about being sure. There's so much interference, what with the dust from the quake, plus Uncle Sam jamming the radio and radar signals.'

'Go and find somewhere to lie down. You'll be a lot more use to us with a few hours' sleep under your belt.'

Kroll didn't move, probably too tired even to get up. Half an hour ago Dima had watched Vladimir go out into the hallway, glance in the direction of the stairs and then, as if the climb were too much for him, flop on to one of the pale beige leather couches. Both he and the leather gave a satisfied sigh: a minute later he was snoring like the distant rumble of another earthquake. Gregorin and Zirak were in the kitchen, helping themselves to Gazul's beers out of an abnormally large American fridge. He could hear them discussing whether the integral ice-making machine should be able to dispense a choice of ice cube size. Amara had gone to her room with a bottle of whisky and the Gulf edition of *Cosmopolitan* magazine.

Dima had tried four times to reach Paliov on the satphone. He had failed every time. Paliov had said not to try and contact him, only to wait for a call from him. He continued to stare at the map, as if it might now deliver better news. Three devices: three separate suitcase nuclear bombs. And one possibly already in American hands. Right now they'd be crawling all over it. Situation rooms from the White House to the Pentagon to Langley would be soaking up whatever intelligence they could extract from it, before discussing threat levels and proportionate responses. What was the proportionate response to a nuclear bomb? Death to imperialists and former communists alike, thought Dima: what difference did it make if you all ended up as dust?

Was Paliov really unavailable, or had he been retired? Fallen on his sword, or been pushed? In Moscow, anything was possible.

Dima glanced at the scanner, battered and scorched but still functioning, just. It looked like a typical piece of shit Russian technology. Built to survive an arctic winter but disinclined to offer a precision reading unless it felt like it. Every thirty minutes it spat out a map reference and on a tiny green screen showed the direction of the bombs' movements from the last point they were logged as stationary. If that was the bank, and Kroll said he couldn't even be sure of *that*, then one of the nukes had been moved to the northwest outskirts of the city. In other words, the American base. The other two, seemingly travelling together, were being taken somewhere due north of the capital, but that was all mountains with hardly any roads.

Eighty to a hundred men had died at the compound and he now had even less of an idea of Kaffarov's whereabouts than he had when they were back in Moscow looking at the satellite images. He tried Paliov for the sixth time. The satphone said his number was still unobtainable.

He called the main GRU field emergency number. He hadn't used it in twenty years, but like his mother's birthday it was a number he never forgot.

'*Speak slowly, state call-sign, mission status and ID code followed by hash.*'

An automated response: the GRU was moving with the times! But this was a black op, deniable. No one had given him any of the above. He pressed the hash key and waited some more.

'*You have entered incorrectly.*'

Being Russia, and being the GRU, there would, of course, be someone behind the voice, listening.

Dima cleared his throat and spoke in his best Chechen.

'*Regarding the incriminating pictures of Secretary Timofayev and the schoolgirl . . . .*'

The voice was clipped, weary, instantly recognisable.

'*Who is this?*'

'*Smolenk! How heartwarming to hear your voice. So glad some things are constant in an ever-changing world.*'

What the man had done to condemn himself to a life as the GRU's out-of-hours phone operator didn't bear thinking about.

'*Dima Mayakovsky for Senior Strategist Omorova.*'

'*Do you have accreditation?*'

'*No, no, this is a black op; just put me through to her.*'

'*Do you know what time it is here?*'

A massive explosion followed by a blast from three low-flying jets obliterated all sound. Kroll jerked awake again, spilling more ash. It was a miracle he never caught fire.

Smolenk suddenly sounded concerned.

'*Are you under fire?*'

He glanced at Vladimir on the couch surrounded by beer cans and the semi-conscious Kroll.

'*Yes, we're all being killed: get on with it.*'

'*I will post a message in her inbox. You're not authorised to speak to staff after hours.*'

Dima sighed. You could be in the middle of an actual nuclear meltdown and this lot would be demanding your lunch ticket reference numbers.

'*Then I'm calling the CIA in Langley. At least they'll want to talk to me.*'

He sighed. '*You people.*'

The line went dead, then there were several clicks.

'*Comrade Mayakovsky, this is a surprise.*' Even at three a.m. Omorova's voice had an invitingly velvet tone.

'*I'm sorry about the time.*'

A couple of seconds passed before she spoke.

'*We thought you were all dead.*'

'*I've got a – situation. I can't raise Paliov.*'

'*No one's seen him all day. We've all been reassigned.*'

They both knew what that meant. Mission aborted.

'*Kaffarov was gone before we even got to the compound. Did anyone report that?*'

Her voice suddenly became more formal.

'*I've got no information about that.*'

'*The missiles that hit the chopper over the compound. Do you where they came from?*'

'*I have no information about that either.*'

Dima felt he was about to vent his anger on her, the person least responsible for the debacle.

'*Sixty of our best men were fried.*'

Silence: she was sticking to protocol. They both knew they were being listened to.

'*Thank you, Omorova. Goodnight.*'

Dima needed space to think, to work out his next move. Gregorin and Zirak appeared in the study. They glanced at each other. Dima could only assume they'd been discussing whether to go on with the mission. That was all he needed. Wanting to destroy something, he picked up the satphone, about to hurl it to the floor when another call came through. A blocked number – on a scrambler, from an untraceable line. He gave Vladimir a shove to wake him and put it on speaker so they could all hear. It was Omorova. She spoke fast.

'*We were told everyone was lost, that the choppers collided. Paliov has been held personally responsible for bungling the mission. Timofayev has taken control. If they know you're not dead they're behaving as if you are.*'

'*What about Kaffarov? Two days ago Paliov was desperate to get him back.*'

'*No one's talking about him, or the bombs. Al Bashir's believed dead, killed by US forces. Be very careful Mayakovsky: the GRU isn't the place it was.*'

Gregorin broke the silence.

'Is that it then? They're giving up?'

'What?' Vladimir was wide awake now.

Kroll looked away. He already knew what Dima's answer would be.

Dima glared at Gregorin.

'Have I said that?'

Zirak jerked his chin up, which he always did when out of his comfort zone.

'It's not an unreasonable question, Dima. We don't seem to have got any nearer to Kaffarov or the nukes.'

Gregorin was next. 'Where's that leave us? We're government servants. Those bastards in Mosow pull the plug, they're not going to pay.'

Zirak said, 'We don't see how we can go on from here.'

Dima looked at the two of them. They were younger than him, younger than Kroll and Vladimir: Spetsnaz staff officers, with careers and futures. Dima knew what was going through their heads. The thrilling assignment they had jumped to sign up to thirty-six hours ago had turned to shit. All support for it from Moscow seemed to have vanished. The most likely outcome was that they'd get killed either by the PLR or the Americans. As if to confirm the precariousness of their situation, another tremor shook the house.

He took a deep breath.

'You're right. The most dangerous thing a good Spetsnaz can do is put their faith in a comrade. Assume the worst, and avoid disappointment. Trust no one. Above all, look after yourself. Congratulations, you've passed the test.'

Zirak, not sure where this was going, glanced at Gregorin, who was staring fixedly at the floor.

Dima pressed on. 'This is the life you chose. A Spetsnaz. I don't need to remind you what that means. You have no life beyond what you are here to do. You are here because you were selected, because of your strength both mental and physical, your loyalty and commitment. You've given up so much to be here. There is no life outside . . .'

He could see his words falling to the ground like spent bullets, his own doubt resonating inside them. How could he convince them of the rightness of the cause when he was losing his own faith? He had given his life to Spetsnaz and it had spat him out, a used shell of a man. What did he have to show for the years? One woman, loved and lost. A child he'd never seen. All for the good of the

Motherland. Kroll, Vladimir, they weren't much of an advertisement either. He looked round at Kroll. He had fallen asleep again, the scanner still blinking on his lap. Vladimir was sitting up now, finishing another beer.

'Well, I don't mind,' he said. 'I'll do anything so long as I don't have to go back inside. Oh, hey, Mrs Gazul.'

Dima looked up. Amara was standing in the doorway. She walked up to the desk, looked down at the papers and with a slightly chipped dark red fingernail, pointed at a blank space on the map.

'There.'

'What?'

'Kaffarov's mountain retreat.'

They all looked at her.

Dima said, 'You've been there?'

She nodded. 'Sure. For the skiing.'

37

Northwest Tehran

Cole had thrown down the gauntlet: come back with Bashir or don't come back at all, he seemed to be saying. Or had Blackburn imagined that? He had lost count of the hours he had gone without sleep. The last two days had been relentless. He had neutralised an IED, smoked Al Bashir out of his lair and secured the nuke. Why was Cole singling him out?

All this ran through his head as he and Campo flattened themselves against the perimeter wall that ran round the edge of the shopping mall roof. They had exited the Osprey into a hail of fire from what seemed like all corners of the LZ. In four seconds he saw four men go down, as tracer lit up the sky above the Osprey. He and Campo followed instructions and made for the west corner, jinking left and right as they ran. They crushed themselves up against the edge of the perimeter wall, soaked in sweat and gulping in oxygen. But for the last hour they were pinned down by fire from two PLR gun emplacements either side of them.

'Fuck our luck,' screamed Campo in a fit of exhausted rage. 'Fuck this war. Fuck the PLR. I see that Bashir I'm going to cut his fucking head off.'

Blackburn gripped his arm as they lay in the tiny area of cover they enjoyed, looked him hard in the face. 'Just stay cool, Campo. We'll get out of this, okay?'

Campo looked blank for a few seconds then nodded half-heartedly. They listened to the radio chatter of the men who had reached the floors below, systematically clearing every room, every space, finding no one.

Campo was still cursing. 'Fucking intel's fucked. They drop us into PLR central and there's nobody home and we're gonna get fried.'

Blackburn gripped his friend's shoulder. 'Cool it Campo. Think. They wouldn't be defending if there wasn't something to defend.'

There was a mad look in Campo's eyes. He threw down his M4. One engagement too far. Blackburn cursed Cole for sending them back in. He grasped Campo by the upper arms and shook him. 'You want to die here? No. Do you want to get home in one piece? Yes. How are you going to do that? By getting this done.'

There were tears in Campo's eyes.

'It's okay. You're only human. One day you're a hero doesn't mean the next you're not going to have a meltdown. This isn't the movies. I need you bro. You need me, if we're going to get out of this.'

Campo took several breaths, nodded, picked up his gun. 'Yeah, okay.'

The quake had torn away a whole section of the mall. When the firing subsided, they took a look over the edge into the void and saw the silhouettes of figures balanced precariously, as if undecided whether to jump. I must be losing it, thought Blackburn, until Campo put him right.

'Fuckin' mannequins. It's a goddam dress shop.'

The realisation cheered Campo. Blackburn, still not sure, allowed himself to look a split second longer than he should have and a volley of shots skimmed his helmet. But just before he ducked he caught sight of an SUV, a Land Cruiser, parked among a row of dumpsters as if for camouflage, lights off but exhaust coming from the rear – occupied. He raised his M4 and peered at it through the night sight. One occupant. Then to the left he saw a second figure moving towards it. He nudged Campo.

'Guy's alone. Our HVT should have a whole entourage with him.'

But Blackburn wasn't listening. The man was jogging in a lumbering kind of way towards the Land Cruiser, not a young man. A burst of tracer lit his face. That was all he needed. The same face that looked out from a hundred posters he'd seen since they'd entered

Iran, the same face he had seen on the bank vault security monitor. Al Bashir.

'Okay, he's mine.'

Blackburn didn't call it in. Instead he trained his sight on the occupant of the SUV, a younger guy sitting in the driver's seat. A clean shot: the driver slumped forward as the side window exploded. Al Bashir reeled back, nearly lost his balance, then wheeled round to look in the direction of the shot before he moved towards the Land Cruiser.

Campo raised his M4. Blackburn shook his head. He ran along the perimeter wall, jumped the gap on to the section of the mall that the quake had separated, then down on to the lid of a dumpster, which broke his fall. He paused for a second to see Al Bashir reach the driver's door, heave the wounded man out of the driver's seat and let him fall on to the tarmac. Then he took a step over him and slid behind the wheel.

Blackburn ran along the edge of the roof to get closer to the Land Cruiser but Al Bashir slammed the shift into drive. With tyres screaming, the vehicle bolted out from its cover by the dumpsters. Blackburn took aim, shot out a rear tyre, but the four-wheel drive vehicle didn't falter. He followed the vehicle in his sights, took another shot, missed, prepared to take another, when he saw it reach the gate where a shelled tank was still smouldering. Without slowing, Al Bashir swung the Land Cruiser into such a sharp right that it nearly toppled over. He then headed back towards the mall, disappearing from view behind a row of containers. Blackburn, as if powered by another force, vaulted on to the top of the nearest containers to get a better shot, only to find the vehicle headed straight towards him, too close to fire at. As Al Bashir slowed to take another right Blackburn leapt, landing sprawled across the windscreen. He grabbed a wiper. It immediately came off in his hand. He lunged at the door mirror as Al Bashir threw the Land Cruiser into a series of snaking swerves. Blackburn scrabbled with his legs, trying desperately to keep from sliding off the hood and under the front wheels. The windshield disintegrated as Bashir took a shot at his unexpected passenger. The bullet zinged past

Blackburn's left ear, the blast deafening him. Enraged, he slammed a fist through the remaining screen and grabbed Bashir's gun arm. The gun discharged again.

Whatever it was Bashir ran into Blackburn never saw. The impact catapulted him on to the tarmac. As Bashir, dazed, struggled to engage reverse, Blackburn got back on his feet, wrenched open the door and grabbed the PLR leader with both hands. They fell in a heap beside the Land Cruiser, their faces inches apart.

The first he knew that Bashir had taken a bullet was the bubbling, bloody phlegm that oozed from his mouth and nostrils.

Campo was rushing towards them. 'Good fucking job, man.'

Blackburn screamed back at him. 'He's hit, he's hit. Adrenalin.'

Campo threw him a sachet which he tore open before banging the needle through Bashir's tunic straight into his chest. He overheard Campo on the radio. '*HVT in custody, wounded, preparing to move to extraction point.*'

Fuck preparing to move, thought Blackburn. He's dying. Al Bashir's eyes swivelled up under his drooping lids. Blackburn pumped his chest, wiped the blood off his chin and performed mouth to mouth. Al Bashir jerked back into consciousness, panting wheezy bubbles of blood, but he managed a smile.

'Should you be going to all this trouble? Or are you planning to bring me to justice?'

He coughed up the blood pooling in his mouth. Blackburn looked for the entry wound, found it in his neck. Blood was pulsing out of it. Blackburn jammed his thumb in it, yelling to Campo.

'Tourniquet!'

'Forget about me, soldier. It's you who are done for. All of you.'

His eyes swivelled again. Blackburn pumped his chest, banging life back into him.

'The suitcase devices – the nukes. Where?'

He shook his head slowly. 'It's not me you should be concerned about. I am history. The baton has passed . . .'

Campo was on his knees beside Blackburn, stripping the plastic off a tourniquet. 'He's bleeding out, stop him talking.'

'Try all you want soldier, whatever happens to me you are done for, my friend.'

Blackburn put his face close. 'The other one who you were with, taking the nukes.'

He nodded. 'Very good, yes. He will destroy you.'

Campo tried to apply the dressing. 'He's fucking lost it. He's talking shit.'

Blackburn hushed him. 'A name. Give me his name.'

'His name is death, my friend.' He coughed up more blood. 'Sol-man.'

'Solman?'

Bashir's voice was now no more than a gurgling whisper. He used a breath for each syllable. 'Sol ... o ... mon.'

After that there were no more breaths.

38

Vladimir leapt up and brushed some quake dust off the couch. Kroll offered her a cigarette. She draped herself across the beige leather: although she looked drained Dima noticed that she had refreshed her make-up. He wondered what she was hoping to get out of all this, presumably not a fling with any of this lot. Women like her made sure they went up in the world, not down.

'The snow was very good. He even had a private ski-lift. It's a protected area, for wildlife.' She snorted. 'He got special dispensation, a favour from the government. I think it once belonged to the Shah.'

'And you've met him.'

'Several times. Gazul always told me to be very nice, very attentive. "Whatever he wants to talk about, listen – like this".' She did a faintly sinister wide-eyed stare. '"Without him we are nothing." That was his belief. I don't know why, that sort of thing they never discussed in front of me. I thought it might be drugs. He always had plenty. One of his wives died of an overdose, his girlfriend told me.'

Dima was looking at Amara with a stare that was almost as intense as hers had been.

'The place: describe it please.'

'It's well hidden, up a track that only a 4x4 can go, but also there is a helipad.'

'Where?'

'In the grounds. It looks like a Swiss chalet, you know, like Alpine, but it's made of concrete and is cut' – she made a chopping motion – 'into the mountain. Kaffarov calls it his Kelsten something.'

She shrugged. Dima rose excitedly to his feet.

'His *Kehlsteinhaus* ... the Eagle's Nest!'

Everyone looked nonplussed.

'So?' said Vladimir.

'Hitler's secret retreat at the top of the Kehlstein mountain,' said Kroll. 'Built by Martin Bormann for his fiftieth birthday, cost: thirty million Reichsmarks. Only Hitler hardly ever stayed there.'

He and Dima looked at each other.

'Because he was afraid of heights!'

Amara shrugged again. Some people had no sense of history.

'Sorry,' said Dima. 'Go on.'

She shrugged.

'How many guards will he have with him?'

'I don't know – some North Koreans, I think.'

'The infamous Yin and Yang.'

'They never speak. And some others who walked round waving their Uzis. Always guns, guns, guns, wherever you went.' She shivered. 'She said he always sleeps with one under his pillow.'

'And?'

'That's it.'

'We're going to need a bit more than that,' said Kroll.

'Please think, Amara: how many floors? Where are the vehicles kept? Are there guards on the perimeter wall? How high is it?'

'How would I know? I'm not a bloody tour guide. I just stayed there a few times.'

'What's she called, your friend?'

'Kristen.'

'Oh, yes, I remember now. She's Austrian.' Dima laughed. 'An Alpine mistress to go with the chalet: he's got the matching set!'

'She doesn't like to be called that.'

'Whatever. Has she ever sent you anything? Directions? A map?'

'Of course not. I always went with Gazul and he knows where it is. Knew.'

Dima wondered what she could make of her life now he was gone, but there was no time to think about that now.

'Kristen is very sweet, always happy, never trouble. Gazul was always saying to me, "Why can't you be like Kristen? Kristen is always smiling".'

Dima frowned. Did she miss the guy or not?

'Kristen is always smiling because she is always stoned all the time. Without her, those trips would have been bo-*ring*. We used to have a good laugh together. One time we – hang on, I'll show you.'

She got up and opened the bottom right-hand drawer of the desk. 'Here it is.'

She reached in and lifted out a white silk-covered photo album.

Vladimir, Zirak and Gregorin gathered round.

'This may not be the best time for wedding snaps,' said Zirak.

But it was something better than that: far better.

'Oh my God . . .' said Dima.

She opened it: the first page showed several shots of herself and an attractive blonde, leaning out of the window of a turret, waving. Then page after page of holiday photos, taken by her and Kristen, and by the look of it some of the guards, showing the entire layout of the Eagle's Nest.

The miserable widow had come good after all. Dima put an arm round her and kissed her.

'All right,' she said. 'But not the rest of you tramps.'

'Look,' said Zirak. 'She's even got Yin and Yang.'

The two Koreans gazed self-consciously at the camera, their Uzis clearly in view.

'Bloody hell,' said Kroll. 'It really does look like the original. Hang on a sec . . .'

He put the scanner carefully to one side and rebooted the laptop:

Welcome to the Kehlsteinhaus . . . it said. *Historical landmark, Museum and Restaurant.*

The two buildings were identical. Kroll looked round at them all, smiled and clicked on *Map.*

39

A door led from the kitchen to the garage. Kroll ran his hand over the hood of the black Chevy SUV with tinted glass.

'Everyone loves an American 4x4,' said Kroll. 'If they have no taste. Maybe we could pass ourselves off as US Special Forces.'

'It's not exactly inconspicuous.'

'Right now anything with wheels that isn't an APC is conspicuous.'

'I like it,' said Vladimir. 'It's bigger than my old cell.'

Kroll opened a door.

'It seats five easy.'

'Six. Amara's fleeing for her life with her loyal security detail: that's us.'

'Kaffarov's going to buy that?'

'He doesn't have to. It's just to help us get past the guards. She'll call Kristen from the gate.'

'How do we know she's even there?'

Dima smiled.

'Amara called her on Gazul's satphone: she said to come right over.'

He looked at Gregorin and Zirak.

'Anybody want to bail out?'

No one did. There was just one thought chipping away at the back of Dima's mind: what *did* Amara want out of all this? And when the time came for her to ask for it, would he want to comply?

40

Camp Firefly, Outskirts of Tehran

A dirty orange sun was seeping through the smoke and dust over the east side of Tehran. Inside the tent, Blackburn faced his interrogators across a folding table. It was just gone 0700. He had been allowed three hours' sleep before being roused for questioning.

Lieutenant Cody Andrews from the US Military Police Corps did the smiling. Captain Craig Dershowitz, Marine Intelligence, did the writing.

'Sorry about getting you up so early.' Andrews' smile widened. 'We'd just like to get this done while it's all fresh in your mind.'

Or too tired to figure whether I'm digging myself a great big hole, thought Black. Outside, Cole was waiting, doing his best to listen in on the proceedings.

Black recalled the events in the bank, the contents of the vault, the maps of New York and Paris, the circled locations and the two men on the security monitor.

'Bashir and one other, right?'

'Like I said, Sir.'

Dershowitz maintained an expression of deep disdain.

'And you believe that the second man was the guy in the videos.'

'Solomon, yes, Sir.'

Dershowitz renounced his vow of silence.

'Solomon who?'

'Just Solomon. Bashir spelled it out as he was dying.'

Dershowitz waved a pen in the air.

'A first name, a last name, a codename ...?'

'He didn't say. He died.'

Dershowitz suddenly snorted. 'Sure he wasn't saying *Salaam*?'

175

Andrews put his head on one side as if he was trying to make up his mind which dessert to order.

'Kinda strange name for a PLR, or an Iranian for that matter.'

'Maybe if he'd lived another minute I'd have asked him that.'

'Moving on to your motivation, Sergeant. You were pretty pissed about what happened to Harker.'

'Is that surprising?'

'And we understand you've been given some rough treatment by his buddies?'

Black shrugged. 'It didn't amount to anything, Sir.'

Dershowitz was evidently reading more into this than was good for him.

'The bullet that killed him was from his own gun. What reason do you think he had for shooting himself?'

Black had the sensation of a man who was about to add two and two and get seven.

'He had just fired it at me. I grabbed his arm through the windshield.'

'When you were on the hood, holding on to the wiper.'

Andrews grinned, trying to lift the mood.

'Superhero stuff, huh?'

The mood didn't lift.

Dershowitz leaned forward.

'Let's see. You're with Harker, and he gets executed. You're in the bank, Bashir leaves. You're on the guy's hood under orders to take him alive and he shoots himself. I'm seeing a kind of pattern here, Black.'

'What kind of pattern's that?'

'Like you're not having a great war, Sergeant Blackburn. You want to go home or something?'

Black looked at them. He could feel his face burning, his fingernails grinding his palms. He was damned if he was going to let on how they were getting to him. *Talk to yourself*, his mother had said. *When you feel bad or wronged, you're your own best buddy.* I'm trying Mom, he told himself. I just don't think it's working.

176

'I grabbed his forearm above the wrist. At that moment the vehicle struck something which drove him forward on to the gun. It discharged. Ask Campo. Sir.'

'You think Campo will back you up?'

'He'll tell you the truth.'

'You've seen to that, huh?'

Black had had enough. He slammed his fist down on the table. Dershowitz's laptop and coffee jumped an inch into the air.

'Look, am I under arrest or what, because if not, Sir, I would like to get back to doing the job I'm here to do, Sir. I brought you the nuke, I've ID'd the executioner. I've brought you the results of my interrogation of Bashir as he was expiring. I got you a name!'

Andrews' smile looked disarmingly real.

'Good to see the fight hasn't gone out of you, soldier,' he said.

Cole was still waiting outside. He had a satphone to his ear, but Blackburn guessed he had been listening to every word.

'How did it go?'

'How do you think?'

Cole took a lungful of hot dusty air and blew it out through pursed lips.

'I've been thinking.'

Great, thought Black: what now? In the last few days he had felt his respect for Cole, a soldier he had once deeply admired, crumble away.

'I think we should press the reset button, huh?'

He ventured a smile. Cole didn't do smiles, so this one looked as though he was at the dentist. He backed it up by gripping Black's shoulder and following alongside as Blackburn walked back to his crew. After a few paces, Blackburn came to a halt. He looked around him at the buzz of the camp. One Osprey was preparing to land as another was taking off. Two AA guns were trained on the sky. Men, machines and weapons were moving in all directions: the US Marine Corps doing what it knew best. The Marine Corps that had been his guiding force all his life. He took a breath, straightened himself and gave his Lieutenant a brisk salute.

'Whatever you say, Sir.'

What kind of an answer was that? he asked himself, as he walked on alone.

41

'Weird shit, huh? As if we haven't got enough on our minds, just fighting the freakin' war.'

That was all Campo would say about it.

Black had tried to hang around outside the 'interrogation tent', as he now thought of it, to be there when Campo emerged. But Cole had called him to the briefing. As they crowded round the map table he caught sight of Campo arriving and moved over to his side. He looked shaken. His body language said *Don't talk to me*.

'Listen up, guys. Who likes to ski?'

Cole's mood had changed, as if someone had given him a shot of something. In fact, he sounded completely different. Did he know something? Was it because of something Campo had told them? Blackburn told himself to calm down: all he'd had to do was tell the truth. But Andrews and Dershowitz had treated him as if he had something to hide. They'd made him feel like a criminal.

If Cole was expecting laughter he didn't get it. But he carried on looking pleased with himself.

'Thanks to our liberating the PLR's nuclear device, intel have run a side-by-side comparison test with the signals it's been giving off against a pair of pulses that have been picked up coming from here.'

He tapped a pencilled mark high on the southern face of the Alborz mountain range to the north of the city.

'There's nothing marked on our maps, but Bigbird is showing us this.'

He laid out a satellite shot of a large building surrounded by trees, tucked into a mountain slope.

'Fuck's that?'

Cole unrolled a copy of an old set of plans. It looked like a

Swiss chalet, with overhanging gables and shutters on the windows. Quaint.

'It looks like *The Sound of Music*,' said Matkovic.

'Yeah, the hills are alive – with somethin'!'

'A loud tickin'!'

'What we're looking at here, gentlemen, is the favourite holiday home of the late Mohammad Rezâ Shâh Pahlavi, one time Shah of Iran. Since it was a gift from his admirers back home, some far-sighted archivist in Langley had the presence of mind to file away a copy of the plans.'

Black's attention was wandering. Another day, another crazy mission. He looked over at Campo, who didn't look as if he was taking in a word of what Cole was saying either. What had they asked him in there? What had they said? Whatever it was it had spooked Campo, who briefly met his gaze – distant, wary. Holy fuck, Blackburn thought, is this me or them?

'You got all that, Sergeant Black?'

His attention snapped back to the briefing.

'Yessir.'

Cole looked at him for a beat.

'Okay, gentlemen, get to it. Black, over here.'

Campo filed out with the rest of the platoon. Blackburn went over to Cole.

'Want to know why I'm looking pleased? Because the Colonel's looking pleased. He's happy, I'm happy. He's happy because the Pentagon's happy that we found that nuke. We get the other two …'

His arms went up as if to catch a giant volley ball.

'So let's draw a line under everything and go to work. Roger?'

Black looked at him. What kind of mind fuck was this? *When shit happens you make me the scapegoat, and when I deliver, you bask in the glory.*

He jogged up to Campo, who was sucking on a cigarette and talking to Montez and Matkovic. He stopped and looked uncomfortable.

'Cole says we did good, finding the nuke: the Pentagon wants to make us all generals.'

Campo left it a second before he responded. 'Cool.'

'How was it with those two fuckbrains?'

Campo flicked his cigarette away.

'I didn't see the shot, okay? You were on the vehicle. You had your hand in the cab. I'm not lying to them.'

Black felt a sudden surge of rage. He grabbed Campo's lapels.

'Hey, I didn't say shit about lying. You saw what you saw. Who said anything about lying?'

'"Why does Blackburn want you to lie for him? Is it because of Harker?" That's what they asked. What do I say to that?'

'Whadya mean, what do you say? You say No! You say *No*! I did not ask you to lie! What the fuck's wrong with you, man?!'

He was possessed by an overwhelming urge to hurt Campo, to smash him against the side of the building and go on smashing.

Montes separated them.

'Guys, let's be cool. We got work to do.'

He was frozen in position, as if still holding Campo's lapels. Blackburn let his hands drop. Campo stepped back, looking at him as if he was crazy. Was this how it started? Losing it, for real? He couldn't remember a time in his life when he felt so alone.

42

Dima drove, even though he was the one who had had the least sleep. In fact, no sleep. Zirak was beside him in the front, and Gregorin in the cargo space, ready to fire on anyone thinking of giving chase.

Amara wanted to sit in the front as befitted her status as sole female and owner of the car, but he had insisted she go in the back, in the middle between Vladimir and Kroll, two human shields to protect her. If she thought they were going to try anything, she was wrong: they were far more interested in her picnic bag.

'Some for you, and some for you: don't be greedy,' she said, sharing out the cheese.

'You've given him more,' said Kroll.

'That's because he's bigger than you. Now be a good boy and eat up.'

Vladimir chomped triumphantly.

'I used to get this at home,' muttered Kroll.

There was a raw beauty to the dawn. The dust curtain gave the sun's rays on the mountains ahead an extra golden glow. At this time the road network would normally be choked with vehicles trying to beat Tehran's legendary traffic jams. They said that it took so long to get to meetings, people did their business deals across the lanes. Today it was deserted, the usual clutter of cars and buses gone, leaving behind a sad and strange serenity. A German shepherd, its coat dusty, saw them coming and ran towards them, tail wagging, hoping. Vladimir gave Kroll a meaningful look.

'You fucking barbarian,' said Kroll. 'Amara, you should give his food to the civilised among us.'

'Can you peasants please remember there's a lady present?'

182

He caught sight of Amara in the rear view mirror. She was smiling.

When he had alerted her to the dangers of the plan, her reaction had surprised her.

'It's only fair to warn you there may be some shooting.'

'What, with real guns? My husband shot a guest at our own wedding reception. You think I'm going to burst into tears and run away? Why do you think women are so weak all the time? I thought Russian women were meant to be tough.'

'I don't know. I promised personally to deliver you back to your father, so I guess I don't want to let him down.'

She had shrugged. 'Let's do this one step at a time.'

They passed Sepehr Airport. The set-up, which was basic at the best of times, now lay in pieces. The Americans had done their worst. An Airbus sat on the runway, broken in two like a rotten log. Three smaller jets were completely burned out. The control tower had taken a direct hit. They took the Tello Road past the Imam Khomeini Sports Complex, where Dima had once put on a boxing contest for his trainee Revolutionary Guards. How many of those men were now PLR?

He looked again at Amara, her husband dead, her whole life in Tehran cut from under her. What future did she have? What future did anyone in Iran have right now? Those bombs, just their presence in the country could be devastating, never mind if they were used. What had Bashir intended with them? Was he about to find out?

After Nasirabad, the road, which had been getting steadily rougher, turned into a track. They were climbing up a long, tree-lined valley: either side of them the mountain slopes reared up – barren, lifeless, forbidding, an awesome beauty all of their own. In winter they were completely different, a snowy wonderland, teeming with skiiers. He had skied near here many times. His free pass and social working hours made him an attractive proposition. There were many women willing to enjoy his company, influential, well-connected women who in turn provided him with invaluable insights into the ruling groups and the vicissitudes of local politics. All of his relationships, except one, had had a mercenary angle. So much so that it had become a reflex. If I spend time with this or that woman what will she bring me? What's the benefit? No wonder he had ended up alone.

As they bumped along the track up into the mountains these thoughts took him right away from the job in hand. Amara's tap on his shoulder brought him back. From the seat behind she pointed at the gates up a steep ramp to the left. Dima slowed down about ten metres away and then pulled to a halt. They checked out the gun nests on either side of the gates. Two men in each: one with binoculars, the other with a machine-gun. They were NSVs – a universal anti-infantry, anti-aircraft, anti-everything weapon, discontinued after the collapse of the USSR, made under licence in Iran. Except those were probably the original Russian models, courtesy of Kaffarov.

'They should recognise the car,' said Amara. 'I mustn't look like a prisoner.'

'Then you do the talking.'

Her outfit looked pretty convincing. She had taken a silk suit and wrenched off one of the sleeves and all of the buttons of her blouse, consistent with someone having grabbed her. Now the tied tails of the front held it closed. The trainers on her feet looked incongruous – but what would you wear for a post-quake, possibly pre-nuclear getaway?

They politely let her out, Dima nudging Vladimir to stand up straight.

'Wait near the car. Let them come to you. The further in we can get before trouble starts, the better.' She did exactly as she was told, trembling and looking for all the world like a woman whose house had just survived a brutal looting, whose virtue had even been compromised. The tears rolled down her cheeks as if she'd told them to. What a natural, thought Dima: she could have a bright future in the GRU.

A guard came forward, his Kalashnikov on his hip.

Amara practically threw herself on him.

'Tell Kristen it's Amara.'

He nodded at the Chevy.

'My own security detail.' She pressed a hand against her chest. 'I said no, but Gazul insisted. They saved my life.'

'Where is your husband now, ma'am?'

She touched him on the arm and shook her head, letting her hair fall over her eyes: she *was* good.

He walked back to his post, picked up a phone. A few seconds later the gates whirred open. Dima shifted into Drive and they rolled through. They were in.

43

Black and Montes watched through a starboard window as a pair of F-16s screamed past the Osprey.

'They better leave something for us!' shouted Chaffin over the roar of the rotors.

Black continued to watch until they turned into silver specks at the end of their ascending vapour trails.

'They're taking out the perimeter AAs and any other hardware they can lock on to. Plus any stray air cover they might have up there.'

'We any closer to knowing who or what's gonna be waiting for us?' said Campo, as if he now knew how to zero in on Black's weak spot.

Black didn't know. His crew always looked to him for the answers. If he had one, he'd give it to them. If he hadn't he'd give them some possibles. Always *something*. They thought of him as the smartest: the guy who was going to get home, get to college and go up in the world, be a teacher like his Mom, maybe. But Blackburn didn't know where he was going. His judgement had been shaken. Nothing in the world looked how it used to. Campo, his former friend, sat staring out at the sky. He'd almost killed him earlier. He had to hold it together. Who or what was waiting for them? Perhaps only God. Perhaps nothing. He thought of his father, in the Vietcong's cage in the water, from brave soldier to terrified teenager: what had he expected to face in the end?

The images from the CCTV screen in the bank vault flashed back to him. Bashir had been easy to ID. The more he thought about the second man, the more a voice in his head clamoured for attention. A guy cuts a Marine's head off with a sword on the Iraqi border; thirty-six hours later he's moving nukes around with Al Bashir in downtown Tehran. Andrews and Dershowitz hadn't looked convinced. Now Blackburn was having his own doubts. Felt himself headed into a whole tunnel of self-doubt: not a good way to be going into a mission.

The mountains reared up like a great barren wall, the only patches of green being the vegetation down below in the valleys. Blackburn tried to imagine the hard, sunbaked rock covered with snow, shut his eyes for a moment and took himself back to a day out with his family, swooping down Blacktail Mountain in Montana, breaking the rules and going straight down. The trick was knowing when to break them.

'LZ three miles. Prepare rope!'

44

The distance from the gate to the chalet was two hundred metres. Dima drove at walking pace to maximise the time they had to take in the buildings and scan the surroundings.

Kroll piped up from the back.

'Hey, guess what – both nuke signals just stopped.'

'Is the scanner fucked again?'

'Nope. Still getting a signal from the third device.'

'Any ideas?'

'Could be underground. In some kind of vault.'

As they got closer to the house they saw a Mercedes G-Wagen: black with black glass. Kaffarov's? There were two other vehicles, a brand new Range Rover Evoque and a battered 1990s Peugeot.

Amara pointed.

'The Range Rover – that's Kristen's.'

'So she's free to come and go?'

'Only with minders.'

'For the world's most notorious arms dealer, he's not exactly overburdened with security,' said Kroll. 'Either he's smart enough to know that it just provokes the wrong sort of attention, or he's mad enough to think he's untouchable. Maybe both.'

'Facts would be a lot more useful than speculation,' said Dima.

'Only trying to help.'

'Right,' said Dima. 'First golden rule: stay in touch.'

Each of them had a radio headset. The plan was to send in Amara, with Zirak and Gregorin. They would scope the place, give Dima a sitrep and pinpoint Kaffarov. It was the sort of operation Dima relished: a plan made on the hoof using whatever available assets there were – in this case Amara and a small tight crew of utterly

188

dependable men all capable of thinking on their feet. They had stayed with him on this, when many saner people would have bailed out. He watched them walk up to the house. The young blonde from the photos waved ecstatically from one of the balconies.

It all looked much, much too easy, he thought.

The first rocket landed exactly where Kristen was standing, as if it had been aimed right at her. She didn't even have time to react. One moment she was waving, then she was gone. The balcony disappeared in a cloud of atomised concrete that engulfed Gregorin, Zirak and Amara below. He heard Amara scream, then the second rocket smashed into the mountainside fifty metres away. Dima felt himself flying backwards, then cartwheeling, until a wooden fence brought him to a halt just in time to see the two gun towers flattened by another strike.

Dima was up first, looking for Kroll and Vladimir. They were pulling each other to their feet. He pointed at the downed gun towers.

'Get to the AAs. See if they still work. Whoever's up there, stop them – now!'

He was moving towards the chalet, not thinking about Gregorin and Zirak or Amara and Kristen: only Kaffarov and the nukes. That's what he'd come for. He'd made it this far, paid too high a price not to collect his prize. No one was going to take it from him now.

He picked up speed as he got to the pile of rubble, and found some steps, half broken, jutting out from the facade. He scrambled up them on to a chunk of balcony that immediately broke away when he stepped on to it, nearly sending him crashing to the ground with it. He could hear someone screaming under the rubble. A fire had broken out inside the building, belching acrid smoke. No mask, shit. All the kit was still in the SUV. All he had was his AK and a knife. He climbed through a window, grabbed a shredded curtain which he tore a strip from and wrapped it over his face.

A big drawing room, with nice paintings on the walls. A Matisse. And a Gauguin: two voluptuous island girls, topless, gazing out at him. Could they be real? Maybe that was what the non-Muslim heaven looked like: quite possibly not virgins, but he wasn't fussy. He saw a giant marble chess board on a glass coffee table the size of a lake: a game midway through. No players in sight: white two moves from checkmate. From a doorway, a huge man with cheeks that squeezed his eyes into slits was aiming an Uzi at him. Yin or Yang? Dima would never know. His knife thudded into the man's carotid artery, making a mess of Gauguin's Tahitians. He hoped it was a fake.

Dima jumped on him, retrieved the knife, grabbed the Uzi and tore off his radio. Another blast echoed deep inside the building – the boiler or a fuel tank? The floor lurched and half a wall collapsed, sending a huge mirror down like a guillotine on to the expiring Korean. He saw the chess set glide away: game over. Four rooms on this floor. Two completely blown away. Kaffarov could be under the rubble as well. Two more – a library. He didn't dare think about what precious first editions might be in there. A desk and a laptop, but a small one, white. Kristen's? Check it later. He found the internal stairs. Intact. Took them three at a stride. Outside he heard the AA guns. A short sharp burst. Someone conserving their ammunition: Vladimir. He marvelled at how you could identify someone by the way they shot.

Bedrooms: one untouched, fresh flowers in a vase. Roses. A swimsuit on the carpet – wet. Tch, tch. A towel as well. Young people today, never clear up after themselves. His mother's voice. You would have liked this room, mother. Silk cushions, triple-mirror dresser with matching curtain along the front: all the things you never had. A masked man in each of the mirrors. Himself. The en suite bathroom all marble: massive.

A rumble from outside, high up. Helicopter? There was a pad on the roof. Wrong noise. Plane? Both: Osprey. Keep the Marines away, Vladimir: I'm not done here yet.

Seven more bedrooms: all empty. They'd seen the G-Wagen: Kaffarov had to be somewhere. No sign of an office, nor even another laptop. Where was it all? Kaffarov never stopped, always trading, always in demand. Food, water and weapons, the three basic needs of humanity, in his case definitely not in that order.

The engines were close, slowing now. The Osprey doing its magic trick, switching from flight to hover, a fourteen-second process: fourteen seconds to take aim. *Bam.* Right on cue, another burst of AA fire, then an explosion, engine revs rising to a scream, struggling to do the work of the stricken second engine.

And suddenly Dima was down, smothered by a huge bulk. How did something that big move so fast, so quietly? His face grated against brickdust. Heat pressed in on him, and garlic sweat. The lone remaining twin was perched on top of him. From behind a hand curved round his forehead, gripping his brow, fingertips pressing against his eyeballs. He tried to open one eyelid, saw a window. Outside was the Osprey, its bulk falling to earth, the remaining engine losing the battle. And in extreme close-up, a flash of blade in the other hand curving toward his neck.

45

Dima didn't hear the order. It disappeared under the sound of the Osprey falling among the trees, slamming into the ground and pulling with it more of the half-destroyed chalet. The blade hovered in the air as its owner struggled to reconcile the desire for revenge with the need to obey orders. His boss won that one. The blade disappeared, for now.

'Hold up his head.'

Yin or Yang wrenched Dima's head up and to one side. Kaffarov bent down slightly and Dima got his first close-up look: a Tajik, dark-haired and pale-skinned with a thin neck and a pronounced chin. Without all the hired muscle he might be a pushover, but right now Dima lacked the opportunity to find out.

'He doesn't look American. Take him to the pool.'

'Thanks, but I haven't got my swimming kit,' said Dima.

The twin yanked him up by the scruff of his coat and dragged him across the room like a recalcitrant dog. A door, with nothing to distinguish it as such, opened silently in the wall. And there was the rest of it: a whole parallel universe carved into the mountain behind the facade of the chalet. Dima tried to walk but the twin held him down, so he was forced to let his feet drag behind him, and be pulled along the corridor like a toy.

Another door opened – the gym – and leading off it, a room full of screens. They stopped in the gym. Dima tried to turn his head to see more of the other room, but was yanked forward again. There was a brief glimpse of an aquarium: did people like Kaffarov keep piranhas, or was that only in films? Then he smelled the chlorine. They didn't start with a question. The huge Korean just stuffed his head into the water and held it there. Twenty seconds. A taster.

Yanked him up. Kaffarov's face was close, calm, expressionless, his pupils tiny dots.

'Who sent you?' He spoke in Farsi, then repeated the question in English.

Dima replied in Russian.

'Your girlfriend's under the rubble. If you hurry you might just be able to save her.'

His head went under again: a cold, suffocating horror, no space, no air. Don't try to breathe. How long would it be this time? He counted twenty seconds – and then another. Kaffarov's face was closer this time.

'You are going to tell me exactly who you are, and why you're here, or Yin will drown you.'

'Ah, so it was Yang I killed then. You boys really do look alike.'

'Do it.'

Down he went again. Okay, start counting. The water was tepid, sort of stale. Dima knew what to do. He'd trained for this, come first in his Spetsnaz group for lasting the longest. It was all a matter of relaxing. The more relaxed you were, the less energy you used. Keep counting. Entire extra seconds could be gone without that next lungful. Learning how to suffer through all the misery and punishment of his training, being thrown naked on to the hard frozen snow and made to fight, the beatings, the humiliation, all about controlling pain, managing anger, channelling it into patience, kneading it into raw aggression, conserved for just the right moment.

The trick was not to care, to keep counting but just give in to it. So I'll die: so what? I've had my moments. The record for staying under water was eleven minutes thirty-five seconds. His best was just under eight. But that was after a really good sleep. I should have fucked that receptionist, he thought: she had red hair and smelled of apples. That would have been a good memory to go out on.

Three minutes. He had glimpsed the pool, seen that this was the deep end. What else could he use? Focus on the surroundings, the hand pressing down, where Yin's weight on top of him was distributed, the knees on his shoulders, not his lower arms which were free. Dima inched them round until his hands could grasp the edge of the pool. Four minutes. Not as good as he was. He needed that lungful of air right now.

He let his muscles go, stopped resisting, and used the weight of his head, which he had been pushing against the twin's hand, to pull him further down, boosted by the leverage from his hands on the edge. With an extra pull he pushed himself deeper. Yin lost his balance, keeled over Dima and hit the water: not what he was expecting. Dima plunged a hand down, grabbed the knife from his pudgy hand, brought it straight up under Yin's flailing ribcage and plunged, then twisted, then plunged again. He felt a wall of muscle, withdrew and plunged once more.

46

There was a collective shout of pain in the Osprey as they felt the jolt. The AA fire took the tip of the starboard rotor off, stalling the engine before the flames started. The ramp doors were already opening for a fast exit, but the door gunners had been blown away. Not by a hail of fire but by short sharp bursts expertly aimed. The F-16s had reported the AA guns neutralised. Mistake. So many mistakes in warfare, Blackburn now understood. It was a miracle anybody survived, let alone triumphed.

The port engine revs rose as it sucked at the air, trying to compensate, but the Osprey was halfway through its transition from flight to hover. Blackburn felt the craft climb and then hang for a tantalising few seconds before it gave up the fight and started its progression downwards. The pilot did what he could but the ground rushed towards them. Men frozen into position clung to the grab handles on the fuselage interior. Futile. Blackburn lurched towards the open ramp, tripped and slid headfirst. He smashed through several trees he never had time to identify, but boy did he love those trees. The arms of angels breaking his fall. His arrival back on earth was still painful though and he blacked out for several seconds. Further down the hill, he saw the Osprey roll on to its side: the wings, with their still-spinning rotors, snapped off like bits of a plastic kit.

He looked up at the chalet, the plans of which he had memorised down to the last room. But at first sight it was unrecognisable, the whole facade and all of the verandas smashed off by the rocket. If there's anyone alive in there it will be a miracle, thought Black. But he knew there were rooms far into the rock. He had to get there. He didn't think about the casualties. If he went back to the Osprey and tried to help, Cole might accuse him of flunking out again. Well fuck you, Cole, if you die because no one helped you, it's your fault. In fact I hope you do die.

Where had this come from? At school he had been the mediator, the breaker-up of fights. The one willing to see the other side. On this assignment – excess baggage. From now on he was travelling light. He picked up his M4, checked it and took off for the rubble.

47

The bodyguard's vast form turned slowly as he sank, the blood pumping out of him forming fine curls as it gradually turned the water from blue to pink. Dima hauled himself out of the pool, gasping for breath. He sucked it in, the stale underground air reeking of chlorine – the best he had ever inhaled. Kaffarov stood over him, holding Yin's Uzi. He may have bought and sold guns – a lot of them – but the way he held it showed that he wasn't in the habit of using one. That was the trouble with delegating: you could become seriously deskilled.

Even so, sprawled there like the catch of the day, Dima was an easy target. Kaffarov might not have had much practice with the Uzi, but he could pick him off no problem. There was nothing Dima could do – except play for time.

'Nice place you've got here. Must be useful having the old panic room to retreat into at times like this.'

Kaffarov didn't respond. Dima suspected he wasn't too keen on the word 'retreat'.

As he got his breath back, he got his first proper look at Kaffarov. A slight man, drooping shoulders. A pointed, foxy face with a couple of days' stubble. Thick eyebrows furrowed in a permanent frown that betrayed a lifelong disinclination to compromise.

'Kristen was pretty badly hurt out there. I don't know if she'll make it: I'm sorry.'

He didn't respond: not even a flicker of regret. But what did he expect from the man who refused to pay the million dollar ransom for his wife, who repeatedly armed every evil or misguided combatant the world over, right down to the child soldiers of Darfur? How lucky for him that the Americans had devoted so much time and money going after Osama, allowing the real monster to spread his weapons of mass destruction unhindered.

'By the way, the Matisse and the Gauguin: I hope you didn't pay too much for them.'

Now he had his attention: money was what mattered to him, not people: of course.

'Why?'

'They're fakes.'

'Bullshit. Who cares what you think?'

'I used to live in Paris: spent a lot of lunchtimes in the Musée d'Orsay: it has a better collection than the Louvre, and fewer tourists.'

Could he appeal to the man's love of art? Doubtful. The paintings were only there because he'd believed them valuable. Kaffarov smiled, a sinister approximation of a smile with no warmth.

'Ah, Paris. Beautiful city. Such a pity.'

What did he mean?

'Look,' said Dima, trying to keep still and look unthreatening. 'I'm not your enemy: I was sent to rescue you and stop the nukes falling into the wrong hands. When we got to the compound, you weren't there. I'm Dima Mayakovsky: one of the good guys.'

'Mayakovsky? You don't look Russian.'

There were definitely pros and cons to that.

'My mother was Armenian. No, really. I am. The Kremlin hired me to keep you safe. Is that so hard to believe?'

'And you have the credentials from them to prove this?'

On a deniable black op? The man was joking. Mind you, he didn't look like someone who enjoyed a laugh.

'A man in my position arouses envy. I have to keep track of my enemies. You have to watch your back all the time in this business.'

Well, you did choose to become an arms dealer, thought Dima. If you want to sleep well at night sell eggs, or oranges.

'By the way, I passed the US Marines on my way in. And I don't think they're here as customers.'

Kaffarov's smirk now twisted up at one end.

'Yes, the Americans seem to think they should have a monopoly of the world's armaments market. So narrow-minded of them.

And – ' he adjusted his grip on the Uzi ' – out of date.'

'You know, those guys have had quite a bit of practice at this stuff. It's only a matter of time before they figure out how to get in here.'

For a man who had the US Marines knocking on his door he wasn't breaking into much of a sweat. Dima glanced at the dead North Korean, turning his pool pink.

'And who's going to guard you now?'

'Do you want to apply for the job?'

It should have been a joke, but his face said otherwise. A rat in a hole too deep to dig his way out alone?

'I can offer very attractive terms.'

Keep humouring him, Dima thought.

'Well, it's the first time I've been offered a job at gunpoint.'

No smile was forthcoming.

'Farouk Al Bashir is dead. I heard it on CNN so it must be true. So I guess the PLR's finished.'

Kaffarov shook his head.

'On the contrary. With Bashir out of the way, the true force of the PLR will be unleashed: 9/11 will just be a footnote in history after what's coming.'

Dima hoped this was an empty boast. He feared it wasn't.

'You don't know it, Dima Mayakovsky, but you're quite naive. I know your exact type. Steeped in the Spetsnaz folklore, never quite able to shake off that old Soviet bullshit.'

He shook his head. 'And here you are, struggling to make a living doing other people's dirty work. There are hundreds of you out there, bitter and twisted after having served the Motherland so faithfully. You should have grasped the opportunity when it was there. I saw the writing on the Berlin Wall. You know what it said? *Every man for himself.*'

Kaffarov was getting into his stride now. He pulled the Uzi in towards him a little: were his arms getting tired?

'I know exactly why you're here. Because some apparatchik in Moscow got to hear that yet another item of supposedly top secret weaponry had found its way on to the open market. You know what his first thought was? *How do I cover my ass?* Sack someone. Find a scapegoat, make them take the fall. Wait. Even better: tell the person you're about to sack to organise a search and rescue operation. It's bound to fail. *Then* sack them. Unfortunately the person you've chosen isn't such a stupid jerk as you hoped: he brings his own men. But you still give him the wrong intelligence. Then boom! Sound familiar?'

Dima felt a surge of rage. Kaffarov knew all along, just as he had suspected. He nodded, pleased with himself.

'I have many friends, Dima. I am a very popular man. Being rich makes you very popular. You should try it someday.'

Dima could feel his patience wearing out. The Uzi was still pointing his way but Kaffarov seemed to have got absorbed by his own smugness. He could see the inferior officer who lurked underneath, who had never succeeded in the military, who had probably taken a fair amount of shit from his more successful peers. How sad that a man of his wealth and influence was wasting time bragging on like this. More than sad: stupid.

Dima kept up a pensive expression, as if he was gratefully absorbing his wisdom. Standing over him, Kaffarov had overlooked the fact that while he was talking, Dima, slumped at the edge of the pool, drenched but no longer out of breath, was slowly letting his left hand slide in the direction of Kaffarov's right foot.

There was a loud *blam* from the other side of the reinforced door. Kaffarov's eyes darted left and Dima lunged, hooking his hand round Kaffarov's ankle and pulling it forward with such a jolt that Kaffarov landed on his back, the impact knocking all the wind out of him. The Uzi flew out of his hand, arced through the air, dropped on to the poolside and, like a lethal game of spin the bottle, revolved several times and came to a stop just out of Kaffarov's reach.

There was another loud thud outside the door. He hoped it might be Kroll and Vladimir, but feared it was the Marines.

Dima sprang up and bent over Kaffarov, a hand tightening round his neck.

'Show me where the nukes are. Now.'

Kaffarov's mouth was moving but no sound was coming out. The complacency had gone, replaced by a look of dismay, as he absorbed what had just happened.

'I told you they're gone.' He nodded in the opposite direction to the door. Dima released his grip so he could get his breath.

'Don't fuck with me. I will most definitely kill you.'

It was an empty threat, because he needed to get him back to Moscow alive. That was the deal. But his skin had turned grey.

'Gone where? Who has them? Talk. Now!'

Kaffarov stretched a hand out as if trying to point further into the bunker. His mouth opened again as if in protest, but his body had surrendered. His chest went rigid as his head flopped forward. Dima locked his hands together, found the correct spot at the base of the sternum and pushed down, hard. Indelibly lodged in the back of his mind was the song they sang during first aid training, to get the rhythm right: *In-out, in-out, my woman likes it hard.* They were meant to sing *For-ward, for-ward! For the Motherland with joy!* but locked up in those huts for three years they had come to prefer the unofficial version. He opened Kaffarov's mouth, held his nose and breathed in three times, then pushed down again. Nothing. There was another explosion outside, bigger this time, and all the lights in the bunker went out. He was in complete darkness.

All that firepower from the greatest forces in the world and the quarry had died of heart failure.

48

As he moved towards the blasted chalet, Blackburn had one thing only on his mind: *Solomon*, the last word uttered by the expiring Bashir. He didn't even know if it was a name at all. He could have been trying to say something else. It hadn't registered with his interrogators. Cole had been unimpressed. Nonetheless, it was the name he had given to the figure he'd seen on the bank's security screen, and to the swordsman he had seen decapitate Harker. *Solomon*. He repeated it over and over. It expanded to cover everything that had conspired against him over the last three days.

He was going to be first in. Campo and Montes sensed it. Blackburn was a man possessed. They could have hung on, waited for Cole, regrouped. Montes had already radioed for full-on Medevac. If Cole was injured, so be it. All of his energy was focused on Solomon and the nukes now. Nothing else in the world mattered. Campo and Montes were with him, but as far as Blackburn was concerned he was on his own.

'Hey, I hear something.' Montes started clawing at the rubble. 'We got injured here.' Campo went to help. Blackburn ignored him, kept moving, climbing the steps to the shattered balcony.

The dead man on the first floor was face down. Western civilian clothes – black T-shirt and pants. Blackburn lifted his head: pudgy oriental features frozen forever into a contortion of pain from the fatal wound that had emptied most of the blood out of his system. He checked for a pulse, just to be sure. None. He glanced at the room. Nothing like he had ever seen before. So much wealth and so much damage. A lump of masonry from the front wall fell away, crashing to the ground below. Think. He called up the plans he had memorised, re-orientated himself. The walls were clad in wood panels, doors leading off to the left but none on the right – none that were visible. The plans he had examined at Firefly had shown that a corridor perpendicular to the landing had been cut into the mountain, leading to a cluster of underground rooms. How did you get in there?

Calm and very focused, he pulled off a glove and ran his hand over the surface. All the way down the left side of the landing, each panel ran floor to ceiling, with a narrow three millimetre gap between each one. No handles or apertures. No infrared devices. The door, if there was one at all, had been expertly concealed. He stood back, looked for any signs of wear. Thirty centimetres from the bottom, on the right-hand side of one crack, just discernible, were three red-brown fingerprints. He wiped a thumb across. They made a smear: fresh. How could they have gotten there? Was the panel beside them a hidden doorway? It had to be. He gave the panel a hard kick. Solid. He would have to blow it.

He radioed. '*Breaching. Stand by.*'

Campo came back. '*Roger that.*'

He applied the grenade launcher to his M4, transforming his rifle into a door buster. The shock could bring down more of the chalet but it was a risk he had to take. The blast seemed to shake the whole mountain: a thick cloud of dust filled the corridor. It minced the wood panels, exposing the door frame. He inserted another grenade and repeated the process. The second explosion felt even bigger. A lump from the ceiling came loose and before Blackburn could move it crashed down on him, knocking him to the floor. Then the left-hand wall caved, in bringing more of the ceiling with it. When he came to he was in darkness, cut off from the others.

'*Blackburn – talk to us! Over.*' It was Campo.

Blackburn didn't reply. He flicked on his helmet light and in the dusty gloom he could just make out the door – opened by about thirty centimetres. He was quickly up and on it, shouldering it with all his weight, adrenalin pulsing through him, as an instinct stronger than anything he had known before drove him forward into the passage that led to the bunker.

The only light was from his torch. He caught the smell of chlorine, remembered a deep rectangle on the plan which could have been a pool. He paused, trying to hear over the sound of his own pumping pulse. Something. A movement. He kept going forward. He passed a room with screens: presumably the nerve centre. Then ahead he caught the glint of water. He couldn't hear anything but sensed a presence. He was near now, near to what he had come for. He swept the space with the torch beam. A large corpse in the water, same size as the dead guy outside, a second man down on the poolside. And a third, crouching, his drenched clothes glistening in the torchlight, staring back at him.

49

'US Forces! Freeze!' said the voice.

Fuck off, said Dima to himself. *Americans are always so melo-dramatic.* He couldn't see the American, but the American could see him loud and clear. Where were Vladimir, Kroll and the others? He had to assume the worst. He didn't even want to think about Kristen – or Amara, whom he'd promised to deliver back to her father in one piece. He was alone and soaked; the man he had gone through madness to chase down and take alive was lying dead at his feet. And now he had an over-excited American playing cops and robbers with him. This job just gets better by the minute, he thought.

Blackburn examined his quarry through the infra-red torch on his weapon.

'Do – you – speak – English?'

'Sure, if you don't know anything else,' came the fluent reply.

In the dark Dima could guess roughly where the Uzi had finished up, but he was in no position to reach for it.

'On your feet, legs: spread 'em. I'm coming forward, going to search you. You got that?'

No point antagonising him, Dima thought. If he's young and inexperienced he might shoot me by mistake.

'Yes, loud and clear,' he replied, getting slowly to his feet, hands held high.

'Touch the wall, legs apart.'

Judging by the voice, definitely mid-twenties at most, Dima thought. He did what he was told, heard the American approach, felt the hands patting him down, careful, deliberate. Conversation seemed worth a try.

'What happened outside? Are we cut off?'

'Don't talk. Can you identify the deceased?'

'The one on the poolside is Amir Kaffarov. The guy in the pool and the one you might have encountered under the Matisse are his personal bodyguards, Yin and Yang. They're twins, from North Korea. Well, they were.'

There was no response from Blackburn, who seemed to be taking his time. Dima felt the passport he had waved at the PLR roadblock slide smoothly out of his pocket. The separate wads of rials and dollars were next, along with his phone. As Blackburn withdrew it from the sheath strapped to Dima's belt, he bade a sad farewell to the knife that had come in so handy with Yin and Yang.

Dima heard the American's radio buzz: something urgent and incomprehensible. As Blackburn continued the search Dima turned his head very slightly so he could look in the direction of the Uzi, in case some light from the American's helmet torch fell on it, but he felt a hand on his neck.

'Eyes on the wall, please.'

How polite. How many Russians would deploy such pleasantries in this sort of situation? Their idea of courtesy was usually to refrain from kneeing you in the balls. But Blackburn was struggling with his darker side. As his hand closed round the grip of the knife, part of him wanted to exact revenge right now, to plunge the blade into the man's neck and let him know just how it felt.

But he was determined to do this by the book. What differentiated him from his prisoner, he thought, would be his underlying human-ity. That was what distinguished them, the soldier from the exe-cutioner. It was important to let the likes of them see why the American way was superior.

'Okay: turn, keeping your hands up.'

Dima obliged, the helmet torch blasting his face. His wet skin reflected some of the light back on to the American's. Hard to put an age to, anywhere between twenty and thirty, intelligent.

'Okay, give me your name now.'

'Dima Mayakovsky.'

'Not what this passport says. What's your status in the PLR?'

'I'm not with the PLR, I'm from Moscow.'

Dima thought he might as well fill the silence that followed.

'Here to repatriate weapons obtained under false pretences from the Russian Federation.'

'Yeah, right.'

Blackburn was leafing through the apparently well used Iranian passport he had found in Dima's pocket: this was definitely going to work against him.

'Taghi Hosseini it says here.'

Instead of responding, Dima said,

'What brings you here? If you don't mind me asking.'

Blackburn looked at him, not showing his dismay.

'It might be that we have common interests.'

Blackburn snorted; the hatred for the man he called *Solomon* was building.

'I sincerely doubt that.'

'*3–1, you copy over?*'

Campo again.

'*3–1, Blackburn. You receiving in there? Structure in danger of further collapse, over.*'

Blackburn ignored it. Dima could see the stripes on the American's arm.

'Sergeant Blackburn, yes?'

Blackburn didn't answer. If the man carried on trying to ingratiate himself, he might have to take action to shut him up.

'You and I are most probably here for the same thing, the suitcase nukes, right?'

Again, Blackburn didn't respond but it was clear from his face that Dima had touched a nerve. He decided to risk another question.

'How many – two?'

No answer.

Dima pressed on. 'I believe there are three, one of which is already in American hands.'

Blackburn couldn't help himself this time.

'What makes you think that?'

'We had a scanner that followed them from the Metropolitan

Bank in downtown Tehran. One went northwest in the direction of the US encampment, and two came here.'

At the mention of the bank, a cold feeling spread across Blackburn's chest. Was this the confirmation he needed that he was looking at the man who had left the bank with Bashir?

He took a step closer to Dima, watching his eyes as he spoke.

'Your codename is Solomon. Right?'

His captive's eyes widened and his mouth dropped open a fraction. Recognition.

50

Solomon. There were only a very few names Dima had ever known that delivered an emotional kick when said out loud.

The last time had been a year ago, when Kroll mentioned him in connection with the bombing of a hotel in Abu Dhabi, where a Middle East peace delegation was gathered. All those present were wiped out so comprehensively that what little was left had to be buried in one grave. There was also a particularly bloody attack on a party of American aid workers on their way out of Afghanistan. The emphatic denials of responsibility by the local insurgents on both sides of the border, and the mutilations which even for Dima were hard to comprehend, suggested an agenda that went beyond simple hostility to the American presence. Each of the twenty-four victims, it was reported, was made to commit degrading acts on each other before being beheaded with a sword – a hallmark that caused Dima particular disquiet.

Here in this bunker, with Kaffarov dead at his feet, and Sergeant Blackburn pointing his M4 at him, was the last place he expected to hear the name *Solomon*, least of all from the mouth of an American serviceman.

'Say that again?' said Dima, checking that he hadn't misheard.

Blackburn repeated the name, slowly, emphasising each syllable as Bashir had. Dima exhaled a long breath.

'What do you know about Solomon?'

Blackburn kept his gaze on Dima. His voice was almost trembling with rage.

'I know that in the last seventy-two hours a man believed to be of that name was responsible for the beheading of an unarmed American serviceman on the Iraq border, and for the execution by sword of a tank driver. I also know that a man of that name was last seen with Farouk Al Bashir, leaving the Metropolitan Bank in Tehran.'

Dima let this sink in. There was a look of certainty in Blackburn's eyes that was going to be hard to shift. Not only certainty, but the expression of someone battling hard to keep his emotions in check. Whatever Dima said next could be decisive.

He took a breath.

'Okay. I can say two things about Solomon which I don't expect you to believe straight off. One is that I am emphatically not him, and the other is that I can probably tell you more about him than anyone else still living.'

Yeah, right, thought Blackburn, in no mood to doubt that the man standing before him was anyone other than Solomon. But he wanted to be sure first. He hadn't killed in cold blood before. He could do the right thing and hand him over – and then what? He didn't want the conflict raging inside him to show in his face.

'Misfit 3–1 this is Misfit actual, over.'

This time it was Cole.

'Misfit 3–1, give your sitrep, over.'

Dima and Blackburn looked at each other. Blackburn switched off the radio, which was strange, Dima thought. In fact the whole situation was decidedly weird. To be at the Shah's old ski chalet with a dead arms dealer, with a dead Korean in the pool, and now being detained by a US soldier in the collapsed bunker. And if that wasn't strange enough, the mention of Solomon put the cherry right on it.

The building shuddered, sending another shower of concrete fragments raining down on them. They were entombed. Blackburn's comrades were calling him but he had turned off his radio. Whatever was going on here, Dima thought, it was important enough for Blackburn to be disobeying orders. Was the man unhinged? He looked angry but not crazy.

'Say your piece and keep it brief.'

'I'll try. He was a kid when he first surfaced in a refugee camp in Lebanon in the late '80s, claiming to be suffering from amnesia – didn't even remember his name but had a gift for languages. American missionaries thought he was some kind of prodigy, christened

210

him Solomon like the wise king in the Old Testament. They took him home with them to Florida. It didn't go well. He was bullied at school. It went on for months. He bided his time. That's a hallmark of his – he doesn't like to rush things. Then young Solomon exacts his own brand of revenge on his high school tormentors with a machete – not in a frenzy, more surgical. I'll skip the details, but you should know that at least three heads were severed. He disappears – stows away on a merchant ship bound for the Gulf. Roll on two years he's 'Suleiman', fighting with the Mujahideen in Afghanistan – against the Russians. But he wants more. He has no allegiances – except to himself. He gets recruited by the Russians, who realise his potential – ruthless, natural linguist, natural everything, plus a deep hatred of America. So they take him on and train him up as an asset. He can play all the parts: Yank, Arab, Eurasian. He's a secret weapon, but he's also impossible to handle. In the chaos after the Soviet Union collapses he disappears – goes his own way. Then 9/11 happens. The Americans pick him up, lock him in Guantanamo. But Solomon's no fool – guess what he does to get out? He offers his services. Gives them a treasure trove of intelligence on terror outfits, on Russian Intelligence, and next thing he's 'Solomon' again, on the CIA payroll doing black ops.'

Blackburn listened. 'How do you know all this?'

'Because I found him in Afghanistan. I was his GRU handler.'

'*You?*'

Blackburn was silent for a full thirty seconds, digesting what he had just heard. Did he believe him? He needed time to decide if he did, time he didn't have. Eventually he spoke, his voice distant.

'In the bank vault – there were maps.'

'What of?'

'New York. Paris.'

Paris – such a pity. Kaffarov's words came back to Dima. *With Bashir out of the way, the true force of the PLR will be unleashed: 9/11 will just be a footnote in history after what's coming.* Dima, his thoughts whirring, was fighting to keep focused on Sergeant Blackburn and his M4.

Blackburn was also battling to keep his emotions out of his

thoughts. Was this guy for real? What was his true agenda? At least he had the guy contained while he worked out what to do next. Cole was out there somewhere, he would be wanting to know what was happening, scrutinising Blackburn's performance. How he loathed his CO.

He pressed the muzzle of his M4 against Dima's neck.

'Okay, very convincing. Now get down.'

He turned Dima round and pushed him on to his knees.

'I can see how you'd *like* me to be him ...'

'Shuddup!' Blackburn yelled, inches away from Dima's ear.

It couldn't have been the shout that caused it, but it was still echoing in Dima's head when they were engulfed by a much louder noise.

51

It felt as if the whole mountain was caving in on them as plaster, concrete and stone rained down. Dima passed out – for how long, he didn't know. When he came to his head was throbbing hard. His eyes and mouth were caked in dust. At first he couldn't see Blackburn at all. He raised himself – slowly, in case the M4 was still trained on him. He needn't have worried. Blackburn was lying on his side, the concrete beam that had given way pinning him down across his arms and torso. He was conscious, panting hard.

Had Dima not obeyed Blackburn's order and knelt, he would have been crushed to death.

'Can you hear me?'

'Course I can fucking hear you,' Blackburn yelled back.

Dima felt for a hand.

'Okay: I'm going to check your reflexes.'

'Fucking don't touch me, okay?'

'Try to be calm, or you will bleed even faster.'

He was staring ahead, wide-eyed. Dima realised why. The knife. It was inches away from Blackburn's face, the blade pointing right at him. Dima reached down for it. Blackburn let out a huge roar of anguish. Dima hesitated, carried on, picked up the knife.

'Not with the knife, not the knife. Just shoot me okay!'

Dima lifted the knife and Blackburn's breathing reached a crazy pitch.

'Look.' Dima turned so Blackburn could see him slip the knife into the sheath on his belt. There was another loud thud from somewhere near the way in to the bunker. All Dima could see was a fresh pile of rubble. Blackburn's comrades trying to blast their way in?

'Give me your torch and I'll check you over, okay.'

'No!'

'Okay, okay. Can you feel your arms and legs?'

Blackburn flexed his limbs.

'Okay, good. Can you wiggle your toes?'

'A bit.'

'Does it hurt?'

'What do you think?'

Dima grasped the lump of concrete and heaved. It wouldn't move. He tried again, putting all the force he could summon into lifting it. It moved about an inch.

'Tell me about the maps. Everything you remember.'

Blackburn's breathing subsided.

'I don't get it.'

'Anything. What kind of maps? As if for a briefing? Were they on a wall? Were any locations highlighted?'

Blackburn didn't speak for several seconds. Dima struggled with the beam.

'On the Paris one – a marker said *Bourse.*' He spelled it out.

'That's the Stock Exchange.'

'You sure about that?'

'Oh yes.'

Blackburn shifted his head and looked up, mystified. Dima slumped down, exhausted.

'You trying to free me?'

'What does it look like?'

'I don't get it.'

'Look: what you saw in that bank vault is probably the most important piece of intelligence anyone's got since they found Bin Laden.'

Dima looked round for inspiration. He saw the Uzi, its muzzle just clear of the rubble, reached over and grabbed it. Blackburn's eyes widened again.

'Shit, my arm's going numb.'

'Okay, let's be intelligent here. I may be able to break up the beam by taking a shot at it.' He examined the Uzi doubtfully.

'No, no: that won't do it.'

Blackburn tried to turn his head just enough to locate the M4. Dima followed his gaze.

'40 mm. It's a risk. You'll have to trust my aim.'

They looked at each other. There was no guarantee the others would find him now. He'd turned off his radio. And if they did, more of the bunker might come down if they tried to blast their way in. Blackburn didn't have any choices left. This Russian was his only hope.

'What do I call you?'

'Dima Mayakovsky.'

'Okay, then, Dima.'

'Before I do it, I'm going to pack some rubble around you to stop the beam dropping on you when it fragments.'

Whatever air conditioning had been ventilating the bunker had stopped a good while before. It was getting hotter and stickier, but Dima worked fast, sweat pouring off him as he shored up the beam. Then he picked up the M4.

'Okay. This is the bit where you really do have to trust me.'

Dima crouched down close to Blackburn, shielding him with his body as he positioned the weapon.

'Close your eyes. There may be some dust.'

He aimed the M4 and fired twice into the concrete.

Nothing happened. Dima emptied two more into the slab. Half the beam lurched. Before it could move any further Dima slid his arms through Blackburn's and hauled him out, then sat him on the edge of the shattered beam. Several seconds passed while they both caught their breath. Blackburn tried to stand. He could. He moved his arms. No serious damage. Elated, he looked round at the rubble-strewn bunker. His eye fell on the Uzi where Dima had put it down to lift him. It was inches away from his hand. Dima saw it too, looked at Blackburn. Blackburn looked at it and back at Dima.

'You are for real.'

'As much as any of us is,' Dima smiled. Blackburn looked like a man who'd just been given his life back.

'We need to get out of here before any more of it comes down.'

Dima put the M4 in Blackburn's hands.

'A soldier should never become separated from his weapon.'

Dima's brain was in overdrive. Processing the implications of what Blackburn had told him had set it racing. Solomon – back to haunt him, bent on vengeance. Beheading American soldiers, a personal nuclear arsenal, the maps Blackburn described, and Kaffarov's words, *9/11 will be just a footnote* . . .

It all added up for Dima. He knew what Solomon was capable of. Blackburn had seen it for himself. He looked at the young American, full of sincerity. Blackburn's righteous indignation at what he had seen, his mission to right the wrong. Easy to be cynical about his sense of purpose, in a world of Solomons and Kaffarovs, where loyalties were bought and sold to the highest bidder, where money, power and vengeance were the prime motivations. He was trying to plot a way forward when another explosive thud came from near the door, followed by a fresh cloud of dust. Through it came a torch beam. They were no longer alone.

52

The Lieutenant was in a rage: that much was clear.

'Congratulations, Blackburn. You found your man. Glad to see you got your priorities right.'

Blackburn said nothing.

'Campo and Montes figured you must be dead since there's at least two buried in the rubble out there.'

The news hit Dima like another explosion. Zirak and Gregorin . . .

Cole glared at Dima.

'So: the executioner. You've made quite a name for yourself.'

Dima didn't respond. When in doubt do absolutely nothing, just think fast and watch hard. The Uzi was half a metre from his foot. He tried to read the Lieutenant: earnest, well-bred, committed, he guessed, here because he wanted to be. In for the long haul. But with something else going on. It was all in Blackburn's intriguing reaction to his superior officer, as if being rescued by him was the last thing in the world he wanted right now.

Cole stepped closer, eyeing Dima.

'As good a place as any to end this.'

Blackburn said nothing. The dust had turned his face to a mask. A very unpleasant thought started forming in Dima's mind.

'Say, Blackburn. It looks pretty unstable in here. Should get ourselves out before it caves.'

'Sir,' said Blackburn. But he made no move. The M4 felt like a betrayal in his hands.

'You're very quiet, Blackburn. Guess I know what you're thinking: now's your chance. Well soldier, you've earned it. You go right ahead. Do what you have to do. Your secret'll be safe with me.'

I can't believe this is happening, thought Dima, realising what Cole was intimating. He glanced at the Uzi.

Cole stepped up to Blackburn and shouted in his ear.

'Hey Blackburn, you hearing me? I'm giving you a chance.'

What a cunt, thought Dima.

Blackburn was frozen to the spot, his M4 now drooping in his hands. In front of him, two men, his CO and his tormentor, telling him to kill the stranger who had just saved his life. And if this man was right about Solomon . . . What happened next took less than a second, but it was a very packed less than a second. Dima, his reflexes taking over, sprang towards the Uzi. Cole, having concluded that Blackburn didn't have the stomach for it, took aim at Dima. But the weapon that went off wasn't Cole's. And the man that went down wasn't Dima. The shot seemed to fill the whole bunker. Cole's expression became one of exaggerated surprise as he sank to his knees, moving through dismay, to indignation, and finally to horror.

He stayed upright for a few more agonising seconds, then his eyes glazed and he slumped forward on to the rubble.

Dima, Uzi in hand, wheeled round to face Blackburn. He had seen that look before: Gregorin describing the elimination of his bullying comrade – a certain serenity that follows particularly sweet revenge. He shook his head as if he still didn't quite believe it. But there was no question, the young American looked as though a great weight had just been lifted from him.

Dima stepped forward and grasped his saviour by the shoulder.

'Thank you, comrade. I think we're quits.'

53

Dima had no idea how they were going to get out of the bunker. In the two hours he had been in there, he had faced Yang, then Kaffarov, followed by Blackburn and Cole. And he had heard about Solomon. Survival was what concentrated his mind now. Escape – he didn't want to tempt providence by even considering it. But with the US Marines outside wondering about the fate of first Blackburn and now Cole, it was only a matter of time before another of them tried to make an entrance. That or another beam smashing down and crushing them to death.

Blackburn was ahead of him.

'I've seen plans to this place. There was some kind of shaft running out through the rear of the bunker. It exits the other side of the mountain. If we can find the entrance.'

Together they made their way over the rubble and broken beams. Through a small antechamber they found a metal door similar to the one concealed behind the panelling in the chalet. Although it wasn't locked, it looked as though it hadn't been used in a long time. Blackburn pointed his torch into the darkness.

'Guess this is it.'

Dima half expected Blackburn to bid him farewell and return to his comrades. But Blackburn hadn't worked out a plan either. He took off his helmet and wiped his forehead. He was drenched in sweat, which was now forming up into drops on his chin and the end of his nose. His mind was spinning.

'What just happened . . . I don't know . . .'

The energy seemed to be running out of him as fast as the sweat. Dima felt for him. He could go back the way he came in, put a good story together, maybe chuck a grenade into the bunker as he left: he had a good chance of picking up right where he was. Cole would be MIA. But they both knew that the Marine Corps would do its damnedest to find their Lieutenant's body and extract it – and then they would find the M4 bullet in him …

Dima put a hand on his shoulder. 'This much I can say about Solomon. You put what I've told you with what you know and take that back to your superiors. They're not going to want to hear it at first. Even if one of them makes an inquiry about him to Langley, they're quite likely to tell him to fuck off. Solomon is an untouchable as far as they're concerned. They're not going to pull him in and wreck years of what they consider to be high value infiltration just on the say-so of a Marine with a hunch. You are going to have to work hard to convince them. Solomon finds his way to America with one of those bombs, he's going to need someone on his case. You've seen the maps, you've seen first-hand how he operates and you've seen the device. And you have what I've told you.'

There was another massive blast and the bunker collapsed completely, sending a huge choking cloud of dust and smoke rolling towards them. They retreated into the tunnel to get away from it – and kept going. Neither of them said anything as they travelled what must have been half a mile underground.

The tunnel was fairly smooth underfoot, but snaked left and right. The ceiling was low and they had to stoop. The air was stale and damp, but cooler. Blackburn's helmet torch showed them the way. They stumbled along in complete silence.

Like the one at the entrance to the tunnel, the door at the end was wide open – but the rusty scar across the floor and the blast marks around the old-fashioned locking mechanism suggested that it had been recently prised open, and whoever had come through hadn't bothered to shut it.

They took their time to let their eyes adjust to the blinding daylight. The exit, half-shrouded in shrubbery, was into a small valley of cypresses. A few metres below the mouth of the tunnel was a track with a fork. To the right it led southeast, up towards a cleft in the mountains, to the left it dropped into a valley and curved north.

Dima studied the ground: fresh tyre tracks. Someone had been here recently and made a turn right by the entrance.

54

It was just before three, the hottest part of the day. The air gushing into the tunnel felt as if it was coming from an open oven. Dima went first, motioning to Blackburn to stay back until he signalled him. He surveyed the area around the mouth of the tunnel: a few cypress trees, a track that ran from the southeast going north. Apart from a half-ruined stone shed about two hundred metres away, there were no signs of habitation. He examined the ground.

'What are you looking for?'

'Tracks. And they're recent. Look.'

Blackburn crouched down with him.

'See the way those blades of grass are broken but still green. And here.' He circled an area in the dust. 'Tyre track, wide tread: pick-up or SUV.'

Dima's phone was still on him. He felt it buzz in his pocket. Kroll.

'*Welcome back from the underground. Who's your new sidekick?*'

'*Where are you?*' Dima asked in English.

'*See the shed?*'

'*Are we clear to move?*'

'*Uncle Sam's still on the other side of the hill, but no one else.*'

Dima and Blackburn made their way over to the remains of the shed. Some camo netting had been spread between the walls for cover. Inside was a beaten-up Toyota Land Cruiser. Kroll and Vladimir appeared from behind a wall. Vladimir had a makeshift bandage on his head, and Kroll a strip of shirt tied round his arm. For Dima, the relief of seeing them was overshadowed by what he knew was coming next.

Vladimir spoke first.

'Zirak and Gregorin didn't make it. Nor Kristen.'

'Amara?'

He nodded at the rear seat of the Land Cruiser.

'She's a bit banged up, nothing broken. The Americans dug her out, then when the rest of the chalet collapsed they forgot about her. We'd legged it when they turned their fire on the AAs, but we maintained surveillance until we spotted her, then we lifted the truck.'

Kroll beckoned Dima over to the SUV. He looked at the bundle curled up on the rear seat: dusty, dishevelled and in shock, but alive.

Kroll spoke first. 'Kristen had shown her the escape route on her first visit. So once we'd found it we decided to hang out in case you showed up. We didn't know if you would, obviously.'

Vladimir was glaring at Blackburn. Dima gestured at his new comrade.

'Among other things, he saved my life. Give him some water.'

Kroll passed them a bottle of water each.

'We're fresh out of sparkling.'

As they drank it down he shook a cigarette out of a pack.

Dima gave them the essentials of what had happened. Out of deference to Blackburn he skipped the business with Cole.

'But we have a far more urgent situation: it's called Solomon.'

Kroll's lighter paused in mid-air.

'Go ahead and light it. You'll probably need another after what I'm about to tell you.'

They sat in the shade of the camo net while Dima gave them the highlights of Blackburn's story – the beheading, the maps and the remaining nuke in the bank vault. When he had finished, Kroll hung his head.

'I think I'd rather go back to prison,' said Vladimir.

Kroll drew heavily on his cigarette and gave Dima a look. 'I hope that's not your "Anyone for Paris?" face.'

Dima ignored him. 'We don't know how long we've got: put that down as a known unknown. Whether Solomon has his own people already in place there and in New York, just waiting for the nukes to be delivered – that joins a long list of unknown unknowns.'

'Yeah, like who in Moscow tipped off Kaffarov.'

Kroll wasn't one to hide his indignation.

Dima turned to Blackburn.

'I guess this is the moment you decide what you're going to do.'

Blackburn looked pale, still stunned by the events of the last half hour. Eventually he spoke.

'There's only one choice. I have to get back to my company.'

'What condition was the chalet in when you left?' Dima asked.

Kroll made a tumbling gesture with his hands.

'They backed off after the rest of the front collapsed. Don't think anyone's going back in there.'

Blackburn and Dima exchanged a look. Blackburn set the water bottle down.

'Guess it's time.'

Vladimir turned to Dima. 'And that's not a problem for us? We don't want the US Army on our tail.'

They all looked at Dima. Blackburn could go back to his superiors with a version of what had just happened and they could come right after them.

It was Blackburn who broke the silence, suddenly calm and resolute. He addressed Kroll and Vladimir. 'Your comrade saved my life today. And he witnessed something that would put me behind bars for the rest of my life. We have a mutual interest in each other's survival.'

Dima turned to Blackburn, who had got to his feet.

'Sure you wouldn't rather stick with us?'

It was the first time he'd seen a smile on Blackburn's face. Suddenly he looked much younger.

'I'm flattered by your offer, Dima. But I think I might cramp your style.'

Dima looked at the track that led up to the cleft between the two mountains.

'Well, would you like us to see you to the top?'

'I think I better do this one alone – should an Osprey show up.'

Dima shook his hand. 'One question, if it's not too personal. How old are you?'

'I think we're well past that point. Twenty-five next Thanks-giving.'

Twenty-five years since Paris, Dima thought. The young man in the photograph – they would be the same age.

'You mind how you go, Sergeant Blackburn.'

Blackburn saluted him then shook hands with the others. The three of them watched the young Marine until he was not much more than a speck on the mountainside.

Eventually Kroll broke the silence.

'Are you going to tell us just what the fuck that was all about?'

55

Kroll drove, Vladimir drank, Dima slept: the three of them side-by-side on the bench seat up front. Amara, still fast asleep, had the whole of the back seat to herself. After what she had been through in the last twenty-four hours, no one was going to move her. It was hot and sticky inside the Land Cruiser. They kept the air conditioning off to save fuel but even with the windows open the humid night air that gushed in seemed to have retained the previous day's heat.

Dima slept fitfully. Too frequently he was jolted back to consciousness by a pothole, or Kroll swerving to avoid stray cattle or lumps of rubble from the quake. And when he did sleep his dreams were disturbing, weirdly edited versions of scenes replayed from the last twenty-four hours. He knew it was inevitable that his brain had to process it all, but that didn't make it any less unpleasant. Yin and Yang, Kaffarov and Cole, each made an appearance, re-enacting their roles, each time with different outcomes. He felt Yin's grip as he held him underwater, unrelenting and strong as iron, until he felt the life ebbing from him. That woke him up. Then Blackburn was there again, not reacting this time, and Cole's gun exploded in Dima's face, blinding him with a fatal white flash.

Then more distant memories floated back into view. Solomon, when Dima first met him – still a teenager, but with that look he recognised from boy soldiers in Africa, of having seen too much, too soon. His brooding, heavy brow, high cheekbones, olive skin: the calculating eyes that were never still. The brilliant fearless teenager with no past and no name he could call his own. Dima wondered if he had ever found out who he really was. He knew it troubled him not knowing.

'How can I choose whose side to be on?' he had said, when the boy inside him was still alive, before it had been extinguished by hate.

'You're on your own side,' Dima had replied, struggling to find him some consolation. 'Fight for yourself: you are your own cause.'

More than any other, this was the one piece of Dima's advice Solomon had taken to heart – if he had such a thing as a heart. As Solomon's trainer and then his handler, Dima had made an effort to befriend him, to establish trust, but Solomon was having none of it. Friendship, he said, was a weakness and a distraction: the first real sign that he was shedding his humanity, like a creature remaking itself. He took himself so seriously that some of his peers teased him. They soon regretted it. He seldom lost his temper but could extract the energy from his own anger, like a solar panel absorbs the sun, storing it for later use. And that could come at any time in the future – three days, three weeks, even years later. Nothing gave Solomon more pleasure than watching the dismay build on a victim's face as it gradually dawned on them why they were being punished. He was brilliant at deception. His mastery of languages, his gift of mimicry, bettered even Dima's, and the terrorist cells he was sent to infiltrate were invariably won over by his willingness to undertake whatever initiation rite was demanded to prove his loyalty, no matter how brutal. He was a chilling adversary. And one Dima had not expected to face – until now.

They kept to the mountains until they were well clear of the Americans, then dropped down to the Tehran–Tabriz road they had taken two days before. Apart from several vehicles abandoned during the exodus from Tehran, it was deserted. They came across a bus that had come off the road and slid down a bank. But there was no sign of the passengers, or the rest of the multitude who had left their homes and livelihoods behind in the shattered capital.

At Miyaneh, southeast of Tabriz, Kroll said,

'We're almost out of juice.'

It was three a.m.

'I guess the fun had to end sometime,' said Dima. 'They've got gas coming out of their ears in these bloody places, but can you find any when you need it?'

The entire town was shuttered, but a vast impromptu camp had sprung up in the parking lot of a shopping mall, with hundreds sleeping in their cars. They woke a few of them up and offered cash for whatever was left in their tanks, but all swore they were as good as empty. They sputtered on a little further, then the tank ran dry. They found a plastic can in the trunk, and leaving Kroll with Amara, Vladimir and Dima walked on until they came to a gas station.

'Nice and quiet,' said Vladimir.

But they were not alone. A gang of raw-looking PLR recruits appeared out of the shadows and raised their AKs. One look at them and you could see the lack of experience, the volatile combination of fear and the lack of impulse control.

'You'd think just one thing could be straightforward, wouldn't you,' said Dima as he identified the leader, a jittery youth in cheap Adidas knock-offs and a red and white scarf round his face. He must have copied his look from an Al Qaeda training video.

'No gas!' they shouted, firing their weapons in the air.

Then why guard it, if there was nothing to guard?

'Hi lads,' said Vladimir. 'Just going to fill up, then be on our way.' He held up the can and waggled it.

'Come on, grandad, if you want some!' shouted one.

'Let's cut his prick off: he won't be needing it,' said another.

'The youth of today really are growing up too fast,' said Dima.

'Bollocks to this,' said Vladimir.

Somewhat the worse for the dodgy Azerbaijani vodka he'd found in the Land Cruiser, he lifted his Makarov and fired upwards, hitting the leader in the arm.

'Was that your idea of a warning shot?' said Dima.

'You know I shoot better when I'm drunk.'

The youths fled and they pushed the Land Cruiser the last few metres, Amara still snoring peacefully as they filled up.

As they pulled back on to the Tabriz road, Dima called Darwish. At least he had good news for someone: his daughter was okay and was coming home, and her evil husband was no more. Which was about the sum total of their achievements over the last forty-eight hours.

Darwish took a long time to answer. When he did he sounded bleary. It was five a.m, after all.

'*Your little girl is on her way back to you.*'

That woke him up. For a few seconds he didn't speak. Then he said,

'*I am forever in your debt.*'

'*Story of your life. Where are you?*'

'*I must make arrangements. I shall call you right back.*'

Five minutes passed. Dima's phone rang.

'*Okay. I am taking Anara away for a few days. I need to give her a break after her ordeal.*' Darwish gave him details of an airstrip outside Tabriz. '*How long till you are there?*'

Dima glanced at the map.

'*About an hour.*'

'*And is my Anara truly okay?*'

'*Truly,*' said Dima. '*Are you all right?*'

'*Yes, yes: just tired.*'

56

Blackburn made it to the apex of the ridge which separated the valley to the north and the Tehran basin to the south. All the way up they had watched him go. He looked back for the last time at the now almost invisible Russians and hesitated.

There are points in your life, he thought, where one decision changes the whole course of it. Enlisting had been one. He could have stayed home, gone to grad school, got a job and settled down, maybe even married Charlene. But that decision now seemed insignificant compared to the one he had made an hour ago. He had shot and killed his own CO, an unimaginable act. How had he come to that? Had he let his emotions get the better of him, going against all his training, or was he standing up for what was right? He had prevented Cole from killing Dima after all, and in cold blood. He had killed his superior officer to save the life of a man he had known for less than two hours. An enemy combatant who had saved him only moments before.

And what really counted now was what Dima Mayakovsky had told him about Solomon. What it added up to – the consequences for the world – were too terrifying to contemplate.

Could Dima and his rough band of brothers stop a nuclear apocalypse? Would anyone believe Blackburn if he told them New York was a target? His own authorities seemed determined to mistrust him, to ascribe the worst possible motives to whatever he did. If he looked honestly deep into himself, he was glad there'd been a reason to kill Cole.

Standing on the ridge, he took one last look into the northern valley. By now Dima and his men were just specks. Were they still watching him? He couldn't tell. Then he turned to the south where

Tehran, the ruined city, stretched out in the distance. And much nearer, the chalet and his comrades – what was left of them.

He was fantastically tired, hungry and thirsty, the afternoon sun sucking up all his moisture and energy. He kept moving, one foot in front of the other, until he eventually dropped down off the mountain and what was visible of the front of the chalet. Which wasn't much at all. As he approached, he felt as though he was going back to the beginning of the day, to when he was a different man. Would they be able to tell?

'Well, will you look at that!' Montes ran forward.

Blackburn looked at him as an alien might look on his first human. He embraced his old buddy, but it was as if their entire shared past had been erased by what had happened in the bunker. All their reminiscing about home, the banter and the horseplay, their sharing of their plans for the future when they got out, all gone – vanished under the rubble and the secret buried beneath. He could tell no one about Cole.

Looking at Montes, Blackburn knew then that he would never be the same. He had enlisted in a bid to get closer to understanding his father and the great weight he carried around with him after Vietnam. But Blackburn had got something else he never bargained for: his own terrible burden.

Matkovic came towards them.

'Man, we so thought you were gone.'

'So did I,' said Blackburn.

'You know what happened to Cole?'

Just like that. This would be the question that would haunt him from now onwards. He knew it would be put to him a hundred times more to come. Eyes watching him as he gave his response. He knew then that the idea that they would take him at his word and that somehow it would never be investigated, was hopeless.

The site around the chalet was being cleared. The casualties from the crash-landed Osprey had all been Medevac'd. The place was crawling with recovery crew. A requisitioned excavator was clawing at the rubble.

'Over here, Blackburn! We need your help.'

Over the hood of a Humvee, Major Johnson, Cole's CO, spread out a copy of the chalet plans Blackburn had seen at Firefly. 'Got to figure out where Lieutenant Cole could be.'

Blackburn hadn't expected this.

'Sir, he's dead.'

The Major looked up and frowned.

'How do you know that Sergeant? He could be in an air pocket for all we know.'

Johnson smoothed out the plans. Blackburn knew exactly where Cole was, in the area between the pool and the room with the screens.

'Sir, the collapse was comprehensive.'

He drew a circle with his finger all round the area of the pool.

The Major stared at the plans.

'How come you got out then, soldier?'

He pointed at the two narrow lines that ran from the back of the bunker.

'Seeing that my entry point had collapsed, Sir, I had already made my way to the rear, to this escape tunnel.'

'And where was Lieutenant Cole?'

This is it, thought Blackburn. The answer that decides the rest of my life. Before, he had thought of himself as an honourable man. What, now, did that mean?

'I don't know, Sir. The whole thing was coming down, so I just got out.'

The Major rubbed his chin.

'Well, I'm not gonna be writing his mother saying we left him there.'

He stared at the plans for a few more moments then looked back up at Blackburn.

'I'm shipping you back to Spartacus. You're pretty banged up, kid. They'll take your report there.'

It was a long time since anyone had called him kid. It certainly hadn't been in Cole's vocabulary. He wanted to say out loud right then. *Know what, Sir? Cole was a bastard and a bully and he was going to die one way or another*. He was glad he didn't. It wouldn't have come out right.

He saw Campo coming towards them. Blackburn detached himself from the group forming around the Major. Campo just stared. No greeting, no brotherly thump on the back: just standing, looking at Blackburn like he'd seen a ghost.

'Oh, man. This is too weird.' Campo nodded at the remains of the chalet. 'It was a real mess in there. And you walk right out.'

Blackburn felt he deserved an explanation, or part of one.

'The tunnel out the back of the bunker. We saw it on the plan, remember?'

Campo shook his head.

'Man you're something else. Your radio goes dead. We hear some big rock fall. Cole goes in. You come out . . .'

'I was lucky. Guess you were too.'

'Yeah, maybe,' said Campo, doubtfully.

They walked further away from the Major. Campo pulled out a flattened pack of cigarettes, shook one out, lit it, drew heavily and blew out a long plume of smoke.

'And you didn't see him at all?'

'In the bunker? No, why?'

Campo shrugged.

'Just askin'.'

Blackburn shook his head.

'What?'

'Because after Cole went in, I called for a sitrep and couldn't raise him on the radio . . .'

'And? It was all coming down in there, you know, like a landslide.'

'Well there was this thud, like a muffled shot, not like some shit falling or anything.'

'I didn't hear anything like that,' said Blackburn.

Campo said nothing, but just kicked at the dirt with his boot.

So this is how it's going to be, thought Blackburn. He had never felt so alone.

57

'We have a problem.'

'Wow. What could that be like?' Kroll's cynicism was working overtime.

'Darwish's tone, the arrangement. Plus he called her A*n*ara. Twice.'

'He's under a lot of stress.'

They both knew it was something else altogether. That he wasn't the sort of man to make a careless mistake, let alone about a member of his own family. Maybe he was being watched so closely that all he could do was mispronounce his own daughter's name – a slip so small that whoever was in the room with him wouldn't notice, but which he knew Dima would pick up straight away. He hoped the bleariness was nerves, nothing worse. Had he put the phone down so he could receive instructions from his captors? It sounded like a trap – unsubtle, inelegant and typical of the way certain people operated. Exactly which people they couldn't say, yet.

'He said he's taking her away – from an airstrip? Where to?'

'Maybe to his family.'

'They're all either dead or still here. This doesn't smell right.'

'Great,' said Kroll as they pulled back on to the road. 'And you're going to want to rescue him.'

Amara stirred from her deep sleep. Her eyes opened, closed and opened again, suddenly widening as she focused on Dima's face. Lit by nothing more than the car's interior light he did look a bit like a ghost.

'I thought you were dead.'

'I'm indestructible.'

She frowned, puzzled, then flinched with pain.

234

'Where are we?'

'Not far from home. I spoke to your father. He's expecting us.'

Now she was upright he nodded at the space beside her. Kroll came to a stop so Dima could climb into the back. For several minutes they drove on in silence. He glanced at Amara, her whole life turned upside down by them.

'I'm sorry about Gazul. After all, he was your—.'

She held up a hand, took in a deep breath and let it out slowly, then shook her head.

'It was a mistake. Don't ever tell my father I said this: he was right about him.'

'You helped us so much – taking us to the chalet.'

She looked down.

'Kristen's dead, isn't she?'

'Sorry. Along with my two comrades.'

'Such a strange job you have. I bet you don't have a wife or family.'

There was a pause before he answered that one. 'It's better that way,' he said, thinking of the life he had once imagined with Camille.

'You know, in Iran for a young widow, it's not good. Do you think I could find work in Moscow? I heard there's plenty of work in Moscow for young women.'

'Not the sort your father would approve of.'

'You're as bad as him. Now you see why I had to get away.'

58

They stopped about half a kilometre away from the airstrip and parked behind a storage shed.

'You stay with Amara in the vehicle,' Dima said to Kroll. 'While we check this out.'

Dima and Vladimir crossed a field of aubergines to the perimeter fence.

'What do you reckon?' Vladimir gave Dima the binoculars.

'Can't see Darwish – or anyone.'

There was a single hangar, a few sheds and a mast with a windsock at the top, hanging limp in the static night air. Parked in front of a makeshift terminal were a couple of Fokker F-27s belonging to a small regional airline and a very clean Kamov Ka-266 helicopter with no markings.

'Look at that. No ID of any kind.'

'Nice people always have numbers on their choppers.'

'Whoever they are they knew we were coming all right,' said Vladimir. 'But who told them? Darwish?'

'Never.'

'He was trying to warn us though.'

'Well, who then?'

Dima had a ghost of a suspicion, buried at the back of his mind, which he kept to himself. He was still burying it when they were suddenly dazzled by an enormous spotlight from inside the hangar.

'Shit!'

They sprinted back across the field towards the Land Cruiser. They were almost on it when they realised it was surrounded.

'Drop your weapons. On the ground!'

236

Dima couldn't think of a better idea so they first dropped the guns and then themselves. The road smelled faintly of oil and animal shit. He tried to get a glimpse of the two armed figures running towards them but they had face masks on.

'Face down.'

One of them swung his boot against Dima's temple as he rolled over trying to see the Land Cruiser. They pulled his hands behind his back and bound his wrists with zip cuffs.

'Face down!'

'I think there's been a bit of a misunderstanding,' said Dima. 'If you'd just let me explain—.'

Another boot in his ribs put paid to the rest of the sentence. A GAZ jeep zoomed towards them from the airstrip and slewed to a halt beside them. Two more men got out and grabbed Dima and Vladimir while the boot man jumped round the Land Cruiser, shoved Kroll on to the passenger seat and got behind the wheel.

'Someone really, really doesn't like us,' said Vladimir.

They drove in convoy to the small terminal. Two more men who had been lounging against the chopper now came towards them: black pants and T-shirts under black jackets, PP-2000 submachine guns dangling from their hands – and a look of triumph on their faces.

Vladimir turned to Dima.

'Do you think we should tell them they look like James Bond extras?'

'Depressing isn't it? So unoriginal.'

'I'm bored with Russians being the bad guys all the time. But hey, if they are the bad guys, doesn't that make us the good guys?'

'Good point.'

'Shut the fuck up, you stupid prick,' said the shorter of the two. His cheeks were pockmarked from bad adolescent acne and his eyes were red-rimmed from too many late nights. He was the marginally less hideous looking of the two, which wasn't saying much, with an 'all the girls want to fuck me' smirk.

In your dreams, thought Dima.

'Are we going for a ride in the helicopter? I can't wait to see the hollowed-out volcano,' said Vladimir.

The taller one, who reminded Dima of a weasel he'd seen in a cartoon film, pulled out his brand new Grach police issue pistol and smashed the grip against Vladimir's cheek.

'They also fire bullets through the pointy end,' said Vladimir. 'Want me to show you?'

'Shut it,' said Weasel, 'before I smash every bone in your body.'

The two men in masks pulled Kroll from the Land Cruiser. Where the fuck was Amara? The three of them were marched into the terminal building, where they watched as the jeep men eviscerated the Land Cruiser. One took out the spare wheel, slashed the lining of the rear compartment and peered into the corners. The other one looked under the hood, then tore off the door trim and even ripped out the headlining.

'I get it,' said Vladimir. 'It's a drug bust!'

'Unless it's the ultra portable WMDs they're hoping for,' Dima replied.

'What, the ones I swallowed?' said Kroll.

'Seriously, they don't really think *we* have them?'

The search seemed not to be producing results. Weasel waved the search party back to the jeep and took several determined steps towards Dima, finishing with his face almost touching his.

'Suppose you stop trying to be clever, and just tell us what you've done with them.'

'The snacks? We finished them on the way. Is the airport café not open yet?'

Dima looked at Kroll: his expression was now unreadable. Where *was* Amara?

Dima heard a door open behind them: two more men in black. Beside him, head bowed and bloody was Darwish. He was half frogmarched, half dragged to a table and dropped into a chair.

Darwish's face was almost unrecognisable. The flesh around his eyes was so battered and swollen his eyelids were just bloody slits.

His nose had been broken and his lips were split and oozing. A clotted icicle of blood and saliva hung from his chin.

'Hold up your hand: splay your fingers.'

Darwish, utterly defeated, complied.

Weasel turned to Vladimir. 'You want to see how accurate the Grach is? Watch.' He fired. Darwish's hand flew back, knocking him off the chair.

'Not really much of a challenge,' said Dima. 'A real man gives his opponent a fair chance.'

'Get up you fuck,' ordered the third man. He was bigger than Weasel and very bald.

'Any more jokes?' he demanded. 'Or shall we just get to the bombs?'

'Sure. They're on their way to Paris and New York, with a former Spetsnaz non-national, codename Solomon or Suleiman, depending which side he chooses to be on. They came from the late Amir Kaffarov, purveyor of Russian arms to the highest bidder. How do I know he's dead? Because he died in my arms. Of a heart attack, oddly enough.'

'Can't you do better than that? You sold them on obviously. Oh, did I forget to say? You're under arrest for illegal arms trading.'

Dima, surging with rage, could feel the zip cuff cutting into his wrists.

'Then I have the right to remain silent.'

'You have the right to *fuck all.*'

He turned to Darwish who was clutching the bloody stump of what was left of his thumb.

'Your pal Mayakovsky's not playing ball. Put your other hand up.'

Darwish was shaking, tears running from his blood-rimmed eye slits, as the shot rang out.

They all looked round. The left half of Weasel's head had dissolved into a sticky shower of blood and brain. Dima lunged for the PP-2000 on Weasel's shoulder and took out Shorty with two short, sharp bursts of fire. Baldy scurried away through the rear of the terminal in a hail of fire from Vladimir, who had grabbed Shorty's gun as he fell. Vladimir kept on after him while Dima and Kroll raced for positions to take out the GAZ boys, who were leaping out of its four doors. Only then did he catch sight of Amara, gun still frozen in her firing stance. She let the gun fall and ran to her father.

'Back at the Land Cruiser while we were waiting for you, she went for a pee,' said Kroll. 'I gave her the Makarov, just in case.'

The Land Cruiser erupted in a ball of flame, the victim of an unhelpful round from one of the falling GAZ men. A second later the jeep exploded. Dima ran back to Amara, who was gingerly embracing her injured father.

'The chopper. Just try and get there. Kroll will cover you.'

He yelled to Kroll and pointed at them as he ran back to the chopper, detouring to one of the downed GAZ guys to scoop up his AK. How long since he had piloted a helicopter? Like carrying a tray of water, he'd complained to an instructor. Don't think about it, just do it. This one looked brand new. Showroom condition. First problem: the doors were locked. No time to figure that out. A carefully aimed shot blew a huge chunk off the door where the handle was. He levered himself in. Jesus, it all looked so unfamiliar. Okay, just concentrate ...

Collective control left of the seat, like a handbrake, the one that made it go up and down. Leave down. Cyclic control, the stick in front, unlocked. Master fuel valve in. Electrics on. Transmission light, check, clutch light, check. Fuel cut-off out – or was it in to start? Try with it in. Throttle twist grip on the end of the collective – half open. Fuel boost on. Starter. Dima pushed the switch forward. Fuck – nothing. He went through the routine again. Fuel cut-off out. Fuel boost off this time. He could see Amara struggling across the apron with her father. Opened the throttle wider. Engine starter again. Another explosion outside. A big ball of flame from the back of the terminal. What the fuck was that? Not Vladimir. Where are you Vladimir? Heard the whine of the rotor shafts – then nothing. Kroll had two AKs, firing both at once from each hip. Good old Kroll.

He tried the starter again. Better hope it's not flooded. *It's not a car, dickhead!* He shut the throttle, tried the starter one more time. *Do it, you piece of Russian shit.* The engine whistled into life and the rotors started painfully slowly. What are you, a fucking hour hand on a clock? He twisted the throttle wide open and the revs climbed to two thousand. The rotors whipped the air, flapping the broken door. He reached back and slid the rear door open so the rest could climb in more easily. Kroll was working his way towards him, his back to the chopper, still firing, covering Amara and Darwish as they converged under the rotors. No Vladimir.

He could feel the blades grabbing at the air, ready to fly. Dima pulled on the collective, depressing the right pedal to counteract the torque generated by increasing the pitch of the blades. Just like riding a bicycle – except so not. Nonetheless, he gave himself a mental pat on the back for remembering. He kept pulling on the collective until the chopper started to feel lighter on its skids and turn. More pedal to keep it straight.

Darwish, his remaining strength gone, slumped against the open door. Kroll helped Amara load him in. Come on, Vladimir. Out from beside the hangar, a limping figure approached. Dima prodded Kroll.

'Help him.'

Vladimir was dragging an injured left foot. Kroll dropped back on to the ground and with difficulty scooped him into the chopper. As soon as they were airborne, Dima shoved the stick forward – too much – so the nose tipped as if it had tripped on its own skids. He pulled back again – too much – and they lurched back. *Fly with pressures not movements*, he remembered his instructor shouting. He found level but then they lurched to the left. As the broken door swung open there was one of the masked men gripping the skid.

'Got a message for your commander, when you've scraped him off the ground. Hands are very delicate things, and thumbs indispensable.'

Gripping the stick between his knees (definitely not in the manual) Dima lifted the PP-2000 and fired a round into the man's left hand. The hand vanished. But he was still there. Dima fired into his right hand and he was gone.

At fifteen knots he felt the shudder that told him they had passed through ETL into full forward flight. Time to ease off the collective and lose pedal pressure but force the cyclic forward. Dima felt a surge of relief as the chopper powered forward and climbed into the sky.

'Now: which way's Russia?'

59

The Osprey back to Spartacus smelled of aviation fuel, medicine and vomit. The casualties were strapped down on stretchers, slotted into the framework of the hold to form bunks. The walls were draped with tubes. The medics were in the small folding jump seats that lined the sides of the hold, where they could check on their patients and adjust the drips hooked up to the overhead bars. Once in the air they paced the aisle in their beige overalls and blue plastic gloves, like mechanics with unusually gentle hands. One or two of those men weren't going to make it. Blackburn thought of Cole, under the rubble, with his bullet in him. This wasn't even friendly fire, it was vengeance.

Blackburn was on a jump seat at the back beside Ableson, a young staff officer on Major Johnson's team. Ableson was one of those thin, clever ones who fought their war from behind a laptop screen. He said nothing at all to Blackburn the whole two hour flight, which was fine with Blackburn. Eventually he noticed a spare stretcher and asked Ableson if he could use it.

He went straight to sleep, and dreamed that he was a kid again in his own bed, sick and hot but feeling safe, his mother smiling, coming in with French toast and hot milk. *'There's a nuke headed for New York, Mom,'* he said. *'We gotta stop it.'* She put a finger to her lips, still smiling. *'Hush now. Eat.'*

When they landed at Spartacus it was night. He offered to help unload the casualties, but Ableson hustled him away. After the camp outside Tehran, Spartacus felt like a giant military city teeming with personnel and kit. A place that a week ago had been almost like home was a hostile environment now.

'I need to get cleaned up,' he said to Ableson.

'Later: they're waiting for you. Need something to eat?'

Blackburn instinctively turned towards the canteen but Abelson steered him away.

'I'll bring you something.'

He escorted Blackburn to an unmarked Portakabin.

Somehow he needed to get the message across about Solomon.

Inside, waiting for him: Dershowitz and Andrews. Blackburn's heart couldn't sink much further but it managed a few more inches. Dershowitz was peering at his laptop and Andrews had a cell phone pressed to his ear. They were as he had left them, as if they had been waiting there for him the whole time, waiting to take him down. His own private apocalypse.

60

FOB Spartacus, Iraqi Kurdistan

Dershowitz glanced up at him and frowned.

'You look like you need to clean up a little, kid.'

'I was told to come straight here. And if it's all the same to you, Sir, could you refer to me by name? I'm Sergeant Blackburn.'

'Sure, kid,' he smirked.

Andrews pocketed his cell.

'Okay. So talk us through your day.'

'Bad day at Black Rock, huh?' said Dershowitz.

'What?'

Blackburn wasn't sure what that was a reference to, but it wasn't good.

'And if it's all the same to *you*, kid, you can call me *Sir*, when you answer.' Dershowitz slammed the table hard with the flat of his hand as he said 'Sir'.

'Yes, Sir. Sorry, Sir.'

Andrews looked as though he was suppressing a bad case of wind.

'Just go from the top.'

He described the scene when he got out of the Osprey, climbing the avalanche of rubble from the shelled chalet and finding the door that led into the rear bunker.

'Whoa. Hold up,' said Andrews, making a stop sign with his hand. 'Need to get a handle on your motivations. You took yourself off pretty fast into that wrecked building. That not a little reckless?'

He looked down and began typing furiously.

'The conditions were such that it appeared the building might have contained an HVT and was liable to cave in.'

'So in you went.' Andrews with his smile again. 'And was anybody home?'

They wanted detail. He gave it to them.

'Sir, there were three fatalities. All recently deceased. One on the first floor of the house and two in the bunker, one of whom was in the pool, the other at the side. I concluded they had been struck by falling masonry during the bombardment.'

Dershowitz spoke without looking up.

'So now you're a pathologist. Lot of strings to your bow, Blackburn.'

'Let's talk about Lieutenant Cole. What happened?' asked Andrews.

He looked from one to the other.

'It's a simple question.'

He decided to focus on Dershowitz, the more aggressive of the two. These men listened to liars for a living. Simple question. Simple answer.

'I don't know what happened to him, Sir. There was a further collapse. I figured my best chance was to find the escape passage I had seen on the plans.'

Dershowitz smiled. Blackburn didn't know which was worse, his smile or his stony silence. The smile with the silence wasn't much fun either.

Ableson knocked and entered without waiting. He was carrying a Coke and a burger wrapped in waxed paper.

'Get the fuck out. Can't you see we're busy here?'

Blackburn almost felt relieved that he wasn't the only focus of Dershowitz's ire.

'Tell me about Cole.'

'What about him, Sir?'

Dershowitz frowned.

'What's that supposed to mean, "What about him"? He's your CO for fuck's sake. Don't you give a shit?'

He picked up a waste bin and swept the Coke and burger into it.

Blackburn could feel the anger exploding inside him. He refused to give them the satisfaction of showing it. He had to stay in control. His head was pulsing with pain. He was by nature a truth teller. His mother always praised him for this, regardless of the misdemeanour.

'*Well, Henry, I'm not pleased with what you've done but it's good that you have owned up.*'

'Your buddy Campo says he lost radio contact with you after you entered the bunker. He says he reported it to your commanding officer and that he, Lieutenant Cole, bravely decided to attempt to rescue you.'

'There was a fall in the front of the chalet shortly after I lost contact with Campo, Sir. It was at that point that I decided that it was neither safe nor possible for me to go back the way I came and so I resolved to find an alternative exit, based on my reading of the plans we were supplied with.'

They stared at him blankly. Blackburn gave a shrug.

'I had found the WMD in the bank in Tehran along with evidence suggesting two more. We had intel suggesting the chalet was a possible location – I wanted to finish the job I started in the bank.'

'This isn't a job interview, kid. Enough with the self-regarding rhetoric. Your CO died trying to rescue you.'

Rescue you. . . . Like fuck. But what could he say?

None of them said anything for several seconds.

Why are you so suspicious of me? Blackburn wanted to ask. What have I done that is so wrong? And the answer came straight back. You have killed your superior officer. That's about as bad as it gets.

'Sir, the last time we spoke I told you about Solomon. That was the name on Bashir's lips when he died. And as it's the only clue we have about the remaining two nukes, I have reason to believe that we should take that name very seriously. May I remind you about the maps I found in the bank vault, of Paris, and New York?'

Neither of them were listening. Andrews had been studying his laptop. He gestured at Dershowitz and they both stared at the screen. Suddenly his face brightened.

'Ah, there you go.'

He angled it in Dershowitz's direction, whose eyes widened so much they looked as if they were about to pop out of their sockets.

'Blackburn, you are so fucked.'

61

Northern Iran Airspace

Kroll sat up front beside Dima. In the back, Vladimir raided the police helicopter's first aid kit and set about attending to Darwish, who was laid out on the floor of the rear compartment.

'We could really do with some blood. Anyone?'

He crashed against the bulkhead as Dima threw the chopper into a tight left.

'Sorry everyone. Power lines.'

Kroll gripped the sides of his seat with white knuckles.

'When did you last fly one of these?'

'You want to drive?'

'You know I hate these things.'

'Do something useful. I want to talk to Omorova.'

'Well, if you've got a hard on, it'll have to wait.'

Dima dictated the private number she had used last time they spoke. When Kroll got a line he patched her into Dima's headset.

Her voice had the same sleepy quality as last time.

'Do you always have to call in the middle of the night? It's getting to be a habit.'

'It's when I seem to miss you most. I'll work on it.'

'What's all that noise?'

'A helicopter I borrowed.'

'You're going up in the world. How's the mission going?'

'Terrible. Kaffarov's dead. The nukes are AWOL. Some goons tried to ambush us.'

'There's an alert out for you. You'll enjoy this – "wanted in connection with the trafficking of nuclear weapons".'

He heaved on the stick to clear another power line, his brain trying to compute what he was hearing.

'*So why are you talking to me? Doesn't sound like a good career move.*'

She sighed rather attractively.

'*My career's going nowhere. Everyone on the operation's been sidelined.*'

'*I have to see Paliov.*'

'*He's been put under house arrest. I'd stay out of Moscow airspace if I were you.*'

'*Just tell me where he is. And I need as much as you can glean on an ex-Spetsnaz CIA asset lately allied to the PLR, name Solomon aka Suleiman. Please?*'

'*I need to get back to sleep.*'

'*Would you believe me if I said the future of the world depends on it?*'

'*Okay, okay. Call me later.*'

She hung up.

Vladimir leaned over Dima's seat and lifted one of his cans.

'Darwish has gone. I'm sorry.'

How in God's name do we tell Amara, thought Dima, but he followed Vladimir's gaze: she was bent over her father's body, silently weeping.

62

As well as keeping clear of power lines, Dima had a lot on his mind as he flew north. The thrill of lifting the goons' own chopper had ebbed away as he digested the news about Darwish. His death rekindled his determination for some kind of payback. Darwish must not have died in vain: that much at least he owed his old friend. What Omorova had told him meant that the sense of freedom the helicopter offered was temporary. In the air he was a target. He needed to get out of the sky, and into something else that would get him back into Moscow unnoticed. Kroll had overheard the conversation on his headset. He knew what they were up against.

'So now we're outlaws. Guess we can say bye-bye to any remuneration for this jaunt.'

Dima braced himself for a volley of Kroll moaning.

'I never said it would be straightforward.'

'I was hoping to take the kids to Eurodisney.'

'Yeah, right. Their mothers won't even open the door to you.'

'They could have come too. I had it all worked out.'

The slow motion car crash that was Kroll's personal life was the last thing Dima needed to hear about right now.

'When you quit moaning, got any ideas?'

Kroll's face brightened.

'Well, this chopper's worth a bit. We could trade it.'

'Hilarious.'

'I'm serious. Bilasuvar. Its only fifty odd ks across the Azeri border. By the time anyone's noticed us we'll be out of the sky.'

That's what Dima loved about Kroll. Always ready with the least likely solution to a problem.

Bilasuvar. In Soviet times it had been a graveyard for air force hardware so old, useless or obsolete it couldn't be persuaded to stay in the sky. Since Azerbaijan had got its independence, it had become a major centre for spare parts and aluminium recycling. It also did a roaring trade in aircraft of dubious provenance.

It was a long shot, but it was all they had.

The sky was lightening in the east as they crossed the border. Dima stayed low to keep off anyone's radar. His mind wandered to Blackburn. The US Military were bound to want to know what happened to Cole. How much would he tell them? How much would they believe? Would he be handed over to the CIA? For Darwish, for Blackburn and for himself, stopping Solomon was the only option, if it wasn't already too late.

'Will you look at that?'

Kroll was suddenly a kid again, revitalised by the sight of a cornucopia of Cold War hardware. Surrounded by a flock of Mil helicopters of all types were half a dozen Tupolev-95 'Bears', that would have spent their lives annoying NATO up and down the North Sea, and maybe as many as twenty MiG-15s, the first Soviet jet fighter with Rolls Royce-inspired engines. How considerate of the Brits to share their knowhow. Dima felt the mixed messages of Soviet nostalgia. In retrospect he knew the Soviet Union was fucked, but it seemed like a good idea at the time.

'Surely with that lot we really ought to have won the Cold War,' said Kroll, peering at the graveyard below.

'We did: it was just the wrong "we".'

'Well, let's hope they've got some decent wheels down there.'

Dima put the Kamov down in a gap between some corrugated iron sheds and a giant wingless Ilyushin Il-76 transporter. A gang of labourers were slicing at the fuselage with chainsaws, like ants consuming some huge prey. Three men wearing tattoos and oil-stained overalls emerged from the sheds, with AKs at the ready, one prominently out in front.

'Jesus,' said Kroll. 'Get a load of this.'

'I've had warmer welcomes.'

Devoid of government markings and battle scarred as it was, the shiny new Kamov still reeked of officialdom.

'Turn round and fuck off back to Moscow unless you want a bullet in the bollocks!' yelled the largest of the three, an unlit cheroot flapping between his brown teeth.

'Maybe Mad Max here thinks we're from the tax office.'

Dima and Kroll lowered themselves slowly on to the ground, hands raised. A cocktail of rust, engine oil and unwashed bodies wafted in through the gap where Dima had shot off the door.

'Mmm-hmh!' Kroll inhaled appreciatively.

'It smells a lot better than that car you live in,' said Dima.

'We're just passing through,' said Kroll, 'and we wondered if—.'

'Shut up and stand over there.'

Dima nudged Kroll as they went.

'They don't call it the Wild East for nothing'.

63

Mad Max looked them up and down, taking in Dima's torn and blood-spattered shirt.

'Who the fuck are you?'

'Doesn't matter. We're looking for a trade,' said Dima neutrally.

Surrounded by the rusting hulks in various stages of dismemberment, the shiny Kamov looked entirely alien. Some of the crew chipping away at the Ilyushin switched off their chainsaws.

'Very funny. Do we look like a street market?'

But Max was leering at the chopper as if it was a lapdancer. For all the bluster, his eyes were saying '*Come to me, baby*.'

'We need a change of transport. Something more – grounded. Two fast, reliable vehicles and the Kamov's yours. You'll never get another deal like it.'

At this, one of the others started towards the chopper. Kroll waved a finger.

'Ah-ah. Look, don't touch.'

Max had caught sight of Amara sitting in the rear, looking blank. His eyes widened even further. He circled the chopper, not sure whether he was believing what he was seeing, then took the cheroot out of his mouth and rolled it ruminatively between two oily orange fingers.

Dima glanced at Kroll, who said: 'My sister.'

Max laughed. 'A man can look, can't he?'

'She's very shy: doesn't like to be stared at.'

'It's a hell of a deal,' said Dima. 'You could retire. Get a nice villa somewhere.'

'I live for my work: why would I want to retire?'

Kroll tried another tack.

'The Chechens would kill for one of these.'

'I think you could have put that better,' Dima said.

'Back to fucking work, you useless shites!' yelled Max. The whole place had ground to a halt at the sight of Amara.

Just visible behind the shed was an S-Class Mercedes: metallic blue with contrasting red front fenders. Dima nodded at it.

'Got any more of those?'

'It's my own personal runaround. But – throw in the sister and you've got a deal.'

Amara looked terrified. Max pulled his head back out of the Kamov, which he'd been checking over. He looked at the row of horrified faces and laughed.

'I'm joking, you idiots! Lost your sense of humour or what?'

'Yeah, good one,' said Vladimir.

'I'll take it. And there's a nice Volvo here. Hardly any miles on it.'

'Just one old lady owner, yeah, I know.'

In spite of himself, Dima smiled. Maybe they were going to get out of this okay. They wrapped Darwish in a tarp and loaded him gently into the rear of the Volvo.

'I was hoping to get the Merc,' said Vladimir.

'You're taking Amara and her father home. Then I'm going to need you in Paris.'

Vladimir's eyes widened. 'We're really going to do this?'

Dima shrugged. 'No choice.'

Although it was not yet nine a.m., Max produced a bottle of vodka from an old-fashioned chest freezer.

He poured the fiery liquid into shot glasses with 'A Gift From Chernobyl' embossed on the sides.

'Valuable antiques, those.'

'Bit early for me,' said Dima, 'But it's the thought that counts. None for you: you're driving,' he said to Vladimir.

There was no time to waste. It was two thousand ks to Moscow. Dima took Amara aside.

'You saved our lives back there. And your father gave his for us. If I get through this—.'

Amara put a slender finger against his lips.

'No promises.'

'Did your father say anything before he—?'

She smiled, the tears welling up.

'Just that he was "very proud".'

They embraced briefly and she got in.

'See you in Paris. Be there by tomorrow night.'

Vladimir nodded. 'Adios Amigos.'

Dima turned to Max, who looked as if Christmas had just come early.

'You never saw us, right?'

'Do we look like informers?'

'Sorry, I didn't mean to insult you.'

'No problem. Take care out there. And take these.' He opened a drawer. 'They might come in handy.'

He handed over a set of jump leads.

64

FOB Spartacus, Iraqi Kurdistan

Two MPs stood at the door. What a waste of their time, thought Blackburn. He could barely stand, let alone make a run for it, but they had still shackled his feet. He was a prisoner now, maybe for ever.

Andrews and Dershowitz had been joined by a third man in combats and a Bruce Springsteen T-shirt. He wasn't introduced, but the other two addressed him as Wes. He had brought with him a field laptop with a hi-def screen.

They played the satellite footage for the third time. The full image included the chalet and the tunnel entrance, but each time they played it Wes zoomed in closer. And with each zoom it seemed to get more, not less, clear.

'Okay, let's see them groundhogs pop out one more time.' Wes had a Texan drawl that was full of the wide outdoors, not suited to a stifling Portakabin full of perspiring men. They watched again. First Dima exiting the tunnel, recceing the hill, turning back to the tunnel, beckoning. Then Blackburn, shielding his eyes from the sudden glare. Dima lifted the phone to his ear.

'Left-handed. Interesting.'

The other two glanced at Wes.

'Guys from those parts save their left for when they've taken a shit.'

He fast-forwarded through Dima and Blackburn's walk to the camo-covered remains of the shed.

'Kinda touching they threw that camo over the Land Cruiser, ain't it, like we're gonna miss it.'

All three of them managed to find that quite funny.

The screen zoomed in on Vladimir and Kroll.

'Kinda hesitant, that greeting. Maybe Doofus here's saying "What the fuck ya gone an' dragged out that there tunnel, boy? Looks to me like you gone and got yourself one United States Marine".'

Dima's hands moved rapidly as he responded.

'And Goofy here's probly sayin', "Uh-uh. This here's a traitor to his country. He ain't no US Marine. Fact is, this here fella ain't even human. He's one great big log of dawg do".'

Wes looked up at Blackburn and laughed appreciatively at his own improvisation.

'Sheesh, we sure get some shit to deal with, these days.'

He shook his head at the screen. 'So "Sergeant" Blackburn. You can if you wish remain silent. What good it's going to do you, I ain't rightly sure, since our people will go on analysing these here bird shots till we pretty much know just exactly what you-all are sayin' down there.'

Blackburn's stomach took another lurch. There wasn't much left in it. He hadn't eaten or drunk anything in six hours, but whatever was left he vomited into the waste bin, over the burger and Coke that Dershowitz had dropped in it.

Wes closed the laptop. The other two sat back. Dershowitz picked something out of his nose and examined it.

'It's a crying shame, Sergeant Blackburn,' said Dershowitz. 'All that expensive training, son of Private Michael Blackburn, US Marine and Viet Vet, grandson of Lieutenant George Blackburn, decorated hero of World War Two: good men who gave themselves in service to their country. So what happened Henry? Where'd it all go wrong?'

65

The Road to Moscow

'So nice to be back on terra firma, and in the bosom of Mother Russia,' said Kroll.

Kroll was driving, one hand draped over the wheel, a can of Coke in the other. They were five hundred ks into the drive to Moscow. Another fifteen hundred to go.

'You know, I think these S-Class W220s are my favourite. This or possibly the W126. I didn't much like the one in between – you know the one that Princess Di—.'

Dima reached a hand round and pressed it against his mouth.

'Two things, friend. One: shut up. Two: you'll be taking off for Paris tonight or tomorrow, so don't get too settled. Concentrate on the road and try not to get pulled over by the cops. They see the Azeri plates they'll think we're human traffickers.'

It was time for Dima to make his first call to Paris. Rossin picked up straight away. Dima tried to imagine him at his favourite table in the Café des Artistes in the Marais, a covert roll-up snagged in the cleft of two fingers and his *Paris Match* and the *Economist* spread out in front of him, for the two sides of his personality.

'*Bonjour. C'est Mayakovsky.*'

He thought he heard the sound of a falling coffee cup.

'*I'm sorry, I don't know anyone of that name.*'

'*Don't be a prick, Rossin.*'

He sighed.

'*Your ugly Russian mug is on all the police and security websites. Apparently you've stolen some WMDs and are bent on starting World War Three – mainly for the purpose of shaming Russia.*'

Dima tried to sound dismissive. '*A clerical error. The guilty party is actually an old mutual friend of ours.*'

'*Who?*'

'*You ready for this? Solomon.*'

He expected a silence. The name tended to provoke one.

'*Goodbye, Dima.*'

'*Wait! Hear me out.*'

'*I'm retired.*'

'*You can't afford to retire. None of us can.*'

'*I just did, thirty seconds ago.*'

'*One last favour, for old time's sake. You'll never hear from me again. Promise, on my mother's grave.*'

'*Your mother died in a gulag. She has no grave.*'

'*Just a few shreds of information. A little surveillance. Nothing more.*'

'*Solomon's dead. We all know that.*'

'*We were wrong. He was biding his time. This is his big Fuck-You to the West. So just please hear me out. The target's the Bourse. He'll be most likely using canteen staff or security as cover – maybe cleaners.*'

'*There'll be over a hundred.*'

'*Check them all out.*'

'*How long have I got?*'

'*Twelve hours.*'

'*Ha ha.*'

'*I can pay.*'

After Dima hung up, Kroll said, 'Speaking of pay . . .'

'We weren't.'

'Well, I've been meaning to—.'

'Remember about "Shut up"? I'll remember you in my will.'

'When's that going to happen?'

'Soon. By tonight I'll almost certainly be dead. Now leave me alone while I talk to Omorova again.'

66

Moscow

There was nothing pretty about the Matruska Bathhouse. It had been built in the 1930s with none of the baroque decor that adorned the other two hundred-odd facilities in the city. But even with its brutalist architecture designed to appeal to the commissariat, Stalin's claim, just before it was due to open, that hygiene was a decadent bourgeois obsession, ensured that it remained mothballed for decades. Dima was fond of it, not only because it reminded him of his youth, but because it was almost entirely patronised by immigrants and gypsies. Despite being at the top of the world's 'Most Wanted' list, he stood as good a chance here as anywhere of going unnoticed.

He gave the steam room ten minutes longer than usual to shift the various layers of grime that had accumulated over the last few days. Then he leapt into the cold pool, did forty lengths and emerged a new man, ready to save the world. He shaved, had a hair cut and a manicure and, after slipping on the special set of clothes Kroll had procured, stepped óut into his favourite city.

He had lived in far more places than your average Russian, been a globetrotter – though the term wouldn't have meant anything to most of his comrades – but this was one city he loved more than any other. And he hoped that when the time came, and in his business who knew when that was, that he would die here in Moscow.

The cab took him to the Liberia Bank of Credit and Commerce. They didn't do much in the way of credit, and commerce was somewhat on the back burner too, but they did a nice line in security deposit boxes. And that was where Dima kept his spare life. Passports: EU, Brazilian and Egyptian; Cash: Euros, US Dollars, some Yen; Amex and Visa cards; and a Makarov with enough ammunition for a small skirmish.

The concierge gave him an odd look. But Dima's mind was elsewhere. He went to the desk and asked for access to his box, giving the name Smolenskovitch, a name he only used at this bank. The bank clerk looked uncomfortable, but beckoned him to follow him into the vault. He had a loose sole on his shoe that slapped the carpet as he strutted ahead. He let Dima into the vault and stood at a safe distance while he watched what was about to happen. Having first clocked the security camera, Dima opened his drawer and found – nothing. Not even his spare French birth certificate. He slammed the drawer shut and marched out past the hapless clerk and past the main desk and the concierge, pushing the revolving door so hard that it was still spinning when he reached the pavement.

He felt a blow to his chest and fell straight down. No one said 'Stop' or 'Freeze'. The team leader had decided to shoot on sight, at close range, to avoid other pedestrians. One to the heart. From a GSh-18 pistol, much noisier than the PSS Silent favoured by the Special Forces, but the operator wasn't interested in being discreet. The twenty-odd pedestrians couldn't have missed it.

A female onlooker screamed and screamed, almost blotting out the siren of the unmarked GAZ mid-size van that slewed to a halt beside the body. Though it was all over in a matter of seconds, some wiseass had managed to pull out their cameraphone, capture the incident and upload it on to YouTube before the van was gone. For good measure the phone guy did a separate shot of the pool of blood spread across the forecourt of the Liberia Bank.

Inside the van, the shooter pulled off her mask and shook out her hair.

'I still can't believe I agreed to this,' said Omorova.

67

It was Blackburn's first time in Baghdad's Green Zone, not that he saw any of it, blindfolded as he now was. What was the point? He asked the MP who changed his plastic zip cuffs for proper shiny metal handcuffs. 'The point, son, is that you're a spy. And we don't want spies seeing stuff they don't need to.'

A spy. And a murderer.

They had found Cole's body. They dug all night and most of the next day, through the rubble, the remains of the chalet and into the bunker until they came upon it. The field pathologist extracted the bullet and the forensic team took about thirty minutes to confirm that the markings on it were consistent with those on several others they had test-fired through Blackburn's confiscated M4. And just to be sure, they dusted the rifle for prints and found only its owner's.

Chester Hain Jnr was a different animal from his subordinate, Wes. Hain looked like a well-born Easterner with an Ivy League education. Plus the demeanour of an American who had lived overseas long enough to have learned how to blend in a little and not draw too much attention to himself: handy in his line of work. He had a faraway look in his eyes, which Blackburn imagined had come from a life trying to read between the lines. Perhaps he could read between the lines of what Blackburn had decided to tell him.

He had nothing to lose now.

'May I talk to you alone, Sir?'

Chester Hain Jnr glanced at the man who Blackburn only knew as Wes, who had never introduced himself, who was chewing on a stick of gum and smacking his lips in a way that Blackburn's mother had trained him out of before he'd even started grade school.

'Wesley?' Hain nodded at the door. Wes stopped chewing, closed his laptop with a firmness that betrayed his humiliation and left without a word.

Suddenly the atmosphere in the room was marginally less stifling, as if fewer people had inhaled and exhaled the air Blackburn was breathing.

Hain poured two glasses of water from a bottle and pushed one towards Blackburn. 'You'll get awful dry in these places. Keep your liquids up just like you did on patrol, okay?'

There was something almost parental about his manner. Blackburn picked up the glass with both hands, the cuffs made that mandatory, drank the contents down in one and set the glass back on the grey metal table between them.

'May I begin?'

Hain folded his arms.

'Shoot.'

He had expected a laptop or a notebook at the very least. Hain just leaned back in his chair with what seemed like all the interest of a customer being read a list of options from his Buick dealer.

Blackburn described every detail he could remember, from the moment he saw Dima. He repeated their conversation verbatim, how they had pooled what they knew about Solomon and what that added up to for Dima. Blackburn described the beam falling and how Dima had struggled to save him, his gun and knife clearly within Blackburn's reach. And then he got to the appearance of Cole. He told Hain everything about his commanding officer's reactions to Harker, to the vault find and to the death of Bashir.

'I believe Cole was testing me, Sir. He was trying to make a point, that he didn't believe I was man enough to execute what he believed was the enemy.'

Blackburn thought it was going well. Hain had barely blinked as he listened. He didn't look away the whole time or change his position. His stillness seemed to be operating like a force field, sucking the details out of Blackburn faster than he could process them. But he'd given up trying to measure his words. He was done for. The best he could hope for was some acknowledgment of the

263

willing co-operation he had given after they'd told him about Cole's bullet.

After Blackburn had finished speaking, Hain looked at him for a few more seconds.

'Thank you for being so candid, Henry.'

Then he sighed.

'Fact is, there are two problems with what you've told me. One is the WMDs. We've done the analysis. The device you recovered appears to be some kind of dummy. There's no fissile material. Whoever sold it may have been some kind of con-artist.'

Hain paused while Blackburn took this in. Then he leaned forward and and put his hands together on the desk as if preparing to pray.

'The other problem you have is that the Russian Federation just issued an international arrest warrant for one Dima Mayakovsky, wanted for the theft of Russian government armaments.'

He got to his feet and went towards the door.

'You shot the wrong guy, Henry.'

68

It was dusk when Kroll surfaced from the Serpukhovskaya Metro Station with a large bouquet of flowers and walked to the apartment building two blocks down. In Brezhnev's time, accommodation in 'Serpo' as it was known was only available to the anointed. Obtaining a toehold was a sure sign to the rest of the commissariat that you were on the up. Today, like many of its ageing inhabitants, Serpo was on the way down, in bad need of a facelift.

Kroll had had a good look round the exterior of the apartment building before entering. Once inside, he flashed a GRU pass which he had helped himself to when they had sprung Bulganov's daughter. It wouldn't work for Paliov's guards but it got him past the concierge. He then proceeded to try to deliver the flowers to one Xenya Moronova. Since Xenya Moronova was the name of his own estranged thirteen-year-old daughter, he knew he wouldn't have much success, but after pressing many bells and offering the bouquet to numerous residents he had a pretty good idea of the strength of Paliov's security detail, as well as the layout of the block.

Twenty minutes later, Dima, in a fresh set of clothes, pulled up in the Merc and picked Kroll up.

'There's an airshaft that the kitchens open on to. We could put a ladder across from the Kasparovs. They are very old and quite deaf—.'

Dima cut him off with a wagging finger. 'You said it was only two guys on the outside. I'm not pussyfooting around. I'll give them the option of legging it or I'll shoot them.'

Kroll sighed. 'If you must.'

Dima glared at him. 'This thing – before we even try to get to Paris – has to move fast now.'

'Speaking of Paris – how are we getting there?'

Dima ignored the question. His mind was elsewhere.

They mounted the stairs and marched up to the guards. As well as the clothes, Dima had a fresh new PSS Silent that Omorova had procured for him. The guards took one look at it and raised their hands. You could have made a bit of an effort, he thought, as he made them lie down for Kroll to handcuff. Dima lifted the XP-9 semi-automatics from their holsters, chucked one to Kroll, pocketed the other. You never knew when a spare gun might come in handy. Kroll escorted the security men to a servicelift, herded them in, shut the door and disabled it.

Paliov was asleep in a chair. In the few days that had passed he looked like he had aged ten years.

He felt Dima's presence and lifted his eyelids slowly as if they were heavy weights. He peered at his visitor. 'I heard you were dead.'

'Yeah, I heard that too.'

'It was on the news.'

'Then it must be true.'

Paliov's eyes started to close. Dima slapped his cheeks. 'They drug you?'

'Probably. Can't think why, I'm practically dead as it is.'

'Timofayev?'

He nodded. 'Seems I've fallen foul of the powers that be.'

'Yeah, well that makes two of us. Did you know the Kaffarov mission was based on corrupted intelligence and was blown before we even took off from Rayazan?'

Paliov came back to life for a moment, a subterranean eruption of anger welling to the surface.

'Timofayev wanted a lightweight team – deniable, disposable. I was determined you'd have the full complement you needed. He *wanted* you to fail.'

Then it subsided. He shook his head.

'What he sees in Kaffarov – and with that WMD ...'

'Kaffarov's dead.'

Paliov's face brightened.

'Don't get too happy. Want to take a guess who's got his bombs?'

He told him. Paliov hung his head. Solomon had been Paliov's project as well, the ultimate agent, gifted, ruthless, no past, no allegiances.

There was a long silence as he absorbed the information. 'Everything I've worked for and now this . . .'

'We had a deal, remember. I'm going to Paris.'

'Ah Paris. Your old haunt.' An inane smile spread across his face. His eyelids started to close again.

'The photographs, remember?'

He frowned. Dima felt an almost uncontrollable urge to throttle him. He settled for another hard smack on the cheek.

'My son, remember? In the pictures. You were going to get me a name and an address.'

Paliov's eyes focused, the muscles in his sagging cheeks tensed. Some of the life came back into him. But the impression was not so much alert as panicked.

'Your son?'

Dima leapt forward, grabbed the old man's shoulders.

'The fucking pictures. You showed them to me. It's why I agreed to go on that fucked-up mission.'

Paliov's hand went up to his mouth.

'It's happening again.' His eyes unfocused.

Dima saw the photographs in his head clear down to every pixel. Camille's features, some of his own. Good looking kid. My son.

'I'm sorry, it's . . .' Then a glimmer of recognition came into his watery eyes. 'Timofayev had them. His people found him. He didn't allow me the details.'

He stared at Paliov with a mixture of fury and despair. This man, once a formidable spymaster, keeper of all secrets, scourge of the West, the focus of all his respect and admiration. He cursed Paliov's decrepitude, cursed himself for not prising the information out of either of them when he had the chance. For a moment he felt the energy that had kept him going these last days evaporating.

He had to keep moving. He had to get to Paris, with or without the information he craved.

'Goodbye Paliov.'

267

'Dima.' Paliov's voice was suddenly much stronger. 'One last favour.'

'I'm fresh out of favours.'

He pointed at the guard's XP-9 that was still in his hand. 'Would you mind if I borrowed that? I think the time has come. I'd ask you to but I've put you through too much.'

Dima froze. Love him or hate him, he had been in his life longer than any other person he had known.

He offered his right hand. Paliov clasped it. Then Dima handed over the pistol, turned and walked to the door.

'Dima.'

He looked over his shoulder. A glimmer of light in Paliov's eyes.

'Your boy. He works at the Bourse.'

69

He heard the shot when he got outside the door. To Dima it meant more than the death of one man: it signalled the end of an era. Paliov had personified a set of values and principles that they had both given their lives to. Love them or hate them – and Dima had done both – they were in his DNA. For all the trouble Paliov had caused him, the lies, the mess and the waste, most of all the lost lives in Kaffarov's compound – despite it all, Dima felt a twinge of regret.

But there was no time to process all that now. As the lift took him down, Paliov's final words reverberated round his head.

He's a trader at the Bourse.

Kroll was waiting for him in the Merc.

'We have a problem.'

'Just for a change.'

'I just got a call from Omorova. Timofayev has demanded to see your corpse. He won't take anyone's word, despite the phone footage. If he doesn't see a body he's going to put the whole city on lockdown and tell the world you're still out there. Armed and dangerous and to be shot on sight.'

Dima looked distracted.

'Omorova doesn't know what to do. She's already taken a big fat risk organising your "shooting".'

70

Renskaya Morgue, Moscow

Friday night is rush hour at Moscow's police morgues. But the Renskaya, one of the oldest in the city, was suspiciously quiet – to anyone familiar with the place, which Andrei Timofayev was not.

A nervous-looking orderly in a white coat, apron and rubber boots led the way down to the basement. The place smelled not of death, but of something unidentifiable and chemical, impersonal. The green paint on the brick walls of the corridors was scored by decades of gurneys, badly steered by drunken or careless porters. There had been no time to prepare the viewing chamber in advance of the Secretary's visit. The tattered curtain across the window through which the corpses could be viewed for identification hung like a string of washing. Timofayev shook his head, as he did whenever he found evidence of Moscow's resemblance to a city in the Third World.

'If you would take a seat, Sir,' said the orderly.

'What for? Do I look like a grieving relative?' Timofayev fluttered a hand at the curtain. 'Get on with it.'

The curtain was drawn back. On a trolley behind the viewing window lay a pale corpse. Just the head and shoulders were showing: the rest was under a sheet – just visible was a corner of the plaster used by pathologists to close up, after they have finished their investigations.

All the colour had drained from the face. The eyes were closed, the head angled slightly towards the window to facilitate identification.

Timofayev glared at the corpse, narrowing his eyes.

'I need a closer look.'

The attendant stepped forward, moving uncomfortably in his large boots.

'I'm sorry, Sir, it's not permitted.'

Timofayev pushed him aside and seized the handle of the door that separated the viewing gallery from the body display area. It was locked.

'Open it. Now!'

The orderly did as he was told and stood back. He had done what he had been bribed to do. Now all he wanted to do was flee. Timofayev strode up to the corpse and peered at it, his face devoid of emotion.

Dima had only stopped shivering when he heard Timofayev's voice. He had conquered the urge to shudder by putting himself in the same state as when he was thrown into the ice-covered lake in his Spetsnaz training, or when he had to fight one of his fellow recruits naked in the snow for the amusement of their instructor, a definite psychopath. He ordered his nerve endings not to respond to the cold, commanded his muscles to obey. Even so, he could still feel the goosebumps on his arms tingling. Bit of a giveaway that. Timofayev's breath was warm and smelled of coffee and something alcoholic. His aftershave blended with the disinfectant that hung in the mortuary air, in a particularly nausea-inducing way. His breaths came in short rapid puffs that sounded like repeated snorts of disdain. He lifted the sheet back to expose the plaster.

And Dima opened his eyes.

Timofayev jumped backwards, crashing into the instrument trolley parked to one side, fumbling for his weapon. Dima sprang up and grabbed his wrist as his hand reached the Beretta.

'You didn't expect me back in Moscow, did you?'

'I don't expect anything of you. You're way past your sell-by date, Mayakovsky. Same as your pathetic old boss.'

Timofayev's eyes drilled into his, seemingly unfazed by the hold Dima had on his wrist. Had Dima wanted to kill him he would have by now but it was information he had come for. All the same, revenge was running a close second and catching up fast.

But with a superhuman force that took Dima completely by surprise, Timofayev wrenched his arm out of his grip and kicked him hard in his naked groin. There was nothing Dima could do but double up on the floor, the pain blotting out any coherent thought except for cursing himself for thinking up this ridiculous stunt.

'See what I mean? You've been running around Iran these last few days, chasing your tail, getting tired, going without food and fluids. You overestimate yourself. It's the same with all you two-dimensional comic book heroes. And then you pay the price.'

Through the fog of agony produced by his traumatised testicles Dima could sense Timofayev preparing to dispatch him. He had to postpone it.

'Solomon's going to make Russia very unpopular. The Americans already know where the WMDs come from.'

'Your information is both inaccurate and out of date,' said Timofayev. 'The Americans have a man in custody who's told them all about you, and they've drawn their own useful though rather unimaginative conclusions. In fact your blundering into them has provided Solomon with a very useful cover.'

'Now you're going to tell me you *want* him to get away with it?'

Dima was not only in physical pain, his whole worldview was crumbling. Would nothing stay still?

'You just don't get it do you, Mayakovsky? The world has moved on. The geopolitical ice is melting. The tectonic plates of power and influence are shifting. America and the West have had their day. They've had it far too good for far too long. New forces in the world are poised to take their place – *are* taking their place, even as I speak. And those of us with the imagination to see this are not going to let it be slowed down by a few feeble old dinosaurs too short-sighted – and weak – to know when it's time for them to die out. You're extinct, Dima. Give it up.'

Dima tried hard to focus on what Timofayev was saying. Concentrating on this pompous speech would help to distract him from the pain while he worked out his next move, if he had one. He was on the freezing floor, naked and unarmed, his head slammed against the wheel of the trolley.

'Paliov warned me about you. He said you didn't know when to stop. I was relying on you screwing up – which you seem to have done rather well.'

Timofayev was getting into his stride. The best Dima could hope for was that he'd relax his concentration, though he didn't come across as the sort who would.

'Were you hoping to wring some information out of me about that orphan boy in Paris?'

Dima didn't feel like dignifying him with an answer, but his silence spoke for itself. He couldn't bear the contempt with which Timofayev spoke about his son, and felt the balance tip towards vengeance.

'Well I don't have any and I never did. I expect some minion in my Ministry may have logged a name and address but we're not obsessive collectors of trivia like our socialist forefathers. It just clogs up the servers. Besides, what would a bright young man do after finding out his father's a failed Soviet agent? Hardly going to do much for his prospects is it? I should leave the boy alone if I were you, to get on with his life.'

Dima struggled to lift himself by grabbing a leg of the trolley, nearly pulling off the cover that was draped over it. He managed to get a grip on the edge of the shelf.

'Go on, pick yourself up. Your story's so sad I might even take pity on you and send you to one of the remaining gulags. You'd like that. It's full of your generation. You can eat boiled onions and reminisce about the good old Soviet days of your youth.'

My generation? thought Dima. The two of them were only a few years apart in age. But they they were worlds apart: at least Dima had some morals, some sense of justice. The sterile android in the suit in front of him, who was sounding off about a new world order, had no belief in anything, no loyalty to any cause other than his own.

He put the flat of his hand on the trolley shelf, felt the instrument under his palm. It would have to do. But a new pain shot up his leg as he tried to lift himself again. He slithered back to the ground and doubled over, closing his hand over the instrument he had grabbed off the shelf, hoping Timofayev hadn't noticed.

He was only dimly aware of what Timofayev was saying now. Evidently the man had quite a lot to get off his chest. Dima was now focused entirely on where Timofayev was standing, how long it would take him to get there from his current position, curled up against the trolley, and whether it was enough. Timofayev had good reflexes, that was apparent. As to whether his aim was as good, Dima would just have to take the risk.

The first part of his strategy was to kick the gurney so the sudden movement caused a microsecond's diversion – enough to get him part of the way.

The first shot from Timofayev's Beretta came almost simultaneously – but by then Dima, having stabilised himself, had sprung up from his crouching position and swiped the gurney, so it pinned Timofayev against the wall as three more shots rang out, hitting the ceiling. With his adversary in position, Dima stabbed the scissors hard into his gun hand. The Beretta spun to the ground.

He pushed him up.

'Sure you haven't just suddenly remembered any information that's unexpectedly come back to you? Want to have another think?'

The scissors caught some of the sinews in Timofayev's palm as Dima extracted them and plunged them into his wrist, severing the radial artery and spraying them both with blood. Timofayev's eyes bulged with shock and a sharp smell of shit cut through the aftershave and disinfectant: a bully. And like all bullies, fatally weak beneath the bluster.

'I ... I ... can help ...'

'We both know that's not going to happen. Last chance now: does anything come to mind ...?'

Timofayev found some last vestige of force and pushed Dima away. As he fell to the ground, he grabbed the gun in his still intact left hand and aimed. Dima was still clutching the scissors. He put all his speed and force into one swing and the points of both blades pierced Timofayev's right eye. Dima thrust them right in, and kept on, forcing them through the back of the socket, until only the handles protruded from the mess.

71

Scooping up the Beretta just as Timofayev's security detail appeared, he took out the first two as they came through the door. He twisted a machine pistol out of the grip of one of the dying guards just as he heard the sound of running men. They came round the corner straight into a hail of bullets from Dima. Leaping over them, he made for the stairs, running into three more. Their momentary hesitation, as they found themselves confronted by a naked man wielding a gun, gave him enough time to down them too. And then he was in the street, naked, covered in Timofayev's blood with just the night, the freezing rain, and – three blocks away – the sirens and blue lights of the police.

He flung himself at a cab dropping off a couple who looked like they were on their first date. At the sight of a naked, rain- and blood-splattered man holding a gun the girl held out her bag like a steak to a rabid dog, averting her eyes and bringing the evening traffic almost to a standstill.

'There's five hundred cash in there! Don't hurt me!'

The boyfriend, Dima noticed, did not leap in front to shield her. First date and last, he thought. He reached inside the bag, pulled out a pack of tissues, pushed past the stunned boyfriend, shooed the taxi driver out of his seat and took off.

It was an old Volga with the usual terrible brakes. The wipers, also well past their prime, made slow and slimy progress across the windscreen, leaving a film that was almost as opaque as the half-frozen rain.

He crossed into the opposite lane, which alerted the drivers of the police cars now on his tail, so he swept back into the left lane and tried to camouflage himself amongst some other cabs. But they weren't going fast enough. He took a right and found himself close to the Paveletsky Station, but a cop car cut him off. He flung the column shift into reverse and backed up a few feet, then rammed the cop car just as its two occupants were getting out. Then he shot up the street he had come out of and into a space between two office blocks. Two drunks were huddled over a bottle. He pulled up beside them, got out and pulled one of them to his feet.

'Your clothes – for this taxi.'

Dima knew the offer would take time to sink in, so he ripped the sodden coat off his back. It would do.

'Got any cash?'

'What? We're the fucking beggars.'

'I'm giving you the taxi.'

Dima waved the machine pistol and they produced fifty roubles.

'All this and you're on the streets. You could find a roof with this.'

They looked at him in disgust. Dima took off down the alley and crossed several more streets, dodging the puddles and dog shit, before disappearing into a Metro station.

72

Bulganov's goons took some persuading. It's not every day an oligarch gets an unannounced visitor who is spattered with blood, wearing nothing but a piss-stained overcoat. They looked him up and down again, as his feet continued to bleed on to the pale mushroom carpet.

'Where are your shoes then?' said the larger of the two.

'He's expecting me.' Dima spelled his name again. 'I just spoke to him. I saved his daughter's life, for fuck's sake.'

Big goon and small goon conferred again and got on the phone, which prompted the arrival of a third. All bulk and no agility, the three of them were about as much use as paperweights. Dima could have floored them in seconds, but having just called in a big favour from their master he thought it might not go over well.

Eventually the private lift pinged behind them.

'You can go up,' said the third paperweight. 'Leave the weapon.'

'Whatever.'

Dima threw it to him: he caught it, but only just.

On the 45th floor Dima got out and Bulganov appeared, barrelling towards him, a large scotch in one hand and a cigar in the other. The apartment smelled of Chanel No. 19 and money.

'Dima! My God, what have they done to you—?'

He got a whiff of the coat and stopped short.

'Christ! Get in the shower, will you? You're not getting on my plane smelling like that.'

The money was Bulganov, but the Chanel...

Omorova was sitting on a white sofa below a small Picasso, her face a mixture of amusement and annoyance. He came forward but she batted him away.

When he emerged from the shower he found a dressing gown

bearing the livery of the British soccer team Bulganov had recently acquired, and put it on. He updated Omorova, who glanced at her watch.

'You've been back in Moscow – what? Seven hours. You're a one-man crime wave.'

He raised his hands in submission.

'I know: it's been hectic.'

'Thanks for my help? Don't even mention it.'

'Of course none of it would have been possible without you. Can I have that kiss now?'

'My career is so over.'

'You're not bailing out?'

'Dima, they probably won't even let me back in the building.'

A butler appeared with a large bourbon for her and a Diet Coke for Dima. One minute you're running naked through the streets, the next you're on the 45th floor standing on silk carpet. A strange life. But then Dima had never had anything he could call normal. He raised his glass to them both, and the Picasso.

She took a big swig and crossed her legs.

'Do that again,' said Dima.

'Piss off. Here's your stuff.'

She opened her bag and produced the contents of his safety deposit box.

'You think of everything.'

'Someone has to.'

He did a quick inventory of the currencies and picked up the passports.

'Ah, hello, old friends.'

'I caught up with your man Rossin in Paris. He's looked at all the staff at the Bourse: domestic and security, all clean.'

'He should check all the maintenance people – heating, plumbing. That size of building, at that age – it probably needs a whole army to keep it going. And what about the computers? Capitalism never sleeps. They must have a round-the-clock team of IT geeks as well.'

Omorova opened a laptop. 'We need to know about any sightings of Solomon on recent trips to Paris. Chances are he's been there to recce as well as to set up some kind of team. He won't be starting from scratch. He's very meticulous. If he's there he's only been there a few days, so he's bound to choose somewhere he knows to operate from. My guess is he won't be staying somewhere unfamiliar that he has to check out, or that means he's having to look over his shoulder.'

Dima nodded. 'Yeah, but we can't assume that. We can't assume anything. He could come through the front door posing as a fund manager, an oil trader, someone in derivatives. He's extremely plausible whether he's playing Lebanese, American, Israeli ...'

Omorova smiled. 'Better than you?'

Suddenly he wished she was coming with him. But equally, there was an aspect of this mission he didn't want to have to explain. He was travelling back in time to a place in his life he thought he had put behind him. Also, in part of his mind he had already written off the quest as hopeless. Trying to find one man and a bomb in a major capital city with just four people to help ... Possibly, now, only three.

She sighed, as if reading his mind.

'And you're still not officially off the wanted list. Timofayev wouldn't sanction it until ...' Her voice trailed away. 'There's still a covert shoot to kill directive against you with all the European security agencies.' She read from a printout. '"The CIS will not, repeat not, protest in the event that the target does not survive arrest." Nicely put, eh?'

Dima shrugged. He hadn't expected anything less.

'What are the Americans saying?'

'Ah. Want the rest of the bad news?'

'Bring it on.'

'Langley are putting it out that a US Marine is under arrest for the murder of his commanding officer – in Iran ...'

Dima winced.

'Go on.'

'They don't want it known at all that a Russian was there at the time. It just makes it more complicated for them. But our back channel communications with them are saying that the prisoner has corroborated claims by the Russian security services that one Dima

Mayakovsky is at large and is a potential threat in the European mainland.'

He shook his head.

'The poor guy probably didn't have anywhere else to go.'

'How come he's not claiming you shot his CO?' said Bulganov.

'He had a terrible choice – either deny me and forget what I'd told him about Solomon, or come clean and try to get his message across. He could have saved himself.'

'Such honesty, such selflessness ...' His voice trailed away. Bulganov was baffled.

Omorova frowned, thinking. 'You were only with him for what, an hour?'

'You can learn a lot about someone in that time. It would be good if he knew I was still out there. Is there anything you could do?'

He looked out of the window. Below, he could see the lights of the new Moscow glittering all the way to the horizon.

'He saved my life so I could get this done. I cannot fail.'

73

Blackburn wasn't sure what he felt about being back in America. All he had seen of it so far was at Andrews Air Force base, when they transferred him from the windowless plane to the windowless truck. From the stairs he saw a vast expanse of tarmac, those strange-shaped vehicles that only inhabit airfields and an American flag hanging limp in the humid air. Not realising who he was, a woman, one of the ground crew, looked up as a pretty young woman might at a handsome young man, and gave him the sort of winning smile that brought an instant lump to his throat. Would any woman ever look at him like that again?

He travelled the seven hours to Fort Donaldson in a cubicle inside a prison truck. There was a toilet under the seat so he didn't have to be let out. A letterbox in the door opened once or twice and a hand offered him a Hershey bar and a bottle of water. There was a window but it had been painted out. Already he felt desperate for the sight of just a bit of sky or a single tree.

Once at Donaldson he was escorted straight to the MP's facility and into an interview room. A small man with a moustache and big black-rimmed glasses sat at a metal desk, head down, peering at a thick file. He whipped off the glasses and stood up.

'I'm Schwab, your lawyer.'

The hand Blackburn was offered felt cold and dry, but it was a hand nonetheless. No one had offered him a hand to shake in a long time.

His small mouth twitched into a cautious smile. He knitted his fingers together and leaned over the file. His voice dropped to almost a whisper.

'I'm the only friend you got right now so the more you confide in me, the more I'll be able to do for you.'

Blackburn didn't react. He didn't feel like confiding. He'd said it all – three, four times he couldn't remember – to a variety of different people, half of whose names or jobs he never discovered. Bleary and jet-lagged from the flight, not knowing what time it was, he gazed doubtfully at Schwab.

'What is it exactly that you do?'

Schwab looked thrown.

'I mean – when you're not defending me.'

Schwab's mouth twitched. He pushed his glasses up his nose with an index finger.

'I defend the un-defendable. Someone's got to.'

It was a joke of sorts, but it fell way short of Blackburn, who didn't even know whether he still had a sense of humour. Then without warning, Schwab dropped his bombshell.

'Wanna talk to your Mom?'

74

Schwab dialled and waited. He didn't have to wait long. He had already been in contact. Blackburn imagined his mother cradling the phone in two hands, as he'd seen her do many times, as if it could bring the person closer.

'*Hello, baby.*'

Her voice was clear and strong, as if she'd been practising what to say for days – which she probably had.

'*I know I've only got two minutes but I want you to know that your father and I love you very much and we believe in you – whatever. Okay?*'

'*Mom?*'

'*Yes, darling?*'

Her voice cracked as she heard her son speak for the first time since hearing he'd been jailed.

'*Is Dad there?*'

'*Sure darling, he's right here. I'll put him on.*'

He could hear the phone being handed over. A hushed exchange about what to say. After a moment he heard his father clear his throat.

'*Well son, least you won't be getting killed out there now.*'

There was an urgency in Blackburn's voice. '*Dad,*' he said. '*I found out.*'

'*What's that son?*'

His father sounded like he had aged a decade, baffled by his son's tone. Blackburn pressed on. There wasn't much time.

'*Dad, I know how it was. I know how it was for you in Vietnam. I think it's what's been sustaining me over the last few—. I understand now.*'

There was a pause at the other end, and a whispered exchange he couldn't make out.

'Sorry, son: I'm afraid I just don't know what you mean.'

'What you went through—. It's what I enlisted for – to know what it was like for you.'

The silence on the other end of the phone said it all.

Blackburn tried to think of what else to say. Nothing came. The weight bearing down on his soul grew even greater. He passed the phone back to Schwab, who looked mystified.

'Ok-ay. You done?'

Blackburn nodded. He had long imagined the moment of tenderness he had craved with his father – two men seeing eye-to-eye for the first time. But all his father could be thinking right now was *Is my son a killer?*

Schwab let the receiver fall back on to its cradle. Then he put his big square case on the table and took out a second vast dark grey file.

How could so much paperwork have accumulated in such a short time?

'Let's get started.'

'On what?'

Schwab stared at his new client. Here we go, he thought.

'I've already said all I can remember. I'm guilty. I'm as good as dead.'

Blackburn lowered his head until it rested on the desk.

75

A little after ten-thirty p.m. they were being wafted towards Moscow's Domodedovo Airport in Bulganov's Rolls. Cocooned in the rear, Dima wondered whether the unnatural absence of noise was due to the bulletproof glass, or because his ears had been damaged by all the shooting. Kroll sat up front with the chauffeur, observing every gauge and dial on the dashboard with undisguised pleasure. In the back with Dima and Omorova was Bulganov himself.

He had been a last-minute recruit to the mission. Dima was a marked man. A contract was out on him. Shoot on sight. Getting out of Moscow and into Paris, with an international warrant out for his arrest, all this was only possible with Bulganov's influence – and his private jet. He lit a fresh cigar and blew two plumes of exhaust from his nostrils, his eyes gleaming with excitement. Bulganov was no friend of the current regime in the Kremlin; Dima knew he had pushed at an open door. But as always, Bulganov had his price. As they were getting into the car he told Dima what it was.

'I get to go all the way with you, okay? Or there's no deal.'

'Of course,' lied Dima.

Omorova had given him a sphinx-like look which said, *Let this guy play goodies and baddies with you? You can't be serious*, and Dima responded with a dismissive frown which said *Don't be crazy: of course I won't*. He had no idea how to stop him, but felt sure a way to get Bulganov off his back would emerge once they were in Paris. After all, dealing with the unexpected was what he was trained for.

Perhaps Omorova's presence was fuelling Bulganov's expansive mood. He was on a roll. 'You know the trouble with post-Soviet Russia? Everybody can be shown to have stolen something from somewhere.' He took another quick puff on his cigar, filling the car with yet more smoke. 'It's a fact. Me – I'm far richer than I ever dreamed, but I also know that all the bulletproof glass in the world can't stop me being thrown into prison if I fall foul of the Kremlin. Therefore I have to have something on them so they leave me alone.'

He glanced approvingly at Omorova.

'I'm right aren't I, Katya?'

Dima realised he hadn't even found out her first name. Hopeless. She projected her best smile at Bulganov. If anyone could persuade him to stay in Moscow it was her. But Bulganov was loving every second.

'You know, I envy you Dima.'

This is getting ridiculous, thought Dima. Maybe he's showing off in front of her.

'You do these things. You don't give a shit about the money. Having money's a burden. It doesn't leave you alone. It's like a baby. Needs twenty-four/seven attention. You – you don't have a thing to worry about. You're free.'

Dima decided not to engage. There was too much on his mind right now. Solomon was taking up more and more of his headspace. By the end of Monday, all their problems and disappointments could be dwarfed by unimaginable catastrophe – and there would be no one for him to find in Paris.

There was also one other matter on his mind: Blackburn. He'd paid a high price for saving Dima's life. He leaned across to Omorova. 'You think the message will get through?'

Omorova sighed.

'I can't guarantee it. It's been a long time since anyone's used that channel. We'll just have to hope.'

The Rolls swept through the airport VIP gate and on towards Bulganov's waiting jet.

76

George Jacobs had worked on the base for longer than anyone could remember. In fact, he was the longest-serving civilian staffer on Donaldson. He'd arrived there at the age of sixteen and now he was fifty-eight. He worked hard, kept out of trouble, had always been helpful. 'No job too menial, that's me,' was his trademark response to any request. Always willing, always positive, he usually went about his work with a song on his lips, often the classics. He knew the whole of Cole Porter and everything Buddy Holly ever sang, and Sinatra too.

He had tended the gardens until his handlers decided that it would be more useful if he worked inside, so he got himself transferred to cleaner. But because he was so handy they upgraded him to maintenance. From then on, he toured the whole facility fixing window catches, sticking down sticking-up floor tiles, unblocking blocked air-conditioning ducts. And he went about his business with so little fuss that most times people didn't even notice he was there. Exactly as he'd been told to do by the group of people he knew only as Cousin Hal.

Everything he'd done in his entire career was just so he could watch what was coming in and going out. Planes, hardware. He had an encyclopaedic knowledge of all forms of military transport. He could look at a Humvee fifty yards away and quote the chassis number to the nearest hundred. He could tell a Seattle-made C-130 from a Missouri-made C-130. Who wanted to know? He never asked. Don't ask, just deliver. That was the deal. What made George so good at his job was that he never asked: he just did it.

So when the latest Hal called him and they met at the Taco Bell on 45 he wasn't prepared for what was coming.

'Something a little different', said Hal. 'You up for it?'

'You know me,' said George, tucking into caramel apple empanada, his favourite.

'There's a guy in the stockade. You ever go in there?'

'Sure but I can't see him. He's in solitary.'

'You pass by his cell?'

'Sure.'

'There anyone in the corridor when you pass?'

'Sometimes.'

'They pay you much attention?'

'Nope.'

'You like singing, yeah?'

When Hal said one of those things it creeped him out that they knew so much about him.

'Sure I like to sing.' He was about to list his top ten when Hal cut in.

'Got a new song for you to sing.'

And Hal told him the words.

77

Blackburn lay on his pallet, listening to the sound of nothing. The only interruption came about every half an hour. There were footsteps but he never saw whose. The meal trolley was the most exciting sound of the day. Its squeaky wheels stopped only once as they progressed down the corridor: he was the only detainee.

The humming was different. So different, he decided it was just another voice in his head. *Da de da de dad a. Dad de da de dad a.* An old voice. It reminded him of his grandfather. It was accompanied by a scraping sound – and then steps – a stepladder. *Da de da de dad a. Dad de da de dad a.* Then some words.

I'm flying to Paris, I'm keeping my promise. I'll be there tomorrow. Da de da . . . Do not, repeat, do not despair.

George didn't think it was much of a song. *April in Paris*, now that was a song. But he sang it like he was told, as he examined the aircon ducts that ran along the ceiling of the corridor. He was a bit unsure about cleaning them because he knew they'd not been touched in years and once he got started – well, it could be one of those jobs that went on and on. But that's what Hal wanted. Reasons for him to be there more than once. He was due some overtime, so he told the site manager he'd try and get as much as he could done over the weekend.

78

Paris

It was two a.m. when Bulganov's Lear descended through thick cloud into Paris airspace. The cloud was emptying its load on to Charles De Gaulle runway number two as they thumped on to the ground, and the pilot coaxed the brakes to bring them to a halt.

The airport VIP crew met them with umbrellas and escorted them to the waiting VIP coach. When you travelled with Bulganov it was VIP all the way. His first step on Parisian terra firma and Dima's pulse shifted up a gear. The clock was really ticking now. He and Kroll were in matching black Hugo Boss suits, borrowed from Bulganov's Moscow security detail. Dima's fitted better than Kroll's, which was a little short in the leg and with his loping gait made him look like a gangly, prematurely-aged adolescent.

They had their Iranian passports ready – there hadn't been any time to prepare fresh ones, but such was Bulganov's clout that they were greeted by the French immigration team like old friends. They weren't even asked to remove their preposterous dark glasses.

'For a minute there I thought they were going to kiss us on both cheeks,' said Kroll.'

'Don't get too used to it,' snapped Dima.

'No need to snap,' scolded Kroll.

For all the drive into Paris Dima said nothing. He sat staring out of the window into the rainy night, memories flooding back, mixed with anticipation about what was without doubt the assignment of his life. So much at stake, failure wasn't an option. The photographs, tantalisingly thrust in front of him by Paliov. No name – just the place his son worked. And the cruellest irony of all, that it was Solomon's target.

Bulganov's apartment was just off the Champs Elysées. As the

Rolls came to a stop Dima saw it. Parked up on the kerb, a dog-eared Renault Espace people-mover with smoked glass windows and no hubcaps. Rossin might as well have had the words 'Danger – Surveillance' stencilled along the side.

'So when do we start?' said Bulganov, rubbing his hands.

'You get some rest while we hook up with our local fixer.'

Bulganov looked a little disappointed, but given the late hour and the weather, it didn't seem like a bad option.

'There's a keypad there,' he pointed out. 'Just tap in 7474 if you change your mind and want somewhere a bit more comfortable to stay.'

'What does he think this is,' said Kroll under his breath. 'A weekend break?'

Bulganov disappeared into the building and the side door of the Espace slid open. Rossin leapt out and embraced his old friend, kissing him on both cheeks.

'It's been too long.'

'That's not what you said on the phone.'

In the ten years since Dima had seen him, Rossin had aged twenty. He had put on about thirty pounds. His dark French-Algerian features had shrivelled a little but the lively eyes suggested he hadn't lost his appetite for the game.

'Step into my office. I have interesting things to show you.'

The interior of the Espace smelled of coffee, garlic, cigarette ash and mildew.

'First let me say I have been extremely careful, in view of your current status. Naturally, any whiff of our previous association could prejudice my investigations.'

Dima felt the same impatience he always experienced in his dealings with Rossin.

'Let's just cut to the chase, okay?'

'There have been some significant developments but I must warn you – there is a great deal of danger associated with this mission.'

'I think I'm aware of that,' said Dima.

'Your man is very, *very* clever. This you must know. As you are aware, I have the very best channels with which to access files of the DGSE, the DCRI, the DPSD . . .'

Dima headed him off.

'And all their files on him are wiped.'

Rossin nodded and wagged a finger.

'In fact there's no evidence any of them ever had any record of him. He's done an extremely good job of covering his tracks. However!' A light came into his eyes. 'The Service Central de la Sécurité des Systèmes d'Informations—.' He interrupted himself to grab a quick breath. 'They showed me a link to a North African extremist group, Force Noir, which he supposedly infiltrated in the late '90s up in Clichy-sous-Bois.'

'Nice part of town.'

Dima remembered it: grim anonymous towers of substandard housing decked in graffiti and satellite dishes. And no white faces.

Rossin nodded, his mouth turned downwards in a Gallic show of distaste.

'One of the worst – on fire through most of the summer of '05. Not so bad now since Sarkozy cracked down on them.' He opened his laptop. 'So we did a little surveillance of a couple of blocks where we knew they were active.' He struck a key like a concert pianist at the start of a concerto. 'Et – voilà!'

Dima peered at the screen: Solomon. Exactly as he remembered him and exactly how Marine Sergeant Henry Blackburn had described him. A tall figure, heavy brow, high cheekbones and dark empty eyes. Hard to put an age or nationality to. The perfect twenty-first century triple agent turned terrorist. He felt his pulse accelerate again and the muscles in his chest tighten.

'That's him.'

He turned the laptop towards Kroll, who bent his head close to the screen. Rossin eased it back towards him.

'There's more.'

Rossin scrolled slowly through shots of three more men coming either in or out of the same block.

'Bernard, Syco, Ramon. They don't seem to have surnames. They're all on file.'

'Syco's my favourite,' said Kroll, looking at the biggest and ugliest of the three.

'When were these taken?'

'Yesterday.'

'Good work. You have a log?'

Rossin opened another window and read off the times.

'Solomon – enters at three-thirty, shortly after the other three have arrived. They are all believed to be inhabiting an apartment on the ninth floor. Solomon leaves at eight. We followed him to a small hotel in the Rue Marcellin Berthelot, about four ks from there. He's registered there as Zayed Trahore, good Algerian name. But he goes back to the apartment an hour later and I'm betting he is still there.'

Rossin allowed himself a small triumphant smirk before he ploughed on. There's a man, thought Dima, who loves his work.

'Now comes the most interesting part. A Citroen van with the livery of an air freight company called Cargotrak made a delivery there at nine-thirty last night. Not a good time to be out on the streets there, I might add. Syco and Ramon carried a box about the size of a small fridge into the building.'

Dima looked at Kroll. 'Jesus. He flew it in on a cargo plane.'

Kroll let a slow breath out.

'Better bet than excess baggage, if you grease the right palms.'

Rossin raised a finger.

'Cargotrak has a long standing contract with the CIA for shipments to Afghanistan and neighbouring destinations. As I say, your man is a clever one.'

Kroll booted up Shenk's scanner.

'What's that?' Rossin looked suddenly worried.

'Just our insurance.'

Kroll compared the co-ordinates with the map of Paris on the iPad he'd borrowed from Omorova.

'Looks good.'

Dima frowned into space.

'Right. Better get on with it. Where's Vladimir?'

'At the hotel.'

'I hope it's near Clichy.'

Rossin smiled. 'Three blocks from Solomon's. And full of local atmosphere.'

'Has he got the necessary?'

'All sorted.'

79

'Do you never sleep?'

Vladimir gave a good look through the spy hole before he let them in.

'I put my head on the pillow forty-five minutes ago.'

Dima gave his comrade a brotherly hug. 'What's a pillow?'

He looked round the room. A small lightweight arsenal awaited them: three Glock 9 mm machine pistols, a pack of stun grenades, three high-power torches, night vision goggles, Vladimir's favourite rappelling kit.

Dima lifted the ropes.

'Did you need these to get out of Iran?'

'Amara persuaded me to stay for the funeral. I needed them to get out of her bedroom.'

'So she's coming to terms with her loss.'

'She was quite pissed off that she couldn't come to Paris with me.'

'You didn't tell her anything, did you?'

'I'm Siberian, not stupid.'

'You sober enough for this next bit?'

'If I have to be.'

Dima turned to Rossin. 'If we need you—.'

Rossin shook his head. 'I'm out of town the next couple of days.'

'I thought you said you'd retired.'

Rossin shrugged. 'It's as you said: none of us retire.'

They travelled in a grubby Citroen Xantia Rossin had procured for them. A car with three men in it at three a.m. was a potential magnet for police curiosity, even without a trunk load of weaponry. Kroll did his best to observe the speed limit until he realised that at this hour, no one else on the road was paying any attention to it either.

Close to the Clichy tower block they had to hang back while firemen dealt with a burning car. A squad of police were loading a van with protesting young men. Friday night in the small hours was not the best time to be visiting this neighbourhood.

'Too bad we can't do the apartment and Solomon's hotel simultaneously.'

'It's the bomb I want first. Check the scanner.'

It was pulsing clearly. Dima should have been more elated, but something was troubling him, something he couldn't put his finger on.

'Let's hope it doesn't slip away from us again.'

The entrance to the block was wide open, any outer doors it had once had being long gone. So was the lift.

'Nine stories. Fuck,' said Vladimir.

'Do you good. Come on.'

Three floors up they stepped over a couple zoned out on substances. Syringes crunched underfoot. Several apartments were doorless and burned out. Some that did have doors sounded like they wouldn't have them much longer, judging by the arguments underway inside. On floor eight they were confronted by a posse of young men, their faces covered, each with a pistol.

'Turn round if you don't want to die.'

'We're busy: fuck off out the way,' said Dima and, without even raising his Glock, shot the gun out of the leader's hand.

The man folded into a ball and the others melted into an empty doorway.

Floor nine. Apartment six. They checked the scanner one more time. A bright green pulsing light. Dima put his night vision lenses on. The other two followed. They examined the door carefully. Then Dima and Vladimir stood either side ready to rush in when Kroll shot out the lock.

Dima fired a few rounds as he burst in – high in case he caught the bomb. There wasn't much to the flat: bedroom, living room, kitchen and bathroom. Every wall was sprayed with graffiti swirls. It stank of urine. There was nobody home.

'Fuck. We've got the wrong one,' said Kroll.

'No we haven't,' said Vladimir. He was in the bathroom, pointing at a small pulsing green light. It was coming from the bomb's signaller all right. But it wasn't attached to any suitcase nuke.

80

The next time he heard the footsteps Blackburn was on his feet. The slot his food came through had a small gap down one side that let a sliver of light in from the corridor. He wanted to press his face up close to it, to see if he could catch a glimpse of the singer. But then there was the camera in the ceiling watching him twenty-four/seven. Schwab told him he was on suicide watch. He was pretty sure he had dreamed the song. How could Dima be sending him a message? How could he know where he was?

But what if the person *was* giving him a message from Dima? Blackburn could blow him wide open if he tried to speak. So he whistled the tune.

No response. Just the scraping of the ladder, then the steps.

He whistled again.

Nothing.

George went to his truck. He often went back to it during the day to pick up a fresh pack of Winstons. But he didn't want a cigarette. He took out the emergency use, once only Pay As You Go cell phone and called Hal.

'He answered the whistle. What do I do?'

'You going back near him?'

'Can do.'

'Sing again – only this time it's I'm here in Paris.'

Thirty minutes passed. Or something like that. Blackburn had no means of knowing. The steps again. And the ladder. And then the song.

I'm here in Paris.

81

Dima tried to contain his surging rage. Tried and failed. Anger leads to mistakes, he had always told his recruits. And mistakes can cost you your life.

Had he not been so exhausted, had it not been so long since his head had touched a pillow, had he not been so consumed with anticipation about the nameless young man in the photograph, he would perhaps have had the good sense to leave the signaller right where it was. You've seen what you've seen. Stop, look and leave.

But he didn't. He reached down, clasped it in his gloved hand and picked it up.

Only once it was in his hand did he see the wires. And then the flash blotted everything out.

82

The MedCenter team on Donaldson were short-staffed on the weekend. Jackie Douglis, a locum at Saint Elizabeth's, had been drafted in to cover. Boy was she bored. ER was Jackie's thing. That had been her plan since Sixth Grade and she was almost there. But sitting around in a half-deserted Marine base on a warm weekend wasn't her idea of how to further her career. Besides, her friend Stacey was having a yard party and she was missing it.

The alarm made her jump. Wayne, the big sleepy-looking orderly waddled in.

'We got a meltdown in the Brig.'

She didn't know what a meltdown meant or what the Brig was for that matter. But it sounded interesting and she sure was in need of some distraction. So she followed along out of the MedCenter across the tarmac. There was a scrum of men in uniform crammed into the corridor. The bars on the doors told her what the Brig was. Some of them were kneeling down. Had someone collapsed, needed CPR? She began the timing rhythm in her head.

But the young man on the floor wasn't in need of CPR. He was being knelt on by two guards as a third wrestled him into a set of leg irons.

One of them turned and saw Wayne.

'Got a shot?'

Jackie saw Wayne fumbling with a syringe.

'Hey, lemme through! I'm a doctor!' she yelled for the first time in her life. All her life she'd been waiting to say those words for real.

83

Paris

The smell of urine brought Dima round. He remembered the apartment stank of it. It caught in his throat and along with the dust made him choke. But he couldn't see the apartment, he couldn't see anything. Nor could he move. There was another smell as well. Something burning. Then he remembered what had happened. And that brought him back to full consciousness. Rage at his own mistake. Okay, this time get it right. One thing at a time. He flexed his toes, check. Fingers, check. His nose was bleeding: he could feel the sticky warmth over his face and he could taste the blood. But he was trapped, buried.

'I have to get out of here,' he said out loud.

He called out, using the little strength he had, but there was nowhere for the sound to go. He tried straightening his legs and found that his head moved forward a little when he did. He discovered new areas of pain though, in his thigh and his left arm. His gun arm. Well he wasn't too bad with his right. Think positively. That's the only thing to do. Negative gets you nowhere.

Solomon had to have known they were coming. Known they were looking for the nuke, and that they had a scanner to track its signal. A fresh burst of rage engulfed him and he pushed forward again. Something gave and a cloud of plaster dust convulsed him in a coughing fit. His whole chest burned with it.

Something lifted and a sharp beam of light speared his face.

'Fucking fuck. He's here!' called Kroll.

Dima peered at him, ghostly not only from the reflected torchlight but also the plaster he was covered in.

'What the fuck did you do that for? You trying to kill us all?'

'Just get me out of here, okay?'

301

He could hear the sirens of the emergency services. The sound gave him a much needed charge of energy. Kroll and Vladimir hauled him to his feet. They felt like rubber.

There was only one explanation. Rossin.

84

Jackie Douglis didn't take long to figure that the young man on the floor was in need of her help. For one he was dehydrated, that much was clear from his complexion and the yellowing whites of his eyes. He clearly hadn't been taking food and as far as she was concerned, whatever the guards had told her about him having killed someone, in her world at least you were innocent until proven guilty.

The senior guard, Halberry, didn't help matters by calling her *Little Lady*. He may have been twice her age and old enough to be her father and all that crap, but this was the twenty-first century and he needed to get with it.

Eventually they came to an understanding whereby the inmate would be transferred to the medical unit secure room for observation and to undergo rehydration. He would have to be shackled. That was non-negotiable and Jackie conceded that yes, she didn't know anything about this young man and that was one battle that she wasn't going to win. But life in the Donaldson MedCenter had suddenly got a whole lot more interesting.

Eventually she shooed all the guards away and they were alone. She gave him a proper examination. Suddenly he spoke.

'Doctor Douglis.'

Jackie was still not used to being addressed like that, but it sounded good. She looked at the young man whose name was Blackburn and smiled. His eyes came alive.

'You smiled.'

'I did.'

She smiled again.

'Thank you,' said the young sergeant. 'I didn't think I'd ever see one of those again.'

Four hours later, her head spinning from the tale she had just heard from the shackled soldier, she reluctantly left him in the care of the night shift. She went to bed to the sound of his story in her head, a story of nuclear bombs in suitcases, of Russians and terrorists … Two hours later, still unable to sleep, she decided to call her father.

'I'm sorry honey, his committee is pulling an all-nighter,' said Senator Joseph M. Douglis's PA, Sheila Perkis, aka Bulletproof – because nothing got past her. So now she seemed to have control of his private number – well, Jackie would see about that.

She emailed him to call. Emergency!

Two seconds later he called.

'Honey, you okay?'

Thank God for his Blackberry addiction. Jackie told him what Sergeant Blackburn had told her.

'I hate to tell you, Hon, but the world is full of folk with all kind of stories. Guys out there in the war zone – it can get to them.'

'Then I'm calling the New York Times: *"Senate Security Committee member's daughter discovers bomb threat to New York, but her Dad didn't want to know". Kind of a mouthful, but I guess they'll get a headline out of it.'*

Joe Douglis felt a tap on his shoulder from the usher. They were back in session. He let out a long sigh of defeat. She was headstrong all right – even worse than her mother.

'Just leave it with me, okay, honey?'

'Promise?'

'Promise.'

'Now?'

'I've said I promise.'

When Jackie Douglis returned to Donaldson next morning, Sergeant Henry Blackburn was gone. All she could discover was that a special team had arrived unannounced by air and flown him out. Destination unknown.

85

Paris

This time Dima drove while Kroll and Vladimir tried to brace themselves. He hurled the Xantia at the Paris streets, throwing it into extreme broadsides and drifts rather than so much as touch the brakes. He didn't know for sure that Rossin still lived at the same address and he doubted he would still be there, but right now he didn't have a better idea.

Timofayev could have tipped off Solomon, but Rossin?

Solomon had been his best pupil, bar none. He soaked up everything Dima could teach him as if he already knew it and was just getting a refresher. He had answers before Dima had finished the question; he grasped techniques first time and never needed to practise. He could stab kick and punch more accurately and with more force than any other trainee. He solved whatever challenge Dima threw at him with an effortless ease that was intimidating. More than once it felt to Dima as if Solomon could see into his head and anticipate just what was coming. And right now he felt it again. Solomon, always a step ahead.

Dima brought the Xantia to a halt broadside in front of Rossin's Espace. He was out of the car before it had stopped, wrenching open Rossin's door and pulling him out on to the pavement. Before the Frenchman hit the ground Dima had a knife at his neck. Rossin's eyes bulged like they were about to pop their sockets. Dima caught a glimpse of the Espace interior. It was stuffed with luggage.

'I think your trip's just been called off.'

'Dima, please. I-I don't understand.'

Dima gripped the Frenchman's throat with one hand and applied the knife with the other. 'You don't understand why we're still alive?'

It was all Dima could do not to plunge the knife right into his neck but he'd made enough mistakes for one night. Rossin needed to get the message fast. He flicked the blade up and sliced off an earlobe.

Rossin squealed like a pig until Dima put the flat of the blade against his mouth, the point half up his nostril.

'Where is he – NOW!'

Saliva was running down Rossin's cheek mingling with the steady course of blood oozing from his ear.

'Headed for the airport. He's going to New York.'

'What about Paris? What about the Bourse?'

He shook his head. 'The Bourse is under extra guard. They had a tip off.'

'The nukes. Have they been shipped?'

Rossin nodded. Then stopped.

'I don't know. I don't—.'

'What flight's he on?'

'Atlantis – it's one of those all business class—.'

'Why should I believe you?'

Dima pressed the knife harder against his ear.

'He told me. He said it was leaving at seven a.m.'

Kroll was already on the phone to Omorova, checking the flight.

'Under what name?'

'I don't know. That's the God's truth.'

Dima put his face closer.

'OK, last question: why?'

Rossin swallowed, tears saliva and blood messing up his shirt.

'Please. He made it impossible for me. Dima – you know what he's like. You can't refuse. You understand, Dima. You know me. I'm not cut out for the hard stuff. Surveillance – that's me.'

It was a huge effort of will not to shove the knife right into his neck and have done with it but that would just mean more mess to clear up. He let go and Rossin crumpled to the ground. He looked at his watch – broken in the blast. He lifted Rossin's. Five-fifteen. An hour and forty-five minutes.

He turned to Kroll, who had his cellphone pressed to an ear.

'You want the passenger manifest?'

'No time. You sort this lot out. Get his laptop – everything on it. Grill him for all he's got. Kill him if he doesn't co-operate. I'm going to the airport.'

'You'll never get past security.'

'I'll take Bulganov. I knew he'd come in handy.'

86

'What is this?' A look of disgust suffused Bulganov's face when he saw the scuffed Citroen. Having just been dragged from his bed after three hours' sleep he was not at his best.

'It's what us ordinary mortals use for transport. Get in.'

Dima brought him up to date as he drove.

'Where do I fit in?'

Bulganov's appetite for the chase seemed to have cooled overnight.

'Just use your magic cards to get us through security. He's going to be in the Atlantis VIP lounge and if we miss him there we'll find him at the gate.'

'But I'm not booked in.'

'You are. Omorova sorted it. Plus one bodyguard. Except we're not going to fly.'

Dima had also helped himself to some of Bulganov's wardrobe. Even with a famous oligarch in tow he couldn't have got past security covered in plaster dust and Rossin's blood.

'Have you thought how you're going to stop him?'

'They still have metal cutlery in VIP lounges? Otherwise I'll have to disarm some airport security.'

'We'll make ourselves terribly unpopular.'

'So? We're Russians. We always get to be the bad guys.'

87

The last thing Blackburn remembered was Jackie's smile. He clung on to the memory like it was a lifebelt that kept him from being sucked back into oblivion. After her smile, there were other faces. Then nothing, then the sensation of travel – on a stretcher still, but in the air, because he felt his ears pop. Now he was in a wheelchair, dazed from a chemical sleep, going up in a lift. He had heard traffic, horns, growling diesels, a city definitely.

Someone slapped his face. Not hard, but enough to feel hostile. But he was well used to hostility now. Maybe he was immune. He had heard that song. It was a message from Dima. He was on the case. *He wanted me to know.*

The room had windows but the lower glass was frosted. Two yellowy fluorescents gave the grey-green walls a sickly glow. There was a strong smell of cigarette ash.

'Okay, Henry. Good flight?'

Blackburn focused on the man who had appeared in front of him. Grey, close-cropped hair, light stubble that seemed to cover his head and half his face. Thick neck, big shoulders. A quarterback's build.

'What time is it?'

'Good. Glad to see you're still able to think. Just gone two p.m. Welcome to the Big Apple.'

He leaned down.

'I'm Agent Whistler, with Homeland Security. I'm hearing you've got an idea someone's going to nuke the world's favourite city.'

Blackburn didn't respond.

'Eight hours ago I get a call says there's a Marine in detention in the brig in Donaldson for taking out his CO, and he's got one crazy

309

story to tell. And this is coming from a US Senator no less. Friends in high places, Henry.'

'I don't know anything about that part.'

'Well, that's the part that matters because we sure as hell wouldn't of wasted tax dollars air-freighting you to New York if the Senator hadn't told us to. So now you're here we may as well kill a little time going over your story.'

Each time Blackburn told his tale he thought it sounded less believable. An evil mastermind, a former CIA asset gone rogue, bent on the destruction of the West, with simultaneous nuclear detonations in Paris and New York, together with the sum total of his and Dima's pooled information – Blackburn's sighting of the maps, the name on Bashir's dying lips and Dima's knowledge of Solomon. All the time he was speaking, Whistler stared out of the unfrosted half of the window, the morning sun bouncing off his glistening forehead. Blackburn couldn't tell if he was paying attention or not. Maybe he was just going through the motions because someone had told him to. When he was done, Whistler turned and faced him.

'So here's what I'm getting from this. Stop me when I go off piste. You saw two maps in a Tehran bank vault: Paris and New York. Paris one's got a big 'X marks the spot' right over the stock exchange.'

'It was an inked circle.'

'Whatever. And there's another mark on New York, right on Times Square. Any dates, times?'

'Two bombs the same day – maximum chaos. Like 9/11.'

'Your theory.'

'Dima's.'

'And he's the expert right? He's the one spun the yarn about this scheming devil. This ain't a comic book and you sure ain't no superhero, Blackburn.'

'I saw him slice the head off an American Marine. I saw his face, I saw his eyes. I saw the same man leave the Tehran Bank with a pair of nukes.'

Whistler looked down, studied a broken fingernail, then picked at it.

'Some story son. And your Russian pal, Dima. Why you covering for him, huh?'

'I'm not covering for anyone.'

'You killed your own CO to save his neck. I call that covering.'

Blackburn felt what little patience he had left draining away.'

'Hey Whistler, why are you guys covering for Solomon?'

Whistler wheeled round, his lips almost curling with distaste.

'Son, we ask the questions.'

'Well I've got no more answers. Why doesn't anyone go and check out Solomon? Does having been a CIA asset make him an untouchable?'

'Son—.'

'I AM NOT YOUR FUCKING SON.'

'Solomon is a deep cover CIA asset. There is no question—.'

'Is that how you're going to explain it to your Senator when a nuke goes off on Wall Street? "Sir, there was no question in our mind so we DIDN'T FUCKING CHECK".'

The outburst made Blackburn feel faint, but he kept his eyes fixed on Whistler. Something had to give. He owed it to Dima. He owed it to himself.

88

Dima's driving had shot Bulganov's nerves but he was wide awake
when they pulled into the VIP parking area. Two heavies came
forward to wave them away but Bulganov's ID and VIP card did
the trick. 'Pardon, Monsieur.'

'Only trying to do their job,' said Bulganov.

'Aren't we all?' said Dima.

An Atlantis steward was waiting with their tickets.

'The flight leaves in twenty minutes. Do you have bags to check?'

'We're travelling light.'

Dima told Bulganov to hang back. He needed to do this alone
and he needed full concentration. His heart was thumping. He was
Doctor Frankenstein seeking to reclaim his monster. The lounge
was all grey leather and glass tables. A lot more restrained than
Bulganov's penthouse, but this was France not Russia. Twenty or so
passengers, almost all men, several hunched over laptops, some at
computer terminals, several on the phone, a few lounging in comfy
chairs. All this at five in the morning. When do people sleep?
thought Dima. When did *I* sleep?

Dima scanned the lounge, methodically eliminating each passenger until he got to the one who was furthest from the door. His
face was obscured by a *Wall Street Journal*, but there was something
about the hands, the frame – indelibly imprinted on his memory.
As Dima came nearer the paper was lowered. For the first time in
twenty years, they faced each other.

If anything he looked younger. Perhaps he had had some work
done on his face. His hair was a bit longer than before, parted in the
centre and still jet black, as were his eyebrows. The cheekbones
showed a few broken blood vessels and the whites of his eyes were

312

pinkish and bloodshot. The suit was tailored and the white shirt open halfway down his chest was more consistent with a playboy than a West-hating terrorist.

Solomon glared at him through half-closed eyes, one eyebrow raised a little as if weary of being approached by yet another annoying interloper, rather than the person who had moulded him into a lethal asset.

Solomon spoke first. 'You don't give up, do you?'

Dima felt an uncomfortable mixture of hatred and tenderness. It was hard not to erase entirely your positive feelings for someone you once regarded as close. But judging by Solomon's expression it was all too clear that the feeling wasn't mutual.

'You know me.' Dima nodded at the surroundings – the rich men awaiting an expensive flight. 'You've done all right, it seems. Is this what you wanted?'

Solomon looked away. 'What I want, Mayakovsky, is something you could not possibly appreciate.'

'Not being a psychopath.'

He gave a weary shrug. 'The world is out of balance. Something has to give.'

He folded up the paper and placed it neatly on the table beside him. Then he folded his hands in his lap. Each movement had a precision that seemed robotic. That's what he is, Dima thought – a machine, inhabiting a human form.

He smiled a thin smile. 'When I heard you were on my trail I was amused. I hadn't given you a second thought for – oh – longer than I can remember. So I decided to do a little research on you.'

Over the PA came the announcement that the Atlantis flight to JFK was ready to board.

Dima found his voice. 'There's not much to research.'

Solomon's eyebrows rose. 'You've certainly gone down in the world, that's true, despite giving up alchohol – or have you lapsed? But there was much you never told me, Dima, when I was your eager pupil. I never imagined for example that you had once loved a woman, that you had even fathered a child.'

Solomon's lips curved into a thin smile. 'So very nearly the family

313

man. How very touching. And how sad you never knew him. He's at the Bourse, as you know. A nice boy, looks like you.'

Dima's heart was smashing against his ribs, as if it was about to punch its way out of his chest.

'Timofayev's dead. I killed him. So's Kaffarov. It's over. You're on your own.'

Solomon smirked. 'You've forgotten, Dima, I was always on my own. I've never acted otherwise.'

'You've missed your chance in Paris. You think you'll get lucky in New York?'

He frowned, dismayed, his eyes glinting now. 'Whatever do you mean? I never miss anything. Surely you remember that?'

Solomon's eyes were wells of deathly black. 'You know what I'm most disappointed about? That I didn't arrange for an occasion to slice your irritating head off your sad old shoulders with a nice sharp blade. It would have given me such pleasure to watch you die.'

He started to get up. Dima lunged forward and grabbed his neck with both hands. Solomon's crushing grip closed round his wrists. Immediately an alarm sounded and out of nowhere half a dozen security goons surged towards them. Four of them lifted Dima off and forced him to the ground.

Solomon straightened his suit and turned towards the other passengers hurrying away from the melee. Then he stopped and came back, bending down so his face was just inches from Dima's.

'Poor old Mayakovsky. Always in the wrong place. You should have been at the Bourse trying to save your son.' He glanced at his watch. 'Too bad you'll never have that reunion. Ten-thirty and—.' He snapped his fingers in the air. 'Au revoir, Paris.'

314

89

It was twenty minutes since Whistler had put in a call to Langley and he was still on hold. The CIA operative supposedly in charge of Homeland Security Liaison had called in sick and no one had been called to deputise.

'*So much for joined-up intelligence,*' Whistler said to the Vivaldi coming out of his cell phone.

The person who did pick up had to go away and double-check Whistler's credentials before routing him to a department called Asset Registry. He asked a dreamy-sounding woman called Cheryl for available background on asset codename Solomon and was told that it wasn't available '*at this time*'.

'*What time would it be available then, Cheryl?*'

She snorted. '*Like never. You don't have the clearance, Hon.*'

Whistler had had enough of being given the run-around. Blackburn had thrown down the gauntlet. What *would* Whistler say if Blackburn had something? How would it feel to be the one who dismissed him? He often thought of those guys who chose not to follow up on the suspicious trainee pilots who went on to down the Twin Towers. Would he have done the same? Would he want to live with that?

So Whistler did something that was bound to earn him a reprimand. He called Senator Douglis's office and asked to speak to him. To his amazement he was put straight through.

'*Sir, I'm the agent detailed to follow up on Sergeant Blackburn.*'

'*Very good to hear from you, Agent Whistler. How can I help?*'

Whistler told him the gist and the Senator said he'd get right on to it. Three minutes later his cellphone chirped. It was the Deputy Director of Homeland Security, a man he had never met.

315

'*Whistler, you trying to get yourself fired?*'

'*Sir, I'd rather be fired for trying to get a question answered than be the one who didn't ask the question.*'

Half an hour passed. Whistler took Blackburn a cup of coffee.

'I want you to know that I just put my career on the line because of you.'

Blackburn didn't respond. He was too busy experiencing the first cup of coffee he'd had since this whole nightmare started.

Another half an hour passed and three men he had never seen before came in, accompanied by Whistler's immediate boss, Dumphrey, red-faced and still in his golfing kit. All three had the same grim expression. The shortest and baldest one carried a large ring binder of ID photos.

'Okay. Let's do it.'

'This better be worth it, Whistler, or you are in so much shit.' whispered Dumphrey.

90

'Okay, okay, okay. Just give me a minute, gentlemen.'

Bulganov was discovering depths of humility he didn't know he had.

'Gentlemen, I apologise. We are Russian. We are an excitable people. When we have our falling out – it can be bad. Thank the Lord God no one was armed – thanks to your rigorous security. If you wish me to get the Interior Minister on the phone I will make a personal apology right now.'

The hint that Bulganov had friends in high places stalled them for a moment. But Officer Giraud, Senior Airport Security Officer at Charles De Gaulle, wasn't one to have rank pulled on him by some fat cat Russian oligarch.

Giraud ignored Bulganov for the moment. He was giving Dima a close look. The man was a mess. He appeared to have dust in his hair. There was a faint smell of urine. He had examined the Iranian passport, heard Bulganov's quick-witted account of him being a fugitive from the regime. And he wasn't convinced. Besides, he thought he had seen this face somewhere. He would have to check.

Dima was silently cursing himself for the futile attack on Solomon. Another mistake. He was unravelling. But crowding out all coherent thought was what Solomon had just told him.

He wouldn't have given up on the Bourse because of the security. Solomon never gave up on anything. Either he had already placed the bomb before the guard was doubled or he had gone in there as part of the guard.

Bulganov was still trying to negotiate.

'If you would consider, on this occasion making an exception and releasing my man back into my custody, I will be forever indebted to you …'

Giraud was taking no notice. He was looking at a mugshot image on his iPhone. His eyes suddenly widened. 'Dima Mayakovsky. You are coming with us.'

91

The one in charge of the ring binder was Gordon, from the CIA's New York office. Smaller and fatter than Whistler, but oozing the natural superiority of Langley's finest.

'Gentlemen, if you would stand away from the desk when I open the binder, thank you. These are classified images. I don't need to remind you this is a highly unusual situation we find ourselves in, showing photos of CIA assets to a felon.'

Whistler heard his boss let out an indignant sigh before complying.

Gordon placed the binder on the table in front of Blackburn. They all watched as he turned the pages. There were fifty mug shots in the binder. Blackburn took his time. Despite the coffee, whatever they had sedated him with was still coursing through his system, weighing down his eyelids. He recalled Harker's turbanned executioner. He remembered the face on the bank security screen. Solomon, the name Al Bashir had uttered with his dying breath. He turned the pages, examining each face one by one.

One of the Homeland guys sighed and glanced at his watch. He was going to take his time. He was going to get this right if it was the last useful thing he ever did.

92

Nine-thirty. They cuffed Dima and put him in the back of the Renault, between two airport security officers. A third officer sat up front beside the driver. The sun was up. The downtown expressway was filling with rush hour traffic that grudgingly parted at the sound of the siren. Dima closed his eyes. All the better to concentrate. Less than an hour. Solomon had planted the device – or his people had. It could be anywhere in the building. It would have been smuggled in disguised as – what? Some kind of delivery – a container, a box. Something that no one would be surprised by.

Was there more that Rossin knew? If there was, Kroll would find it. The Cargotrak van – had it been used to deliver the bomb to the Bourse? Bernard, Syco, Ramon. How much did they know?

They were headed into the centre. The Eiffel Tower came into view, they tore round the Arc de Triomphe, weaving through the traffic. The driver was enjoying himself. One of the toughs next to Dima told him to ease up, but he didn't. Dima kept very still, didn't complain or protest. Always a challenge to keep your guard up when your quarry goes passive. He was saving himself for the right moment. None of them had seatbelts on. That was useful. He had spotted the driver's firearm in a holster under his right armpit. He watched the road for a moment, when they were closing in on another vehicle. There needed to be some impact. A truck, laden with building materials. Dima took a deep breath to oxygenate himself before putting all the force he could muster into his legs. Lunging forward, he threw his cuffed wrists over the driver's head and with his knee against the seat he yanked the cuff chain tight, moving his hands back and forth to grind the chain into the man's neck as he tensed his neck muscles to resist. The driver's head snapped back and his hands left the wheel. The two guards each side of Dima clawed at him, but a microsecond later the Peugeot ploughed into the truck.

The noise of the collision was drowned by the explosion of the inflating airbags, which pushed the driver and his front-seat passenger firmly back in their seats. At the same time, the driver's seat buffered Dima. When the airbags deflated, a second or so later, the driver fell forward, his body limp. The front airbags couldn't do much for the burly, unbelted passengers. The guard on Dima's right went over the front passenger's head and was half out of the windscreen, crushing the man in front as the seat folded beneath him as he went. Dima released the driver from his stranglehold and dived for his pistol, flicking off the safety catch and firing it into his side before it was out of the holster. The guard on his left was still conscious. He already had his gun half out. Nothing else for it. Dima blasted him in the temple, blood splattering the cloth interior, then patted his pockets and found the keys to the cuffs, plus – also handy – his airport security ID. He reached past him to open the door, booted him out of the car, then climbed over him and out. A pedestrian was staring open-mouthed at the scene. Dima waved the gun at him with one hand, and the keys with the other.

'Open these or you're dead. Now!'

Bending his head slightly as if to avoid being shot, the young man took the keys with trembling hands and undid the cuffs.

'And give me your phone.'

A new iPhone.

'Sorry. Hope it's insured.'

Dima was off, running now in the direction of the Bourse – but it was more than a mile away. He dialled Kroll as he ran. The street was choked with traffic. He leapt into the road in front of a girl on a scooter.

Kroll picked up.

'Hang on.'

He showed her the gun.

'*Mademoiselle, je suis désolé.*'

She dismounted, her hands upturned and her eyes wide.

'You'll find it near the Bourse.'

He jumped on and sped off down the pavement, which was less congested than the street, steering one-handed, phone in the other.

'I just heard from Bulganov,' said Kroll.

'Call the Bourse security. There is definitely, repeat definitely, a bomb in there. Persuade them to get everyone out. Something must have been planted in there. Unobtrusive. Grill Rossin. Maybe he knows something.'

Pedestrians flattened themselves against shopfronts as Dima tore down the pavement. Ahead, the Bourse loomed over the surrounding streets, a neoclassical monument to the creation of wealth. Its pale, timeless columns looked invulnerable.

Dima ditched the scooter, almost pulling it with him as he ran. His cell rang again. Kroll.

'Dima! It's in a photocopier.'

'How many offices have they got in there? It's going to be like looking for a needle in a fucking haystack.'

'The police alert says "Shoot on sight". You'll never get in the building.'

'I'm going to try.'

Kroll's next words were just audible before his voice was blotted out by sirens.

'The copier, could be an Imajquik. Logo's blue and red.'

93

New York City

Blackburn turned the pages slowly, struggling to take in each face. Something about the nature of those mug shots gave them all the same sort of blank, impassive look. But then they were meant to be unmemorable. They'd been trained to give as little of themselves away as they could, to blend in and disappear.

'Gentlemen, please.'

Gordon gestured at Whistler and Dumphrey, who had edged forward. 'Let's give the guy some space. We've come this far, we don't want any mistakes.'

Blackburn kept looking. The room was so quiet that all he could hear was the hum of the traffic somewhere far below. New York at work, but for how much longer? He tried once more to conjure up the face in the Harker footage, the face on the security screen. The image in his memory was bleaching out, as if Solomon was willing it to fade.

He got to the last page. He recognised none of them as Solomon. He looked up, felt the atmosphere in the room change.

Then he turned the book over and started again from the back. On the fifth from the last page there were only three mugshots and one blank space. He paused at the page and looked up again.

'Ah, for fuck's sake,' groaned Dumphrey.

Blackburn just kept looking at them, his finger on the page. Under the blank space was the serial number: 240156 L.

'Now you want us to think Langley doctored the book.'

Whistler found the idea amusing. Gordon didn't. He clenched his chubby fists, little white dots showing on the tips of his knuckles.

'That's an outrageous suggestion.'

Blackburn tried to keep his voice steady, but anger and frustration gave it an alien vibrato. He dropped it to a whisper.

'Solomon isn't here. He's your agent. But he's not here. Why?'

Dumphrey sighed and looked at the others.

'I think I've had enough of this freak.'

94

Dima mounted the steps, tucking the gun out of sight and holding the airport security pass in his hand. Two armed guards blocked his way. He held up the pass as he walked quickly towards them, not stopping.

'Security chief's office, quick! You've got a suspect package in there.'

They seemed about to stop and question him, then thought better of it.

'First floor: top of the stairs.'

Beyond the massive ancient doors the trading floor was swarming with men in those loose-fitting red jackets. The walls were ablaze with lines of orange and yellow prices.

Nine forty-four. Dima hit the grand marble stairs running, barely taking in the rich gold panelling. He slammed his hand against the first fire alarm he saw. Nothing: disabled. Solomon wanted everyone at their posts for maximum carnage. He turned round and headed for the basement, where he almost collided with a man in overalls.

'Where do your deliveries come in?'

'The cargo dock. But you can't just—.'

He ran through some double doors, his eyes scanning everything. In the cargo dock, a fork-lift truck, several trolleys and boxes stacked on pallets. And in a glass booth, three men hunched over mugs of coffee.

'Sorry to disturb you. I'm looking for an Imajquik photocopier, delivered by Cargotrak.'

None of them looked up.

'We're on our break,' said one.

Dima was tempted to shoot all three, but he needed their help.

'Cock-up our end. Sent you the wrong model. Need it back or my life's not worth living.'

One of them stopped chewing and looked at the others.

'Like he said. We're on our break.'

Faces glazed as they chewed and gulped.

'Just tell me where it is and I'll find it.'

They looked at each other. One sniggered.

'It?'

'Yeah, what d'you mean, *it?*'

'Guys – I'm in a hurry here.'

'You got authorisation? This is a global financial trading institution, friend. Only authorised contractors.'

They exchanged the complacent looks of men with safe jobs and generous pensions. It would serve the French right if they were all blown up, thought Dima: their love of bureaucracy was downright pathological.

Dima grabbed the nearest one by his shirt collar. Hot coffee spewed out of his mug across the other two. He put the airport goon's gun against his temple, grinding it left and right, twisting his overfed skin over the muzzle.

'This is my authorisation.'

The other two leapt out of their chairs cowering.

'There's – they've been coming in all week.'

'Four over the weekend.'

'That's better.'

Nothing like a gun to the head to inspire sudden helpfulness.

'They went up to the second floor.'

'And the third.'

95

Dima considered his options as he ran up the flight of stairs. No alarm. No way of evacuating – even if he got anyone to believe him. Start screaming 'Terrorist bomb! Get out!' and he risked arousing the attention of security, who would most likely shoot him on sight.

He had to just keep looking, knowing that every second brought detonation closer. He got Kroll on his mobile.

'Second floor. Get here, now!'

He reached the second floor and ran straight into the first room he saw. Five women looked up at him from their screens.

'Any photocopiers – newly delivered?'

They all looked blank. He ran to the next room: more people at screens.

'Sure,' said one, pointing. Dima wheeled round. In the corner, to the left of the door, a woman was lifting the lid on a grey machine and placing a piece of paper on the glass.

'Don't!' screamed Dima. He leapt forward and pulled her arm away.

'Excuse me,' said the woman, wrenching herself free. 'I was here first.'

She jabbed a button on the console. The machine whirred, produced its copy, and she pushed past him to the door.

'Some people have no manners.'

The next two rooms each had a copier. Both had been used. Could it be in a functioning machine? No way.

In the fifth room he found a lone woman. He came in so fast she shrieked and leapt out of her seat.

'New photocopiers – from Imajquik?'

A look of recognition.

'Are you from maintenance?'

She smiled. 'You want Adam's office – upstairs.'

'Where upstairs?'

'You look – is everything all right?'

'Just – tell me where.'

'Adam Levalle, Deputy Director of Communications.'

Dima took the stairs three at a time, and burst through the door marked Director of Communications. Another woman, on the phone: young, dark, pretty and indignant. She frowned, putting her hand over the phone.

'Have you an appointment?'

'Photocopier!' said Dima, struggling for breath. 'Where is it?'

Dima scanned the room. None in sight.

She sighed, pointed at a pair of closed double doors, and went back to her call.

'You'll have to come back though. Monsieur Levalle's on a call.'

Dima marched towards the doors. She dropped the phone as if it were infected, got out of her chair and came forward to intercept him.

'Did you hear what I said? And where's your ID?'

He pushed her gently back into her seat with a look that suggested she should stay there, and pushed open the doors.

A smart office: wood panelling, a desk, a meeting table and chairs, nice leather ones. A young man was on the phone, his face half-hidden by the receiver. The woman was persistent. She grabbed Dima by the elbow.

'Sir – you can't.'

Adam Levalle, Deputy Director of Communications looked up: a clear, bright face, full of promise – instantly recognisable.

Dima froze.

96

Gordon, Whistler and Dumphrey exchanged glances.

Whistler spoke first.

'Well, does he exist or not, this Solomon?'

Gordon was hanging on to the threads of his authority.

'I have to make a call. Is there somewhere I—?'

Dumphrey exploded.

'Well, make it here then, and make it fast. Either this is the biggest goddamn hoax since Adolf Hitler's Diary – or we're about to have World War Three.'

Gordon called Langley and waited while the call-holding music wafted out of his phone. Then he suddenly straightened himself. *'Sir, Good Afternoon ... Yes Sir, yes but ...* I need identification on Asset 240156 L.'

His cheeks reddened. *'Yes I understand Sir, sorry to have troubled ...'*

Gordon looked deflated.

'240156 L is on deep cover long term. His image is not available at this time.'

He looked thunderously at Whistler, who was enjoying Gordon's humiliation.

'My advice is that you continue your interrogation a little more forcefully until you have something useful and STOP JERKING US AROUND!'

Dumphrey slammed the table with the flat of his hand.

'Okay, I'm calling time on this.'

97

Paris

Adam Levalle finished his call and looked at the strongly-built, dishevelled stranger who stood before him, breathing rapidly. He clearly didn't belong in the building. He looked exhausted, yet on high alert.

'I'm sorry, Sir: this – person – just burst in here, babbling about the photocopier. Shall I call security?'

Dima struggled to breathe. Paliov's photographs: the young man on the bridge, in the park. *Solomon saw them too.* And sending the bomb to him, to Dima's son, was all part of his plan.

'Ah,' said Adam Levalle and nodded at the copier. 'Shouldn't be in here anyway. We hardly use them these days.' He smiled. 'The paperless office. Supposedly.'

'And he pushed me.'

'Thanks, Colette: I'll take it from here.'

Dima snapped back into the moment. Took his eyes off Adam. Went towards the copier.

'Has anyone touched it?'

'Colette said it doesn't work. I looked for a plug but—.'

The clock on the wall said ten to ten. He turned back to Adam.

'You need to leave. Get far away from here. As far as you possibly can.'

Adam Levalle was not the sort of person who just did what he was told, especially in his own office. And the unannounced stranger's intensity, his appearance, like someone who had come through a lot to reach this spot, at this particular moment, aroused his curiosity. Clearly there had to be a reason.

Dima examined the machine. No power connection. No wires. He turned back to Adam.

'I can't raise the alarm. It's been sabotaged. And I can't defuse it. If you do what I tell you, it could save your life. Does the Bourse have a bomb shelter?'

Adam Levalle nodded.

'Go there now. Take as many as you can, quickly. Don't wait if they protest. And do not let anyone try to stop you. Please – just go.' Dima, arms spread, was trying to herd them towards the door.

Colette stood her ground. 'Sir, this man has no ID. I think I should call security.'

'What are you going to do?' Adam asked him, unfazed, curious.

'I have to get this away from here – as far away as possible. Please do as I say.'

Dima's eyes were on fire now.

Adam considered this.

'You'll need some help. I think there's a trolley – in the stationery store down the hall.'

Colette's hand was on the phone.

'I'm calling security.'

Dima strode across the room, prised the receiver from her hand.

'Okay, now listen. Inside this copier is a bomb. We have minutes – if we're lucky – to save the lives of everyone in this building and in Paris. If you get security they will detain me and I'll resist and they'll end up shooting me and everyone in the city will die.'

'But – who are you?'

'Yes,' said Adam. 'Who are you?'

Dima could hear rapid footsteps outside. He took a step towards Adam, and breathed in, daring himself to say the name.

'Was your mother's name Camille?'

Adam frowning, nodded. 'My ... my natural mother yes, but she's – how do you know that?'

'Then if nothing else, do this for her.'

98

Adam and Dima wheeled the copier along the corridor and into a lift. Adam kept glancing at the intense stranger who had just burst into his life, warning of imminent apocalypse. And who, mystifyingly, seemed to know a detail from his life that he had shared with very few people.

'Can I ask you how you knew—?'

Dima interrupted. 'Just let's get through this.' He couldn't tempt fate by imagining anything beyond the next few minutes.

Kroll materialised in front of them, breathless from running up the stairs. As soon as Dima saw him he waved the young man away.

'Go Adam – go to the shelter,' Dima shouted, waving Kroll forward. 'Go there and don't come out until there's some kind of all clear.' He pushed him away as Kroll took his side of the trolley.

'Strange location to plant it. I'd have thought a better place would be closer to the ground. Closer to the foundations, more likely to demolish everything in one go. On the other hand, it isn't a conventional bomb . . .'

It was Kroll's trademark way of handling tension – to talk incessantly, until Dima shut him up. But Dima had tuned him right out. He wasn't hearing anything. He was thinking about where and how. He did notice that Kroll was wearing identical overalls to the unhelpful men in the cargo dock – though with a telltale small redringed hole in the chest.

It was cramped in the servicelift. The copier took up almost all of the space. Kroll squashed up against the doors and jabbed Basement. The best bet was back to the cargo dock and whatever van they could hijack. The lift struggled into action. It was old and slow. Agonisingly slow.

Dima was squashed against the rear, Kroll against the doors. He was still going on, apparently unbothered by the imminent apocalyptic danger inches from them.

'You know, Dima, after this one, I'm really thinking of taking a break. After all, the kids are growing up. Absent fathers and all that. If I showed their mothers that I was really making an effort, showed real willing, I think things could be different. What do you think? Maybe do a little work for Bulganov. Nothing too arduous, you know ...'

Dima wasn't taking it in. His head was already hammering from an overdose of adrenalin.

The doors opened. For a millisecond the world stood still as Dima looked from Kroll to the open doors and back to Kroll: three guards, and three slugs that smashed straight into his friend before he could even raise his pistol. He'd shielded Dima, buying him an extra split second in which to aim and fire three double taps – one into each guard's centre mass. In two seconds all three dropped like liquid, one after the other. Kroll's body blocked the trolley. Dima could only climb over the copier to his friend, who still had a faraway look in his lifeless eyes, the memory of his kids embedded in his expression.

'Goodbye, dear friend.'

Dima moved the body to one side and grabbed one of the guard's weapons and spare mags as he pushed the trolley forward, scooting it as fast as he dared towards the cargo dock. No time for any niceties now. Everyone in his path was a target. He manoeuvred the trolley through a set of double doors and into the cargo dock. An electrician's van was just pulling out. He raced round the trolley, grabbed the door and wrenched it open. The driver didn't look old enough to own a licence, let alone be in charge of a Transit van.

'Turn it off. Out. Now!'

The youth obliged.

'Don't move.'

Dima looked round for more available hands. The glass booth

was empty except for one body – undressed: Kroll's source of overalls. He saw a movement behind a stack of boxes.

'Come out!' He fired a warning shot to speed things up.

Another of the unhelpful men from the glass booth appeared. He looked like he had been sick.

'Over here. Get this thing into the van.'

Two more guards appeared. Dima took them down in two short bursts. The youth was crying now.

'Just put the copier in the fucking van or you're next.'

Dima prodded the boy with his gun. They got the doors open but both of them had lost their strength.

'You two – that end,' he shouted, grabbing the other end himself. Together they hefted one corner on to the Transit's load bed then Dima pushed the copier all the way in.

'Do nothing to get in my way or you're dead, okay?' The youth nodded eagerly.

Dima leapt into the driving seat and was off, accelerating down the ramp and out of the rear of the building. Ten past ten. He headed southwest down Rue de Richelieu, passing the Louvre on his left. Lights on, hazards flashing, gun and steering wheel in his left hand, his right hand on the horn. At the Quai des Tuileries he went right, into the oncoming traffic. At least they could see him and see that he wasn't getting out of their way. He had to get out, get as far out as he could. It had been so long. All his intimate memory of Paris was either faded or out of date. Think! Where could he find somewhere empty, in Paris, in the time he had left?

Two police vans were now heading towards him, straddling the lanes. Nowhere to go. A question of nerve. He'd have more than them. He headed for the gap between them. They parted at the last second, but he crossed a junction and clipped a bus as he swerved left trying to avoid it, sideswiping a Citroen and scraping off the nearside mirror. The Citroen span round like a toy, taking out three more cars and starting a full scale pile-up. He jammed on the brakes, threw the Transit into reverse, crossed the reservation and continued. On the Voie Georges-Pompidou now, hitting a hundred plus kph.

Madness. At any point someone could smash into him and that would be the end. But every metre he travelled was moving the epicentre further away from the heart of Paris. And further away from Adam Levalle.

99

Blackburn was on his feet, a hood over his head, being marched down a corridor by two goons. For a brief moment, when he was allowed to look at the mugshots, he had dared to think the tide had turned and they had taken him seriously. It didn't last.

He could hear Whistler and Gordon behind. Their tone suggested that they were arguing, but from under the hood he couldn't make out what they were saying.

'Where am I going?'

'To the special place where we get you to tell us the whole truth real fast,' said one of the goons.

The other chipped in. 'Ever thought you were drowning? No? Well you're about to find out just what it's like.'

They entered a lift that plunged them downwards. The next corridor was colder, the floor bare concrete, the sounds bounced and echoed against the hard unyielding surfaces. A door swung closed behind him. The room was dark. The sliver of light coming under the hood had disappeared. Blackburn could smell water, chlorinated like a swimming pool. Suddenly the hood was whipped off and there in front of him was a gurney, at one end a bucket. The goons had gone. Two men stood either side, their faces shrouded by ski masks. One held a large transparent bottle with a tube stuck in it.

'Wanna change your mind before you lie down?'

Two cell phones went off simultaneously, one playing the *Hawaii Five-O* theme, the other the *Stars and Stripes*. Blackburn looked round to see both Gordon and Whistler listening, faces blank with dismay. The ski mask men were both behind the gurney. Laid on a narrow table to one side were several ratchet straps and a night stick.

'Holy mother of fuck,' said Gordon.

336

One of the ski mask men shifted his weight, impatient. 'We good to go, right?'

Whistler was frozen, open-mouthed. Eventually he spoke. 'It's Paris. Full nuclear alert.'

Blackburn's thoughts were a blur. Just when he had reached the point where he was seriously doubting his sanity, Paris was happening. New York was next. Blackburn looked at the men in the ski masks, the gurney waiting for him. The news had gone through him like a lightning bolt. His whole body jolted into life. No, he said to himself. This is *not* as far as it goes.

He lunged forward and with both arms outstretched shoved the gurney hard so it slammed against both the ski mask men, pushing them over. Then, twisting to the right, he snatched up the nightstick and swung it at Gordon, smashing it against his skull so hard that he dropped on to the floor in a heap. Whistler was in a corner, nowhere to go. He reached into his jacket but Blackburn landed the stick right on the back of his hand and his M9 dropped to the ground. He lifted his other to protect himself. Blackburn kicked the gun towards himself, grabbed it, and was about to land the stick hard on Whistler's nose when he paused.

'What's it to be, Whistler? You don't want to be the guy who did nothing while New York was wiped off the map?'

He didn't respond.

'Paris is probably burning already. Walk me out of here, you could be the man who helped save your city. Unless you'd rather be found dead in a black ops torture chamber.'

After the institutional greys and khakis of the various rooms he had been incarcerated in, the frenzy of glitz and flashing colours was an assault on Blackburn's senses. He stood at the north end of the square, a few yards from the red 'M' of the subway entrance, wearing nothing but the tunic he had been flown to New York in – under the biker kit Whistler had ridden to work in that morning. Whistler had been a good choice of accomplice. He had enough imagination – just – to give Blackburn the benefit of the doubt. That was generous, since Blackburn knew he could still fail. What did he expect – to

337

find the second shiny suitcase parked next to the *Good Morning America* studios? The zipper news crawl on the side of the building made no mention of Paris.

He made another tour of the area. It was full of people: tourists, shoppers, commuters, families with children. He thought of his first visit – as an eight-year-old with his parents. His mother had steered him away from a doorway below a lit-up picture of a girl in a bikini holding a cocktail. He'd thought she looked pretty. Now the doorway and the whole block had been replaced by the M&Ms store. It was getting towards rush hour. He would stay here till midnight and beyond if necessary.

A half hour passed. The stream of people heading for the subway was getting bigger. Through the throng of departing office workers a giant clown waddled towards him, leering madly. Blackburn moved to the left. Whoever was inside the suit thought it would be funny if he moved the same way. Blackburn turned away and the clown mimicked his move a second time. A little girl giggled and pointed. Wired to snapping point, Blackburn felt like punching him to the ground. Instead he turned a full 180 degrees just in time to see a familiar figure pause at the top of the 40th and Broadway subway entrance in front of Citibank. Their eyes locked briefly. Blackburn scanned the face, the black eyes, the high cheekbones and the heavy brow.

And then Solomon dived down the stairs into the darkness.

100

Dima still had no plan. And just five minutes left. Just keep going, keep going, and thinking. The Seine now on his left. He could ditch in there if he could get to it – but the barriers – he'd have to find some kind of ramp. Quai Saint-Exupéry now, passing Pont d'Issy-les-Moulineaux. Barges moored along the river. A police Peugeot in the mirror closing in on him. They wouldn't risk firing, there was too much traffic. A round slammed into the rear window. Wrong.

He wove between cars and trucks, came up on the nearside of a transporter laden with Toyotas. The cop Peugeot was on the other side of it. Dima floored the accelerator as far as it would go, got ahead then jammed on the brakes. The transporter driver swerved to the right, his trailer jack-knifing across the carriageway and tipping its load on to the road, one of the Toyotas smashing on to the cops' roof.

The Quai du Point du Jour turned into the Quai Georges Gorse and curved west following the river's tight turn at Ile Seguin, once the site of the Renault factory – the whole crescent-shaped island given over to the plant. Five thousand workers had churned out cars day and night. Now it was deserted, the factory walls flattened. A connecting bridge was coming up – no intersection. Dima threw the Transit into a right which took him north, then a left, and then another. Ahead now was the bridge to the island, with gates across it. At least that meant nobody was home. He braced himself and charged at the gates, bouncing over them as they burst and fell – then headed for what he guessed was the centre of the island and slammed to a halt.

Five minutes left. Five minutes to live. Five minutes to try and stop it. He opened the rear doors, climbed in, and with all his force pushed the copier out on to the dirt. It fell on its side, bursting the casing and exposing the device. No detonation. He kicked the shards of the copier away, then grabbed the electrician's tool bag: now concentrate, Dima, and get to work.

All his emotion was shut down now – his mind just a processor, making choices, decisions, not even thinking about Adam Levalle.

The shiny aluminium casing gave no apparent sign of a way in. No labels, no serial numbers, no clues of any kind. Inside would be a tube with two pieces of uranium. When rammed together by a detonator – that would cause the blast. With some sort of firing unit to do the business and a timer to tell it when.

On one of the narrower sides he found a rectangular panel. He got a chisel from the tool bag and prised it open. He'd defused IEDs in Afghanistan but that was a long while ago. And he'd been trained to do it with the skill and patience of a watchmaker – but there was no time for craftsmanship. The timer was under the panel, an LED display –'04.10'. Four minutes, ten seconds. Solomon – obsessed with timekeeping – no wonder the rest of the world had made him so full of hate.

Three minutes, fifty seconds. He grabbed a claw hammer and tried levering out the timer. It wouldn't budge. Solidly welded to an inner frame, it looked like high tensile steel. It might only be small, but even this size was enough to devastate the city and everyone in it.

He thought about Blackburn: had they finally listened to him? If this went off maybe they'd believe him – but you never knew with Americans. Once they'd made up their minds about something, or someone, they didn't like to change them.

Okay, forget the timer: go for the detonator. He jumped back into the van. More tools – but nothing that looked useful. Wait – the van itself. He fell into the driving seat and turned on the ignition. Nothing. It was on a slight incline. He pushed his whole weight against the thing and moved it a few metres away, then set the van rolling, with just enough momentum to get over it. Push and steer, and just hope to God it worked. The rear wheels met the outer casing, dented it and split a seam. Good enough. He worked on that with the claw hammer for a full thirty seconds. Sirens now, a whole squadron, coming down the Rue Troyon. What took them so long?

01.50. One minute fifty seconds on the LED. Get to the detonator now – fused solid to the tubes. Someone really didn't want this tampered with.

Out of the corner of his eye he saw a row of blue flashing lights. One or the other – not long now. At least he'd have company for the end. He got the claw hammer between the detonator and the tubes. It wasn't moving though. Come on Dima! 00.48 now. One more idea. The cop cars were on the bridge. He looked down, and wondered if, just maybe, your focus gets that little bit sharper when you're sure you're going to die. He threw the hammer away, grasped the detonator in one bare hand, the rest of the device in the other, squeezed the detonator and twisted. 00.09, 00.08. Tighter! The whole detonator – it was attached like an oil cap on an engine – it turned a fraction, then some more. 04, 03, 02 . . .

Game over. Dima thought he saw 00.00. A fraction of a second while the mechanism showed its deadly signal. Then the brightest, whitest flash. And a sensation of flying, but no landing.

Epilogue

In the Bois de Boulogne, the leaves were rustling in the breeze, which was pleasant. Several tables away a small dog was refusing to stop yapping. The more pieces of cake its owner fed it the more it barked. Vladimir let out a low groan.

'I'm afraid I'm going to have to shoot her.'

'Do something to take his mind off it.' Omorova said, lifting her gaze from her iPad so Dima could read her lips.

'I'm off duty,' said Dima from behind his dark glasses. 'It's Sunday. I'm here relaxing in Paris. And since I can't hear anything because my eardrums are still shot, I'm fine thank you very much.'

He raised the binoculars again and scanned the promenading couples.

'You know, you could be arrested for that.'

'Whatever you think I'm doing, you're wrong.'

Under their coffee cups and Ricard glasses was a *Herald Tribune*. Vladimir nodded at the headline. *Marine Bomb Hero Cleared*.

'You think they made it up – so as not to be outdone?' He read out the rest. '"*Nuke terrorist slain after Subway chase.*" Come on. One minute Blackburn's in the slammer for icing his CO. Next he's jumping the tracks chasing down public enemy number one on the New York Subway. Do me a favour.'

'America has a free press. They don't make stuff up. You have to believe they can do things like that. That's why they run the world. Besides, I know my pal Blackburn is a man of infinite resource. That's why I personally selected him for the job.'

'Now *you're* making stuff up. He's the one told you it was Solomon.'

'And you knew him for what – two hours?'

'I've had romances shorter than that.'

Omorova looked at Vladimir, a trace of disgust in her otherwise sphinx-like expression, then smiled at Dima.

'You proved one thing wrong – about us Ruskies always being the bad guys. In fact, it would be a good starting point for your memoirs. Could be a bestseller.'

'Except I'd have to make up the last bit. I don't remember a thing about it.'

'The detonator blew, the rest didn't because you'd detached it. You saved Paris.'

'Yeah, but the French aren't too happy with our role as their saviours. That's why they majored on all the damage we did on the way.'

Dima found what he was looking for, put down the binoculars, grabbed his stick and heaved himself up from the table.

Omorova wagged a finger. 'Steady now, we don't want to have to scrape you off the tarmac a second time.'

'Where's he off to?' asked Vladimir.

'Unfinished business, I think,' said Omorova.

Dima hadn't worked out anything about what would happen as he struggled forward, the cast on his broken leg chafing. He hadn't prepared a speech. He opted just to go with the flow, see where the conversation went and maybe – or maybe not. And that was just as well because what he had failed to spot as he tracked Adam Levalle and his girlfriend through the binoculars was the older couple not far behind.

'Hey!'

Adam waved when he spotted Dima.

'Well, this is a surprise.'

He grasped Dima's hand, shook it hard, then embraced him. His girlfriend smiled.

'Natalie, this is Dima – Mayakovsky.'

Adam turned to the older couple behind him, who were deep in conversation.

'Dima, please – let me introduce you to my parents.'

'Hey Mom, Dad – meet the Saviour of Paris. And my new hero.'

But Dima could find no words.

FIN